LOC

Kerry Wilkinson is a bit less of an accidental author than he once was. His debut, *Locked In*, the first title in the detective Jessica Daniel series, was written as a challenge to himself but, after self-publishing, it became a UK Number One Kindle bestseller within three months of release. His three initial Jessica Daniel books sold over 250,000 copies in under six months, making him Amazon UK's top-selling author for the final quarter of 2011.

Kerry has a degree in journalism and works for a national media company. He was born in Somerset but now lives in Lancashire.

For more information about Kerry and his books visit:

Website: www.kerrywilkinson.com or
www.panmacmillan.com
Twitter: www.twitter.com/kerrywk
Facebook: www.facebook.com/JessicaDanielBooks

Or you can email Kerry at

kerryawilkinson@googlemail.com

By Kerry Wilkinson

LOCKED IN

VIGILANTE

THE WOMAN IN BLACK

THINK OF THE CHILDREN

PLAYING WITH FIRE

THICKER THAN WATER

BEHIND CLOSED DOORS

CROSSING THE LINE

KERRY WILKINSON

LOCKED IN

PAN BOOKS

First published by Kerry Wilkinson 2011

This edition published 2013 by Pan Books
an imprint of Pan Macmillan
20 New Wharf Road, London N1 9RR
Associated companies throughout the world
www.panmacmillan.com

ISBN 978-1-4472-2564-5

7 9 8

A CIP catalogue record for this book is available from the British Library.

Typeset by Ellipsis Digital Limited, Glasgow
Printed and bound by CPI Group (UK) Ltd, Croydon, CR0 4YY

Visit **www.panmacmillan.com** to read more about all our books
and to buy them. You will also find features, author interviews and
news of any author events, and you can sign up for e-newsletters
so that you're always first to hear about our new releases.

LOCKED IN

THREE DAYS AGO

The killer used a gloved hand to try the front-door handle one final time and make sure it was locked. The back door and windows had already been checked and there was definitely no way in – a good thing considering the body was already dead on the bed upstairs.

Now the first part was complete, the months of careful planning that led to this night finally seemed worth it. Getting into a locked house and back out again wasn't simple on the surface but, once the idea had been struck upon, everything had happened so easily.

The hardest part had been the final act. Until the moment the life had been choked out of the victim, the killer hadn't been sure they could actually complete the deed. Murdering someone wasn't easy but it had been necessary.

There was no regret, no feelings of anything really. The victim certainly deserved it, as would the others to come.

1

Jessica Daniel screwed her eyes tightly shut and thought about how much she hated morning people. For some, the dawn sun spilling through ridiculously thin curtains would herald a bright new day full of opportunity but, for her, it was just a reminder she *still* hadn't asked her land-lord to fix some better blinds.

Admitting she had lost the battle to stay asleep, she fumbled around for her mobile phone on the table next to the bed. It was always the first point of call in the morning, if only to remind her how little she had going on in her life. She opened her eyes slowly and struggled with the device's unlock button, before bashing away at the suppos-edly touch-screen front. It only seemed to function to any great degree if your definition of 'touch' was actually 'poke very hard until it does what you want'.

She had no texts, no missed calls and the only emails were ones offering her enhancements she definitely wouldn't be needing without far more invasive and complicated sur-gery first.

Marvellous.

Jessica went to put the phone back on the nightstand but, before she could, it started to ring. She cursed herself for setting the ringtone to some upbeat pop tune she didn't even like; the chirpy song really wasn't suitable for this time of the morning. Her eyes were still seeing a hazy grey around the edges but the caller ID clearly showed Detective Inspector Jack Cole's name. Jessica looked across at the digital alarm clock next to the bed which flashed 06.51. She was pretty sure it was a Saturday too, which made things worse.

She had been promoted to detective sergeant eight weeks ago and calls like this were something she knew she was going to have to get used to. When people were in a more junior position they could often get away with working regular shifts. Early-morning wake-up calls could now be expected more often.

'Hello,' Jessica said into her phone, trying not to sound too groggy.

Cole didn't sound much more awake than she did, which at least didn't mark him down as a morning person either. He told her 'something big' had happened but he wasn't completely sure of the details and tried to give her an address.

She would happily have described herself as messy and disorganised but the one thing she had remembered to do in the past two months was keep a pad and pen next to her bed for a moment like this. Cole started to give her the details and she tried to write them down. At first she thought her eyes were still struggling with the early hour but then realised her confusion was down to the fact the pen wasn't working.

'Hang on, hang on,' she said irritably, opening the drawer underneath her nightstand just in case there was a spare pen there.

There wasn't.

It was typical that even when she had gone out of her way to be organised, things didn't quite work out. She asked the inspector to send her a text message with the details instead and then hung up.

Cole was Jessica's immediate superior and had been promoted at the same time she had. She had always got on fine with him when they had been in more junior roles. He was a decent guy but perhaps a bit too nice. He was about as normal a bloke as you could ever meet; one of those people whose descriptions you hated when taking statements from a witness. He was average height and weight, with sensible short brown hair and always wore regular unassuming clothes. He didn't wear glasses or sport any distinguishing scars or facial hair. Even his voice was exactly as you would expect.

In fact, the only thing not really regulation about Jack was that he had what most officers didn't seem to – a proper family life. He was in his mid-forties and married, seemingly happily, with two children. He had family days out with them, still took his wife out for meals and to the cinema, and booked his time off sensibly so they could all have weekends away together. Unlike pretty much every other officer, he didn't drink and Jessica had never heard him swear. Perhaps that was normal to most people but it was anything but for the job they had.

Cole liked working from his desk and saw any real interaction with criminals, witnesses or anyone outside of the station as something he would rather not be involved with. To some it showed he didn't like to get his hands dirty but Jessica understood he had strengths in different areas.

Sitting on the edge of her bed, Jessica ran her hands through her long dark-blonde hair thinking that it needed a wash, as it always seemed to. There was definitely not going to be time for that this morning. She pulled it back into a loose ponytail and hunted around her room for some suitable clothes.

She thought most of her colleagues took 'plain clothes' a bit too literally. Even the younger blokes seemed to take the title 'detective' as a chance to start clocking up department-store loyalty points with a wardrobe seemingly consisting of identikit dull suit jackets and pairs of chinos. The only difference between the younger guys and the veterans seemed to be the width of their ties. The new guys would start off with skinny monstrosities around their necks but their neckwear seemed to become wider the longer they spent turning up in those dreary suits.

Jessica knew she couldn't take things too far and still wore a suit to work each day but at least it wasn't the same one with an egg stain on the pocket, unlike a certain colleague or two she could think of. She also made sure she dressed something like her age – she was almost thirty-one after all. Hunting through her wardrobe, Jessica pulled out a light grey suit to put on and, just to be a hypocrite, a blouse straight from the floor.

Jessica lived in the Hulme district, just south of the main centre of Manchester. It wasn't too bad, far enough away from the pubs and clubs and the full-on student areas to be able to sleep through the early hours – and only ten minutes' drive to her team's Longsight base. Far more important than all of that was the fact it was close enough to the curry mile to pick up a good Madras without too much hassle.

Cole had messaged Jessica an address in Gorton, in the east of the city. It took her just over fifteen minutes to drive, despite the roads being fairly quiet. There wasn't too much in the way of traffic but, as ever, the traffic lights constantly seemed to be red. She also nearly ran over some student type who looked like she was making the dreaded Saturday morning walk of shame. There didn't seem to be any other reason for a girl in a short purple dress to be walking bare-footed across a main road holding impossibly tall heels in her hand. Jessica wondered if the girl had actually had a good night as she crunched down through the car's gears after swerving around her.

Jessica's bright red K-reg Fiat Punto was her pride and sometimes-joy, even if it didn't give her much pleasure on the cold winter mornings when it wouldn't start no matter how much she kicked and swore at it. She had been given it as a present for passing her theory test from her mum and dad over ten years ago and had learned to drive in it. It was an attachment to easier, less serious days. How it was still on the road was a mystery far beyond Jessica's detective skills. The exhaust was perhaps the only thing loud enough to wake up her flatmate and best friend Caroline, while the MOTs were expensive and the piss-taking from colleagues was relentless.

Even her dad gave her stick about it. 'We only bought that as a first car,' he would say to her. 'You earn a decent salary now . . .'

Well she earned a *salary* now, that was for sure, and, as long as they could get her from A to B, or at least close to 'B', she wasn't that bothered about cars. In an emergency, she had access to the patrol's pool of vehicles and, rusting heap or not, it was at least *her* rusting heap.

Jessica pulled up behind two patrol cars outside the address. It wasn't too far off the main road, fairly close to the speedway stadium. Luckily her supervisor had sent the basic directions too. She got out and walked towards the plain-clothes officer she recognised by the house's gate.

Detective Constable David Rowlands had a grin on his face. 'I didn't know if they were calling you in but then I heard the exhaust on that heap you drive from half a mile away.'

'It's come to something when someone with hair like *that* takes the piss out of anything,' Jessica fired back with a grin, flicking him the V just for good measure.

'I was still asleep when I got called in,' he protested as a way of explaining why his usually spiky and gelled hair was instead decidedly fluffy and floppy.

Rowlands was younger than she was, still not out of his twenties, and tall with spiky jet-black hair – plus the customary skinny tie. He certainly fancied himself with the opposite sex and had a sharp mouth with a cheeky, dimpled smile that meant it was hard to get angry with him. Even with his constant bragging about various con-quests and his obvious cockiness, Jessica had taken an instant liking to him when he had joined the squad a few months after she had.

He had once tried it on with her late one evening a year

or so ago. To be honest, given his reputation, she would have been bloody annoyed if he hadn't at some point or another. She hadn't been receptive but that wasn't the point. They had both been drinking after a rare result; some woman who had been sent down for stealing from her own mother. Rowlands wasn't the type to take her rejection too seriously and, if anything, they were better mates afterwards. He was certainly one of the few members of the Criminal Investigation Department she would go out for a drink with.

Jessica breezed past him, ducking under the police tape, to enter the small front garden of the semi-detached house, thinking it was quite a nice-looking place. Not all the houses in this area were as well kept. The red brickwork looked fairly clean, as did the upstairs and downstairs bay windows. The only thing spoiling the illusion of middle-class fulfilment was the bright white double-glazed front door just about hanging on to its bottom hinge.

Rowlands followed her under the tape. 'Who did this?' Jessica asked, nodding at the door as they stepped towards it.

'Our lot. The tactical entry boys came down this morning.'

'Bit early for them, wasn't it?'

'I guess but they get called out to all sorts.'

'What's inside?'

'You'll see . . .'

Rowlands stopped by the front door while a uniformed officer in the hallway pointed Jessica up the stairs. The house looked as nicely decorated on the inside as it was tidy on the outside with prominent plush shaggy carpets and ornaments in the hallway.

Jessica found Cole outside one of the bedrooms. He had his back to the room facing the stairs as she got to the top. 'Scene of Crime boys are on their way,' is all he said as he moved aside for Jessica to have a look.

The first thing she noticed was how bright the room was. The bay window to her right had blinds that were fixed into the frames but they were only partly closed. The early-morning sun poured into the room, illuminating the magnolia walls and light yellow sheets on the king-size bed opposite.

Jessica first saw a pile of clothes on the floor. She thought it was similar to her own floordrobe but, as her eyes flicked across the room, she saw the body.

She was glad she hadn't had breakfast that morning.

A woman was lying on her side half underneath bed covers that were pulled back to her waist. Her eyes were bulging and her face was a light grey, almost pale blue colour. Deep cut marks were visible around her neck and had bled over the covers. The dark red liquid had pooled and set underneath her, matting into her blonde hair and the sheets. 'Oh,' Jessica said.

'Oh indeed,' Cole replied behind her.

2

Jessica had seen bodies in all types of horrific situations – people beaten so badly you didn't know if they were male or female, limbs contorted at almost incomprehensible angles and worse. Parts of the training programme had been pretty grim but it was something that came with the job. While you were working in uniform, you also saw plenty of things most people wouldn't want to. Some could handle it better than others.

She hadn't seen too many bodies in a state like the victim's though and it looked as if the dead woman had been there for a day or two. The deep, vicious choke gouges in her neck had almost certainly been caused by some kind of thick wire and the colour of her skin made the cause of death pretty clear, even before the Scene of Crime team arrived.

Jessica knew that the SOCOs would have their hands full considering it was a Saturday morning. Scene of Crime teams were a mix of civilians and serving officers and worked citywide, meaning the hours and travelling distances were awful. Saturday and Sunday mornings were by far the worst times, cleaning up the mess of various revellers' nights out and the inevitable alcohol-related carnage that came with it.

Various television shows made investigating crime

scenes seem like a glamorous occupation but Jessica doubted whether darting around Manchester, usually in the rain, and tidying up one drunken mess after another would quite reach the same heights.

She didn't enter the room any further as she could see all she needed to from the doorway and didn't want to risk contaminating anything. She turned back around to face her DI, who was still looking away. 'That's pretty nasty. Do we know who she is?' Jessica asked.

'Probably. The house is owned by someone called Yvonne Christensen. One of her friends called in two days ago saying she'd not seen her in a couple of days and that no one seemed to be home, even though her car was still parked outside. Uniform were around yesterday and couldn't get any type of response. They came back this morning with the tactical entry lot.'

'Bit early for them, isn't it?'

'They had already been out at another job raiding some place for drugs. You know what everyone's like with budgets. I guess someone figured they'd get two jobs done for the price of one.'

Jessica let his answer hang for a few moments, before replying. 'Does anyone else live here?'

'We're not sure yet. It looks like the body has been there for a couple of days so probably not.'

Cole didn't turn around the whole time he talked. He was leaning with both hands on the banisters at the top of the stairs. 'This one's going to be ours,' he said quietly.

It was only a few words but Jessica understood it was more what he implied than what he explicitly said. She knew he wouldn't really want too much to do with the grim details but would help out in his own way and direct operations from the station. The groundwork would be hers.

'So who's the friend?' Jessica asked.

'Someone she goes to one of those weight clubs with. They live a few doors down. Uniform are with her now but she doesn't know yet. Dave has her name.'

That was his second implication: 'Go tell her'.

Jessica walked around him back down the stairs. The interior design seemed far gloomier than it had moments before and she met Rowlands by the front door. 'Do you have the details of the friend who called this in?' Jessica asked.

He ummed as he pulled a notebook out from his pocket and flicked through the pages. 'Stephanie Wilson,' he said, folding the book back up and putting it away. 'She lives just down the road.'

'Are you ready to go talk to her?'

'Yep.'

'Let's hope she's not too traumatised or your hair's going to tip her over the edge.'

Despite their joking, they both knew it was time to be serious. The two of them ducked back under the police tape outside the house and Rowlands pointed for them to turn right. Mrs Wilson lived on the same street but on the other side of the road around a hundred yards away. Jessica thought the sun was surprisingly warm considering the time of the day and the fact it wasn't yet summer. She noticed there were a few obvious curtain-twitches as they walked down the road, which was little surprise considering the patrol cars outside the victim's house and the obvious police presence. The ones hoping for a show would be sadly disappointed when the body was removed under a cover later on.

Perhaps it was because she was so used to actually attending crime scenes but Jessica never really understood the interest that came when police attended an incident. She didn't get the types of people who slowed down for motorway accidents just in case there was blood or something else to get excited about, or those who crowded around vicious fight scenes. When you had seen some of the sights police officers had to each day, and dealt with the aftermath, Jessica didn't believe most people would be so keen to get in line for a good view.

Rowlands rang the doorbell of Stephanie Wilson's house, which set off an overly cheery 'Greensleeves' chime not really appropriate for the moment. The door was answered by a uniformed officer, who led them through to the kitchen.

The basic layout of the house seemed to be identical to that of the victim's home. There was a stairway just inside the front door with a hallway running alongside it straight to the kitchen. A couple were sitting at a small round dining table in the kitchen with mugs of tea in front of them. There wasn't an awful lot of room but the two officers were pointed to the remaining two seats around the table, while the constable picked up a third mug from the side and went through to the living room.

Mrs Wilson was a lot larger than her husband, with

short shoulder-length greying hair. Jessica would have guessed she was in her early fifties but she was never that great with ages. The woman wasn't massively overweight but, compared to her short unimposing partner, she seemed a lot larger than she was.

It was the man who stood up to shake their hands and introduce himself. He was clearly nervous as he spoke. He kept one hand on his wife's shoulder to reassure her and talked quickly, barely pausing to breathe, while his wife didn't even look up from the table. 'Hi, I'm Ray and this is Steph. It was Steph's idea to call you, wasn't it, dear?'

He looked down towards her but she didn't respond. He continued speaking as he sat back down. 'I wasn't sure whether we should dial 999. I didn't want to waste your time. You always see those articles about people phoning up because they've lost their slippers or whatever.'

Jessica took a deep breath herself, perhaps subconsciously affected by Ray's non-stop opening. 'I'm afraid we have some bad news for you.'

She paused but Stephanie didn't give her a chance to add any more. She looked up for the first time from the table, directly at Jessica. 'Yvonne is dead, isn't she?'

There wasn't too much point in trying to tone things down. 'Yes, she is.'

The woman let out a little sob that seemed to have been building, while her husband reached to put his arm around her, making soothing noises as he did so.

'I'm afraid we are going to have to ask you about anything you might have seen and why you contacted us,' Jessica added.

They had to be careful in moments such as this with balancing someone's grief against needing to act as quickly as possible. Given the state of the body, it looked as if they had already lost a day or two. Jessica let the words hang as the woman blew her nose on a tissue offered by Rowlands and took a sip of tea.

'We always go to this slimming club at the local school on a Wednesday,' Stephanie said. 'We began going together at the start of the year. Yvonne had split from her husband at the end of last year and I . . . well, I could do with losing a few pounds.'

Rowlands had his notebook out and was writing while Jessica listened as the woman continued. 'She'd lost around eight pounds but I'd lost over a stone. I couldn't believe it. We usually have a brew and a natter, then go to get weighed. I had texted her Tuesday morning, just some stupid joke, and she replied to say: "See you tomorrow".'

Stephanie paused for another sip of tea. 'But the next day she didn't seem to be around. I'd texted her in the afternoon, just to check times, but I'd not heard back. Then I went around at five o'clock anyway, like usual, but there was no answer. Her car was on the road outside; it still is, so I didn't think she'd gone anywhere. No one was answering the door and I could hear her phone going off inside when I called it. I tried shouting through the letterbox in case she'd hurt herself but there was no answer. I looked through the windows but couldn't see anything and then tried the front door but it was locked.'

'Does she live on her own?' Jessica asked.

'Yes. Her husband Eric moved out not long before

Christmas. He's shacked up with some other woman some-where and James is off at university. I've tried to be there for her but yes, she's on her own.'

'Is James her son?'

'Yes, only child. You should've seen her on the day he first went off to university. Crying 'cos her little baby had grown up.'

'I don't suppose you have any contact details for Eric, do you? We'll need them if you do.'

Stephanie slid her chair backwards with a screech, stretching towards a handbag on one of the counters. She reached in and took out a mobile phone. 'I have a mobile number for him. I don't know where he lives though. I texted him on Thursday before I called you, just to see if he'd seen her.'

'Had he?'

'I only got a one-word reply.'

Stephanie held up the phone for the officers to see the simple answer: 'No'.

'I was surprised I got that to be honest,' Stephanie added. 'That's when I called you. I didn't really know what else to do. It wasn't like her to say nothing if she was going away and . . . I just felt something was wrong. You do, don't you?'

Jessica nodded while Rowlands took down the number for Eric Christensen then handed the page to her.

Stephanie tailed off tearfully . 'I guess I'm just glad it wasn't me that found her . . .'

Jessica started to say something hopefully reassuring but stopped herself and thought for a moment. 'I'm sorry, can you repeat that?'

17

The woman breathed in and her sobs slowed for a moment. She took a second to compose herself and then made eye contact with Jessica. 'It's just that, if Yvonne's front door hadn't have been locked, it might have been me that found her the other day.'

Jessica narrowed her eyes slightly and leant back into her chair, feeling a slight tingle down her spine. 'So, you don't have a key then?' she asked to make sure.

'No. She would leave me one to watch the house if she was on holiday but that was it.'

Jessica offered her thanks and sympathy and told Rowlands to hang around to make sure Mr and Mrs Wilson were okay. She walked as quickly as she could back down the street to the victim's house, weaving in between the parked squad cars and ducked under the police tape, striding towards the busted front door.

The Scene of Crime team had arrived. Usually it was only one person who attended but, on this occasion, word had obviously gone out that it wouldn't be so straightforward. Someone Jessica didn't recognise was wearing a white paper suit just inside the hallway, while a second person was disappearing up the stairs. The one in the hall started to say something but Jessica ignored him, nudging past and pushing on towards the door at the back of the hall that led into the rest of the house.

Cole came out of the kitchen just as she reached the already open hallway door. 'Are you okay?' he asked but she didn't react.

She looked at the wall to the right of the doorway, wanting to make sure she had been right about what she thought she had seen when she was going up the stairs earlier. At the time it hadn't registered fully but she could now see what was in front of her: a row of hooks with keys hanging from them. On the right one was a set of car keys attached to a fob but it was what was hanging next to it she was interested in.

Cole looked at her bemused as Jessica went to the paper-suited person still by the doorway and asked for a rubber glove. She returned to the rack and carefully took the key ring hanging on the left hook. It had two keys on it. 'What are you . . .?' Cole started to say before tailing off.

Jessica took the key to the front door, still just about hanging on to the frame after being smashed through by the police. It was a big, heavy double-glazed door, the type that needed the handle pulling up so it would lock. She crouched down and wiggled the key into the lock, turning it just to make sure it was the right one.

She then quickly hopped up, striding back past the paper-suited officer and Cole into the kitchen. She walked purposefully past the immaculately clean stove and work-tops to the back door before trying the handle. It was locked but the second key on the key ring fitted and turned. Cole was now behind her next to the door and spoke more forcefully this time. 'What are you doing?'

Jessica paused for a moment before replying. 'Well, Sir, if the front door had to be broken down because it was locked but the key was hanging in the hallway the whole time, then how did the killer get in – or back out?'

3

It hadn't taken long to establish that every window in the house was also secured from the inside. There was no sign of forced entry, none of the locks had been damaged, nothing was broken and no obvious items had been stolen. There was still a flatscreen television on the wall and a laptop computer on a desk in the living room. Jessica knew that didn't mean other things hadn't been taken but, with a standard burglary, something like a laptop – light, mobile and worth a few quid – would have been one of the first things out the door. Yvonne Christensen's mobile phone, which had been heard ringing, was on the nightstand next to the bed as well. It wasn't a top-of-the-range model but she knew some scroat somewhere would have paid a tenner for it.

Jessica left Cole, who said he was going to have to phone his wife, and walked back to the Wilsons' house, asking Rowlands to come outside.

'Why did you dash off like that?' he asked.

'It was when Mrs Wilson said she couldn't let herself into the victim's house. When we were over there I remembered some keys hanging in the hallway but the front door was locked because we had to smash it down. I figured that, if her best friend didn't have a key, then how did whoever killed her get in? The back door and windows are all locked too.'

'So you reckon it was the husband then?'

Jessica let out a long 'hmmm' noise. 'Maybe but that doesn't make much sense either. Firstly, we don't know if he has a key any longer but, even if he does, if you were going to kill your partner, you wouldn't make it obvious, would you? If you knew you were one of a few people with a way in, you'd hide the fact that was how you'd done it. You could fake a burglary or something like that but it's all so clean in there. It's not like it's one of those old-fashioned doors that just lock when you pull them shut, you actually have to try to secure it.'

'Could she have let someone in?'

'Possibly but how did they lock it when they were back out again given her key is in the hallway?'

'Maybe whoever did it secured everything to get a few days' head start?'

'If they did then it's not the husband. I phoned him a minute ago and asked if we could come pick him up. I didn't tell him his wife was dead but he's definitely around and gave me the address.'

She handed a piece of paper over to Rowlands then continued talking. 'Can you take one of the liaison officers and tell him the news – then bring him to the station? Ask which university his son goes to because someone's going to have to tell him too. We're going to have to find out who has a key for that house.'

Rowlands took one of the marked cars as Jessica walked back towards the victim's house to ask Cole what he wanted to do next. He was just ducking under the tape by the edge of the garden as she approached. 'I was supposed to be taking the kids to the zoo today,' he said.

'I don't know why criminals can't just stick to office hours,' Jessica replied with a grin.

'I've been saying that for years; if you're going to commit a crime, can you at least have the decency to do it between nine and five, preferably Monday to Friday.'

Humour was frequently dark in the station. Perhaps to an outsider it would seem as if they were uncaring towards victims and other people that came through the doors. If the general public knew some of the comments that were made about them behind their backs, there would be uproar. Really, it was just the way members of the force coped. At any given time you could find yourself dealing with the lowest types of human life committing horrendous acts on some of the most vulnerable people imaginable. You had to care but it was essential you had some kind of detachment too. It was the banter and dark jokes that made that possible and fuelled people to work together.

Jessica gave a small laugh. 'Dave's off to pick up the husband. Have they found anything inside?'

'I don't think so, you know how long it all takes.'

Jessica nodded but was struggling to get her head around everything. 'The thing is, even if they find a sample from the husband or the son, it wouldn't necessarily show anything because they both lived here until fairly recently. Unless the victim is a habitual deep cleaner, there is always going to be some trace of them in the house.'

'It depends what they find, doesn't it? Blood under nails or something like that would be a good lead.'

Jessica blew out through her teeth and shook her head slightly. 'Maybe.'

She knew the forensic testing often gave them their best leads but sometimes it could throw up as many questions as answers. If the victim had scratched the attacker and there was a trace of them on her it would give the police a solid start but leads as concrete as that were rare. Just showing the husband had recently been in the house wouldn't be enough and, after that, even if they did find blood or hair from someone else, they would still be hoping for a match on the National DNA Database.

Anyone who was arrested on suspicion of committing a crime had their mouth swabbed and details stored. If a person had never been in trouble, a sample taken from a crime scene could sit for years until paired with someone. The testing methods were great for ruling people out of an inquiry but you still had to do police work the old-fashioned way if you didn't get a match.

'No need to be so negative,' Cole said with a smile and wink. 'Usually it's someone the victim knows.'

Jessica gave a small smile but it wasn't sincere. 'I know but you'd make it less obvious. There's something not right here. Did you ask about any estimated time for results?'

'No, the hairnet brigade get a bit snotty if you start pushing them. Things move slowly at the weekend anyway. If we're lucky, we might get a formal identification plus a time and confirmed cause of death by Monday.

I'll phone the chief inspector so he knows what's going on and he'll put a call in to say this is a priority. It doesn't stop them being under-staffed though.'

'Aren't we all?'

'Either way, some of the forensics guys are going to have to come in on a Sunday to wade through it all.'

'I'm glad I'm not making that phone call. Someone's going to get an earful.' Jessica paused briefly and then added: 'Are we both going back to the station to talk to the husband?'

'Yes, there's not much more we can do here. Scene of Crime are doing their thing and officers are knocking on doors to ask if anyone saw or heard anything in the last few days.'

Jessica looked back down the street towards the Wilsons' house. 'There were lots of curtains twitching this morning but I doubt any of them were watching when it might have been some use.'

'Always the way, isn't it?'

Jessica never failed to be amazed by how many people apparently didn't see anything when some kids were terrorising an old lady or some guy was beating his missus up.

'Shall I meet you back at the station?' she asked.

'Yes, you head off and I'll see you there.'

The journey to the main base at Longsight wasn't a long one but the traffic had started to back up on the main roads as people woke up and realised that, for once, the sun was shining and they could actually go and do something with the day. It made a change from cowering from the rain in any case. Jessica often thought sunny days in the north seemed to bring out two types of people – those who hopped in the car and raced to the coast and those who went to the pub.

She parked at the front of the station and walked through to the canteen. Their base had been renovated relatively recently and its sandy brick colour on the outside was still visible, unlike a lot of the local stations where the dirt had long since taken hold. It was two floors high but also had a basement that housed the incident room, as well as a separate area for the cells. Many officers also worked down there who didn't have set desks. The top floor was where the chief inspector's office was, along with a lot of storage and some other administration areas.

On the ground floor the main door opened straight into the reception where the desk sergeant would handle anyone who had been arrested. Some would be processed and put in the cells, while others would either be bailed to reappear or occasionally just given an on-the-spot fine or a bit of a talking to. Also on the floor were many of the slightly more senior officers' individual offices plus the canteen, the media area and the interview rooms.

The canteen didn't have the greatest choice at the best of times but there was never any hot food available on a Saturday, so Jessica crouched in front of a vending machine before settling for a sandwich that seemed to have the least curled-up corners. She then made her way through to one of the station's two interview rooms.

Cole was already in there, setting up the recording equipment. Eric Christensen wouldn't be under arrest but he would be cautioned and interviewed plus told he could have a legal representative if he wanted. Unless time was absolutely paramount or someone's life was at stake, all interviews were supposed to be done at the station and documented.

Each interview was recorded onto three tapes. The master would almost certainly never be listened to. It was there solely as a backup to prevent any allegations of tampering. It usually had a yellow seal around it to show it had not been opened since the interview. One of the copies would be for the police to use, while the third was the suspect's.

Jessica swallowed a mouthful of sandwich. 'We must single-handedly be the only organisation in the world keeping the manufacturers of cassette tapes in business.'

Cole jammed the final tape in the machine and looked around at her. 'I've been saying for ages it's ridiculous.'

Jessica pointed at the device. 'I can get a better quality recording on my phone than off this thing. Did I tell you about the case I was at the other month?'

'Go on.'

'At the magistrates' court we had some guy up for handling stolen goods. The quality of the recording wasn't good enough and the written log was incomplete so the whole thing fell apart. I was sitting at the back as the defence ripped us apart.'

'Shame it's not me that sorts out the budgets,' Cole said with a smile.

As he finished talking, there was a knock at the door and Rowlands entered with two men just behind him. The first was wearing a suit and Jessica recognised him as one of the duty solicitors. His role was to offer free legal advice to people that had to be interviewed. That would often happen over the phone but, in serious cases, it was always in person. There were only a few duties for the area, so they were all familiar faces.

That meant the man behind him had to be Eric Christensen. He was tall and blond and casually dressed in a pair of jeans and light-fitting shirt. On first impression, Jessica wouldn't have said he looked upset at hearing of his wife's death but he certainly seemed subdued.

Cole gave Eric Christensen the standard caution and the rest of the interview itself went pretty much as she suspected it would. The man said he was shocked by his wife's death but insisted he would never have meant her any ill will. He explained their divorce was going to be a formality as they had separated five months ago and said they had simply drifted apart over the years. Now that James had gone to university, they no longer saw the need to stay together for him.

He was seeing someone new who lived in Bolton and said he had been out with her on Tuesday night, playing snooker with friends on Wednesday, in with his partner on the Thursday, and then out again last night. He claimed he didn't have a door key to his old house and, as far as he was aware, Yvonne and James were the only people who did.

The husband was bailed without conditions but told to contact the police if anything occurred to him. He had asked if he could tell his son about Yvonne's death. It was an awkward decision but Jessica guessed there was never a good way to be told your mother was dead, whether in person by someone in uniform or over the phone by your father. Either way an officer from the local area was going to be sent out to speak to James, if only to formally exclude him from the inquiry.

When the room was empty except for the two officers, Cole looked to her and raised his eyebrows. 'What do you reckon? Do you think he's our guy?'

'It's not as if he was thinking through his answers – everything was natural. We can get someone checking the alibi but I'd be surprised if it wasn't solid. He answered all the questions too, even the intimate ones.'

'I know. He's either got nothing to do with it or is one of the most natural liars I've ever seen. The son seems unlikely too. Unless there's a huge life insurance policy, neither of them seems to have a motive either.'

Eric had told them James went to Bournemouth University. It was a nine- or ten-hour round trip but his father reckoned he had gone that far just to get away from them.

'He fell in with the wrong crowd a few years ago, then me and his mum were arguing all the time,' he said. 'He couldn't have really found somewhere further away, could he?'

Jessica knew the logistics of getting from Bournemouth to Manchester and back again wouldn't be impossible but James would surely have been missed if he had disappeared for that length of time.

'He didn't give us much else to go on, did he?' Jessica said.

'No, it sounds like he has just moved in with his new girlfriend and wants to get on with his life.' They tidied up the room and walked through to reception. 'Are you heading home?' Cole asked.

'I guess so. Is there anything you want me to do here?'

'No, I'll call the higher-ups then get off myself. We've got officers going door-to-door and we're not going to get any results from the labs through until Monday at the earliest. There's not much more we can do.'

Jessica said goodbye to the desk sergeant and asked him to call her mobile if anything interesting happened. She walked out of the station on her own, taking her phone out to check for any new messages. It was now late afternoon and, though the sun was still out, it had lost much of its heat. She shivered slightly but, as she did, for the second time that day, the phone started to ring while in her hand. She shook her head, thinking she should definitely change the ringtone to something less energetic, and looked at the screen to see who was calling.

There was no name displayed, just a mobile number she didn't recognise. She jabbed at the screen to answer. 'Hello.'

The man's voice on the other end was slightly shaky and whoever it was sounded nervous. 'Is that Detective Sergeant Jessica Daniel?'

'Yes, who's this?'

The person paused for a moment. 'I'm just calling to talk about the dead body you found this morning.'

4

Garry Ashford was not happy. The alarm on his phone he
didn't remember setting had gone off and he couldn't get
back to sleep. As he lay in bed, he didn't think an electrical item could be smug but his phone certainly looked
close to it as it showed him in big LED characters that it
was one in the afternoon. There was no way he would
have set an alarm for that time on a Saturday, not after
being out until three in the morning, so someone was
taking the piss.

It didn't help that he was being charged thirty-five
pounds a month for the privilege either.

His head throbbed slightly as he remembered the
previous evening. Not only had he endured a bad week
but he had spent nearly seventy quid the night before
and ended up in the same position he always did with the
opposite sex – precisely nowhere. As one of his supposed
mates had pointed out in the taxi a few hours ago, this
was more than a sexual barren spell; it was becoming a life
choice.

Garry threw the duvet off and went to the window to
see what the day had to offer him. Opening the curtains,
he was surprised to see the bright light of the sun shining
into the room. Nice day or not, there wasn't an awful lot
the sunlight could do about his shambles of a home. He

had never been sure whether his rented accommodation actually counted as a flat, a bedsit or a hovel.

Everything was in one room, or two if you counted the fact that the bathroom had a door that didn't quite shut all the way. In the main room, which also doubled as the kitchen and dining room, his bed folded out from the sofa. It didn't matter whether you used it as a couch or a bed though; either way the springs had gone. He had a small old-fashioned portable television on a nearby table with an indoor aerial that never seemed to work properly planted on top pointing at the window. There was a cooker and microwave next to a sink a few feet away and a dining table with two plastic garden chairs in the centre of the room. On the other side of the bed was a chest of drawers that was, for some reason, the largest item of furniture in the entire flat. Aside from the faded flowery wallpaper, that was it for the main room.

The bathroom had a shower cubicle, laughably called a 'suite' in the advert he had answered. It had long since been taken over by a black, mouldy damp-type substance Garry was in no rush to have a fight with. If that wasn't bad enough, the toilet had a cracked seat and there was no sink in the bathroom; he had to use the one in the kitchen.

Although he knew it was awful, it was cheap and placed perfectly for his needs. It was very close to the centre of Manchester towards the back of the Oldham Street area, above a shop. Or, as one of his less-eloquent friends put it, 'Where all those artsy pricks live'. Its location meant he could walk to work and manage to get to all the bars on his doorstep without too many problems. Even if he did need a taxi home every now and then, it didn't cost too much.

Garry ran his hands through his thick black straggly shoulder-length hair. There had been a time when he thought longish hair would give him a rock-star look all the girls would go for. All these years down the line and that thinking had definitely gone out of the window but he still couldn't be bothered to get it cut.

He looked at the scene in front of him and thought that, even though his choice of home wasn't that appealing, he probably wasn't helping himself. Clothes were strewn over most of the free floor space, while the sink that was supposed to act as somewhere to prepare food, clean dishes and wash his hands, was overflowing with a mix of pots, pans, cups, plates and a folded-up pizza box.

'Right,' he said out loud to the empty room. 'Let's get this mutha sorted.'

It wasn't the type of thing he would have said if anyone else was present.

Garry was fairly slim and unimposing with his hair his most striking feature. His pasty frame was covered only by a pair of blue boxer shorts he had worn the whole of the previous day then slept in overnight. He put on some music to play through his phone, the rock tracks blending into one and sounding tinny through the device's underwhelming speaker. Garry could hear them well enough and, safe in the knowledge he was on his own, he sang along to the words he knew, made up the ones he didn't, played a bit of air-guitar and danced around in a way he never would on a night out.

Slowly but surely the scuffed wooden floor began to become visible. Clothes were shoved into the oversized chest of drawers or dropped in a giant supermarket carrier bag he had kept so he could do his own laundry.

As he was finishing, the playlist of songs he had set up on his phone came to an end and the room went quiet. Not knowing what to do with the rest of the day, Garry folded his bed back into the sofa and flicked on the TV. The indoor aerial was, as usual, not giving much of a signal into the cheap digital box he had hooked up. He fumbled around with it but the television just kept spewing out a hum of dissatisfaction. Annoyed, he turned it off and picked his phone up, skimming through his contacts until he got to a certain name.

Mark Llewellyn was one of the quieter people he knew and, although Garry fancied a drink and a chat, he didn't really want to spend the rest of the day in the pub. He dialled the number and, after a brief conversation, the pair arranged to meet at his local in half an hour.

It dawned on him that spending his Saturday afternoons in the pub was hardly embracing life but he didn't have much else better to do.

Garry had already drunk a third of his pint when Mark slid into the booth opposite him, plonking a full glass of beer on the table between them. The pub was only two minutes' walk from Garry's flat and usually full of locals. Because it was away from the main street, the tourists didn't really see it, although most would have opted for a significantly posher bar anyway. It was a mile or so away from the student district and, whenever he went for a drink, Garry was convinced he was the youngest person there.

'You all right, mate?' Mark asked.

'Not too bad, just work and that.' Garry's tone clearly gave his mood away.

Mark had picked up his drink but put it back down to avoid spilling it as he laughed. 'Blimey, it can't be that bad? Want to talk about it?'

'Maybe. It's a bit girly, isn't it?'

Mark looked at him and laughed again. 'What, talking? You really have got problems.'

Garry knew Mark through a mutual friend but, because they lived in close proximity to each other, they often went for a quiet drink together. They shared quite a bit in common but Mark earned a very good salary, which was a little intimidating. Garry pushed his hair behind his ears and took another mouthful from his drink.

'You just think things are going to be better than this, don't you?'

'How do you mean?'

'Well, I always wanted to be a journalist. You watch all these programmes and read the papers and everyone seems to be doing something worthwhile. I wanted to be a travel writer. From what I thought, you'd just be sent off to explore the world and get to stay in all these plush hotels and flirt with the exotic barmaids. You'd send through a few hundred words then move on to the next place.'

'I don't think most jobs are like that,' his friend laughed.

34

'I know but I want to do things like go to the football and interview the players and so on. As it is, I can't even get into movies for free.'

'Why should you be able to?'

'Well, someone's got to review these things.'

'Not you though?'

'No chance.'

'So what do you do? I thought you at least got to interview some famous people?'

'Sort of. You remember that reality TV girl who slept with that guy? You know that presenter bloke? It was all over the news.'

Mark looked blankly at him and shook his head. 'That's not the most accurate portrayal of someone I've ever heard.'

'Well, I don't know their names.'

'Neither do I from that description.'

'Whatever,' Garry said shaking his head. 'Anyway, I went to interview her. She had a book she was supposed to be promoting but talked in one- and two-word answers. If that's how she spoke then God knows how bad the writing was. Aside from her own fingernails, she wasn't interested in anything. After fifteen minutes of not answering questions, she was whisked off to some other appointment by her PA.'

'Was she hot though?'

Garry smiled. 'In a glowing orange radioactive-type way.'

'You're too picky.'

'I wish I had the opportunity to be fussy.'

Mark finished another mouthful of his drink then laughed again.

'You don't know the half of it,' Garry continued. 'Most of the time I get stuck talking to councillors about all sorts of nonsense.'

'That does sound pretty boring. What's the name of your paper again?'

'The *Manchester Morning Herald*. I've worked there for eighteen months now. How many front-page stories do you reckon I've had in that time?'

'I have no idea. I don't really look at papers to be honest. Twenty?'

'Two – and both of them were about how often people's bins get emptied.'

'Ooh, big-time.'

It was Garry's turn to laugh. 'I know but it's mad out there. People will put up with most things: gangs on the streets, giant pot holes in their roads, rising crime rates, you name it. But stop emptying their bins every week and it all kicks off.'

'Funnily enough, my dad was moaning about his bins over the phone the other week.'

Garry flailed his arms around and banged his pint on the table as if to emphasise the point. 'See what I mean? It's crazy and these are the people I'm out talking to every day.'

'Go on then, tell me about your worst encounter.'

After a drink to calm himself, Garry continued. 'Do you remember how freezing it was last winter with all the snow and everything? On the coldest day for six years, I got sent out onto the streets to ask people their views on local government.'

Mark spat half a mouthful of beer back into his glass. 'Bloody hell, mate, no wonder you're annoyed.'

'That's not even the worst bit. Most people told me to eff off or whatever, or just ignored me. It was about eleven in the morning and there were these kids who I'm sure should have been in school. They were about thirteen or something. Anyway, they were standing just across the street shouting "kiddy-fiddler" and "paedo" at me.'

'What did you say back?'

'Nothing, I mean what kind of funny comeback is there to that?'

'Hmm, good point. I might remember that next time my boss is giving me a hard time.'

'What, you're going to call him a "paedo"?'

'Well, as you pointed out, what's he going to say back?'

'Probably "you're fired".'

Mark seemed to be in a perpetual state of laughter but Garry could hardly blame him. 'Why don't you just quit and look for something else?' his friend asked.

'I don't know. There's not much out there. Besides, I keep telling myself it's going to get better. I don't want to end up having to move back with my mum and dad. It can't get much worse than a twenty-five-year-old moving back in with his parents.'

'If your mum's anything like mine, at least you'd get your washing done for free.'

Garry laughed half-heartedly. 'That's one thing I guess.'

'You know what you need? A girlfriend or a big story –

or both.' Mark stood up after downing the rest of his drink and shook his glass. 'You want another?'

'Yeah, go on. Same as usual.'

Mark walked off to the bar and Garry slumped back into the seat thinking about his parents. He came from a small town just outside Ipswich, the kind of place that was great to live as a kid. All his mates lived within a few minutes of his house and there were loads of wide-open spaces to kick a ball around and get into trouble. But it was also the type of area that became decidedly duller as you got older. Everyone pretty much knew everyone else and, no matter who you were, your parents would always end up finding out anything you got up to.

His mother's inquisitorial technique was often as basic as, 'Is there anything you would like to tell me, Garry?' It was hardly 'Columbo' but, given the number of things some nosy neighbour could have spotted him being up to, he frequently confessed to things she had no knowledge of.

If that wasn't bad enough, the pubs wouldn't serve anyone under age because they knew who everyone was. There was nowhere to hang out or buy fast food and not even a decent cinema or bowling alley. All of that, along with the fact that none of the girls you had grown up with were now remotely interested in you, meant by the time you reached eighteen, you were desperate for a chance to get out into the real world.

University had given him that option. Garry was at least pretty good at school, albeit lazy, but he had earned the A-level grades needed to study journalism at Liverpool, which was exactly what he wanted. As with most teenagers, he had seen plenty of enormously appealing American movies about college life and thought university would provide something similar. In a way it did but only if you saw yourself as one of those anonymous kids in the back of the parties in all those films.

He had a reasonable time living on campus, made a few good mates he was still in contact with and got a decent grade at the end of it all. He even had an on-off girlfriend for a few months, although the 'off' part was definitely her choice, before becoming her permanent decision.

Like most people about to graduate, he had left the job-hunting a tad late, although he resolved pretty quickly he didn't have any intention of returning to his home area. Big cities were definitely for him and he had spent two years in Liverpool, somehow making a living from free-lancing around and doing a bit of bar work cash-in-hand. Generally he didn't do much of any note but then he got his big break, or so he thought.

He responded to an advert to become a junior reporter on the *Herald* and miraculously didn't mess up the interview. He even had his hair cut for the occasion, albeit not that short. After eighteen months, he was gradually coming to the conclusion he had made a huge mistake.

Garry looked over to see Mark still standing in line at the bar and then heard his phone ringing. The number wasn't one he was familiar with but he answered anyway. 'Hello?'

The caller introduced themselves.

Garry was confused at first, asking why they were calling from a different number but, by the time the person on the other end had finished telling him their story, the reason was obvious.

5

Considering she had been woken up early and had a strong suspicion the biggest case of her career was hurtling towards a dead end, Jessica knew she was in a mood her flatmate Caroline would describe as 'particularly sweary'.

The phone call wasn't helping. 'I'm sorry, what did you say your name was?' she asked the man on the other end of the line, who was definitely going on her shit-list when she hung up. It was a fairly short list, consisting of the DCI, one of her ex-boyfriends and the pervy bloke who ran the chip shop at the bottom of her road.

'My name is Garry Ashford,' came the reply. 'I work for the *Manchester Morning Herald*. I wanted to ask you about the body you found this morning.'

Jessica knew the media hadn't been given any information yet. Later on, they would be told a standard line about a body being found and tests being done. If the son had been informed, they might even be given the name of the victim. Next week would be when the media were brought in and asked to cooperate. They would get the details of the victim and asked to give out a phone number for members of the public to call if they thought they had information.

Manning that line was definitely the worst job when you were a constable. Trying to pull out anything remotely useful from the mass of nonsense calls you had to wade through was a nightmare. Everything had to be followed up just in case that one piece of information you had deemed useless actually ended up being something vital. Someone would have to oversee the operation and Jessica thought it was a job that had Rowlands's name all over it.

'Which body are you talking about?' Jessica asked, wondering if straight-batting the caller would work.

'Hang on, let me check. Er, somebody Christ or something . . . sorry, I can't read my own writing. Er, Yvonne, Yvonne Christensen.'

Those words meant there would be two names finding their way onto Jessica's shit-list. First, this journalist, second, whoever leaked him the name. Everything released to the media by the police had to go through the press office. They got decidedly annoyed if something they hadn't approved ended up in the papers or on television. Working with the media was even part of the training nowadays and, worse than that, the DCI would be annoyed if he didn't get his chance to go on television and make an appeal.

'How did you get that name?' Jessica asked.

'You know I can't tell you that. I've got to protect my sources and all that.'

So he wasn't just a know-it-all, he was a cocky sod too, thought Jessica. 'Look, I'm going to have to refer you to the press office. There's no one in at the moment but I know there will be a statement going out later. If you phone their main number, somebody will come back to you in a bit.'

Jessica thought she was keeping her temper pretty well in check. The press-office speech was something she had given to people in the past, usually when she was far more junior and didn't know any information even if she wanted to give it out.

'I figured that,' Garry replied. 'But I thought they would probably only be giving out basic information later and thought I'd ask someone who might actually know something.'

'Right . . . how did you get my number?'

Garry lowered his voice. 'I know a guy at the phone company who can get numbers for me.'

He was really getting on her nerves now.

'I wonder if you could pass him on a message for me. Have you still got you pen handy?' Jessica didn't wait for the caller to answer before continuing. 'Tell whoever got you that number that they *will* be fired and possibly prosecuted. Can you spell "prosecuted" or does it have too many letters for you?'

Even if he was telling the truth, Jessica was fully aware she had no way of knowing who this journalist's 'guy' was – let alone a way of getting him fired – but she might as well try to get someone sweating a bit.

'Okay,' Garry said dismissively. 'I'll tell them that . . . so do you want to make a comment then?'

'No.'

The cheeky swine had gone right to the top of her list with that flippant remark.

Jessica hung up abruptly after considering sending the journalist packing with a two-word goodbye. She wondered if she should tip off Cole but thought that the journalist would have already gone over her if he was going to. Besides he was probably just full of it. One of those Scene of Crime people, or someone in uniform, had just blabbed and he was trying it on, seeing if she let anything slip. She would wait for the Sunday paper and then decide if she was going to hunt him down and make his life difficult.

As much as Jessica wanted to get on with the case, CID struggled with weekends simply because of everyone else's working patterns. Courts, coroners, solicitors' offices, forensics, their own press office and all kinds of other departments were either closed or trying to run with a cut-down weekend workforce. While uniformed officers had many more call-outs and lots more work to do across Friday nights, Saturdays and Sundays, plain-clothes officers were often left catching up with paperwork.

She had been planning on going home and possibly getting something to eat with Caroline but knew she wouldn't be the best company given her mood. After her talk with the journalist, Jessica went back into the station to catch up on some paperwork, figuring it would be one less thing to do the following week. The desk sergeant was clearly confused, seeing as Saturdays were usually the day when plain-clothes officers were battling to get out of the door, rather than back in it.

She had her own office but wanted a bit of company. Rowlands was on the main floor doing some paperwork of his own so she went and sat opposite him. 'Wotcha,' she said.

'You're way too old to be talking like that.'

'Oi. How are you doing anyway? Did Eric Christensen get home okay?'

'I assume so. Someone took him in a car to identify the body then they were going to drop him back.' Rowlands paused for a moment, looking up at her across the table. 'How are *you*? Isn't it this week that . . . ?' He tailed off.

As much as they bickered and joked with each other, there really was affection under the surface, albeit strictly platonic. 'Yeah, Monday.'

'How long has it been?'

'Eight months.'

'Do you still miss him?'

'Of course.'

Everyone who first joined CID started as a detective constable after spending around two years in training and a period before that in uniform. Generally, being a new DC meant you were the first point of call when the teas needed to be made or you could possibly be sent on a biscuit run on a quiet day. Woe betide a freshly recruited constable who brought back a packet of custard creams from a mid-morning dash to the local supermarket. Even hardened criminals didn't get as much abuse as some unfortunate new recruit returning with something that didn't have chocolate on it.

You learned pretty quickly.

On top of that really important work, you also got all the jobs no one else wanted. You would get the vast array of forms to fill in and handle the rest of the paperwork to file, sending it off to wherever it was needed. You would have to hunt through the mountains of papers or computer files to fulfil the freedom-of-information requests. You might have to work with the press office if you really annoyed someone, or perhaps liaise with other police forces around the country and make the endless hours of phone calls to rule people out from inquiries. If you were really unlucky, you could even get the task of hunting through hours of CCTV, phone logs or anything else in an attempt to find a breakthrough.

Every now and then you were actually responsible for a decent lead, something that might get an expression that wasn't just a scowl from an inspector or chief inspector if you were really lucky. If you got a 'well done' or someone bought you a pint, you knew you'd had a really good day.

Those months were the initiation ritual where you found out whether you actually wanted the job, or whether you were up to it. Not everyone was.

After her introduction to the department, Jessica had been assigned to help out Detective Inspector Harry Thomas around two years ago. Despite his position, he was still eager to get out into the thick of the action. Desks weren't for him and neither was the brown-nosing, which was why he hadn't even tried for anything like a promotion. At first it was just a shadowing exercise set up by bosses looking to tick boxes and perhaps have a laugh among themselves. She was in her late twenties, emerging from five years of working in uniform and taking exams to qualify.

Harry was two ranks above her and twenty years older.

He was an old-fashioned detective with not much hair, a paunch belly and a north-east accent – even though he hadn't lived north of Manchester since he was a child. He also had a supposed attitude problem, certainly when it came to anyone in authority above him.

It had most likely been their DCI's little joke at first – pair the new girl with the grumpy old guy who has sat at the same desk for a decade and see how much she wanted to be a detective then.

In fact, their partnership turned into a firm friendship and mutual respect. She liked how he got results and was completely committed to getting bad guys off the streets. He liked . . . well, she wasn't sure. It wasn't the type of conversation they would ever have had – feelings and all that. It would have been like confiding in your dad. Either way, he had put up with her for long enough and, for Harry, that was as close as it ever got to giving someone his approval.

'I know you and Harry were close but I didn't really know the guy,' Rowlands said. 'He always seemed a bit grumpy and people went on about leaving him be. I don't think they really knew what to make of it when he took you under his wing.'

Jessica nodded. 'He was certainly grouchy but I think it was just his way. When you got past that he had a really dry sense of humour.'

'Is that where you got all your dirty jokes from?'

'Only the good ones,' Jessica grinned. 'The thing was he had contacts everywhere. This killing this morning, if I'm honest with you, Dave, I don't really know where to start.

I'm just sitting here hoping forensics strike lucky. Harry would have been out there talking to people he knew. I'd ask him how he had those contacts and he'd just shrug and say he had a pint with them fifteen years ago.'

'Blimey, I was still at school then.'

'Exactly. This one time I was out with him and there was a homeless bloke he bought cans of lager for. He'd just put them down next to him and give the guy a wink. I didn't know why he'd done it but he just said, "You'll see." Then, two weeks later we went back to the same guy. He was in the same window wearing the same clothes and Harry went and sat next to him on the ground.'

'What, in his suit?'

'Yeah, it was mad. I just kind of hung around on the other side of the path not knowing where to look. He gave the guy this brown envelope or something, had a quick word and then walked off again. I asked him what was going on and it turned out this homeless guy had witnessed some incident a few nights previous. People don't notice him because they think he's asleep or passed out or whatever. Later on, Harry goes and arrests some other bloke and the case we're working on is all sorted.'

'That's quality.'

'I know. Things like that happened all the time but most people didn't get to see him work.'

'Has he told you what actually happened with . . . y'know?'

'I've not spoken to him in five months. He doesn't answer his phone and, assuming he hasn't moved, he doesn't open his front door either.'

'People have been saying he didn't cooperate with the investigation.'

'Who knows? I think he just feels embarrassed by it all.'

'Surely it wasn't his fault he got stabbed?'

Jessica sighed. 'The thing is, Dave, I just don't know.'

Eight months ago, Harry had gone to the pub after shift for a late drink. She didn't know for certain but Jessica assumed it was something he did most nights. In general Harry wouldn't go near the police pubs; he preferred the ones far more dimly lit where the landlord was happy to let his clientele hang around after closing for a cheeky final drink. Or five.

The drinking never seemed to affect Harry's work and, other than the job, there wasn't much they had in common but Jessica had seen him mellow somewhat. After they had been working together for six months, she had even persuaded him to go to the same pub the rest of the crew went to. He had let her buy him a drink: 'Not that Scotch shite, a proper drink, bourbon,' is what he had told her to order.

That is exactly what he had been drinking when some boozed-up thug knifed him in a dingy pub at the end of a bright September day. He survived but spent weeks in hospital and never returned to the force. Jessica had visited him but he wasn't the same person.

Faced with the mandatory counselling sessions before being allowed to return fully, he took early retirement. He didn't even seem that interested in helping the police's own investigation. Whether it was the shame of drinking himself into a vulnerable position or simply not being able to defend himself, she didn't know.

'From what the papers said, it sounded pretty clear cut,' Rowlands said. 'We got the guy's fingerprints and the knife and everything.'

'The prosecution are using me as a character witness at some point. I know people were saying Harry hadn't co-operated properly with them but they didn't tell me any of that when we met up last week.'

'But if they've got the knife and everything, what else do they need?'

Jessica shrugged. 'From what the lawyer said, the problem is the CCTV from the pub is more or less unusable. There were plenty of people in there at the time but mysteriously they all seemed to be in the toilets at the same time.'

'Oh right, like that then.'

'Exactly, no one wants to say anything.'

Tom Carpenter was someone who couldn't handle his drink and happened to carry a knife in his back pocket. Regardless of the witness problems, his fingerprints had been all over the knife left sticking out of Harry's guts. A string of low-level thefts meant they'd had no problems identifying who he was.

At the time Carpenter might not have realised he had stabbed a police officer but, when the papers and news programmes got hold of the story and started flashing his photo around, there weren't too many places to hide and he handed himself in.

Jessica hadn't known how to take the news when she found out. She had certainly done plenty of hard graft working with Harry but he had always been fair with her. The years of exams you had to take before getting onto CID could teach you the things you might need to be a detective but Harry had helped her *become* one. He had introduced her to his sources and shown her how to find her own. He told her which journalists you could trust and which ones you should nip to the public lavatories to avoid, even if they were on fire. It was almost as if he opened her eyes to the city itself.

Cole had been promoted when it was clear Harry wasn't coming back and it was a sad fact she had almost certainly been promoted to detective sergeant to fill a gap left by him walking away. It had seemed like a quick promotion but a lack of recruitment in the local area meant sergeants were getting younger all the time. In theory it meant she got to supervise the detective constables but in practice, she still took orders and was given only slightly better jobs to do.

Jessica didn't want to talk about things any longer. 'You may as well get off, Dave. I've got a few things to sort out then I'll be following you.'

'Are you sure?'

'Yeah, just sort that bloody hair out when you get home. You look ridiculous.'

Rowlands laughed. 'You're one to talk. It still looks as if you only got out of bed twenty minutes ago.'

'Whatever, see you Monday.'

After the constable had left, Jessica tried phoning Harry

to see how he was feeling ahead of the court case. As expected, he didn't pick up. She had been around to his flat twice in those months too but there had been no answer. Whether he was in or not, she didn't know. Seemingly he wasn't in any kind of contact with anyone from the station. She sent him a text message just in case.

With little else to go on, she thought contacting a locksmith would be a good idea, just to ask how easy it could be to break through a double-glazed door or window without a key. She picked a name from the Yellow Pages classifieds and called. His advert claimed he worked '24/7' – but he said he would only be available to talk to her if she had an actual job that needed doing.

In other words, he wanted a few quid.

He did reluctantly agree that he could spare her 'a few minutes' on his lunch break on Monday so she arranged to meet him at his house, which was a short drive from the station. Jessica could have kept ploughing through the phone book to find someone who would speak to her today but she just wasn't in the mood any longer.

6

The next morning Jessica was sitting in her flat's kitchen eating some toast and reading the Sunday edition of the *Herald*. She didn't usually buy a newspaper but, given the phone call from the reporter the previous day, she had been out to the local shop to pick one up.

There was a small article under the main story on the front page that basically rehashed the media release she'd helped the press officer write the evening before. The officer had been 'working from home' so it had been a short conversation but at least the paper had played ball. Garry Ashford's name was nowhere to be seen either and Jessica concluded he was clearly all talk. Some of the national papers had a paragraph or two on their websites but there was no way she was going to buy all the papers just to check what had gone in.

She used her phone to search the Internet for the victim's name but it hadn't turned up any news stories of note, certainly nothing that related to the case. At least that meant the department were still on top of things and she wasn't going to have to explain to the DCI why his television appearance would be upstaged.

As she was reading, her flatmate Caroline came into the kitchen wearing a white dressing gown and fluffy pink slippers that looked like piglets.

'Morning,' Jessica said. 'I didn't think you'd be up this early. I tried to be quiet, not that it would make much difference.'

Jessica was always amazed by her friend's ability to sleep through anything. If there was an overnight alien invasion, she thought Caroline would just wake up after eight hours of uninterrupted slumber and wonder who the grey-headed extra-terrestrial with the probe was.

Caroline laughed. 'If I had the choice of my superpower of being able to sleep through anything, or yours of being able to eat any old shite and not get fat, I'd rather have yours.'

Jessica knew her friend had a point. Saturday fry-ups and regular curries were just the start; she had never really put on weight, even as a child. Now approaching her dreaded thirty-somethings, she had been telling herself she had to start eating properly but hadn't got around to it.

'Anyway,' Caroline added. 'I don't know why I'm up. I guess I just fancied doing something.'

'You're not turning into a morning person, are you?'

'I hope not. I *hate* those people.'

Caroline Morrison was Jessica's oldest and best friend. She was slim with naturally slightly olive skin plus long brown hair and wide brown eyes to match. If she was honest, Jessica had always been a tad jealous of her friend's looks and especially those eyes. Caroline really was pretty whether she put any effort into her appearance or not. A few years ago, when they used to go out a lot more often than they ever managed now, Jessica always felt the need to wear more make-up and spend longer on her own hair

in order to not be the 'ugly friend'. She didn't feel un-
attractive but, compared to Caroline, she was always likely
to be second choice.

At that time Jessica was frustrated her skin was frequently pale, her hair wasn't completely blonde, while her
hazel eyes weren't quite any colour. Some days they seemed
green, others brown or grey. She wasn't bothered by anything like that now; Harry's stabbing and subsequent
downward spiral had matured her in a way she couldn't
have expected.

Caroline nodded towards the toast in Jessica's hand.
'Any bread left?'

'Yeah, you might have to cut the mouldy bits off
though.'

'Eew . . . oh is that . . . ?'

Caroline had noticed the main picture on the paper's
front page above the murder story. Jessica closed the pages
and scowled at the photo. 'Yes. Peter Hunt.'

'Is that because the court case starts tomorrow?'

'I tried not to read it but probably.'

When Tom Carpenter, the man who stabbed Harry,
handed himself in, it wasn't the police he had come to,
instead it was someone altogether more sinister – Hunt.
Lawyers weren't that popular with police officers in any
case but Hunt was truly the scourge of the Greater Manchester Police force.

He was a lawyer who delighted in taking on cases to
defend anyone with a high-enough profile to get his photo
into the papers and on the news bulletins. There may have
been rifts between colleagues in her department but the

one thing everyone Jessica worked with was united on was that Hunt was as low, if not lower, than the people he represented.

It didn't help that he was from the south. Being a lawyer was Hunt's first crime, while having coiffured blond bouffant hair was another. But being born in Cambridge and speaking with a southern accent was an altogether bigger one. The fact he represented all manner of hooligans and law-breakers was the final straw.

Public Enemy Number One for the force wasn't anyone among the array of drug dealers, gang members and other ne'er-do-wells that blighted their life, it was Hunt. Even the DCI, disliked by most of the officers under his care because of his pomposity and adhesion to strict form-filling, had it in for the lawyer. It was rumoured he himself regularly checked the status of Hunt's tax disc just in case he'd forgotten to renew it on the £250,000 Bentley he drove around in.

'I saw him on TV last week,' Caroline said. 'He was on one of the news channels talking about some book he's got out.'

'He's always somewhere giving his version of the truth. He was in the paper last week because he was launching some campaign with one of the local MPs. One of the younger lads set up a dartboard with the picture on. It was very popular.'

'I wouldn't have thought you had a good enough aim to get him in the face?'

'Who said I was aiming for his head? It was a full-length photo.'

Caroline smiled. 'You really don't like him do you?'

'He's an arse.' Jessica didn't like bringing work home but had ranted to Caroline about Hunt a few times in the past.

When she and Harry had first met, he had been working on a case against Frank Worrall, a well-known local crook. Money-laundering is what they had tried to get him on but people-trafficking, prostitution, loan-sharking or the odd beating could have been options too. Worrall was involved in many things that caused misery for others but proving it was never going to be easy. As well as the year of on-off work Harry had already put into it, Jessica had helped with some of the final bits and pieces before the Crown Prosecution Service had been called in.

Worrall was no fool and had an army of people working under him. The dealers on the street were easy to pick up but they were always careful not to be caught with any significant amount of drugs on them. They were always out of court quickly, never turned anybody else in and, even if they had wanted to, they wouldn't have known it was Worrall at the top of the tree. Eventually CID, along with the over-arching Serious Crime Division, had brought Worrall in and been given that go-ahead to charge by the CPS, who must have thought there was a case.

But they hadn't counted on Peter Hunt.

A year ago in court, Hunt had painted Harry and the rest of the force as bitter, target-driven incompetents with a vendetta. Worrall's wife had cried in the witness stand and told the jury what a good man her husband was. She sobbed as she spoke of him grafting every day to provide for her and their children, while Hunt had even handed her a box of tissues to emphasise the point. The kids were also present at the back with the grandparents towards the trial's conclusion to ramp up the pressure and Worrall himself spoke about inheriting his father's building business and how he had just wanted to do his dad proud. He insisted the police had it all wrong and he didn't understand why they had it in for him.

Even Jessica had to admit it was a masterful performance.

Against the emotion of those performances, the paper trail the police had put together was always going to be a hard sell. The jury had the choice of either the crying wife and scared-looking children at the back – or a complicated series of circumstantial transactions that could be implicating. When it came down to picking between the sharp-speaking, good-looking lawyer or tired officers reading from a notebook, there had barely been a contest.

The eight men and four women acquitted Worrall on all counts with Hunt leading the now free man out onto the steps of the court house with their arms aloft. He told the live news broadcasts that proving Worrall's innocence was the highlight of his career and that the police would have to rethink the way they ran investigations.

If that wasn't enough to fully put himself in the force's sights, when he had taken the Carpenter case, he had not only managed to get the man bail but had negotiated the CPS down from an attempted murder charge to one of wounding with intent – or section eighteen grievous bodily harm in legal terms.

Harry's lack of cooperation hadn't helped but Hunt had stood up in pre-trial court and vouched for the accused, saying he would be personally responsible for him between that date and the main trial. Carpenter had been free to walk the streets on bail for the past eight months.

Jessica wasn't bothered by Hunt's hair, his birthplace or his occupation but, even for him, trying to get this guy off was low.

She folded the paper over and put it down on the table. Given the anger she felt at the giant photo of Hunt, she decided there was only one thing for it that evening. Harry had given her many pieces of advice but one of the things she pledged to remember was about keeping a normal life away from the job.

'Do you fancy going out later?' Jessica asked.

'It's a Sunday. Aren't you at work tomorrow?'

'Yes but we don't have to go crazy, do we?'

'All right but not that pub at the end of the road.'

Jessica nodded. 'Okay, fine. We should probably clean this place up a bit before we go out.'

'Is that your way of asking me to do it?'

'Maybe . . . I'll clean my room though.'

Caroline laughed. 'You sound as if you're eight years old.'

When the two of them had first moved in, Caroline had gone for the bedroom with the more girly colours while Jessica was happy with the one that had a light blue tone to it. Caroline's had lilac walls and she had bought herself a matching duvet cover, while Jessica was using the same bedding she'd had for as long as she could remember.

The walls may have been a pale blue but her sheets were dark brown. Her room was consistently the messier of the two as well, with most of her clothes left on the floor.

'So we're agreed,' Jessica said. 'You tidy the hallway, kitchen and living room and I'll pick up the clothes from my floor.'

'Whatever – as long as you buy the wine later.'

'I did say I didn't want to come here . . .'

Jessica knew her friend didn't really like the pub closest to their flat but she didn't fancy going into the city centre; there would be too much temptation to turn a relaxing night into something not really appropriate considering how much she would have to deal with the next day. This way she could sneak in something from one of the takeaways on the way home too, although she hadn't mentioned that part when she and Caroline had made plans to go out.

'I know but it's close and it's not *that* bad,' Jessica replied.

'Maybe not that bad for someone as cheap as you,' Caroline said with a huge grin.

'Right and whose top are you wearing?'

'I wouldn't dare wear something of mine in a place like this.'

The two women giggled to each other as the bottle-and-a-half of cheap wine they had gone through was beginning to take its toll.

'I think you should give me the top anyway,' Caroline continued.

'Why would I do that?'

'I distinctly remember lending you fifteen quid for a taxi a few years ago when you were going out with that Graham fella and I'm pretty sure I never got it back.'

That was possibly true, although money had never been an issue between them. Jessica hadn't had much of a pay increase until very recently. Meanwhile, Caroline was enjoying a successful advertising career with one of the local agencies. She had been earning good money for a few years, certainly enough to move out of their flat if she so chose.

They laughed again. 'Eew, Graham.'

Caroline and Jessica came from roughly the same place not far from Carlisle, a hundred miles or so to the north of Manchester. They hadn't really had any contact with each other until they started sixth-form college when they were both sixteen. On the very first day, they had ended up sitting together in a history class.

Jessica often thought it was funny how one small, seemingly inconsequential, decision could have such a bearing on the rest of your life.

They were both only children and, since bonding through that, they had been more or less inseparable. They had spent a year travelling through parts of south-east Asia when they turned eighteen. Caroline had applied to go to university in Manchester and, although Jessica wasn't interested in further education, the pair had both moved to the city upon their return. They didn't live together at first. Caroline stayed in university accommodation for her first year, while Jessica found a flat close to where they currently lived. By the time Caroline had finished the first year of her course, the two of them moved into the same flat they still lived in.

Caroline had spent three years studying, while Jessica tried to find something she was interested in doing. She applied to the police on a bit of a whim. While a lot of people joined the force because they had a family member who also worked in the emergency or security services somewhere, this was far from the case for Jessica. Her parents managed a post office in their home town, which was certainly something that did run in the family. Her father's father had bought the building and started the business almost sixty years ago. There was never really any chance of Jessica hanging around to take over the reins and both of her parents knew it. They never pressured her though and still ran the place, happily looking ahead to retirement in a few years. Jessica usually found time to visit her parents once every couple of months but spoke to them regularly on the phone.

Perhaps the reason the two had remained so close was that Caroline's parents had both died within a few months of each other not long after she graduated. It hadn't been much of a surprise; her mother and father were quite a bit older than Jessica's parents and her dad had been ill for a while. Not long after he died, her mother did too. Caroline had been devastated but took heart from the fact they had both seen her graduate, the first in her family to do so.

'So, new boyfriend then?' Jessica said.

'Yep.'

'Let's hear it then.'

'Do you remember a few months ago when I went over in those heels?'

'Of course,' Jessica laughed. 'It was really funny.'

'Thanks for the sympathy; I could have broken my neck.'

'Honestly, if there was any neck-breaking involved, I would have definitely laughed a little less.'

'Anyway, I really like that pair, so I took them to that place on Gorton Market where they mend shoes. There was this lad who worked on the stall . . .'

'You dirty tart.'

They giggled again. 'We had a few drinks and have been seeing each other since then. We're going out again some time this week.'

Jessica understood that meant her friend had been spending time with him when she claimed she was at the gym or somewhere else inconsequential but didn't mind. 'As long as you don't dump me to move in with this obvious weirdo, then I hope you have a good time.'

'Weirdo?'

'He went out with you.'

'Oi.'

They both laughed some more. 'What's his name then?' Jessica asked.

'Randall. Randall Anderson.'

'Randall? What sort of name is that?'

'I dunno. I kind of like it. It's a bit different.'

'Hmm . . . Caroline Morrison-Anderson. I guess it does have a ring to it.'

'Don't start . . .'

The fact neither of them had really had time for a serious relationship was perhaps the biggest reason neither Caroline nor Jessica had decided to move into their own place. Of course they actually liked living together but, with neither of them having a heavy commitment, there had never been too much need to hunt for a new place to live.

Jessica felt the wine taking hold and, as the final orders bell rang, she pulled her phone out from her bag. 'I'm just going to check the Internet to see what's in tomorrow's paper.'

She thumbed away at the screen, flicking through her bookmarks before finding the *Herald*'s news site. The front page loaded and she pinched the screen to zoom in, before slamming her free hand down on the table.

'What's up?' Caroline asked.

Jessica just about kept her temper intact. 'Garry Ashford. Whoever he is, I am going to string him up.'

7

Sunday night hadn't ended in the way Jessica thought it would. The top headline on the *Herald*'s website had read: 'MURDERED IN HER OWN HOME'. Underneath that was: 'LOCKED DOOR MYSTERY' and the byline: 'EXCLUSIVE by Garry Ashford'.

Pretty much all the details were there: the victim's name, the fact the house was locked and that the police had taken two days to respond to Stephanie Wilson's concerns. That sounded bad straight away. The journalist had also spoken to Mrs Wilson, who had blabbed pretty much everything she had already told them.

Worse than that, he had quoted her: 'Detective Sergeant Jessica Daniel insisted she had no extra comment to make.' There was even a complimentary line about her being 'trusted to head up the inquiry'. That write-up almost certainly meant her bosses were going to think she was the leak. They were going to hit the roof and, seeing as the journalist had phoned her the day before, if Internal Investigations were involved, they would see his phone number on her records.

Jessica still had Garry's details in her mobile's previous callers list and, figuring she could be in enough trouble already, phoned him back as she left the pub to walk home. She wasn't sure whether to go straight in with the full barrage of swear words or to build up in a particularly obscene crescendo. Afterwards, she couldn't quite recall the full details of the one-sided conversation but definitely remembered promising to do something not at all pleasant with his lower intestines and quite possibly inventing a host of new curses.

She had arrived at the station earlier than usual on the Monday to be greeted by a hard copy of the paper sitting on the reception desk in front of that morning's desk sergeant. The headline was the same on the print version as it was online, except the article itself was even more terrible than she thought. Jessica saw that, in the absence of any photos of the victim, they had used a picture of her. Worse still, it was a horrible passport-type photo the press office had taken to use on the force's website.

Under a big banner headline about a murder, she was there grinning like an idiot. Just as she thought her morning couldn't get much worse, Jessica saw Detective Chief Inspector William Aylesbury bounding through the big double doors into reception.

Most people called William would have the good grace to let you call them 'Will' or 'Bill'. A huge majority would even prefer it but not the DCI. She called him 'Sir' of course but, when he introduced himself to anyone, he would pronounce every last syllable of Will. I. Am. Ay. Les. Bury. He would roll the letter 'r' as if he were royalty.

He was certainly one of those types who followed the family trade into the police force. His father and grandfather had been senior officers in the Met, while his son had recently joined Greater Manchester Police's uniformed ranks based at a different station. She had no doubt he would be superintendent in no time with the current one, DSI Dominic Davies, well-known to be retiring in under twelve months.

He was in his early fifties with short grey hair but could have passed for someone ten years younger given the way he looked after himself. He was tall and imposing when he wanted to be and almost always perfectly turned out with expensive-looking suits.

'Been making friends with the press, have we?' Aylesbury said, indicating the paper in Jessica's hand that she hadn't been quick enough to put down.

He beckoned her into a meeting along with Cole and the woman in charge of press relations. Jessica told them she had spoken to Garry Ashford on Saturday afternoon but only because he had called her. She explained she had not given away any details and didn't know how the information had appeared in that morning's paper, although pointed out there were plenty of people who had been at the crime scene.

She was pretty sure Cole believed her but Aylesbury was far too hard to read and the press officer definitely didn't buy it. The woman stared daggers throughout the meeting but, given she was outranked by everyone present, that was about as much dissatisfaction as she could get away with. Jessica's opinion of the DCI improved a tiny amount when he dismissed the press officer and told her and Cole he would inform Internal Investigations there was no need to be involved.

They had the powers to start an inquiry regardless of

what the chief inspector thought but seeing as nothing had been leaked that was likely to compromise the inquiry – and that he was backing her for now – it seemed probable they would listen to his advice.

That meeting led straight into a second one with the three of them, which was how her morning would have started if it wasn't for the newspaper story. The next discussion was about how the case would run. Aylesbury confirmed Cole would work from the station with Jessica reporting directly to the inspector, who would keep him up to date.

After that the three of them went downstairs for the main team briefing. They were standing at the front of the station's large meeting room, with no natural sunlight in the basement hall – the only illumination being provided by bright white strip lighting. Sometimes on the night shift, officers would come to sit in this room just to be kept awake. The whole of the station's force had been called in to be told what was happening, including most of the uniformed officers. A couple of detectives from neighbouring districts had been loaned to the station, as often happened with murder cases. In all, there were between twenty and thirty people sitting on uncomfortable-looking plastic chairs, or standing near the doors at the back, sipping on cups of coffee, waiting to be filled in.

Behind the three of them were two huge whiteboards pinned to the wall. At the top in the middle of the left-hand one was an enlarged photo of Yvonne Christensen's neck wounds, next to a recent photo to show how she had usually looked. Her name was written underneath in marker pen, along with the husband and son's in smaller writing under that.

Jessica thought Aylesbury sounded quite impressive as he spoke, despite his over-pronunciation. He started by reminding everyone of their responsibilities in not talking to the media without prior permission, then thanked everyone for being there and said he had every faith they would catch the person responsible. He told them Cole would be their link person at the station and then handed the floor over to Jessica.

He gave her a full introduction for the benefit of the visiting officers but they would have known exactly who she was because of the ridiculous photo of her gurning on the front of that morning's paper. Jessica thanked her boss, ignoring the murmurings of amusement from the officers standing in front of her, and then explained how the house had been found locked up.

After that, she moved on to the morning's developments. 'We've got the initial results back from the labs but there's not an awful lot to go on,' she said. 'We know Yvonne Christensen was killed some time late on Tuesday night or in the early hours of Wednesday which all fits in with Stephanie Wilson's timings. She was strangled with some type of steel rope or wire but we don't have anything more specific on that. They have been running tests on the bed sheets and the body but haven't yet found any samples that don't belong to the victim.'

'Do we know why she was in the bedroom?' someone asked.

Cole answered. 'Probably. If you were being strangled,

the obvious thing you would do is try to pull away the other person's hands or the rope but there are no cuts to the victim's fingers. Given that and the estimated time of death, it seems likely she was throttled in her sleep. If she did wake up, it would have been too late.'

Jessica nodded along and then carried on speaking. 'Obviously this makes it more difficult to figure out what actually happened. Even if the victim had let someone in we wouldn't know how he or she got out. Because of the findings, it seems very unlikely the killer was a person she opened the door to. The obvious answer is that either her estranged husband or son was involved. As far as we know they are the only family members still alive but there are no life insurance policies in place and no other obvious motive.'

Jessica paused for breath. 'Since Saturday, we have been able to pretty much rule out the husband Eric and son James. Confirming their respective alibis was complicated because of the period between the time of death and the body being found. James is at university in Bournemouth and, given the distance along with everything we've been able to verify, there aren't any gaps long enough for him to have come up here and been able to return again.'

Jessica looked at Cole and raised her eyebrows. He took the hint and picked up the story. 'James does at least have a set of keys which he showed to our colleagues down south but he insists they are kept with his other keys and are always on his person or somewhere nearby. Eric Christensen, on the other hand, says he gave his set back to his wife when he moved out. We don't know if this is true but his alibis for the past few days certainly do check out.'

He looked back to Jessica, who turned again to face the floor and spoke. 'Essentially, with the lab teams not coming up with anything and the only family members we know of unlikely to be involved, we don't have an awful lot to go on. We're not even sure how the killer got in and out, let alone who it was. We've examined all the usual things and know there is no basement, while the attic is full of junk. There was certainly no one hiding up there waiting for us to clear out.'

'Can you cross over from the attached property?' someone asked from the floor.

'No, good thinking though. It is semi-detached but the brickwork goes all the way up to the top. It was one of the last things we checked.'

Jessica asked the assembled officers if anyone had any suggestions for how someone could have managed it. One constable got a laugh by putting forward the name of a popular TV magician, with a sensible suggestion to look at the previous owners. It had already been established the Christensens had lived in the place for just over five years but theoretically the previous owners might have kept a key. It seemed unlikely but it was something that should be formally ruled out.

'Did the door-to-door inquiries come up with anything?' one of the constables asked.

Jessica and Cole snorted at the same time. 'Nope,' Jessica said while Cole expanded. 'The best we got was one neighbour at the other end of the street who thinks they saw the same person walk past their house three or four times in a short period. She was a little elderly and it could be the postman for all we know. Her description was fairly bland and didn't really give us too much but they are going to work with the profilers today to get something onto the evening news. It does seem a long shot though.'

Someone made a crack that any picture without a gormless grin being on the front of tomorrow's papers would be an improvement. Jessica made a mental note so she could give the joker something tedious to do when the jobs were given out. She had read the witness's description and doubted there was anything in it but thought it perfectly summed up Cole himself, given the normality of it.

Cole continued. 'We've set up a phone line for people to call in with information but we haven't had anything yet, despite the media coverage.'

Neither the inspector nor Jessica had anything further to add, so Aylesbury told everyone there was going to be a press conference in the station at three in the afternoon and pressed the point they should all look busy. He sent them on their way with a slightly cheesy attempt at inspiring them into action. It was probably better than what Jessica could have managed, so she was grateful for it.

As the floor thinned out with various people being given their jobs for the week, Jessica waved Rowlands over and told him he was coming with her to the locksmith.

The two of them walked out to the car park at the back of the station. The morning had taken a lot longer than Jessica thought it would but at least things now seemed to be moving. She wished she had thought to bring a jacket to work, her trouser suit offering little resistance to the chilly spring breeze as they walked towards the car pool. Saturday's warm weather seemed long gone and Rowlands must have taken one look at the morning's grey skies and thought ahead as he was wearing a long trench coat to guard against the cold, while his hair was back to its full spikiness.

'We're not going in yours, are we?' Rowlands said sarcastically as they reached the bank of vehicles.

Jessica grinned and shivered at the same time. 'I'm not sure, we do need something to distract from your flasher's mac.'

'Careful with that smile, there might be a *Herald* photographer around.'

Jessica thought she might as well remind the locksmith who they were if he started looking at his watch too quickly so they took one of the marked police cars. She told Rowlands the address and said he could drive. Her mood was better than it had been in days but she still couldn't be bothered with the other idiots on the road. Sometimes being in a marked car simply aggravated things. You could always tell the worst drivers; they were the ones who slammed on their brakes and pretended they were doing the speed limit the minute they saw you in their mirror.

The journey wouldn't take very long but they had barely reached the bottom of the road when Jessica's phone rang.

'Will you change that bloody ringtone?' Rowlands moaned as she fumbled in her bag for the device.

The caller was one of the other officers from the station.

They had done some checking on the house's previous owners. The couple that owned it before had emigrated to Canada when they moved out five years ago and were still living there.

'Not a bad alibi,' Jessica said to the caller. She hadn't thought the previous occupiers would be a serious avenue to explore but also hadn't reckoned another lead would fall through quite so quickly.

She hung up and turned to Rowlands. 'Perhaps we should see if that TV magician has an alibi after all?'

8

The locksmith's white van with company branding was parked on his drive, making the house Rowlands and Jessica were looking for easily identifiable. Just to fit the stereotype, he even had a red-top tabloid flopped across the dashboard as they walked around it to get to the front door. The man invited them in and offered to make some tea. Jessica never really drank hot drinks when she was younger but when you joined the force it became almost inescapable. Every time you went to a house to interview someone you were offered one and whenever you were on a training course you would have tea shoved down your throat at every opportunity.

One of Harry's favourite places to get himself out of the station, aside from the pub, was a cafe which refused to serve coffee. On questioning this, the owner had told Jessica: 'This is England, we drink tea. The French drink coffee.' She didn't really get that statement then or now. Even when you were at your desk in the station, whoever you were sitting next to seemed to ask at least once every hour or so if you fancied a tea from the machine. Whether what the machine spewed out could be classed as 'tea' was another issue, of course. She would love to get forensics involved in that particular investigation.

After their phone call, Jessica thought it would be a

quick ten-minute trip where the locksmith would want them back out the door as soon as possible. But, far from keeping an eye on his watch, he actually seemed to enjoy showing off his knowledge. He talked about multipoint locks, five-lever dead locks, security hinges, double-locking handles and all types of other things that generally washed over the two of them. Rowlands wrote it all down but he might as well have written down 'super special double-locking lock locks that can't be opened, not even with special fairy dust' for all the use it was to Jessica.

'Could someone pick this type of lock?' Jessica asked.

The guy rocked back in his chair, almost spilling the cup of tea he was cradling, and laughed as if she had just told a particularly funny joke no one else got. 'You've been watching too much TV, love.'

She forced Rowlands to ask about a skeleton key, although that brought even more laughter. The locksmith's point was pretty clear – as long as they had been fitted correctly, it was more or less impossible to break through double-glazed doors and windows that were secured.

Aside from the fact their visit hadn't really got them anywhere, being called 'love' was the final straw for Jessica. They said their goodbyes and set off back to the station, Rowlands clearly trying to suppress a smirk at the term of affection she had been called.

The desk sergeant pulled Jessica to one side as soon as they arrived back at Longsight. 'Has anyone told you about what's happened in court this morning?'

She hadn't forgotten that Harry's case was beginning that day; it had been in the back of her mind all morning. With so much going on, and the fact Harry was still ignoring her, there didn't seem much she could do. She was supposed to be acting as a prosecution character witness at some point during the proceedings. It was booked into her schedule that she would appear but she wasn't completely sure when that would be. Most cases were allocated a set number of days or weeks for a trial and both sides had a rough idea what the order would be. Witnesses had to be booked in, whether civilian or professional, but there could sometimes be a day or two's leeway.

'No, I've been out,' Jessica replied.

'Harry hasn't turned up. They've delayed selecting the jury for now but, if it goes on much longer, the case is in danger of being dismissed. Apparently they can get through the first day or two without him as they have all the photos and the knife and so on but, after that, if there's no Harry they don't really have a case.'

Jessica sighed and cursed under her breath.

'We've sent uniform around to knock on his door but there's no answer. His phone's off too so no one knows where he is,' the desk sergeant added.

'That lawyer guy is going to be furious.'

Jessica had met with the prosecutor heading up the Crown's case on a couple of occasions. First he had come to her to ask what she could offer as a character witness for his side, and then he had returned not too long ago to give her examples of the types of question he would ask her in court. All officers were trained in regards to court procedure but this was a case the CPS really wanted to win. They knew Peter Hunt would be claiming Harry was an alcoholic who had started some sort of fight where Tom Carpenter had defended himself against a violent drunk.

Jessica didn't have to lie to refute that. Harry did drink, sometimes more than he could handle, but she had never seen him get aggressive with it. In fact the opposite was true. He would calm down significantly and start to tell his stories. He was full of tales from the 'old days'. Some of them weren't very politically correct and certainly not in keeping with the modern police force but he certainly knew how to tell a good anecdote.

That was what she would say on the stand; he was a good man and, though she hadn't been present, she didn't believe he was the type of person to instigate something that would end up with him being stabbed. None of that would matter if they couldn't get Harry himself to court.

'Hunt can't believe his luck, of course,' the sergeant added. 'The guy I spoke to reckons he's had a huge grin on him all morning. He's been swanning around like it's already in the bag.'

'Great. Any other good news?'

'The computer system is down again.'

'Again? What's happened this time, did someone stop feeding the hamster?'

'The what?'

'Y'know, giant hamster wheel, powering the station . . . ? All right, forget it.' Her humour was obviously far too advanced for the likes of her colleagues. 'Is the DCI around?'

'Getting ready for the press conference, of course.'

A few years ago, somebody had decided the force wasn't open enough to the general public. They wanted the police to be far friendlier with the media, who would in turn get across a better positive message on their behalf to the general public. To do this, some of the ground-floor offices had been knocked through, repainted and reassigned as an area where they could host press conferences, or bring select members of the media in for cosy briefings.

The major problem had been that, for some reason, that same person had called the new room the 'Longsight Press Pad'. No one really knew what the name was supposed to mean and anyone with any sense would have just called it a media or press room. Even the journalists thought it was ridiculous and, given the negative reaction, the whole initiative had been swiftly forgotten with the police effectively given the green light to go back to treating journalists with the contempt most of them thought they deserved.

Despite that the name had stuck, almost as a badge to remind people not to be so stupid in the future. The Pad was almost full that afternoon, Aylesbury sitting in the middle of a table at the front with the Greater Manchester Police branding across the wall behind him. Cole was on his right, with Jessica sitting on his left. Jessica was sweating and thought that whoever had named the room should have spent more time getting air-conditioning installed and less time coming up with a ludicrous title for it.

There were three local television cameras on tripods at the back of the room blocking the door. If there was a fire in the station they would all no doubt burn – but at least the cameras would have a good angle on it all. In front of them were around fifteen people, some journalists and some seemingly technical people to deal with the audio and visual quality. Jessica recognised a couple of the faces; one or two she had watched on the local television news and another female print journalist she had seen a few times over the years.

In the past, she had never really had cause to speak to the media because there was always someone above her to do the talking. That fact hadn't even crossed her mind as they had spoken about doing the press conference that morning. She didn't really get nervous but might have dressed up a bit if she had known she was going to be on TV. Before she had gone in, one of the uniformed female officers had given her a trick about wearing extra eye make-up to look more 'serious' on camera. Jessica thought the implication was really that she would look more 'awake' on camera but had taken the advice with a quick trip to the toilets before entering the room. Regardless of her efforts, Aylesbury was wearing enough make-up for the three of them.

One face she did make a special point of looking out for was Garry Ashford. She didn't know what he looked like but, as everyone assembled in front of them, she had started to narrow down her list of suspects. She had ruled out the females and the older male journalist who she had seen on TV. There were a couple of technical-type people, which left her with three possible options for who this Ashford character could be.

First was a grossly overweight bloke sitting in the front row. She had never seen him before but he looked as if he was in his early forties. He had short patchy black hair and blotched skin on his face. He was talking to a much younger female journalist next to him who didn't seem too interested in making conversation.

Second was a guy in his late twenties or possibly early thirties. He was tall, good-looking and seemed far too sharply dressed to be a journalist. He had nicely styled brown hair and certainly stood out in the room. He was in the second row of seats, sitting behind the station's press officer, already writing in his notepad and seeming attentive. If this was Garry Ashford, she might just about feel guilty about kicking his arse considering how good-looking he was.

Suspect number three was sitting at the back and had barely looked up since Jessica had started watching him. He was young, maybe mid-twenties, and had shoulder-length scruffy black hair which stood out against his pasty white skin. She stared closely at him and noticed he was wearing a brown tweed-like jacket with elbow patches.

Who the hell was this guy? Tweed? Elbow patches?

He had that kind of look some people seemed to think made them look like a quirky rock star, or tortured writer. It didn't; it made them look like dicks.

As she compared all three 'Garry Ashfords', Jessica hoped this guy was the real one. She would actually enjoy bullying him.

Aylesbury opened the conference, introducing himself and the other two officers and welcoming everyone present.

Without naming names, he criticised 'uninformed report-ing' and said that any leaks should be properly checked with the station's press office. After telling the assembled media off, he then effectively confirmed that every detail already reported by the *Herald* was true.

Each journalist had been given a pack with the photos and details the force was happy to release. It included the phone number members of the public should call if they had any information, as well as the sketch based on the person the neighbour had seen walking past the victim's house a few times the previous weekend. That had only arrived moments before the briefing had begun but the assembled media had been assured they could download a better-quality version from the force's website. Jessica had seen the sketch itself and didn't expect any useful leads. It looked so plain it could really be anyone. Whoever was manning the phone lines the following day would have a lot of useless information to wade through, she thought.

The media were told that Yvonne Christensen's hus-band and son had helped the inquiry but were not suspects and the point was reinforced that the public should feel safe. Aylesbury made a special instance of looking into the camera to emphasise his words and enforce that point as if he was making an Academy Award acceptance speech.

After that he opened the floor to questions. Most of what was asked was simply going over what was already known. The first question came from the obese man at the front, who immediately ruled himself out of Jessica's list of suspects by saying, 'Paul Davies, *Bury Citizen*,' before asking something particularly bland.

One down, two to go.

After a few more questions, the DCI pointed at the hand from the back – suspect number three. The man ruffled his hand through his hair and said: 'Garry Ashford, *Manchester Morning Herald*. I was just wondering why it took the force two days to respond to Stephanie Wilson's concerns?'

Jessica narrowed her eyes and stared at him. 'Got you,' she thought.

9

The last couple of days had seen a complete turnaround for Garry. After the call from his source about Yvonne Christensen's murder, he had phoned the number he had been given for that detective sergeant but not really got anywhere. She seemed like a right moody so-and-so.

When she asked how he had found out her number, he made up something about a friend from a phone company but didn't think she'd bought it. They would struggle to find his source even if they got into his own phone records. The person that contacted him had at least two SIM cards and had called from the unregistered pre-pay one.

After getting a 'no comment' from her, he made the call he had been waiting eighteen months for – to tell his editor he actually had a story of note for him. It was both of their days off and he had never called his boss on his mobile before. He figured this was as good a time as any. Garry reckoned Tom Simpson would have been a good journalist at some point in the past but, being in the job for as long as he had while he worked his way up to editor, he had lost something along the way. Garry had taken a year and a half to become cynical about the industry but his boss had been in the job for over twenty years, so who knows what he thought of it all?

The editor was in charge of managing the paper's content and staff but recently there increasingly seemed to be pressure to make savings. Everyone had seen the memos from management about cost-cutting and, along with the length of time he had been doing the job, Tom Simpson had appeared to lose any courtesy he might have once had.

As editor, his one concern was getting a paper out on time and not getting fired. He frequently swore and bawled out other reporters in the newsroom, warning them that costs had to be brought down and, if they didn't get him better stories, perhaps *they* would be expendable. Some of the older production staff and journalists had told Garry it hadn't always been like that. When Tom had first been promoted to editor eight or nine years ago, the atmosphere had been much better but declining sales, the rise of free content on the Internet, and rifts with management had taken their toll.

One of the older reporters, who was eagerly awaiting retirement in a year or two, had explained to Garry in the pub one evening just why he thought things had got so bad.

'All those government departments and councils and police and fire and everyone else have these bloody press officers now,' he said. 'In the old days you could buy someone a pint and get the full story on everything. It was all cock-ups galore and you could really go to town on these idiots. Now you just get stuck rewriting these nonsense statements about "diversity" and "ethical funding", whatever the hell that means.'

Garry didn't know whether that was right but it was clear the only time the editor's mood seemed to improve was when somebody brought in a story that raised sales.

The finance department and editor received daily figures for how many copies of the paper had been returned by newsagents and street sellers. This allowed them to work out how many copies of the paper had actually been sold. Garry thought his luck had finally turned with his 'bin fury' story. On the back of that, sales had gone up twenty per cent for three straight days. His editor was delighted. He had praised Garry's work ethic in a group email and hovered around his desk for those days asking about follow-up stories. Eventually it had to end – there were only so many articles you could churn out about rubbish before people stopped buying and moved on to something else. Sales dropped to where they were before and Garry had been forgotten about again. In many ways, that had made things worse. Before, he was just some anonymous reporter in the newsroom but after that, he had shown he could get stories that spiked sales, just not consistently.

Garry's editor answered his phone with a 'who's this?' Not even a 'hello' and definitely not a 'hi'.

'This is Garry, Garry Ashford.'

'You do know it's my day off?'

'Yes . . . but I think I have something big for you.'

'You "think" you have something big? I'm on my way to the football.'

Garry stumbled his way through telling his editor about

the phone call he had just received. He talked about the murder and how the body had been found locked in a house as the police took two days to find it. His editor asked for the source and Garry gave it.

'You scruffy little genius! Why didn't you use them before?'

It sounded good-natured but Garry wondered if the 'genius' part outweighed the 'scruffy' comment to actually make it a compliment. He told his boss that his source had never really come up with anything of note before.

His editor didn't sound as if he was really listening anyway. 'Right, right,' he continued. 'Look, get hold of this witness. Just turn up at her door and find out what she told the police, then get into the office tomorrow. No point in wasting something like this for tomorrow's edition – the city's empty on a Sunday. We'll get everyone with a blinding front page on Monday. Blow the nationals out of the water.'

Despite a few pangs of uncertainty about turning up at the front door of a potential witness, Garry did what he was told. He first did a few online searches through his phone to find the correct address. His source had given him Stephanie Wilson's name and the road she lived on but not the exact house number. Luckily, there was a Ray and Stephanie Wilson on the electoral roll, so he knew where he had to go. He had also found them in the online version of the phone book too. Not many people seemed to be in the book now, given the widespread use of mobiles, but the Wilsons were obviously old-fashioned and had a landline number. Garry called it and spoke to the husband, Ray, who seemed delighted the press were involved. They arranged for the journalist to visit the house the following morning.

The interview with Stephanie herself was largely taken over by her husband who, from what he said, had been single-handedly responsible for uncovering the whole story. He kept saying how he had been a journalist in his youth and that it was his idea to call the police.

The way he had spoken, you would have been forgiven for thinking it was he who had uncovered the body and was in the process of cracking the case. Stephanie hadn't said too much and was clearly highly affected by her friend's passing. As Garry managed to coax the truth from her, it became clear her husband had had pretty much nothing to do with any of it. That didn't stop him asking if the paper wanted to send a photographer over to take photos of them both. Garry thought he was a bit of a nuisance but seemed relatively harmless and thanked them both for their time. He had what he needed.

The offices of the *Morning Herald* were spread across two floors midway up one of the taller buildings in the centre of Manchester. Editorial and advertising shared a floor, production and finance occupying the one above it. Other businesses had various floors within the property but the whole place was like a ghost town on a Sunday. Garry used his security pass to get through the staff door at the back and then again for the lift.

He had barely stepped out of the elevator when he

heard his editor's far-too-cheery voice from across the other side of the room: 'Garry.'

While the few heads who happened to be working that day turned to look in his direction, no doubt confused why their boss was so pleased for once, Tom was bounding towards him. Garry started walking towards his desk but his editor caught up and put a fatherly arm around his shoulders, ushering him into his own office. Even when he had been popular in the past, he had never been invited into the editor's office.

Garry had a good look around. The view was as impressive as it could be considering what Manchester had to offer. Garry's usual desk offered various angles of the back of some girl's head who worked in advertising. Admittedly, she looked more attractive from the back than the front but that wasn't the point. The editor ushered him into a plush leather swivel chair, where the mechanism to move the seat up and down actually worked, which was significantly more than you could expect from a chair on the main news floor. He then offered to make Garry a cup of tea.

What on earth was going on?

Garry thought his boss making him a hot drink was perhaps pushing things too far, so declined.

He told his editor how the morning interview had gone and repeated what he had said on the phone the day before. His boss nodded furiously throughout, making the odd note and just repeating 'good, good' over and over. Garry was aware that the magnitude of someone being brutally murdered seemed to be lost in the moment. He was told he could use the editor's own computer to type up the story so, still feeling as if he were in some bizarre alternate universe, he used his notes to do just that.

Garry thought of the victim as he wrote. He was excited about finally being in his editor's good books but didn't want to let that detract from the empathy he felt. Ray Wilson and now his boss both seemingly wanted to use the murder almost as a springboard for their own aims. Ray's were harmless and slightly pathetic but Garry hoped his boss wouldn't push things too far. Yes, it was a big story and he was going to be the one to break it, but he didn't want the fact to be lost that someone had been murdered.

He finished typing and went to find the editor back on the main floor, receiving plenty of odd looks from his colleagues, unsure what he had done to receive such a warm welcome. Tom almost skipped across the newsroom towards him and they both went back into the office. Garry's boss sat in front of the computer and read through what had been written. He nodded frequently and again repeated 'good, good' numerous times. When he was done, he turned back to Garry. 'Top, top work, this, young man. Top work. Need to spice it up a bit in a few places but this is really well done.'

Garry was nervous by what he meant by 'spice it up' but said nothing.

'I think you're just about done for the day,' Tom added. 'Go get yourself a pint and enjoy the evening. You deserve it. We'll get this on the website tonight and then tomorrow your name will be on the front page.'

He was being sent home *early*. Working unpaid over-time was something he had done many times but Garry had never been let go before his shift ended. This really was new ground.

'I reckon there'll be a press conference tomorrow and you'll be right there,' his editor added. 'Maybe you can give your little source a call when you get in? Y'know, see if anything else has happened?'

Garry had no intention of doing that but said he would, picked up his bag and made a beeline for the lift. He moved quickly as he didn't want to risk his invitation to leave early being revoked but also because he didn't want to see the accusing stares from his colleagues as he walked out, wondering why he was suddenly so popular.

They would find out when they saw the front page.

After checking in again with his delighted editor on the Monday morning, Garry had been told he would be going to the press conference over at Longsight mid-afternoon. His editor told him to 'ramp up that two-day cock-up angle'.

What he meant was to ask questions about why it had taken two days for the police to successfully find Yvonne's body after Stephanie Wilson's phone call. Personally, Garry thought it was a bit harsh. The police weren't to know there was a dead body involved and, considering she could have just gone away for a few days, he thought they had done pretty well to act in that time.

Regardless of his own thoughts, he would ask the question. At least with all the other media present DS Daniel couldn't shout at him in quite the way she had on the phone the night before. He found a clean pair of dark trousers and his favourite jacket. He had worn it out a few times after being assured by his friends it made him look interesting. He thought it gave him the air of some type of philosophical deep thinker.

He made sure he was sitting at the back for the briefing, making notes as other people asked their questions, and spotted DS Daniel on the end. She hadn't said much, simply sitting and scowling at the audience in front of her. As he sat waiting to pluck up the courage to put his hand up, he thought she had looked directly at him. Her long almost-blonde hair was swept back out of her face and he thought she looked kind of cute.

That thought began and ended as he asked his question. He saw her looking straight at him, a half-smile on her face with her eyes telling him one thing clearly: 'You're dead meat, sunshine.'

10

Jessica wasn't sure whether she liked Caroline's new boyfriend. Perhaps she felt that way because the investigation was going nowhere and nobody would have impressed her given her mood – or maybe it was because she had arrived home from another unproductive day and found him already in their flat?

Their flat was on the ground floor with another one above them which had been empty for a little while. Unlike some in the area, it was an actual apartment and not just a converted house. They had a small garden at the front but it had been paved over before they moved in and they never did anything in it. As you entered the front door, Jessica's room was immediately on the left, while the entrance to the living room was opposite it. Next to her bedroom was Caroline's, while at the end of the hallway directly opposite the front door was their bathroom. The kitchen was a separate room, with its door opposite Caroline's bedroom. The living room was the biggest in the flat but the two bedrooms were fairly equal in size.

It was a week and a half since Yvonne Christensen's body had been found and Jessica had got precisely nowhere. They had already reached the point where constables from other districts had been returned to their force while officers at Longsight were being moved on to other cases. It really was a disaster, with the finger of blame pointing squarely at her.

Nothing much had happened in the initial investigation with lead after lead finishing in a dead end. The hotline had come up with nothing, except for members of the public wanting a chat or thinking their uncle looked a bit like the e-fit. Someone had even phoned up to say the sketch looked like the officer who had been on the news the night before. They were referring to Cole, which brought plenty of quiet laughs around the station when he wasn't present. All potential leads had been checked but there was nothing of any substance.

The day after the press conference, the *Herald* had gone to town on the force because of the two-day delay in finding the body. There was a big picture of the victim smiling out from the front page, with an editorial inside asking why the body had been 'left to rot'.

'Nice and tactful for the family,' Jessica said to Cole when they had seen the paper.

A few days after that, the force had been blasted again, this time for a lack of progress. The byline on both articles had been 'Garry Ashford'. With the investigation not going anywhere, Jessica would spend parts of her free time thinking up creative ways to make life miserable for the long-haired, tweed-jacket-wearing pain-in-her-arse.

With murders, in a huge majority of cases the killer was someone who knew the victim. In most of them it was either a family member or someone romantically involved. But anyone they knew of who apparently fitted that description with Yvonne Christensen had been ruled out.

They had looked into everyone from the husband, to his new girlfriend, to the son, to the neighbours and even Stephanie and Ray Wilson, just in case. They checked her bank accounts and phone records, all of which seemed normal. No one seemed to have a motive for murdering Yvonne and, even if they had stumbled across a reason, no one – least of all Jessica – had much of an idea how the murder had been pulled off.

With all of that running through her mind, she had driven home in the rain with a clear plan for the evening: take her shoes off and relax in the living room with a bottle of wine.

Jessica really liked her and Caroline's living room. She found it incredibly cosy and relaxing, perfect after a bad day. There was a deep dark brown fabric sofa that allowed her to sink into it. She had fallen asleep on it a fair few times in the past. They had a separate reclining seat made of the same coloured fabric but Jessica much preferred the sofa. There was a glass coffee table in the middle of the seats too, which usually had some selection of celebrity magazines Caroline had bought on it. Jessica pretended she never read them but would often have a flick through when she was alone.

Between the two of them, they didn't really watch too much television and hadn't bothered paying for anything like satellite or cable. Given their jobs, both of them lived pretty busy lives but Jessica had never been much of a television-watcher in any case.

Caroline had plenty of DVD box sets but Jessica only really watched the news and late-night reruns of trashy morning talk shows. Not that she would have admitted the talk-show watching to her colleagues, of course. You would lose plenty of credibility if you confessed that one of your hidden pleasures was staying up at night to see what the results of the previous show's DNA tests would throw up.

But, after arriving back in her flat, there was a man she didn't know sitting on their sofa drinking from a can of lager.

'Er, hello?' Jessica said as his presence caught her by surprise while she had half-kicked off one of her shoes.

'Oh, hi . . . is it Jessica? I'm Randall, Caroline's boyfriend.'

Caroline had re-entered the main room at the sound of the voices. She said she had been changing in her room and added that she hoped Jessica didn't mind Randall coming over. 'It was just that I wanted you both to meet but everyone is always so busy so, in the end, I just invited him over. I hope you don't mind.' Caroline explained.

Jessica didn't mind, well not really, but it would have been nice to have been asked.

As it was they weren't having a bad evening. Randall was decent-looking – just under six feet tall, with a shaven head and blue eyes. He clearly had a decent physique judging by the tight fit of his T-shirt and must work out, though his muscles weren't bulging in a grotesque way. There was some kind of spiky-lettering tattoo visible on the lower half of his right arm but Jessica couldn't figure out what it was. He wasn't really her type; she didn't go for guys who spent so much time working out and tattoos and piercings had never been too appealing. He did seem nice and Caroline could barely take her eyes off him.

Although she preferred the sofa for comfort, Jessica had left it to Randall and Caroline to share while she took the recliner. They half-watched some nonsense game show, laughing at the contestants' lack of knowledge while Caroline tried to get her best friend and boyfriend to interact with each other. The bottle of wine the two women had shared was certainly helping in that regard.

'So, you met over shoes then?' Jessica said after an hour or so of small talk.

Caroline and Randall looked at each other and giggled then had a mini argument over who should tell the story in full. If it had been anyone other than her best mate – and if they didn't look so happy – Jessica would have felt sickened by their show of affection. There was nothing more annoying to her than happy couples.

It was Caroline who spoke. 'He did such a good job fixing them and they *are* my favourite going-out heels.'

She smiled and squeezed her boyfriend's hand.

'Isn't it just a bit of glue?' Jessica asked, not meaning the question to sound quite as blunt as it did. She was moderately interested but probably could have phrased the question better.

Randall laughed. 'Well, yeah. You just take the names, addresses and phone number if they're cute, wait until they're gone, get the old superglue out then charge 'em for the privilege.'

Jessica assumed it was a bit more complicated than that but laughed along.

'Wait, you only get the phone numbers if they're "cute"?' Caroline asked with mock indignation.

'I got yours, didn't I?'

'Oh yeah, that's all right then.'

'At least you've got a story for the grandkids anyway,' Jessica said. 'Grandma fell over and broke her shoes, while Grandpa fixed them for her.'

'Whoa. Who said anything about grandkids?' Caroline laughed.

'Or kids.' Randall joined in.

'And as for getting married . . .' Caroline added.

They were already finishing each other's sentences and, despite the public sentiment being a bit too much for her, Jessica was pleased that her friend seemed happy. She could just do with a lot less of that happiness happening in front of her.

When the giggling had died down and Jessica had poured another glass of wine for each of them, Caroline said to her boyfriend: 'Did I tell you Jessica works for the police?'

'Yes. What is that, local?' he asked.

'Not too far.'

The conversation fizzled out as Caroline yelped due to Randall tickling her. Jessica went back to half-watching the television. Whatever game show it was they had on seemed to be lasting a ridiculous length of time, the contestants definitely not getting any cleverer.

'Are you single?' Randall asked Jessica during an advert break.

'Yep.'

'I've got some mates – I could hook you up with someone.'

'I'm all right, thanks.'

'Come on, it'd be fun the four of us going out.'

Jessica didn't feel comfortable with the conversation.
'Nah, I'm okay. I'm busy at work.'

'Well, if you change your mind . . .'

'. . . You'll be the first person I call.'

Jessica thought she had enough on her plate without
complicating things with dates or boyfriends.

A short while after, Randall stood and asked if he could
get a glass of water.

'Lightweight, are we?' Jessica asked playfully, considering he'd had three cans of lager.

'I've got a bit of a headache coming on.'

'There are painkillers in the drawer under the sink if
you want some?' Jessica said but Caroline cut in. 'Oh, he's
allergic to aspirin and things like that.'

Caroline stood up, pushing her boyfriend back to the
sofa. 'I'll go, you explain.'

Caroline left the room and Jessica said: 'Sounds nasty?'

Randall made a face as if to indicate 'sort of'. 'I've kind
of got used to it. You live with the headaches and so on.
Some people have it really bad, their throats swell up and
within a few minutes they can't breathe. With me it takes
an hour or so.'

Caroline returned and gave her boyfriend a glass of
water, which he drank a few mouthfuls from, then put the
glass on the coffee table.

'So what actually happens?' Jessica asked.

'It's not happened in years because I just stay away from most medicines. Back then, my ears would start to ring slightly, then I'd come out in a rash on my arms. It's only after an hour or so when the inside of my throat begins to swell. That could stop you breathing and kill you in theory.'

Caroline spoke then. 'He had to tell me because if he ever had anything by accident, if I noticed a rash on his arms or anything, I would have to call an ambulance. That's a telltale sign.'

Jessica just nodded but she was glad it wasn't her. 'Must be hard getting over hangovers,' she joked.

Randall got up, saying he had to go to the toilet. He left the room and, as soon as they had heard the bathroom door close, Caroline wasted no time.

'What do you reckon?'

'He seems nice. You seem good together.'

Caroline grinned. 'It helps that he's hot too.'

Jessica grinned back. 'He's not too bad. Bit young for you.'

'Young? I'm only thirty. He's twenty-three, you cheeky mare.'

'That's toyboy territory. Mrs Robinson and all that.'

'It is *not*.'

Both women were now laughing with each other. 'You should take him up on the offer of going out with his mate. It would be fun with the four of us and take your mind off the job, too. You deserve a night away from it all.'

'Nah.'

'Go on . . .'

'Well, maybe. Not now though, I'm busy. Maybe in a few weeks when things have quietened down?'

Having a fun evening in with her friend was beginning to take Jessica's mind off the fact that things were not going well at work.

'I'm glad you like him,' Caroline added.

'He seems like a good laugh.'

'He is. He told me he was quite shy as a kid but says I've brought him out of it. He's quite sensitive when you get him on his own.'

'As long as he treats you all right.'

'Well, if he doesn't I know a police officer that can put him right.'

The flushing of the toilet brought an end to their conversation but, before Randall could return, Jessica's phone rang anyway. She had dumped her bag by her shoes next to the living room doorway and forgotten to take her phone out. She answered just a moment before it would have rung off.

It was Cole telling her that another body had been found.

11

Just because there had been another killing, there would have been no instant reason to link it to the first – until you saw the crime scene. There were so many parallels to the first death. The property was less than half a mile from Yvonne Christensen's but this time the victim was found in an armchair in the living room. It looked as if there had been more of a struggle but there were still deep, vicious wounds in the victim's neck.

The second murder scene was very similar to the first but with one major difference: this time the victim was male.

As Jessica walked into the interview room at Longsight, she didn't know how to feel. She had been at work the entire day and the wine she'd shared with Caroline on an empty stomach was only just wearing off. Any crime scene could be enough to make you feel a bit queasy but, as time edged into the late evening, her stomach was rumbling and she didn't feel quite right. She guessed a large part of that was down to the mixed emotions she was having. A part of her was exhilarated that something was now happening and relieved she wasn't necessarily a failure. Then she felt disgusted with herself, ashamed of her selfish reaction to someone else's death. It was hard to reconcile the two thought processes.

Cole was already sitting at the table opposite the station's duty solicitor, who was next to a terrified-looking young man.

Jonathan Prince still lived at home with his parents, despite being twenty-two. He had come home from work and found the body of Martin Prince, his father, in an armchair which the Scene of Crime officers were now taking photos of.

Cole started the tape and Jessica spoke to confirm everyone's name plus the time and date before pausing for a moment. 'Are you okay, Jonathan?' she asked.

No response.

'Jonathan?'

'Yeah, yeah. I'm okay. Well, sort of . . .' The young man spoke slowly, dazed.

'Okay, Jonathan I have to ask you these questions, all right? I know you've had a horrible time but anything you can tell us will help us find out who did this. Do you understand?'

'Yeah, yeah . . . I know.'

'Can you tell me what you've done today?'

Jonathan took his time and was frequently tearful. The solicitor said he didn't have to do this now but Jonathan wanted to. He said he had got up and gone to work as normal. He was employed as a builder and left the house at half-past six every morning. His mum, who worked as a secretary for the council, was always up at that time too, although he rarely saw his father before he got home. He told them his dad used to work for a printing company but had been laid off a few years ago. He hadn't found work since and rarely left the house.

'He just couldn't find anything to do with himself and no one wanted to give him a chance because of his age. He became a different person. Not bitter . . . just *sad*.'

It was hard not to be touched by the way Jonathan spoke about the father he had found dead just hours before. Jonathan himself had been unemployed for a period after leaving school but had now been in the building trade with a local firm for just over two years. He had thought a few times about moving out but his rent helped pay his parents' mortgage and he didn't want to leave them in a tough situation.

'Okay, this is going to be hard, Jonathan, but can you talk us through finding the body?' Jessica asked.

'It was about three o'clock or so and we were finished for the day. I didn't really have anything on so went to the pub for a bit with a few guys from work. After that, I was just going to go home and play on the PlayStation or something.'

'Did you drive home?'

'No, God no. Got a taxi.'

'And what happened when you got there?'

'I let myself into the house . . .'

This was the part Jessica had been waiting for, even though she was pretty sure what the answer would be. 'So the front door was locked when you arrived?'

'I guess . . .' Jonathan paused and then started nodding emphatically. 'Definitely. It was locked because I still had my keys in my hand.'

'Is it usually locked when you get home?'

'Sometimes. I mean, if my mum has left for work and Dad's not up yet I know she'll leave it locked just in case. It depends if he's out of bed.'

'Okay. What happened then?'

'I'd gone into the living room to say "hello". Usually the first thing you hear when you walk in the front door is the TV but it was quiet. I walked into the room and he was just there . . .'

Jonathan tailed off.

At the crime scene before they came back to the station it had already been established each window and the back door was locked. It was the first thing Jessica had asked to be checked when she arrived. The front door was of course open but Jonathan had told the 999 operators he had let himself in before finding the body. Martin Prince's own house keys had been found next to his wallet upstairs on the nightstand adjacent to his bed.

Again, there was no obvious way in or out.

Jonathan's alibi of being at work all day would be checked with his workmates and boss but, again, Jessica had no doubt it would be legitimate. His mother looked like posing a slightly different problem. Sandra Prince had arrived home as the police were arriving at the scene. When she realised the authorities were entering her house and had the news broken to her about her husband, she had collapsed, unable to accept what she had been told. She had been taken to hospital herself in an ambulance – much to the delight of all the curtain-twitchers on the road, Jessica thought.

Before she had gone in to talk to Jonathan, Jessica had spoken to someone in charge at the local hospital who said Sandra was now conscious but not capable of being interviewed. It sounded like the shock had been too much for her. She had been in the hallway of their house when she fainted as the officers present didn't think it was a good idea for her to see the living room and the state her husband was in. That did mean her handbag had been left in the house. Jessica felt terrible but had looked inside to see if her house keys were in there. They were, of course, as she had known they would be.

They would interview Sandra when the doctors said she was up to it. Given the circumstances – and the fact she had likely been at work all day, which was easy enough to check – she wasn't going to be treated as a suspect. That didn't mean she wouldn't have any useful information though and Jessica would still want to talk to her sooner rather than later.

They released Jonathan and she told one of the uniformed officers to give him a lift to the hospital.

After finishing the interview, someone in uniform had given Jessica a message from Aylesbury that she and Cole should go up to his office. She had only seen him in the station this late once or twice. Counting the basement incident room, the station had three floors. After her promotion, Jessica had been given one of the smaller offices on the ground floor. She shared it with another detective sergeant, Jason Reynolds, who was a big imposing black officer a few years older than her. He was funny and helpful but currently heavily involved in a complex fraud case.

If it wasn't for that, there was a very good chance the murder case would have been given to him instead of her, which was an idea Jessica would have been very receptive to at that moment.

She and Cole took the stairs up to the first floor and made their way past some of the rooms used for storage into the DCI's office.

'What do we reckon,' Aylesbury asked when they were inside, 'is it the same killer?'

It was clearly what both Jessica and Cole had been thinking. Cole spoke first. 'We think so, Sir. Obviously there are no forensics yet but the neck wounds look similar and the house at least seems to have been locked up like the first one.'

'Did you get much useful from the son?'

Jessica spoke this time. 'Not really. He was pretty shaken. He just confirmed he had unlocked the front door to let himself in, then found the body.'

'And all the other windows and doors were locked?'

Jessica and Cole nodded in unison. 'Yes,' Jessica said. 'The house could have been unlocked during the day, we won't know that until we speak to Mrs Prince, but the son says it was locked when he got home in any case.'

'We're going to have to keep this out of the media for now. We can't have talk of a serial killer at this stage, especially one killing people in their own homes. We should at least wait for the lab tests to come back and then maybe we can talk about releasing information. I'll draft a press release with the office, just something about a body being found and so on. You two, keep your mouths shut – and tell all the other officers that too. We can't have this getting out, not like last time.'

They were dismissed with Aylesbury's words ringing in their ears. Jessica walked through the station's reception. She was going to mention something to the desk sergeant about contacting her if any news came through about Sandra Prince but he was talking on his mobile and didn't seem too keen to be bothered. Jessica hung around for a few moments but felt too tired to wait. She hadn't driven in because of the wine she'd had but one of the other officers was going to drop her home. She was walking towards the bay of marked cars when the familiar sound of her ringtone started, muffled from being in her bag. She fished around and pulled out the device. The caller's name was only half a surprise. She had saved the number as something she thought particularly appropriate. 'Tweed wanker' the display said.

Jessica pushed the touch screen to answer and put it to her ear.

'What do you want?'

She didn't know if Garry Ashford knew anything about what had happened that evening but she definitely wasn't going to give away any information by accident.

'Hi, it's Garry Ashford. Can you speak for a minute or two?'

'I know who it bloody is. What do you want?'

'Can I run something by you?'

'What?' Jessica was shouting now. Did he know or didn't he?

'I've got it on good authority another body was found tonight.'

'Whose authority?'

'You know I can't tell you that.'

Suppressing a sigh, Jessica tried to stay calm. 'Like before, you are going to have to talk to the press office. They deal with media requests, not me.'

'Are they going to put out a statement about this murder being linked to the first one?'

Jessica winced. 'I don't know who told you that, Garry, but I think someone's pulling your leg.'

'Or maybe you are now?'

Jessica was fuming, not really knowing how to respond. How could he know? He might have found out a body had been discovered – there had been plenty of people having a nose on the street the Princes lived on – but how could he know how the victim had been killed? Or that the house had been locked?

Either someone involved with the investigation was feeding him information or . . .

'Are you my murderer, Garry?'

'What . . . no. Of course I'm not.'

'You seem to know a lot about the murders. Maybe things only the killer would know?'

'No, no, you've got it wrong. It's not like that.'

Jessica didn't think for a moment he was her man but thought she would give him a bit of his own medicine anyway.

'So what is it like? You've got to look at things from my point of view. I've got some guy who seems to know an awful lot about my case but doesn't seem willing to speak about it. Meanwhile, he's writing stories blasting me and my fellow officers. Maybe I should bring you in for questioning?'

She could almost hear him squirming at the other end.

'No, no. Look, I didn't write all of that. My editor, he . . .'

'He what?' On the other end of the line, Jessica heard the caller give a large sigh.

'Can we meet?'

'Are you asking me on a date? I don't go out with killers, Garry.'

'Not like that. It's just . . . I'd like to talk to you. Two people have died.'

It was the last line which brought an end to the charade between them. Jessica was still annoyed with him but she could hear in his voice that the journalist, like she did, recognised the two dead people were almost becoming a side issue.

'I'm pretty busy at the moment,' she said.

'Just fifteen minutes. Tomorrow afternoon? There's a coffee-shop place near my office.'

'Right, whatever. Text me the address.'

'Great. I'll do it now.'

Before he could end the call, Jessica thought of one final thing. 'Are you still there?'

'Yes.'

'Good. Don't wear the jacket.'

Jessica hung up.

12

There wasn't much coverage in the following day's papers – it had probably been too late for their deadlines. The morning news broadcasts were running with the line fed to them by last night's release and everyone seemed fairly happy that a lid had been kept on the details. Jessica went to see Aylesbury in the morning to give him a brief rundown on her conversation with Garry Ashford the night before. She didn't really want to be part of an internal investigation so thought it was best to tell him she had agreed to meet with the journalist later on that day. The DCI pointed out that, considering there were no test results back from the scene and they had been unable to speak to Sandra Prince, anything in the media about the murders being linked could cause a panic.

'They've already got us looking like blundering incompetents. What with this and the shambles of a court case going on, we're in everyone's sights at the moment.'

A 'shambles' was certainly one way to describe how the case surrounding Harry's stabbing was proceeding. After Harry's no-show on the first day, the prosecution had asked for an adjournment based on 'illness'. Peter Hunt for the defence had vigorously opposed the request but, given the jury had yet to be selected, the judge had reluctantly delayed the case for the rest of the week. Jessica had tried calling Harry but, as usual, there was no answer. Rumours were flying around the station that he would refuse to give evidence and the case would fall apart. With the Christensen investigation going nowhere either, it was a tense time.

The case had begun the week after and Harry had been present each day. After the jury selection and opening argument, it was his turn in the witness box today. Jessica was not allowed to attend because she was a witness and was relying on the desk sergeant – who seemed to know everything that was going on – and the television news.

'What about whoever's leaking this stuff to Ashford?' Jessica asked.

Aylesbury looked at her as if to say, 'I'm not convinced it isn't you'. He didn't follow it up, instead saying: 'For now things are fine but if anything else gets out it will become a matter for the Internal boys.'

The station was buzzing that morning. There was nothing like a body turning up to get everyone moving. Some people would be inspired to find the killer, others by wanting to do something good to progress their own career. Most officers fell somewhere in the middle. A photo of Martin Prince had joined Yvonne's on the incident room's whiteboard to keep everyone's mind focused, while the morning's briefing had gone on much the same lines as what Aylesbury had told her in his office.

He reminded everyone of the need to keep things in-house then Jessica talked the floor through what they knew. Jonathan Prince's alibi had been checked and confirmed and, even though Sandra Prince was still in hospital, it had been verified she had been in work the previous day too. Test results should be coming back later that day but, for now, everyone would operate under the assumption the murder had been carried out in the same way, probably by the same person, as that of Yvonne Christensen. A uniformed officer had been placed at the hospital with Mrs Prince and Jessica would be told when it was fine to interview her. Everyone was very careful not to mention the phrase 'serial killer'. Until it was actually confirmed, those were dirty words.

A phone number had been given out to all media the previous evening and officers were again needed to take calls. Some uniforms were going door-to-door in the area where Martin Prince had lived and another sub-team had been given the job of trying to link the two victims. It was a possibility they had been killed at random but far more likely they had something in common that, if discovered, could lead to a person who might want to murder the pair of them. The first thing they would do would be to contact Eric Christensen and ask him if he actually knew Martin Prince. It was probably too much to ask for but sometimes you overlooked the obvious.

'Find the link, we find the killer,' Jessica told the assembled team.

To say Garry Ashford was nervous about his meeting with DS Daniel was an understatement. One of the first things you were taught as a journalist was to protect your source, so there was no way he would reveal who had given him information about the killer. As for their conversation on the phone the previous evening, he wasn't sure whether she actually thought he was a suspect. If she really did think it was him, she would surely have him arrested so presumably she was just messing?

For now, he hadn't told his editor that he had any extra information about the second killing. The basics had been released to the media and his boss had asked him what else he knew, telling him to get back onto his contact and get the full story. He promised he would and had half told the truth when he said he would be meeting the detective sergeant to talk about the case. He *was* meeting her, of course, but only to confirm the information he already knew was true.

Since his boss's editorial criticising the police the previous week, using Garry's information and byline, he had been a lot more tentative about what information he gave up. He had somehow managed to walk the line of staying in his editor's good books while also feeling as if he hadn't compromised his ethics. It wasn't that he necessarily had a problem with breaking any of the police's embargoes or revealing information they hadn't released but he did feel uncomfortable with how it was being used to bash them in a way that gave little thought to the victims.

He was sitting in a small cafe around the corner from the newspaper's office in the centre of the city. It was an old-fashioned place that looked drastically out of sync surrounded by newly built or renovated glass-fronted buildings. He didn't know but it looked as if it had been there for centuries. It had character and smelled of exotic tea in a way only old cafes could. There were only half-a-dozen heavy round metal tables on the inside, with matching metal chairs that screeched every time they were moved. A couple of tables were also placed on the pavement outside just in case the sun came out. It was where Garry went for lunch a couple of times a week, attracted by its cheap prices and good-looking waitresses. He didn't know if the cafe's manager hired based on looks but it certainly seemed like it.

He ordered a cappuccino and told the blonde server he was waiting for a friend. He had just worn a regular coat over his shirt after the fashion advice he had received the night before. DS Daniel was five minutes late so he checked his phone to see if she had called or sent him a message of explanation. She hadn't but, as he looked back up, he saw her coming through the door with her best scowl on. She spotted him instantly and made her way over to sit opposite.

The waitress made a move as if to come over to their table but the officer gave her a look that quite clearly advised her not to.

'Hello,' Garry said as she sat down.

'Right, I'm here. What do you want?'

DS Daniel looked a little windswept; her long hair had clearly been blown around and she fiddled with it, trying to move it out of her face. For the first time Garry actually noticed her eyes. They were kind of half green, half brown. He liked them but not the way they were looking at him.

'I just wanted to check some things with you.'

'Go on.'

He flicked through his notebook and read from it without looking up. 'I've been told that the body you found last night was killed by the same person who killed Yvonne Christensen. Not only that but both bodies were found in houses that were locked and that you have no idea how the murderer either got in or back out again.'

DS Daniel looked down and took a deep breath then looked back at him. Her expression had changed. She no longer looked angry, just weary. 'Look, I'm not going to ask you who your source is but you can't print this stuff. We don't know if everything you just said is true. People have died. What we want is help finding whoever did it, not sensational headlines that are going to make people panic.'

Garry knew where she was coming from. He agreed with her to some degree but he was a journalist after all. Just because he had been given some information unofficially, he didn't see why it couldn't be used as long as it was done responsibly. 'I didn't write those headlines, my editor did, but you can't expect me just to sit on information when I get it. I have a job to do too.'

'That might be true . . .' DS Daniel tailed off. 'Right, print what you have but if I see the words "serial killer" anywhere in the article . . .' She tailed off again but the implication was clear.

'I'll do what I can but the editor writes the headlines and edits what I write. It's up to him.'

'Fine.'

'So can I quote you?'

'Don't push your luck. I don't trust anyone that can't spell their own name properly.'

'Huh?'

'Garry has one "r", you moron.'

Jessica was sitting on a bus that would take her almost the whole way back to the station. It would leave her with a five-minute walk but she didn't mind that. She hadn't fancied driving into the centre for her talk with the journalist. It was always a nightmare to park and she hadn't planned on spending too long with him.

She was actually quite pleased with the way her meeting had gone. She believed Garry when he said it was his editor who had written the stories up to have a go at the force. When Harry used to take her out, he would speak about the value of journalists. 'Just be careful which ones you trust,' he told her. 'Some of them would screw their own mothers over if it made the front page.' She was a pretty decent judge of character and Garry seemed all right. He actually seemed to care, which was always a good start.

She thought having someone she could trust in the media could be key to finding the link between Yvonne Christensen and Martin Prince.

As she wondered about that, the time the journey was taking was reminding her why she didn't use public transport very often. In terms of distance, it wasn't too far back to the station but the time really added up when the bus waited at every single stop. There was some guy chatting far too loudly on his phone in the seat in front of her, with three teenagers listening to some dreadful dance music through the speaker of one of their phones at the back. Near the front there was a baby strapped into a pushchair crying its eyes out while its mother chatted to her friend in the seat next to her. It was just noise, noise, noise.

She closed her eyes for a moment but couldn't blank any of it out. As she looked towards the rear of the bus, she saw one of the youngsters had just lit a cigarette. She sighed and wondered whether she could be bothered with it.

She took a deep breath. 'Oi,' she snapped at them, pointing at the no smoking sign on the window next to them. They were about three rows behind her.

'What?' the one with the cigarette said, taking his first drag.

'Put it out.' By now most of the other passengers were looking at her.

'Why? What the fuck are you going to do about it?'

This was all she needed. Jessica reached into her inside pocket and pulled out her police identification card, getting up from her seat and walking towards them. She hoped the bus wouldn't stop suddenly or she would stumble and look a right fool. She showed them her credentials, perching on the seat closest to them. 'Just put it out and stop being dicks.'

'You can't talk to us like that,' one of the non-smokers said.

'And you can't smoke on a bus, so put it out and we'll forget it happened, right?'

The kid with the cigarette looked as if he was weighing up his options but eventually stubbed it out on the floor.

'And watch your mouth in future,' she finished, putting her identification away and walking back to her original seat. 'Next time I'll drive,' she mumbled under her breath.

Jessica would not have been in such a hurry to get back to the station if she had known the news that was waiting for her. Firstly the desk sergeant pulled her to one side to update her about Harry's court case. She didn't know who the officer's source was at the Crown Court but whoever it was must have had a front-row seat.

Harry had been called to give evidence that morning but things hadn't gone well. Apparently, he had responded almost entirely with one- and two-word answers to the lawyer prosecuting and only shown any animation when Peter Hunt had begun cross-examination. Before the judge had stepped in, Harry had called Hunt 'scum' and a 'parasite'. He had eventually responded to the questions but, with the jury present for everything, the damage had been done. If he couldn't control himself in a courtroom, then why would they think he could control himself in a pub? Jessica felt so sorry for him. She so wanted to help in the way he had helped her but you couldn't do that if the other person wasn't willing to engage. She decided she would try to call him again that night. He probably wouldn't answer but she didn't want to abandon him.

As soon as she had finished at the front desk and before she could get back to her office, she ran into Rowlands.

'What bad news has my spiky-haired harbinger of doom got for me today then?' she asked.

'Funny you should say that . . .'

'Go on.'

'Sandra Prince. Her doctor won't let us speak to her for at least another twenty-four hours. He says she's not ready for it yet.'

'Great. Anything else?'

'We spoke to Eric Christensen. He says he's never heard of anyone called Prince. We showed him pictures of all three family members and he doesn't know any of them.'

'Has anyone come up with any other link?'

'Nope and door-to-door haven't got anything either.'

'Phone lines?'

'Got a few things to check out but probably not.'

'Are forensics back yet?'

'Just the basics. It looks like it's some kind of steel rope again. It's all on your desk but cause of death and the weapon seem to be the same as before. All the blood matches Martin Prince and, for the moment, they've not got anything else.'

Jessica sighed. 'Right. Do you actually have any good news?'

Rowlands beamed at her. 'Tomorrow night I'm off out with that new girl uniform have hired.'

Jessica rolled her eyes. 'You're a dick.'

13

As Jessica looked through the paper the next morning, she thought the coverage could have been worse. Admittedly not *that* much worse but definitely worse. Once again, all the other papers and TV broadcasts had stuck to the information given out by the press department. She knew the *Herald* was going to print the information Garry Ashford had – she had even told him to write it. In fairness, the phrase 'serial killer' wasn't present at all in that morning's front-page story. The problem was the headline: 'HOUDINI STRANGLER' in giant capital letters. If that didn't get members of the public panicking, then the article explaining how 'Houdini' was breaking into people's locked houses, murdering apparent strangers and getting back out again completely undetected certainly would.

The officer manning the front desk that morning told her they had already had two dozen phone calls from worried members of the public and he didn't even need to say where her first stop of the morning would be. She headed straight up the stairs towards Aylesbury's office. As she walked past the window, she could see Cole already there with Reynolds and a man and woman she didn't recognise dressed in suits. She could make a good guess at who they were.

When you became a police officer you were fully aware

there would be plenty of people who didn't like you. In uniform if all you got was the 'oink' noises and the odd swear word then you had got off quite lightly. Over the course of a career most officers would be spat at or assaulted in some way or another. Being disliked by certain sections of the public was a given – but if you wanted to be *really* hated then you joined the Internal Investigations department. Not only were you disliked by the public for being a police officer, you were also hated by other officers for investigating your own.

Each police force in the country had a set number of officers who had moved from regular duty into the Internal division. The reasons, of course, were to work against corrupt officers. Everyone had heard the stories of the 'old days' where certain members of the force would be paid by various criminals to turn a blind eye to the very acts they were supposed to be preventing. Jessica was sure some of those tales were exaggerated or possibly even based on television shows and movies, rather than fact. Certainly she had never come across any type of double-dealing in her time. Some officers even got a bit edgy if they were offered a free cup of coffee just in case.

Almost everyone in the force would be against those types of practices but changing sides and investigating your own was not a popular way of showing it. In the same way a grass would be ostracised in the criminal world, the Internal Investigators were shunned by a lot of officers.

Leaking information to the media was not as serious as taking money to turn a blind eye of course but, when it affected investigations, it was still treated accordingly. If that information caused a public panic that just made things worse.

Jessica entered Aylesbury's already pretty full office. The room wasn't massive, with a large desk that had a computer and some photographs on top. On the walls were various commendation certificates and the like. The DCI was sitting on his side of the desk with Cole and the two strangers on the other side. Reynolds was standing and, as there were no seats left, Jessica stood near the door.

The two officers she didn't know looked up at her then back down before she could make eye contact with either of them. They were both fairly young, the male maybe early forties with side-parted brown hair and a suit clearly a size too big for him. The female was around the same age with long brown hair tied back into a ponytail.

Aylesbury greeted her presence with a 'DS Daniel'. He paused to let her settle and then continued, acknowledging the two people sitting next to his desk.

'As some of you already know, these are officers Finch and McNiven. They work for Internal Investigations and will be speaking to everyone today about the information leaked to the media. I'm sure you are all aware of what has been in the papers.'

He held up a copy of that morning's *Herald* just to emphasise his point. He was speaking fairly calmly but Jessica could see anger bubbling below the surface. He was probably holding back because of the presence of the Internal officers. She wondered whether the anger was aimed at the leaker or at the people brought in to investigate his officers. She had never quite seen eye-to-eye with the DCI but, when it came to your fellow colleagues, most people would back them over the Internal team.

'We all know the value of using the media but whoever has leaked this information has not only made the force look incredibly stupid but put the investigation at risk. We have not been able to speak to Sandra Prince yet and headlines like this are hardly going to help her condition if she were to see them. People need to feel safe in their homes and to trust us. Recklessly giving information like this out helps no one.'

He made a special point of emphasising the last two words. 'During the day officers Finch and McNiven have been given one of the offices down the hallway from here. They will be talking to pretty much everyone in the station but you three will be spoken to first. At least then it will allow you to get on with the rest of your jobs. You know how these things work.'

No one said anything, not that there was much they could add. Jessica didn't know which officer was Finch and which McNiven but, as the DCI finished speaking, the female of the two looked up from a sheet of paper in front of her and said: 'We wanted to start with DS Daniel if that's okay?'

It was exactly what Jessica had suspected.

Cole and Reynolds filed out of the room back towards the stairs, while she went down the hallway with the two other officers. The male officer led the way, the female walking in between him and Jessica. They went down the passageway, turned left and kept walking until they reached the final room at the back of the building. It was an area Jessica had never really been to. As far as she knew there were only storage rooms back there. The male turned the lights on and Jessica could see it almost certainly was just storage. Boxes with files sticking out of the top had been shoved to the back wall and someone had brought up a table from what looked like the canteen. There was a dusty smell as the male offered her the seat across from them.

The woman started talking first. 'Okay, DS Daniel, I'm Officer McNiven, this is Officer Finch. We're from the GMP's Internal division as you already know. Can I start by asking if you know why you're here today?'

'To be bollocked by you lot,' was what Jessica thought. What she said was: 'So we can all work together to stop information getting into the papers that could harm the case I am working on.'

She made a special point to stress the word 'together'.

Officer McNiven smiled. 'Something like that.' She paused and shuffled through her papers, before continuing. 'Okay, tell us about your relationship with Garry Ashford.'

Jessica told the investigators that she had spoken to him three times on the phone, once on the Saturday after the first victim had been found when he phoned her, once the day after to 'clarify' the article she had seen on the *Herald*'s website and then he had called her again after the second body had been discovered. She left out the part where the middle conversation had been largely an exercise in creative swearing. She then said they'd had a very brief talk in a cafe the previous day.

'How did he get your number?' McNiven asked.

'I don't know.'

'Why did you call him?'

'I wanted to ask who his source was.' A half-truth.

'Why did you meet him yesterday?'

'I wanted to explain why causing a panic was not a good idea. I told Detective Chief Inspector Aylesbury I was going to meet him.'

'Did you give him any information?'

'He already had it. That's why we met.'

'Did you give it to him?'

'What? Information about the second killing? No. I've not given him any tips at all. I wouldn't even let him quote me.'

'Have you ever met or had contact with this journalist before the incidents we have spoken about?'

'No.'

'Why do you think it was you he contacted?'

'I don't know.'

They went around in circles for another five minutes or so with the two officers asking essentially the same questions in a slightly different way. Jessica didn't know anything further to tell them, while they seemingly didn't believe her. They were at a stalemate when Officer McNiven thanked her for her time, said she could leave, and asked if she could send Cole up to meet them.

Jessica stomped her way back past Aylesbury's empty office and down the stairs. She found Cole in his office and told him the bad news.

'You're up. Rosie and Jim want a word.'

She thought about calling Garry to ask what the hell the

headline was all about. Considering the conversations she had just had – and the fact the investigators could and probably would check her phone records – she figured it was a bad idea. He would almost certainly say it was his editor who wrote it anyway. Maybe that was true, maybe not.

She would have to wait until Cole came back down before they could go through the morning briefing. A few more test results had come back but nothing very helpful with yesterday's phone leads chased up and ruled out. She spoke to two of the DCs who were trying to link the two victims. They had come up with nothing of note. Some of the victims' kids had gone to the same school but, given they lived relatively close to each other, that was to be expected. Other than that, it was yet another brick wall.

She went to the canteen to have some breakfast. Although she hadn't expected the Internal team to be waiting at the station for her, she had known it was going to at least be a trip to the DCI's office, so had come straight in that morning. Randall had stayed over for the first time the night before too and she felt a bit awkward after waking up, so left without seeing either him or Caroline. The station's canteen was on the ground floor along the hall from her office. At best the food could be described as 'poor'. Reynolds refused to eat there and claimed he had once needed three days off after eating some stew.

'The tea's bad enough here,' he advised her. 'Don't risk the food too.'

Jessica wasn't as passionate about not eating there as her office-mate but she did try to avoid it where she could. She risked beans on toast, thinking no one could really make a mess of that. As it was, it wasn't too bad. She was sitting on one of the plastic chairs using the Internet on her phone. Word would have flown around the station that the Internal team were interviewing upstairs and it was a good bet everyone would know she was the first person who had been called in. She didn't want to talk about it too much, so was fiddling with the phone's front just to look as if she might be busy to hopefully stop anyone coming up to her.

She had wasted around twenty minutes before the first person tried their luck. One of the DCs assigned to try to link the two victims approached her table. DC Carrie Jones had a very strong Welsh accent that Jessica loved but others didn't. Piss-taking was a given in any work environment. Jessica got it for her car, Rowlands for his hair and girl-chasing, while Carrie Jones got it for her accent.

'I've got some news,' she said.

Jessica couldn't help but smile at her. 'Good news?'

'Good news and bad news.'

'What's the bad news?'

'Sky News, ITV, the BBC and the local radio stations are now also using the phrase "Houdini Strangler".'

The smile disappeared from Jessica's face immediately. She put her hand to her forehead and sighed. 'You could have sugar-coated that a bit.'

'Er, sorry. Do you want the good news?'

'Go on.'

'The hospital has phoned to say you can go see Sandra Prince.'

14

Jessica returned to her office to make a few notes before heading off to the hospital. Reynolds was sitting at his own desk opposite hers. It was clear their office was occupied by two very different people. On Reynolds's side closest to the door, everything was in meticulous piles or filed away. On Jessica's half, papers, notes and files were carefully ordered on the floor, around the bin, under her seat and spilling over from her desk.

Shortly after she had been moved into the same space as him, Reynolds asked why she was so messy.

'To the untrained eye, this may look like a disordered shambles but to an experienced organiser such as myself, there are levels to this filing system you can't even begin to imagine. I know *exactly* where everything is.'

It was more or less true. She knew in the rough area where everything was but 'exactly' was probably pushing it.

Although he had been ranked above her before Jessica was promoted, there had never been any issues between the two of them after she was elevated. He had laughed as she explained her 'filing', while she had spent most of the day giggling when he had told her about taking three days off thanks to the canteen's stew. Their work didn't overlap at the moment and they shared a fun relationship.

As she checked through the papers on her desk for the information they had on Sandra Prince, Cole knocked and entered.

'You're up,' he said to Reynolds.

'What was it like?' Reynolds asked.

'Fine. They didn't really have much to ask me. I'm pretty sure they think it's DS Daniel.' He nodded at her and gave her a wink as if to say he believed her.

Reynolds told them to wish him luck and left the room.

'Now you're done, we can go see Sandra Prince,' Jessica said. 'The hospital called and said it was okay.'

She didn't know if the DI would want to go but figured it was best to assume he would, rather than just head off with someone else in tow.

She was fairly surprised when he replied. 'Let's go.'

The drive to the hospital had been a bit of a nuisance. Rush hour had come and gone but it was Friday and the traffic patterns always seemed to be inconsistent at the end of the week. As per usual it wasn't too sunny in Manchester; grey clouds washed over the city, while winter and spring were still fighting over what the temperature should be. Cole had taken them in a marked car. Jessica thought his driving matched his personality, steady and straightforward, nothing too crazy.

Some guy had obviously not noticed the car's markings as he swerved late across lanes and cut them up. If it were Jessica, she would have unleashed a barrage of 'coarse language', as Caroline might say and then pulled them over.

At the absolute least, she would have given them the inconvenience of having to report to their local police station with all their documents but Cole carried on as if nothing had happened without even beeping the car's horn. In some ways, Jessica thought, his calmness was very disconcerting.

At the hospital their presence was queried by the receptionist. She was young and continued hammering away at her computer's keyboard as she said: 'I've not got a record of you coming.'

The two officers had shown their identification cards and Jessica had put on her best 'Pull your finger out, I'm a police officer don't you know?' face. It hadn't really got them anywhere.

Eventually the receptionist picked up the phone and a nurse had come to escort them. Sandra Prince had her own room on a third-floor ward which had a uniformed officer assigned to it. The nurse told them that Mrs Prince's doctor wanted to speak to them before he would allow them to talk to his patient, so they were left in a small cupboard posing as an office along the hallway from the ward.

Jessica really didn't like hospitals. She'd not had any particular traumatic experience with them as some might have done but she had been on a few call-outs while in uniform. She had once come to see a victim of a domestic violence in this exact hospital. A young girl had had her face smashed in by a jealous ex-boyfriend. Jessica had to take the photos for evidence purposes and every time she came here, she remembered the girl's battered, bruised and swollen face. In the end, the girl had refused to testify in court.

Another time an assault had happened in the hospital itself. Somebody who had fallen down on a night out and was still drunk had tried to start trouble while in the waiting room. Jessica had taken special pleasure in arresting him. Those incidents and more meant she was rarely keen on coming to this place.

Ideally she wouldn't have had to for this case. Usually interviews would be done at the police station so anything that was said would be recorded. But Sandra Prince was not really a suspect and, given her doctor's advice, it had been felt the interview could be done here. Her presence at work had already been confirmed for the whole of the day the murder had taken place. She could have killed her husband in the morning and then left the house but it did seem unlikely given the similarities to the first case. They had to check with Aylesbury but he had told them they could speak to her out of the station.

When the woman's doctor arrived, he told them Mrs Prince had gone into shock after finding out about her husband but had been fully coherent since yesterday evening. He said she had not seen the day's paper or any of the news coverage and asked if there were any more shocks they were going to spring upon her. He also wanted to know if she was under suspicion. If she was, he told them they would have to move her to the station. Technically they didn't have to tell him anyway but they reassured him and he showed them into the Sandra Prince's private room.

The room wasn't massive but certainly bigger than

most people's bedrooms. It was spotlessly clean with a few pieces of medical equipment surrounding two single beds facing the door. One of the beds was empty, while a woman was sitting up in the other. Jonathan Prince was in a chair next to his mother's bed. She had greying curly hair that was cut fairly short. She wore glasses but her skin was almost as pale as the white bed sheets, the tone in stark contrast to the wrinkles in her face. Aside from her colour, there wasn't anything else noticeably wrong. Not that there should have been but she seemed relatively perky when the doctor asked how she was and checked her blood pressure. He then said he would leave them alone but told his patient she could ring the emergency alarm next to her bed at any time.

Jessica arranged two more seats next to the bed for herself and Cole, while he introduced himself and Jessica and explained that, although they were not in the station, he still had to caution her for legal reasons. He told Sandra Prince that she was entitled to have a legal advisor present and that there would be a free one available at the station if that was what she wanted.

Mrs Prince pulled herself up into more of a seated position. She looked at Jonathan, then back at them and said: 'It's okay. I just want to find out who did this.'

Jessica said they were going to have to ask her son to leave the room. Jonathan seemed a little reluctant to go away from his mother but she told him it was fine. He closed the door behind him and Jessica started the interview. 'Could you tell us what happened on the day your husband was killed please, Mrs Prince?'

The woman cleared her throat. 'I always get up for Jonathan. He has to go to work early and, even though he's grown up now, I always think it's nice for him to see someone in the morning. He left and then I had some toast, watched a bit of TV and went to work myself.'

'Did you see your husband that morning at all?'

'Not really. I gave him a kiss goodbye on my way out. I always do that. He was still in bed and half-asleep. He said goodbye back.'

'What time did you leave?'

'Always eight twenty-five exactly.'

'Did you have any contact at all with your husband that day? Call him? Text him?'

Sandra Prince took off her glasses and gave a small laugh. 'Martin couldn't text. He had a mobile but he didn't really know how to use it. He could manage calls but not texts. I didn't call him, no.'

There were tears in her eyes as she spoke. Jessica gave her a few moments until she seemed fully composed. 'Do you remember if you locked the door when you left that morning?'

'I always locked it if Martin wasn't up. If he was out of bed I wouldn't bother but I think sometimes he would sleep a lot during the day. I would always make a point of locking the door when he was still upstairs.'

Jessica looked at Cole, who gave her a half-nod. 'Okay, Mrs Prince,' Jessica said. 'This might sound like a stupid question but do you know of any other way into your house other than by the doors or windows?'

'How do you mean?' She paused and added: 'We have a

cat-flap at the back but it is always locked shut. We used to have a cat but she was run over years ago and we didn't want to replace her. Since then, we've kept it locked.'

'Nothing other than that?'

'No.'

'Do you know of anyone who might want to cause your husband or your family any harm?'

Sandra Prince smiled a little. 'No. Martin didn't really have that much contact with other people. Since he lost his job, he stayed in a lot and I can't think of anyone else. We just kept ourselves to ourselves.'

'Has your husband's behaviour been any different recently?'

Mrs Prince shook her head. 'He didn't go out too often after he was made redundant. Since the burglary, he went out even less. He didn't want to leave the house empty.'

Cole and Jessica looked at each other. Jessica's eyes were wide and she could feel her heart rate rising. 'Since the what?'

'The burglary. We were burgled around this time last year. Someone broke in while we were at a friend's house. They didn't take much but it was just the thought of someone going through your things. Martin wanted to move but we didn't have the money. He hated leaving the place empty after that.'

Jessica felt her stomach lurch as her heart continued to pound. She found it hard to stay in her seat. 'Did the police find who did it?'

'We thought so but the guy was let out.'

Jessica stood up and thanked Sandra Prince for her

time, barely knowing what she was saying as the adrenaline powered through her. She left the room with Cole, thanking Jonathan, who was sitting outside next to the uniformed officer, for his patience.

They didn't say a word until they were outside of the main hospital building. 'How did we miss this?' Cole said to no one in particular. Jessica was already ahead of him. She had taken out her mobile phone and dialled Rowlands. He answered with a standard put-down but she cut across him.

'Are you near a computer?'

'Yes, why?'

'Do you have the Christensens' address near you?'

'Somewhere . . .'

Jessica and Cole were walking towards the car park as she heard Rowlands scrabbling around on the other end. 'Hurry up,' she muttered, not knowing if he still had the phone at his ear.

After a second or two, which seemed a lot longer, he spoke again. 'I have it here.'

'Do a search to find out if their house was ever burgled.'

'Okay, hang on.' Jessica could hear him tapping away in the background. The police's system was notoriously slow. She was now back at the car but standing next to it, leaning on the roof above the passenger door. Cole was opposite her.

'Right, I've got it,' Rowlands said. 'Hang on . . .' She could hear him typing on the keyboard. 'Yep, it was burgled around a year ago.'

15

The drive back to the station seemed to take an awfully long time and Cole's coolness was really beginning to wind Jessica up. She was still buzzing, the excitement of finally finding the link they had been waiting for almost too much to take – both victims had been burgled. Jessica was trying to stay calm but every red traffic light, every queue at a roundabout and every time Cole stopped to bloody well give way made her clench her teeth and bite her tongue. If she had been driving, she would have had the sirens blaring and the lights flashing as she tore down the Stockport Road to get back to the station as quickly as possible.

She had already told Rowlands to get all of the information they had relating to the burglaries either on her desk if they had a hard copy or on her computer screen if they didn't. As they finally arrived back at the station, Jessica barely waited for Cole to park before she had the passenger's door open and was striding towards the main building. She bounded through reception, past the desk sergeant and down the hallway into her empty office.

As she began to scan through the information that had been left on her screen, Jessica could see the burglaries of the Christensens' house and the Princes' had been linked to three others that happened in the same area within a week of each other this time last year. The problem was that, in theory, the crimes were unsolved. Having looked through each of the five incidents and cross-checked with the relevant notes, it was pretty clear the police *had* found their man though.

Wayne Lapham was a name Greater Manchester Police were very familiar with according to his file. As a fifteen-year-old, he had been sent to a young offenders' institution for setting fire to an empty office building. He had spent the past twenty-five years in and out of prison and on probation schemes for various offences including drug possession, thefts, assaults, drunk and disorderly and threatening behaviour. Every eighteen months or so he would be picked up for a new offence and either sent back to prison or handed over to probation for another spell of supervision.

The offence that most interested Jessica was his most recent one. Just over a year ago, police had been called to a pub in the Levenshulme area of the city, just south of Gorton, where the five burglaries had taken place. A man had been attacked with a pint glass but, in the course of investigating that attack, they had ended up searching Lapham who just happened to be in the same pub. Having seen his record Jessica knew full well there was a very good chance the officers had recognised him and were searching him because of who he was. He would have been given a vague reason so he couldn't press charges of harassment but everyone knew how it worked.

While searching him, they found a laptop and two mobile phones in his rucksack. He had first claimed they were his but, after police had been given a warrant to search his house and found the rest of the items taken in the five burglaries, Lapham's story had changed. Then he claimed he had bought everything in a pub for £300 a few nights previously from a man he had never seen before or since.

Jessica smiled as she read that bit, shaking her head. Because *most* people would happily hand over £300 to a stranger in a pub. Obviously the police had delighted in picking holes in his story and the fact he had already changed it once. They charged him with burglary and handed the case over to the CPS for it to go to court. Given his record, he had been denied bail and was left sitting in a jail cell for three months as he waited for the full Crown Court trial.

That was where things got complicated. Although he had been caught with every item that had been stolen, there was no forensic evidence linking him to any of the scenes. Each burglary had been committed in the same way. Given the unseasonably warm weather last year, Lapham – or whoever had prised open an unlocked and slightly ajar window – then made off with anything they could get their hands on.

With evidence linking him to the stolen goods but not the scenes and the CPS nervous over whether they would get a conviction, they offered Lapham's lawyer a concession on the morning of the trial. If his client pleaded guilty to handling stolen goods, they would drop the burglary charges. It was exactly the kind of thing that infuriated officers who worked hard on cases, not to mention victims who wanted to see justice. The one thing it did do was keep conviction rates up, meaning the CPS hit their own targets. Lapham, of course, couldn't believe his luck. He pleaded guilty and walked free that afternoon after the judge ruled the time he had spent in prison on remand was sufficient punishment.

It couldn't be a coincidence that two of the houses that had been burgled had now seen murders happen inside them. Regardless of whether he had been found guilty, Lapham was the man they needed to bring in. Jessica checked the address they had, printed off a copy of his mug shot, went to tell Aylesbury what was going on, and then set off to pick up their only suspect.

This time she would drive.

Uniformed officers had been sent out to check on the three other burglary victims from last year. There was no obvious motive for why a burglar would return to the scene of their crimes and kill the person who lived there but it's not as if they had anything else to go on. Seemingly it was the only link between the two murder victims too.

Cole had thought it best they didn't take marked vehicles, given Lapham's likely attitude towards the police. That meant Jessica taking her own car, along with Rowlands and a uniformed officer. Cole was also driving his vehicle – a spotlessly clean silver 4x4 – along with two other regular constables. Six officers might have seemed a bit over the top but no one knew how Lapham would react to the police turning up at his door, especially given his history with the force. A marked car would also be sent behind them so they could transport their suspect back to the station when they had him. They would radio for the driver to move in when they were ready.

Despite Rowlands's complaints about the sound of her exhaust tipping the suspect off while they were still a mile away, Jessica roared down Alan Turing Way towards Oldham Road on their way out to Moston. It was late afternoon and the Friday traffic had reached its peak with everyone heading off towards the motorway and home. They had barely got out of the station when Jessica left Cole far behind. He had given way at the junction next to the station's exit as she put her foot down, probably cut up the guy behind – who beeped his horn – and then accelerated away through a traffic light that was *definitely* still on amber. Well, probably.

If the roads had been clear, the journey would have taken around twenty minutes but Jessica did it in less than that regardless of the traffic. As she pulled up outside the grubby block of housing-association flats Lapham was supposed to live in, Rowlands admitted he had been impressed, if mildly terrified, by her driving. The uniformed officer in the back didn't say anything but his pale face and relief to get the seatbelt off when she put the handbrake on told the story well enough.

'Should we wait . . . ?' Rowlands began to say but Jessica already had her door open and was making her way around the front of the car. Rowlands looked at the officer in the back seat and shrugged as if to say, 'I know'.

They found the flat number fairly quickly; it was on the ground floor and they established there was no back door. Jessica sent Rowlands towards the rear of the building anyway, just in case Lapham tried to make a run for it out of the window.

After he gave her the message to say he was in position, Jessica, with the uniformed officer by her side, knocked on the door. The wood felt thin and the colour was hard to distinguish. It had probably been blue at some point but it didn't look like it had ever been cleaned. There was no answer but they could hear a television on inside. Jessica knocked again, louder the second time. They heard a female voice from behind the door, then it was opened.

The woman standing in front of them had grimy unwashed brown hair tied back into a ponytail, secured with a ludicrously big flowery pink tie that certainly didn't suit the rest of her appearance. She was wearing a peach-coloured dressing gown with matching slippers, holding a smouldering cigarette in her left hand, with the right one poised on the door.

'Who the fuck are you?' the woman said to Jessica, looking her up and down, before noticing the officer in uniform. 'Oh for—' she continued.

Jessica talked over her. 'Nice to meet you too.' She pulled out her police identification. 'Is Wayne in? We'd like to have a little chat with him.'

'Don't you pigs ever leave him alone? What do you want this time?'

'Is he in? He does live here, doesn't he?'

'He's not here.'

'Are you sure? We could just come in to have a look around . . .' Jessica motioned to put a hand on the front door but the woman pushed it back against her.

'If you've not got a warrant, you ain't coming through. He's not here. Now piss off.'

The woman went to close the door but Jessica stopped her. 'If he's not here, then where is he?'

'I don't know. The pub? The snooker? I don't know where he gets to.'

'*Which* pub?'

'Don't take that fuckin' tone with me,' the woman started but Jessica was losing patience. She pushed the door fully open and squared up to the woman standing in the doorway. Jessica was a couple of inches taller than her and the woman took a step back.

'I'll take whatever tone I want,' Jessica said, sounding as fierce as she could. 'Now tell me where he is or, warrant or no warrant, we'll turn this shithole upside down and see if there's anything we can arrest *you* for.'

The woman was clearly fuming. Jessica knew that much of what she had just said was bluster and was gambling that whoever Lapham's girlfriend was wouldn't know that.

'Fine,' the woman spat. 'He goes to that Prince of Wales pub just over on the main road.' She motioned with her hands the direction she meant but Jessica knew where the place was because they had driven past it on the way in. The woman took a step back towards Jessica in a clear effort to show she wasn't intimidated. 'Now get out of my house, you posh bitch.'

Jessica did just that, thinking it was the first time she had ever been called 'posh'. She had the information she needed and, as Cole hadn't been present, her little bit of grandstanding wouldn't be an issue. The uniformed officer certainly hadn't said anything and Jessica had even seen a half-smirk on his face as they walked back to the car, radioing Rowlands on the way to say they had what they needed.

As they got back to her car together, Cole was parking his wagon behind them. If he was annoyed they had got there first and were on their way back from the flat empty-handed, he didn't mention it. 'Not in?' was all he did say after he opened his driver's-side window with an electric hum.

'Prince of Wales pub around the corner,' Jessica said. 'Let's walk it, then we'll get the marked car to park outside when we know he's there.'

It must have seemed an odd sight as three people in suits and three in uniform walked the few hundred yards to the pub. Jessica showed all of them the mug shot she had printed so they knew who to look for. The pub was on a main road with a concreted car park at the back. Jessica sent two of the three uniformed officers to wait there, leaving Rowlands and the other uniform at the front. She and Cole entered through the heavy wooden door.

The pub looked as if it hadn't been renovated in Jessica's lifetime. Despite the smoking ban being in effect for years now, Jessica could still smell stale cigarettes and the ceiling was covered in the brown and black stains that seemed so familiar before the law. On the walls were framed photos and prints of various local football teams. The carpet was thin and completely bare in places with the stone floor visible. It looked as if it had a red flowery pattern at some stage. Jessica thought it was exactly the type of hole Harry would have loved.

The door opened up into what was essentially one large room with the bar to their right. There were a few railings to try to break the space up but you could more or less see everything from the door. Jessica scanned the room and Cole did the same. There were only around half-a-dozen people in the whole place and she couldn't see Lapham. Cole said 'no' quietly to indicate he couldn't either. He went to check the men's toilets, which were next to the bar, as Jessica sat on a stool in front of the barman.

The server, who was big and bald, towered over her. He had already been eyeing the two of them suspiciously as they walked in and the fact a potential customer had gone to use the toilets without buying a drink was no doubt causing him concern.

'Can I get you . . . ?' he started to say as Jessica took out her identification from her suit pocket. She also removed the printed photo of the suspect from the other pocket and held both items up for the barman to look at.

'Have you seen this man?' she asked.

'Who, Wayne? Yeah, he was in here up until a minute ago. He took some call on his phone then bolted out the back. He left half his pint.' The server indicated a half-finished glass of bitter on the table a few feet away from

Jessica. 'I didn't clean it up 'cos I thought he might be coming back.'

Jessica slammed her hand on the bar, startling not only the barman but at least two of the other customers, who looked over towards her. 'That cow tipped him off.'

16

Jessica could count on the fingers of one hand the number of times she had run since moving into plain clothes. As a kid she had been a pretty good athlete, especially when it came to sprinting. Somewhere in a box at her parents' house would be a certificate or two from her school days. As with most young teenagers, girls especially, the idea of getting sweaty and dirty while at school became less and less appealing as she got older. As she sprinted back to Wayne Lapham's house, Jessica thought that, if she hadn't been so girly when she was thirteen, this run might have been a tad easier.

Cole had come out of the toilets shaking his head as Jessica shouted to him about Lapham leaving. She dashed for the front door and was halfway down the road they had just walked along with Cole, Rowlands and three uniformed officers trailing in her wake. To anyone driving past it must have seemed like a bizarre scene being filmed for a sitcom.

She bounded past Cole's vehicle and her own car, hurdled a hedge and charged towards Lapham's flat. Rowlands arrived out of breath just after Jessica had finished pounding on the front door. She would have shouted out the woman's name if she even knew it, continuing to bang on the door as two of the other officers, Cole, and finally the other officer arrived. Jessica was out of breath herself but adrenaline was flooding through her and the only emotion she had was blind fury.

'She tipped him off,' Jessica said to Cole, and then repeated herself in case anyone was in any doubt as to why she was acting so erratically.

With no answer at the door but no warrant either, she turned to Cole. 'Can we break it down?'

Cole ummed, so Jessica turned to the biggest officer in their party. He was the only one in uniform who didn't look as if he was going to keel over after the run. 'Break it down.'

The officer looked to Cole for approval, so she shouted the second time. 'Just *break it down*.'

The uniformed constable was comfortably over six feet tall and looked as if he could smash through doors like this for fun. He ushered them to one side, took a step back and readied himself to put the full force of his boot through the door when it opened suddenly.

In the doorway stood the woman from before but this time she was fully dressed. The slippers and dressing gown were gone and she was wearing dark blue tracksuit bottoms and some kind of hooded top with the over-the-top hair tie. The woman looked at the officer who had his foot half-raised and then at Jessica. 'What the fuck do you think you're doing?'

Jessica was not in a mood to be mucked about. 'Where is he?'

The woman gave a small grin, her yellowing teeth clearly visible as she goaded the officers. 'Who?'

Jessica ignored the taunt and barged past the woman, who let out a 'hey' as she was sidelined. She opened the first door on her right, which was the bathroom. The whole house was full of varying degrees of junk. Broken computer keyboards and other electrical items that didn't look as if they worked littered the hallway as Jessica went into the kitchen directly opposite the front door. The draining board was piled high with dirty plates and pans and there was more random scrap on the floor. She didn't even know if the other officers had followed her in but Jessica moved into the living room, still hearing the protests of the woman going on behind her.

There was no sign of Lapham.

Jessica made her way back through the living room and kitchen into the hall where she noticed a door she had missed the first time around. In her haste to barge past the woman, she had missed an opening opposite the bathroom.

The woman was arguing with Cole and Jessica could hear the words 'my rights' being shouted. She ignored the noise and went through the door that led into the bedroom. The bed hadn't been made and an enormous flatscreen television hung on the wall facing it. A bright purple duvet cover was on the floor and nothing could be seen under the bed. Jessica got down on her knees and hurled the covers aside, fully expecting to see Wayne Lapham underneath.

He wasn't there.

She moved to the built-in wardrobe and pushed the doors aside, shoving the clothes on the rail out of the way.

He wasn't there either. Jessica swore to herself and then made her way out to the front door where the woman was screaming at the officers still there.

The woman jabbed her finger into Jessica's chest as she pushed past her.

'I'm going to have you. You can't do that. I know my rights,' the woman said.

'Is there anything in this list of "rights" that tells you aiding a criminal is an offence you can go to prison for?' Jessica didn't actually know if you could go to prison for it – but you probably could. It sounded good in any case.

'What are you on about?'

'You do know we can check your phone records?'

That statement clearly rattled the woman, whose confident expression changed instantly.

'Where is he?' Jessica said. 'I'm not going to ask again.'

One of the officers unclipped the handcuffs from his belt with timing Jessica couldn't have wanted to be better. The woman looked at the constable holding the cuffs and then back at Jessica. Her face fell, the snarl finally removed.

'I don't know. He just said "thanks" and hung up.'

Cole spoke next and Jessica wondered why he hadn't said anything before. 'Do you have any idea where he might have gone?'

'Where he always goes,' the woman replied. 'A pub somewhere.'

The officers made their way back to the station in convoy with Jessica following Cole and the marked car they had waiting. Jessica realised she still didn't know the woman's name, or even who she was. Presumably she was a girl-friend or something similar? They could have arrested her for aiding Lapham's escape but she could have made a complaint about Jessica ransacking her house without a warrant. Arresting her wouldn't have done too much good in their attempts to find their suspect in any case. One of the uniformed officers had been left with her in case Lapham returned. She hadn't been too pleased about it but Cole had told her they wouldn't push charges if she cooperated.

Jessica knew it was her mistake. If she hadn't charged in without waiting for Cole to arrive in the first place, some-body could have been left to keep an eye on the woman. That would have made a lot more sense than a leisurely stroll to the pub. She phoned into the station to say they were returning without their suspect and that the press office should try to get a photo of Lapham onto the evening news and into the next day's newspapers if possi-ble. At least that way they could get the whole city looking for their guy. With any luck, if the woman was right about him propping up a bar somewhere, he would return home at closing time and the uniformed officer would have him in custody that night. Jessica knew it was too much to hope for.

The traffic had now all but cleared and for most people it was officially the weekend. Jessica still had to return to the station to explain what had happened. She drove steadily, following Cole, waiting when he waited and giving way when he gave way.

Back at the station, to his credit, Cole backed her when they went to see Aylesbury. No mention had been made of Jessica going in ahead of him and he certainly hadn't tried to push any blame onto her, even though she felt she deserved it. The whole incident hadn't turned into the mess she thought it would, largely because the DCI was ready to go on to the television news that evening to appeal for help finding Lapham. It was as if he couldn't quite believe his luck.

He dismissed the two of them and made his way downstairs to wait for the cameras. Jessica offered a 'thanks' to Cole but he shrugged his shoulders and gave her a half-smile. 'Have a good weekend,' she added.

Caroline had gone out with Randall for the night and Jessica watched the evening news at home on her own. They had invited her but she didn't fancy it. She had been finding reasons to avoid the flat for the past couple of nights in any case. Although last night had been the first time Caroline's boyfriend had stayed over, they had spent most evenings in together that week. Jessica was glad her friend was happy but the lovey-dovey stuff drove her mad. She didn't want to say anything and at least she could now have an evening in by herself.

Jessica flopped into the sofa with her feet curled underneath and watched the news on one local channel before flicking to the other. Aylesbury was in his element. For the first piece he was outside the station as the sun set. He had his best 'this is serious stuff' face on, speaking about the need for the public to be vigilant. He said that some press reports had been wildly inaccurate, added that people shouldn't panic and then went on to say the police were looking for help in finding Wayne Lapham to 'help us with our inquiries'. He didn't once mention the word 'suspect'. The channel then showed the mug shot of Lapham with his name underneath. On the next station, the DCI had moved into the Pad for his interview. He went over much the same information the second time around but, if anything, looked even more sincere, despite sitting on the edge of a desk.

Jessica changed the channel to some reality show spin-off. She wasn't particularly interested but was happy to sit through anything that would take her mind off the day's shambles. The sun had almost set and, even with the flat's curtains open, the room was pretty dark. She was still wearing her work suit but felt warm and a little sleepy, putting her head on the armrest of the sofa and sinking further into it before closing her eyes for a moment.

She awoke with a jump what she thought was a few seconds later. She had finally changed the ringtone of her phone to some rock song she loved from when she was younger. She could hear the tune kicking in but didn't know where the sound was coming from. The television was off and the room was light. She looked at the analogue clock on the wall above the TV but couldn't take in what it was telling her. Disorientated, she tried to sit up and a blanket that had been covering her fell to the floor. The noise stopped and she rubbed her eyes to get a better look at the time. It was sometime around five past nine. Had she really slept all night? Caroline must have come in and switched the set off and put the blanket over her.

She shook her head, trying to wake up, and went to look for her phone. Her bag and shoes were on the floor next to the living-room door as they always were but her phone wasn't in her bag. Jessica hunted around the room, looking under the pile of magazines on the coffee table and then the table itself. Eventually she found the device under the sofa. She thought she had left it in her bag but had long since failed to be surprised by where her phone or keys ever ended up. She had once found her keys in the fridge, so anything was possible.

Jessica thumbed a few buttons and saw she had a missed call from the station's landline number. She called the number back.

The desk sergeant's familiar voice answered. 'I wondered what you were up to. Big night, was it?'

'Not really. What's up?'

'Want to guess who walked into the station half an hour ago?'

'Lapham? Really?'

'Yep. It's not him you'll have to worry about though. Guess who he was with?'

Jessica started to rack her brain but was still too half-asleep for a guessing game. 'Go on.'

'He's downstairs with everyone's favourite lawyer: Peter Hunt.'

17

Jessica's first thought was that Hunt was supposed to be busy dealing with Harry's stabbing case and then she remembered it was Saturday. A second thought then occurred to her; how on earth had a career criminal like Wayne Lapham managed to get one of the best-known defence lawyers in the city, possibly the country, to represent him?

Then the penny dropped.

Lapham had been all over the previous night's news and there was little doubt he would be on the front of most of that day's papers. The chance to represent someone as high-profile as that must have been too much for Hunt to resist. Maybe Lapham had even read about Tom Carpenter handing himself in via Hunt? Or perhaps he had seen something of the Worrall case? Hunt certainly got enough coverage so most of Manchester's underworld must have been aware of him.

Jessica had a peek around Caroline's door and could see two bodies entwined with each other sleeping under a sheet. She thought she would leave them to it and left the house quietly without changing. She had slept in her suit from the day before but reckoned it would do for a Saturday.

At the station, even with a reduced staff for the weekend, Jessica could feel a buzz as she walked in. A couple of officers were hanging around the entrance area and stopped to look at her as she headed towards reception. The sergeant who had phoned called her over and handed her an envelope with her name on it. 'This was dropped in for you,' he said.

Jessica ripped across the top to find a court summons inside. After the trial's start had been delayed, her day at Crown Court was going to be Tuesday. She was not only going to be facing Peter Hunt today but in three days' time as well. She wanted to phone Harry but figured it could wait, doubting he would answer anyway.

'Cole is already in his office,' said the sergeant. 'He said to go see him when you got in. The DCI's upstairs too.'

'A full house then?'

The desk sergeant gave her a wink. 'Just like any other day.'

Jessica went to see Cole first. His office was only two doors down from hers and next to the canteen. It was a room smaller than the office she and Reynolds shared but the inspector did have the space to himself. Jessica knocked once and went in. He was sitting behind the desk typing on the computer but stopped and looked up as she entered.

'Hey,' Jessica said.

'You've heard then?'

'Hunt? Yeah, I got the call. Are we going in together?'

'Yes. I spoke to the DCI already. He was fuming that Hunt was involved but said to play it cool.'

Jessica gave him a small smile. 'That's a given for you anyway.'

'I think he was talking about you.'

Jessica went to the interview room to set up the tape as Cole went to get Wayne Lapham and his solicitor from the holding cells below the station. Although he had come voluntarily, Lapham was still their only suspect in a double murder and had been arrested accordingly. He had been locked in a cell awaiting Jessica's arrival. A few minutes later, he was brought handcuffed into the interview room by Cole and a uniformed officer, Peter Hunt by his side.

Wayne Lapham was short but still had broad shoulders and a fiery look about him. Jessica knew from his file that he was forty but he looked older. He was unshaven, his greying dark hair cropped close to his head with a visible scar across his forehead that ended above his left eye. He was wearing a sweatshirt but with the sleeves rolled up revealing two arms completely covered with tattoos of varying designs. Jessica saw that his tracksuit bottoms had a small hole in one of the knees. Peter Hunt looked immaculate on the other hand. He stood tall next to his client, towering over him in a brown pinstripe suit that appeared to be custom-fitted. He was wearing a white shirt with a wide collar and a thick matching brown tie knotted tight to his neck. His blond hair had no traces of white or grey and was impressively styled almost into a quiff but with something of a side-parting. He was carrying a leather briefcase that looked very expensive.

They couldn't have looked more different.

Lapham was the first to sit, Hunt taking the chair next to him. He put his case down by his side and placed a notepad on the table. Cole sat next to the tape recorder, pressing the buttons to start the recording and, as usual, introduced everyone present and formally cautioned the suspect. Jessica stayed standing while that happened before finally taking her seat directly opposite her only suspect.

Nobody had said a word before Wayne Lapham commented: 'Ye are pretty cute, y'know?' He was looking directly at Jessica and gave her a wink. She noticed that he had an earring in his right ear and another tattoo just below his earlobe. He had a Scottish accent that had mellowed with time but was still noticeable.

Peter Hunt said nothing so Jessica let the silence hang before asking him where he had been during the hours Yvonne Christensen had been killed.

Wayne's reply was forceful, a direct challenge. 'Pub? Home? Sleeping? I dunno. Where were you?'

Cole stepped in. 'Mr Hunt, would you like to *advise* your client?'

Hunt had a neutral expression on his face, looking down at a notepad in front of him. He glanced at his client. 'Just answer as best you can.'

'I'll try again,' Jessica said before repeating the question.

Wayne said nothing but smiled ever so slightly. 'Tuesday at twelve I was at the pub until I went home for tea. I stayed there until midday the next day when I went back to the pub. Simple; if I'm not at home, I'm at the pub.'

His attitude was already pushing Jessica's buttons. 'Not breaking into people's homes then?'

Hunt immediately cut in, looking up from his notes at

Jessica. 'Excuse me. Are you accusing my client of breaking into homes on that day?'

Jessica ignored him, asking where Wayne had been between the times they thought the murder had happened.

Wayne didn't even sound angry, just antagonistic. He hadn't taken his eyes off Jessica once during the interview. 'Are you deaf?'

'Just answer,' Hunt said quietly.

'Home and pub. It's not hard.'

Jessica met his glare. 'The problem is, Wayne, that you're the only link we have to both of these murders. Isn't it funny, you burgle both their houses then a year later they end up dead?'

Wayne slid his chair back slightly, making it screech along the floor. Finally taking his eyes from Jessica he laughed quietly as Hunt spoke again. 'My client has never been found guilty of a burglary. I think you should be careful of who you're accusing.'

Jessica again let it hang in the air, refusing to rise to the retort. 'Okay then, *Wayne*, let's go back to last year. Let's talk about this man in the pub you "bought" all those stolen items from, shall we?'

Hunt moved as if he was about to speak but simply let out a little cough. Jessica met Wayne's gaze again. He had eyes that were a very pale blue, almost grey. His stare was unwavering. 'I don't really remember.'

'Come on, Wayne, this mysterious man is the number one suspect in a double murder. You're our star witness. Do you want to try again?'

'He was a man.'

'That's a start . . .'

'Wearing a baseball cap.'

Jessica said nothing.

'I don't remember any more than that.'

Jessica sighed, looked at Cole, then Hunt, then back at Wayne. 'The problem is that I don't believe you. I don't believe there was a man in the pub. I think *you* stole those items and I think *you* went back to those houses and murdered two innocent people for whatever reason you could come up with.'

She wasn't sure if she did believe that but had nothing else to go on. Hunt spoke louder this time. 'My client has been cleared of those burglaries. *Cleared*. Now if you have any evidence, any single scrap at all that he was at any of those scenes then – or at any of them last week – please produce it. If not, let him go and we can all get back to enjoying the weekend.'

Jessica ignored him. 'How did you get back into those houses a second time?'

No answer.

'How did it feel strangling those victims, Wayne?'

The two of them continued to stare at each other as if Cole and Lapham's lawyer were invisible. 'Did you enjoy it?' Jessica added.

Hunt started to stand up, pulling his pad from the table as if to indicate the interview was over, but his client didn't move.

'Fuck ye,' Wayne said aggressively.

'You'd like that wouldn't you? Violent man like you. Is

that what you got up to in prison? Is that how you got that scar?'

'De-tec-tive!' Hunt was shouting now, standing up to his full height and indicating for his client to do the same. Cole shuffled nervously in the seat next to her but neither Jessica nor Wayne moved. The suspect didn't say a word, continuing to stare at Jessica, neither of them wanting to be the first to look away.

He growled his response. 'Yous have got fuck all on me and yous know it.'

Jessica did know it and trying to wind him up was having the opposite effect. She was allowing herself to be frustrated by his lack of cooperation. 'Who's the girl?' Jessica asked.

Hunt was still standing but, with the obvious lack of movement from his client, had little option other than to sit again.

'What girl?'

'The one at your flat. Wife? Girlfriend? Mistress? Sister? Girlfriend and sister?'

'What's it to ye?'

'Nothing . . . just that when she phoned to tip you off about us looking for you yesterday, that was what we call "obstructing a police constable in execution of their duty". It's a criminal offence, something I know you are very familiar with.'

Cole shuffled nervously and Jessica knew she was on thin ice. 'We've already checked the phone records,' she lied, snapping her fingers. 'I could send an officer around to pick her up like that.'

Wayne finally looked away, peering towards his Hunt. 'Is that true?'

Hunt stumbled over his words. 'I, er, well, I don't know. It could be an offence . . .'

His client was suddenly angry, his cool expression and steely stare gone. Jessica had the feeling she was finally seeing the real Wayne Lapham. 'Why won't ye lot leave us alone? I've not done nothing wrong. Every time I get out and try to get clean I have ye lot banging on my door, stopping me in the street. It's not right.'

He was finally animated; banging on the desk with his cuffed hands, any pretension of coolness gone.

'"Not done nothing" is a double negative, Wayne. Can I take that as a confession?' Jessica smiled.

Hunt cut back in. 'Don't be bloody ridiculous.' He looked to Cole. 'Are these questions going anywhere? If you've got anything at all on my client then charge him. If not, let's end this ridiculous grandstanding.'

Even Hunt's demeanour had slipped with that exchange. Jessica knew she was pushing it. She didn't even know where she was going but hoped her superior wouldn't shut her down. 'The problem is, Wayne, that you *don't* go out and get clean, do you? At the very least you go out and buy a load of stolen gear from some bloke down the pub who you just happen to not remember.'

Wayne was back to staring at her; the calm had returned. 'Ye are even cuter when ye are angry.' He winked at her again.

Cole cut in even before Hunt could. 'Right, this is going

nowhere.' He gave the time and said he was terminating the interview before stopping the tape and getting to his feet. 'Mr Lapham, you are free to leave. I will find the keys to those cuffs and you can go out with your legal representative. Check with the sergeant on the front desk on the way out. He will give your lawyer further instructions regarding police bail. You may have to return at a later date.'

Cole left the room, leaving the door slightly ajar. Hunt was also standing and packing his notepad into his briefcase, shaking his head while making tutting noises. Jessica and Wayne remained sitting, weighing each other up. Jessica finally relented, scraping her chair back, turning around and walking towards the door. Before she could get there, Wayne spoke. 'Detective . . .'

Jessica turned around.

'That is one mighty fine arse ye've got there. I would *love* to have a go on that.' He used both hands, still handcuffed, to grab his crotch. 'I'll bet ye are a real goer, yeah?'

Hunt went to say something but Jessica acted on instinct. She took two strides across the room and leant over the table so she was at eye level around a foot away from him. 'You think you're a real hard man, don't you, Wayne?'

He eyeballed her as Hunt said something about the interview being over. Jessica ignored him and stared directly into Wayne's eyes. 'It must take a really hard man to break into people's houses and take their possessions before getting some slimy shitbag like this to get them off.'

She heard Hunt splutter as Wayne's gaze flickered away

for a fraction of a second, perhaps unnerved by how close they were.

'I don't think you're hard, Wayne. I don't think you're hard at all. I think you're a pathetic little man who's pissed their life away. And do you know what else? I think you're all talk.'

She moved even closer to him, just six inches between them now. 'Do you know how to fight, Wayne? I bet you think you do. Most people start by throwing a few punches.'

Her gaze hadn't shifted but Wayne's had. He had shunted his chair backwards slightly, looking towards his speechless lawyer. Neither Jessica's tone nor eye line had wavered. 'The thing is, Wayne, it's not about how you throw those punches, it's where you target them. For instance, if you punch someone hard in the windpipe, that would crush their larynx. They would go into instant shock. But, because they'd be in shock, they wouldn't quite be aware of how to fight back. Do you know punching someone in the nose isn't really an effective way of breaking it?'

She used her left hand to rub her right palm but otherwise didn't move. Hunt was frozen to the spot, his client desperately looking from side to side. 'The best way to truly put someone out of action is to use the base of your palm to hit upwards through their nose. As well as a crushed larynx, their nose will shatter.'

Jessica finally moved backwards, albeit only half a step. There was silence. Hunt hadn't moved and Wayne was staring back at Jessica not knowing what to say. 'So there you go, Wayne. You think I'm a goer, how about you *fucking* try me?'

Jessica saw a visible bead of sweat appear on his forehead. She held out her hand towards him. 'Just touch me and let's see what happens, shall we?'

18

Jessica was in the ladies' toilets at the station. She locked herself in a cubicle after checking the rest of the facility was empty and sat on the closed seat. Her heart rate had only just started to drop and she felt a complete mess. Her day-old clothes were beginning to get uncomfortable and she had an overwhelming feeling of being trapped. Something had come over her in the interview room that had never happened before.

She sat with her head in her hands and sobbed silently to herself. Jessica didn't even remember everything she had said or done with Wayne Lapham. It was less than five minutes ago but already she could see only flashes of the incident. It was as if she had watched herself from the corner of the room, an out-of-body experience of sorts. She remembered Peter Hunt shouting for an officer and calling her 'out of control'. She remembered Cole returning and looking bemused as she stomped out of the room, past the uniformed officer and down the hallway into the toilets she sat in now. The parts between Cole leaving the room and him returning were patchy.

What on earth had happened? She didn't even know where all that stuff had come from. She had never hurt anyone like that in her life. You got basic combat training in the force but they didn't go out of their way to hurt anybody. She had read a few guides on Internet sites and knew how to look after herself, while Harry had given her those tips about targeting people's windpipes and noses if you were in trouble. She could only assume that, as her emotions had got the best of her, the things she had absorbed had all come out in the most venomous way she could have managed. In some ways it could be fearfully impressive but that wasn't how she felt.

Jessica heard the main bathroom door open and some-one enter. She held her breath and lifted her feet off the ground, though didn't really know why she was doing it. She listened to the other person enter one of the cubicles next to her and waited for the flush and the sound of water gushing from the sinks. Eventually the door went and she was alone again.

Jessica had never really been an emotional person. The last time she remembered crying was when Caroline's parents had died almost a decade ago. Caroline's devasta-tion had affected her significantly but helped them bond. Jessica genuinely felt her friend's pain and they had cried together at the funeral. They were such good friends but also such opposites. Jessica generally didn't get attached but Caroline would cry at everything from videos on the Internet, to movies at the cinema, to articles in the paper and even, on one occasion, an advert on television. While Jessica was fiery and easily angered, Caroline was consis-tently cool and very little fazed her. They constantly ribbed each other about things. If they were watching some TV show with an animal in, Jessica would throw a box of tis-sues at her friend 'just in case you go off again'. Caroline, meanwhile, had devised a sliding scale of Jessica's moods, ranging from 'a tad sweary,' to 'particularly sweary', to 'volcanic sweary'. Who knows what she would have made of her friend's mood in the interview room?

It was all in good humour but Jessica sat wondering if perhaps her temper had become too much of a problem. She was also struggling to figure out why she was crying. Was she upset, embarrassed or even fearful for her future after what had happened? And why had she let Wayne Lapham wind her up so much?

Jessica took a deep breath and stopped to think. In truth, she didn't believe Wayne was the man they were looking for. His list of crimes was long but didn't have anything on it that indicated he was capable of two brutal murders. She also believed his life was as pathetic as visiting the pub and going home, probably with a little bit of criminality on the side. He didn't seem intelligent enough to set up the scenes either. Someone had very cleverly and deliberately covered their tracks by not only making sure they left no trace of themselves with the bodies but also hiding the very way the murders had even been conceived.

Could Wayne Lapham really have figured out a way to get into a house and out again undetected? He was a thug and a bully and Jessica had no doubt he'd broken into those houses a year ago. Sneaking in through partially open windows was his style. Subtlety was something she doubted he could spell, let alone pull off.

That left her wondering about her own behaviour. Why had she threatened him? Whatever the reasons and whether she had simply lost it, she had at least achieved one thing. She had seen it in Wayne's eyes as he panicked and looked to Peter Hunt for assistance. He hadn't touched her, he wouldn't have dared. He was the most scared person in that interview room and, despite his bravado, he was no murderer.

Jessica dried her eyes and unlocked the cubicle's door. She checked herself over in the mirror, smoothed her hair down and retied it into a ponytail, thinking it was definitely getting too long. She straightened her suit and left the room.

The hallway was unnervingly quiet. It was a weekend but, even so, the silence boomed in Jessica's ears. She wasn't due to be in that day but, given the nature of her job and the case itself, was pretty much always ready to come in at short notice. She walked down the hallway towards her office, wondering if she should go home or if there was anything else she could do. Lapham had been released and there would be paperwork to go with that.

As she rounded the corner that would take her to her office, she almost walked straight into Cole. They both stepped back. 'You okay?' he said.

'Yes, I'm fine.'

'What happened in there? Hunt was fuming. He practically ran up to see the chief inspector and then stormed out with Lapham a few minutes later.'

Jessica had pretty much expected that would be the lawyer's reaction. 'Not much. We exchanged words.'

Cole gave her a sideways look as if to imply he knew it

must have been much more than that but he said nothing. 'I think the DCI wants a word.'

'Right.'

Jessica went to head towards the stairs but, as she half-turned, Cole added: 'Do you reckon he's our man?'

She looked back towards him. 'Do you?'

Neither of them said anything but Jessica could tell from her superior's look that he was thinking exactly what she was: 'No'.

She made her way up the stairs and could see Aylesbury in his office through the window. She knocked and he waved her in. 'DS Daniel,' he said, indicating for her to sit down. She did but said nothing. They looked at each other as if waiting for the other to talk first. He eventually broke the silence. 'Is there anything you want to tell me?'

Jessica paused for a moment. 'No, Sir.'

'Are you sure?'

'Yes, Sir.'

Aylesbury nodded slowly, his eyes darting across her as if trying to read her thoughts. 'Cole says Wayne Lapham has been bailed. I think we all know we don't have enough to keep him in.' Jessica nodded but said nothing. 'I think you should go home for the weekend and then we might need to talk again on Monday, yes?'

'Yes, Sir.'

Jessica was back in the exact position she had been in what seemed like barely hours ago – sitting with her feet underneath her on the sofa in her flat, mulling over yet another shambles. It was now early afternoon and the flat was once again empty. Caroline had left her a note on the coffee table in the living room.

'Gone to lunch and shops. Call if you want to join us. X. C.'

Jessica didn't fancy either lunch or shopping. She wondered how many more times she could mess something up before someone stepped in to remove her from the case. There were already rumours the Serious Crime Division were looking to swoop in to hunt the 'Houdini Strangler'. The SCD had been set up a few years previously and dealt with a wide range of crimes. No one in CID was really sure whether what they were working on would fall under the remit of the SCD. Certainly any larger gang crime would usually be referred to them but a lot seemed to come down to how busy the SCD were at any given time. It was often felt that, if they were having a particularly quiet month, they would look for anything decent CID were handling and then take the case on themselves in order to not have their budget cut. They were just one in many confusing layers of law-enforcement where Jessica often felt not even those involved knew who answered to whom. Everyone just fought hard to make sure their own departments looked busy and successful when the time came for budgets to be allocated.

She only knew two things about the upcoming week. First, she would be in Aylesbury's office first thing on Monday, probably for a dressing down, possibly to be taken off the case and maybe to be suspended outright. Second, she was due in court on Tuesday to face Peter

Hunt again. She hoped she would make a better go of it second time around.

Thinking ahead to her court date, she figured now was as good a time as any to phone Harry. It was pushing six months since they had last talked. She flicked through her phone's list of contacts and pressed the call button when it got to 'Harry Thomas'.

It rang once. Twice. Jessica was about to leave a message, as she had done many times, when the line clicked and went silent for a moment. 'Hello,' came a voice from the other end.

'Harry?'

'Yeah.'

'It's Jessica . . . I . . . I didn't think you'd answer.' Silence. 'Are you okay?' she continued.

'How's the case going?'

He clearly didn't want to make small talk but would have seen coverage of the 'Houdini' case in the papers and on the news.

'Not great.'

'Aye, it's a weird one . . .'

Jessica had no idea what came over her but, for the second time that day, she broke into tears. 'Oh, Harry . . .' He didn't say anything but she tearfully continued. 'I don't know what I'm doing. Things are a mess. We've had no leads, no idea how these killings link together and then, when we finally make a connection, I blow it. I let Lapham get away and, even when we got him back, I screw it up and he's back out again.'

'You got him back?'

'He walked into the station with Peter Hunt this morning.'

'Hunt?'

'Yes.'

'What a shitbag.'

Jessica laughed slightly through the tears. 'That's what I said.'

'You said that?'

'Yes.'

'To him?'

'Yeah.'

Jessica could hear Harry laughing. Huge belly laughs and snorts. And then she was giggling too. She had barely heard Harry that happy even when they worked together. 'What did he say?' Harry managed to ask in between the guffaws.

'Nothing really. He didn't get a chance to say anything.'

Harry continued to laugh. 'That is bloody fantastic.'

Jessica grabbed a box of tissues from the table and blew her nose, the tears now gone. She smiled and tried to stop herself joining in but Harry's laugh was infectious. It took a while until both of them had finally stopped. 'Are you okay, Harry?'

'Me? Yeah, I'm just a stubborn, silly old man. Don't you worry about me, detective sergeant.' He had never had the chance to call her that before. It sounded good. He sounded proud.

'We all worry . . .' Harry said nothing, so Jessica swallowed before continuing. 'What happened in court?'

Harry didn't reply for a few moments and she wondered whether he would but then the answer came. 'Nothing. He wound me up.'

'He winds everyone up.'

'Kid's gonna get off.'

Jessica didn't want to acknowledge that, not knowing if it was true. 'What would you do with the case, Harry?'

'Link the bodies. People don't kill at random, not really.'

'We thought Lapham was the link.'

'Do you still think that?'

'No.'

Harry paused again. Jessica didn't know if it was deliberate or if he simply didn't have anything to say. 'Some people will do anything to get themselves ahead, detective sergeant. Or get revenge. Everyone has a dark side. You'd be surprised what can bring it out.'

His statement sounded ominous and Jessica didn't know how to respond directly, so she changed the subject. 'Do you know I'm in on Tuesday?'

'Yes.'

'Do you fancy a drink afterwards?'

'Are you buying?'

'Of course.'

'I'll see you there then.'

19

Considering what happened between Jessica, Wayne Lapham and Peter Hunt had occurred behind closed doors, even she was impressed at how quickly the news had travelled around the station when she arrived on the Monday morning. As she walked through reception, it felt as if all eyes were on her. People were smiling but Jessica found it unnerving. She was so used to the gloomy 'It's Monday and whatever investigation we've got going on is in a complete mess' looks that she didn't know how to react to it all. She didn't even bother to check in with anyone on the front desk, or visit her own office, she headed for the stairs and the DCI's office.

She could see him sitting behind his desk and he looked up to notice her walking past the window before she had a chance to knock on the door. He beckoned her in and indicated towards the seat opposite him. His grey suit looked sharp and newly pressed, while he had a stern, harsh look on his face.

'DS Daniel,' was his greeting, as ever. Jessica sat and waited for her boss to speak. 'On Saturday, I had a very brief conversation with Peter Hunt. Despite it being my day off, I had a further, much longer conversation with Mr Hunt yesterday over the phone. Today, I came into the station to be given a letter that had been hand-delivered by Mr Hunt for my attention.' He paused for a moment, ever the showman. 'Would you like to guess the contents of either those conversations or the letter?'

'No, Sir.'

'In that case, I should give you some good news and bad news – first the bad. Mr Hunt has alleged that in the interview room on Saturday, you threatened his client, Mr Lapham, with violence. He further alleges that your conduct was completely out of order throughout that interview and that you called him . . .' The DCI paused, pulling a letter out of an A4 brown envelope. He scanned down through its contents then continued. '. . . that you called him a "shitbag".'

He looked up from the letter straight at her. 'How do you answer that?'

She didn't answer him directly but instead said: 'What is the good news?'

Aylesbury actually smiled and she saw a twinkle in his eye she had never seen before. 'The good news for you, DS Daniel, is that I have listened to the recording made and, while some of your questioning may have been a little *unconventional*, I certainly could hear no threatening remarks. I have spoken to both Cole and the constable stationed outside of the room at the time, and neither of them are able to corroborate Mr Hunt's version of events. Given that Mr Lapham has also refused to make any statement of any kind relating to what did or did not happen during questioning on Saturday, I have informed Mr Hunt that there is very little more I can do.'

It all clicked into place for Jessica. Cole had stopped the

tape and left the room, leaving the door only slightly ajar. The constable outside heard nothing – or was happy to say that. Lapham, meanwhile, would not want any kind of coverage, either public or otherwise, to indicate he might have been intimidated by a female. That meant it was simply Hunt who was left with a problem.

Aylesbury continued. 'Mr Hunt has indicated in his letter that he would wish to pursue this matter with Detective Superintendent Davies. I spoke with him a short time ago and informed him that I believed there was no basis for any action, especially given the lack of cooperation from Mr Hunt's own client. I should tell you, however, that the superintendent has promised to meet with Mr Hunt at some point this week. He will make a final decision as to whether or not Internal will be called in.'

DSI Davies was their overall boss but was not based at the station and had been winding down to retirement for a while now. On most decisions he deferred to the local DCI and William Aylesbury was one of his particular favourites. Jessica guessed on this occasion Hunt's profile meant a meeting had to be held. She hoped it would just be for courtesy and almost allowed herself a half-smile.

'I just have one more question to ask, DS Daniel,' Aylesbury said, this time giving her the biggest smile she had ever seen him give anyone. 'Did you *really* call him a shitbag?'

Jessica said nothing for a moment, weighing up her options. She wasn't entirely off the hook yet. Given her boss's demeanour, she replied with the half-smile she had been trying to stifle. 'I think it may have been "slimy shitbag", Sir.'

The DCI laughed much like Harry had two days previously and once again Jessica found herself joining in, albeit it not quite so wholeheartedly as she had with Harry.

'I would have *loved* to have seen his face,' the chief inspector managed to say in between guffaws. It didn't take long for the lighthearted moment to pass and Aylesbury looked at Jessica to indicate it was time to be serious again. 'I should of course point out that behaviour like that will not be tolerated and, if you did say anything out of order towards Mr Lapham, that is exactly the type of practice we do not condone.'

'Yes, Sir.'

From there it was straight down to business. With Wayne Lapham released and uncooperative about the mysterious man who sold him the stolen goods in the pub, who they both knew probably didn't exist, they were back to having no suspect.

The morning briefing went much along those lines. They had found one link but there must either be more to it or something else that joined the two victims. Lapham wasn't entirely in the clear either. His mug shot was on the whiteboard with a big question mark underneath it. Officers would be looking into his banking details and phone records to see if there was anything that could link him to the dates or victims. Jessica thought it likely another minor crime or three would be discovered but doubted he would have much more to do with the main investigation.

Jessica had resolved to go back to the crime scenes that

afternoon. The Scene of Crime team had already been over them with little in the way of positive results. The Christensen residence was still boarded up at the front with the husband, who was still technically paying half the mortgage, deciding what to do with the place. It wasn't going to be easy selling a house where someone had recently been murdered inside. Sandra Prince had been discharged from hospital the previous day and Jessica was also going to pay her a visit. It had been her who had first put them on the tail of Wayne Lapham and maybe she had something else tucked away. Jessica had been in such a hurry to get out of the hospital the previous time when she found out about the burglary, she could easily have missed something else. She knew the whole of Tuesday was going to be spent either in court or hanging around outside, so figured it was best to try to make something happen today.

The simmering undertone of the briefing was all about Jessica herself. More officers than ever before had said 'good morning' or 'hi' to her in the hallways. Everyone clearly knew about her incident, or at least the Hunt part of it, and seemed suitably impressed. She had already been offered six separate 'drinks from the machine' which was about as generous as anyone ever got in the station.

The briefing ended and she sent everyone on their way. The investigation was still in somewhat of a mess given the lack of suspect, motive or method but at least everyone was in a good mood. It seemed a silly distinction but sometimes people being positive could make something happen.

Officers had begun to leave the room when Jessica saw

Rowlands calling her over, flicking his head and pulling a face. To others it might seem a somewhat disrespectful way to initiate a conversation but Jessica didn't mind. He was standing near the back of the room, slightly away from any of the other departing officers. She walked over to him, fully expecting some crack about her car, Hunt, or something else that wasn't very funny.

'All right?' she asked.

'I've had a thought.'

'Well, it's been twenty-eight years. It had to happen sometime.'

Rowlands gave a half-smile but didn't take the bait. 'No, seriously.'

'Go on then.'

'There is this guy I used to go to uni with who is now a part-time magician . . .'

'That's a serious thought?'

'No, honestly. Listen, I was asking him about how you could get in and out of something that was locked.'

'Are you taking the piss?'

'We don't have any better ideas, do we?'

Jessica raised her eyebrows but had to concede they didn't. 'What did he say?'

'It was complicated. I think he wants to meet you.'

'You are joking?'

'No, really. Look, it was just a thought.'

'A shit one.'

She instantly felt bad about saying that. Rowlands was a cocky so-and-so but his face fell ever so slightly before returning to its previous state. In the briefings, they constantly encouraged people to 'think outside the box'. That phrase was beyond a cliché but the intent behind it was the same: try to think around a problem rather than just go for it directly. A situation like this, where they genuinely had no idea how the murders had been committed, was exactly the time that type of thinking could possibly come up with a solution. Besides, she knew full well forces in other areas of the country used psychics in their investigations. From her point of view illusionists and psychics were more or less the same, except that magicians were upfront with their deception.

'All right, fine . . .' Rowlands said.

'Look, I'll tell you what. I'm in court tomorrow but come with me back to the scenes later today. If we don't get anything from that, we'll go see your mate on Wednesday. If you tell anyone that's what we're doing, you're on your own.' Jessica didn't want it getting out that she was seemingly desperate enough to stoop to this line of thinking.

'I'll give him a call.'

'He's not a weirdo, is he?'

'At university, he once nailed his trainers to the ceiling of his room in halls. He then set up a webcam and hung from the roof all the while streaming the whole thing over the Internet.'

'Why?'

'He said it was something to do with endurance and showing how differently the mind could work when it was put under stress but I think it was more to impress a girl.'

'Did it?'

'What do you think?'

'Great, not a weirdo at all then.'

Garry Ashford was only a couple of days away from being fully back in his editor's bad books. 'If it bleeds, it leads' had been the media's motto for years and the *Herald*'s recent sales had borne that out. The day of Garry's first exclusive had seen sales double. The attacks on the police force had helped keep the numbers up, while Garry's second big story about the 'Houdini Strangler', which was his editor's headline, had seen numbers almost triple.

It hadn't all been good news for the reporter though. His colleagues had pretty much ostracised him, wondering how the hell some scruffy kid who had done nothing previously had suddenly managed to stumble across such good stories. On the other hand, his editor had been talking of awards, promotions, pay rises and all sorts of other positive things. Garry was fully aware he hadn't yet been elevated, or given any extra money, and wondered how long he could keep his run going.

It was now Monday and it had been made abundantly clear by his editor that he had to come up with something good. His boss had questioned him about his source and asked if there was any more information they could use. It was all very polite on the surface but there was definitely an undertone.

That left Garry with something of a problem. He wasn't going to just make things up and, while he had sent a text to his source's unregistered number, he had not had any response yet. The last time they had spoken, his contact said they would have to talk sparingly and that information would be a little light on the ground for a while.

His meeting with DS Daniel the previous week had gone better than he expected. That said, anything that hadn't ended with him being sworn at and threatened with varying degrees of physical violence would have been better than his previous phone calls with her. She had now slated his dress sense and name, so he thought his actual looks were the only thing she had left to go after him for.

He was supposed to be off over the weekend but received a call from the news editor on Friday evening asking what he knew about Wayne Lapham. He knew as much as anyone else, seeing as he had seen the same media releases and photos as the rest of the office when the police had put out the request for help finding him. Somehow, he had still been told to spend his Saturday getting some background on the investigation's prime suspect. There seemed to be some assumption that he would know what he was doing.

He didn't.

Lapham didn't appear to exist on the electoral roll or in the phone book, which was unsurprising. Garry had texted his source for help but, with no reply, had ended up doing what all journalists hated doing: door-stepping. As part of their appeal, the police had put out information that Lapham had last been seen in the Prince of Wales pub in Moston. Garry didn't really know the area but had found the address of the place on the Internet and taken two buses to get there. He kept the tickets, hoping he would at least get expenses, and armed with a copy of that day's *Herald* – which had a photo of Lapham on the front, had marched into the pub hoping someone would be willing to point him in the right direction.

The barman, who Garry assumed was also the landlord, was a large bald-headed man with intimidating accusing eyes and a deep voice. Garry showed him the paper's front page and started with a polite, 'Hello, I was wondering if . . .' but the barman finished his sentence for him.

'. . . you were wondering if you could buy a drink? Yes, you can.'

Garry had ordered a coke and asked for a receipt. That would be going to the expenses department too. That first drink had got him the information that Lapham had been in the pub the day before and that 'your lot' had been on the phone all morning.

The second drink uncovered the fact that Lapham was often in the pub but wasn't at that exact moment. Garry could see that for himself.

The third coke and first packet of crisps had helped Garry find out that Lapham didn't live too far away and that this place was his local. With each ordered drink, the barman's smile got wider and wider. Garry had always had a weak bladder and needed two trips to the men's room already. In some ways, he thought, it was a bizarre type of torture that he was paying for the privilege of.

Garry's first beer of the day, ordered out of exasperation, and second packet of crisps had finally prised out that Lapham lived in a row of flats not too far away.

'Dunno more than that I'm afraid, mate,' the barman told him after Garry had finished that final drink. Garry thought the word 'mate' was something of a subjective term.

After a third trip to the toilet on his way out, Garry followed the barman's instructions to the row of flats where Lapham apparently lived. He had no answer from the first door, while the man behind the second looked at him as if he had two heads then slammed it in his face. After a rather sweary inquiry as to his identity from the woman behind the third door, he was surprisingly informed this *was* Lapham's house and that the female was his 'fiancée', Marie Hall. Even more astoundingly he was invited in, with the woman promising to tell him how the police were 'stitching up' her partner.

The woman was still in her dressing gown, a particularly peach monstrosity. She invited him into her kitchen and chain-smoked throughout their conversation, which was more of a one-sided rant. Garry thought his flat was a mess but Lapham's made his look like a hospital ward.

Despite the swearing, lack of cohesion and seemingly baseless accusations, Marie had at least given him some useful information. She said some officer had not long been sent back from her place because her fiancé had handed himself in and was currently at the police station being questioned. That was the first Garry knew of it. She reckoned the police had nothing on him and were 'dredging up old things 'cos they've got it in for him'. But she gave him plenty of background on her fiancé and even let Garry borrow a photo 'as long as you bring it back'.

From what she said, Lapham was a misunderstood soul whom the police delighted in picking on.

Garry thought that, although those claims seemed unlikely, behind the bravado, Marie actually did care for Wayne Lapham and was genuinely worried for him. She certainly didn't like the police and more than once went off on a tangent about 'that posh bitch officer forcing her way in here'. Garry didn't push the point but had an idea about who the 'bitch' could have been.

He thanked her for her time and caught the buses back to write the story up. By then news had come out that Wayne Lapham had been released. Garry linked everything together and turned it into something of a profile piece about the investigation's prime suspect. His editor had called and said the piece was okay but sounded disappointed his reporter hadn't got more. Quite what he'd expected, Garry wasn't sure.

It was that tone which had continued into the Monday meeting but perhaps all that was about to change. On Garry's phone was a text from the pre-pay number he had memorised.

'Call me. It's good.'

Garry phoned the number, feverishly taking notes throughout the call. It *was* good. Good enough to wreck the career of a certain detective sergeant.

20

Jessica's day hadn't been too productive. She had first taken Rowlands with her to Yvonne Christensen's boarded-up house. They were let in through the back by the victim's ex-husband, Eric, who had been given his son's keys. Jessica didn't know what she thought she would get from the visit and hadn't expected a flash of inspiration where she discovered something others had missed. Things didn't work like that.

Eric didn't want to enter the house and told them he hadn't been in since the murder. He said he was in the process of organising a company to go in and clean the house up. When that was complete, he would look to put it on the market. Finding a set of cleaners keen enough was proving a problem when he explained the situation.

Jessica wasn't surprised.

The house itself looked more or less the same as it had the last time she had been there. The bed upstairs had been stripped with the sheets taken by the Scene of Crime team. Blood had soaked through to the mattress and was clearly visible.

Jessica and Rowlands walked around the house looking for something that might have been missed. She checked the attic for the first time herself, having seen the report that said there was no connection to the neighbouring property but wanting to check herself for completeness. It was exactly as the account had said – there wasn't much to see with no way in, obvious or not.

She tried to walk herself through what would have happened, the direction Yvonne must have been facing when the wire was wrapped around her neck. She thought about where the killer's feet must have stood and the angle their body must have been at as they held the murder instrument. None of it really helped.

She visited Sandra Prince at her house. It seemed odd that the woman had gone back to living at the property where her husband's murdered body had recently been found but Jessica knew some people did that because there was nowhere else for them to go. The woman wasn't in the best frame of mind but did say she was bemused as to why Wayne Lapham had been released. Sandra hadn't been angry exactly but kept saying that he had already got away with it once, meaning the burglaries. It was hard to argue with her. Jessica asked if she knew of any connection to the Christensen family but Sandra didn't recognise the name or photos.

In terms of the case itself, neither of the visits had really helped but it had focused Jessica's mind on the bodies again with the viciousness of it all. It made her appreciate even more that the person she was looking for was definitely no fool. Setting up this kind of scene took the attention away from themselves because the police were busy trying to find out *how* the murders were carried out, rather than *who* carried them out. As for the why, they had as much idea about that as they did about the other aspects. She didn't believe Lapham could be their killer but the connection he gave to the victims surely couldn't be a coincidence either.

After returning to the station, Jessica checked in with Cole but there was little to report. The victims of the other three burglaries for which Lapham had been convicted of handling stolen goods had been visited again but reported nothing untoward. Jessica went to her office to get rid of some paperwork. Reynolds wasn't in and she had the space to herself but she couldn't focus on the work, her thoughts turned towards her appearance in court the following day and round two with Peter Hunt. Not to mention the case she was working on.

She had just pushed back into her chair and shut her eyes when her phone rang. She picked it up from the desk, looking at Garry Ashford's name on the screen. She had reprogrammed his name properly into her phone after meeting him, reluctantly admitting that perhaps he wasn't that bad after all.

He still dressed like a prat and couldn't spell his own name though.

'Mr Ashford,' she answered. 'How's life in the gutters?'

'Oh . . . hi. Are you alone?'

'Yes but this isn't a sex line. Well, unless you're paying . . .'

'Can I run something by you?'

Jessica's first thought was that another body had been found and somehow the journalist knew about it before she did. Her mind was racing. 'What?'

'At lunch today, I spoke to a lawyer named Peter Hunt.'

Jessica winced at the mention of that name. She was aware that, even if she was exonerated by Aylesbury and the superintendent, there wouldn't be too much they could do if a story about her threatening a suspect got into the papers. The police couldn't be seen to have someone in such a prominent position who was embroiled in a scandal like that. As someone who could work as part of a big investigation, she would be finished, hard evidence or not.

Her response aptly summed up her mood. 'Shit.'

'He was only confirming what I had already heard.'

That was the problem the station's whispers had caused. The legend of what had actually happened in the interview room had grown out of all proportion. In the car on their way to the Christensens' house earlier, Rowlands had asked her about the incident. She hadn't told him much – or anyone for that matter – but he had told her the things he had heard. They ranged from something actually approaching the truth to her having Peter Hunt up against the interview room's wall by the throat. Other versions included her turning the table over and bellowing a string of abuse at both Hunt and Lapham, while somebody else had apparently said she'd attacked the pair of them with a fork from the canteen. She had realised on the journey things had got out of hand. People had obviously been talking and word would have been around most of the Greater Manchester Police force by now. That wasn't even counting the people Peter Hunt had spoken to. It hadn't crossed her mind at the time but this was exactly the kind of thing that could have happened.

'What *have* you heard?' Jessica asked.

Garry's version of events was almost exactly as Jessica remembered. He certainly had a very good source considering there had only been three people in the room and she knew he hadn't got the information from herself or Wayne Lapham. Hunt may have confirmed details but she doubted he would have tipped someone like Garry Ashford off in the first place.

'I can't really talk about it, Garry,' she said after he finished telling her his story.

'I know but I have to ask.'

'What are you going to write?'

'I don't know yet . . . something.'

'You know this could ruin me?' Jessica wasn't sure what to say. It wasn't as if she had been too nice to him before. That had just slipped out.

'Would you like to tell me what happened?'

Jessica didn't know what had come over her in the past few days with the anger in the interview room, plus the emotion in the station's toilet and over the phone with Harry. She had even enjoyed a laugh with the DCI, a person she had never really got on too well with before. And now she told Garry Ashford, a journalist and relative stranger, everything. Once she started speaking, she couldn't stop. He didn't try to interrupt or ask anything, he simply let her talk. She told him how Lapham had got under her skin and that Hunt had let him. She spoke about the investigation itself: how the police had got nowhere and were struggling. They weren't even sure how the murders had happened, let alone who did them.

She even told him about her own feelings of inadequacy amid a complete lack of leads.

If Internal Investigations were listening in, they would have had a field day. When she had finished, there was a short silence.

Garry eventually broke it. 'That was a bit . . . *more* . . . than I expected.'

Suddenly she was laughing again and so was he. 'I don't know why I told you all that,' she added once things had calmed down. 'I could be ruined if all of this got out. They wouldn't trust me to go into an interview room again.'

'What would you like me to do?'

'I don't know.'

'I have an idea but would need your help?'

'Go on . . .'

'Do you think you can trust me?'

'I'm not sure I have much choice.'

Jessica listened as Garry told her to leave it with him but to make sure she got hold of the next day's paper. 'I think I've got a way to keep you and my editor happy,' he said.

Jessica thought that, if he could manage that, he was definitely a lot cleverer than she had previously given him credit for.

Having read the *Herald*'s website on her phone the next morning and then bought the print edition on her way to the station, Jessica was beginning to think she had definitely underestimated Garry Ashford. But if the scruffy little genius had got her off the hook, he had also ensured her colleagues would be taking the piss out of her for weeks.

She had been impressed when she had seen the online version but it was the actual hard copy that really stood out. The front-page banner headline read: 'HOUDINI HUNTER'. She wasn't a fan of the 'Houdini Strangler' label but, good or bad, it had stuck. Garry's front-page piece, which extended over a two-page spread on the inside, was a full profile of her. It was positive throughout, reassuring the public that she was looking out for them and hard on the trail of the killer. After the previous editorials slating the lack of progress, this piece praised the 'behind the scenes efforts'. Very little of the information had actually come from her but, even if it had, it was written so cleverly no one could have known for sure. It quoted 'sources close to Detective Sergeant Daniel' and 'senior members of the team'.

The journalist must have really done his homework the day before. They still didn't have a great photo of her but had come up with one taken a few years previously when she was in uniform. She remembered it being taken but had no idea where the newspaper would have got it from. She definitely looked younger in the shot and she thought more naive too.

Jessica was planning only a brief stop at Longsight to pick up some paperwork on her way to court. It would give her something to do while she was stuck hanging around in the witnesses' waiting room. Court duty was a mixed blessing for officers. On the one hand, you did get a day off work. She thought it was like when the teacher used to wheel in the video player at school and you knew you would get an easy ride for that lesson. The downside was the sheer amount of waiting around you had to do.

At the station, Jessica had walked into a rowdy, sarcastic cheer from the half-a-dozen or so people milling around the reception area. Before she could make her way through to her office, the desk sergeant pointed towards the stairs. 'He wants to see you.'

She wasn't sure if it would be a negative trip to see the DCI. He surely couldn't be annoyed given the force had finally been painted in a good light? Jessica went up the stairs but, as she made her way past his office's window, he didn't appear to be smiling. 'DS Daniel,' he said as she knocked and entered. She instantly noticed a copy of that morning's *Herald* on his desk. 'So you *have* been making friends with the press then?' he added, referring to their initial conversation in reception when details of the first murder had made the papers.

'Not really, Sir. I don't know where he got most of that information.'

'But you know where he got *some* of it . . . ?'

Jessica said nothing but the half-smile on Aylesbury's face indicated he wasn't expecting an answer. He spoke again. 'I talked to Superintendent Davies this morning and he was *particularly* pleased with today's media coverage. Delighted, I would say. He asked me to pass a message on to you.'

Aylesbury paused, presumably waiting to see if Jessica

would bite. She stayed silent, her face neutral and waited for her boss to continue. 'He wanted me to tell you not to worry about either Peter Hunt or any internal investigation. His exact words were, "Tell Ms Daniel I'll handle it".'

Jessica half-smiled. 'Thank you, Sir.'

'I should of course remind you of your responsibilities when dealing with victims, witnesses, suspects and their representatives . . .'

'I understand, Sir.'

'Right then. Enjoy your day in court with Mr Hunt today. I'm sure he will be positively delighted to meet you again so soon.'

21

Manchester has two Crown Courts. Jessica had been to the Minshull Street one in the north of the city centre a few times in the past as that was generally where the cases from her district were heard. But the most serious crimes and anything referred up from magistrates' courts were usually heard at Crown Square. Given it involved a police officer as the victim, Harry's case was always likely to end up there.

The building was largely the same as any other court precinct Jessica had been into. It was disorganised with groups of people anxiously checking boards to make sure they were in the right place, with solicitors and ushers racing from various side rooms to the courts, checking on witnesses and defendants. Other sets of people sat on the uncomfortable-looking plastic chairs, checking their watches and fiddling with mobile phones.

If you were in uniform, court officials generally liked having police witnesses in the various public waiting areas. It offered a clear disincentive for anyone in the room who might want to cause trouble. Jessica was in her regular suit but the prosecutor dealing with Harry's case came enthusiastically bounding across the reception area as if appearing from nowhere. He shook her hand, reintroduced himself and assured her everything in court was going well. That wasn't what she had heard, of course . . .

Harry was nowhere to be seen but, as the prosecutor led her into court one, she saw him sitting at the back in the public gallery. The court itself was a beautiful creation. It had enormous high ceilings with everything exquisitely wood-panelled. The judge's bench at the front was long and ran the full width of the room, with a huge seal on the wall behind it. From his view out onto the court, the jurors sat on his right, with the dock, probation seats and press box on his left. The middle of the room was set aside for the lawyers and assorted legal workers, with the public area at the back. The witness box was between the jurors and the judge.

Jessica went to sit next to Harry at the rear. He looked fairly scruffy in a suit but had no tie and was unshaven with uncombed hair. As she sat, he offered a 'hello' but wouldn't be drawn into any more conversation than that and didn't seem too keen to engage. She wondered if he would still be up for that drink later, or if he even remembered agreeing?

She watched Peter Hunt swan into court with an air suggesting he believed the case was already won. As ever, he was immaculately turned out. He glanced towards her and Harry but acknowledged neither of them before quickly turning away and taking his seat. Being called as a character witness meant Jessica was last in line for the prosecution. Given Harry had self-destructed on the stand, she was possibly a last chance to turn things around before Hunt had the chance to call his own witness, namely Tom Carpenter. The prosecution knew Hunt would claim Harry had provoked a reaction from the accused by threatening him and that, even though a weapon was involved, that knife was a necessary part of Carpenter's job as a joiner. They would say he had just forgotten to take it out of his trousers and things had got out of hand with disastrous consequences.

Jessica watched the twelve jurors enter court from a side room and made snap judgements on all of them. She could instantly tell the two people who weren't too bothered by the case. One of them was fairly young, a man in his early twenties or so. Earphones were just about visible hanging by his neckline, indicating he had only just had the decency, or been told, to turn the music off. He scuffed his feet and looked at the floor throughout, showing no enthusiasm on his way in. There was a woman too, much older in her fifties, who looked utterly bored as they filed in. Jessica thought she was probably annoyed she'd had to put her book down or something like that. When the time came to make a decision, Jessica marked the two of them down as going along with whatever the majority would do – especially if it would get them discharged quicker.

The older man at the front, likely the person who would be foreman, was sharply dressed in a suit, although it wasn't a necessity when you sat on a jury. He was undoubtedly the one who would take the most interest and lead all the discussions in the retiring room. He probably watched a lot of courtroom or police procedural television shows and thought this was his big moment in the sun. He would no doubt be taking copious notes and sticking rigidly to all the judge's instructions about not reading about the case in the media or talking about it outside of the court. He certainly wouldn't have seen her on the front of that morning's paper.

Jessica would have bet money that, although he hadn't spoken about the case, he had told anyone who would listen that he was a juror *on* the case and then insisted he couldn't talk about it. He looked exactly the type who would delight in the fact that he knew things other people didn't – and revelled in letting them know that. Jessica figured he was a good person to get on side. He would vigorously put his point across after they had retired and be hard to sway away from that.

There were two women around Jessica's age sitting on the end of the front row of jurors. It looked as if they had bonded during the course of the case. They spoke quietly together while everyone awaited the judge's arrival. They were exactly the kind of people who would be key swing votes on a jury: interested enough to listen throughout, forthright enough to not be bullied, but open-minded to take on other people's views.

Jessica had no idea if she was right but working as a police officer gave you a pretty good grasp of the type of people you could be dealing with on any given day. She figured the foreman and these two women would be the key people to convince. These two females especially would stick together and argue their points of view. It was often that fair-mindedness that would get others to agree with you.

The judge entered and everyone stood. He was an enormous man, his robes bulging under the strain from his belly. Some people wore their weight well and managed to hide it but the judge definitely did not. His portly, rounded face was red and he looked out of breath merely walking into the room. He nodded to acknowledge the court and everyone sat down.

Jessica was asked to step out of the court as the two sides bickered over some point before she was called back in and introduced by the prosecutor. As she made her way the few feet to the witness box, she felt the jury's eyes on her. She looked over towards them and, as she would have expected, the potential foreman was feverishly making notes, despite the fact she hadn't even taken the oath yet.

As she reached the stand and took a copy of the Bible, she made a special effort to make eye contact with as many of the jurors as she could. The potential foreman was still writing while headphone boy was looking at his feet. She managed to look at the others and held the eyes of the two female jurors on the front row for a fraction of a second longer.

She confirmed her name, age and rank and then began to answer the initial clarification questions. When you appeared as a witness, your side would want to make sure the judge and jury knew you were a reliable, trustworthy person. That often involved a brief rundown of your entire life story and history. It was dull to pretty much everyone involved and, if Jessica had been asked to confirm her conception date, she would have only been half-surprised.

She saw Tom Carpenter in the dock watching her. The first time she had seen him was after the stabbing when he had been questioned after handing himself in. Jessica wasn't involved in that but had seen him walking through the station with Hunt. He looked very different then, unshaven with a sneer and contemptuous look for the officers around him. Now he was smartly turned out in a suit, shirt and dark-coloured tie. He was shaven and had shorter hair. Back then he looked exactly the type to carry a knife ready to stab anyone who looked at him the wrong way. Now he looked the height of suburban respectability, someone you could trust and rely on. If you compared him to Harry's unkempt appearance and demeanour in court, you would easily mistake the accused for the supposed veteran police officer.

Jessica answered each question as clearly as she could, directing her answers towards the jury. The prosecutor's examination was as extensive as it could be. He asked her how long she had known Harry, what her relationship had been with him when she joined CID and other standard questions to establish that she knew him pretty well. Considering Harry kept to himself, she figured she knew as much as anyone. She confirmed she had never seen him act unprofessionally in the course of duty, nor seen him be aggressive.

After the prosecutor had finished speaking, Peter Hunt stood up for the cross-examination. He looked straight at her, the first time she had noticed him do so. If he was annoyed about what had happened a few days previously he didn't show it, speaking with an even tone and steady pace.

He confirmed a few of the details she had already spoken about and made a special point to let her re-emphasise that she had become the person Harry was closest to on the force. The lawyer then asked one of the questions she had been worrying about. 'If you know the victim so well, how many times have you spoken to Mr Thomas in the last six months?'

It sounded odd hearing Harry called 'mister'. He was no longer a detective, so it was technically correct but to her ear didn't sound right. She knew her answer would sound bad but had no intention of lying. 'Once,' she admitted, perhaps slightly more quietly than some of her other responses. She bowed her head almost subconsciously while she said it. In the way legal professionals seemed to be trained to do, Hunt recoiled in mock surprise. Jessica thought that look of horror or shock must come on day one of legal training. Before you opened any books or took any exams, you had to be able to show you could look stunned even when being told information you were already fully aware of. If he did ever get booted out of the legal profession, Hunt could at least go for a job as a daytime soap actor.

'Just the once?'

'Yes.'

Hunt gave a smaller recoil and then looked directly at the jury to make the argument that she couldn't know Harry that well if they had only been in contact once in recent times. She had to concede he had a point.

The man on the end was frantically adding to his notes as Hunt continued. 'In your experience, is Mr Thomas a big drinker?'

'How would you define "big"?'

'Let me rephrase it. Have you ever seen Mr Thomas drink while on the job?'

'Not really.'

'So yes?'

'It's not as simple as that.' Jessica had seen most officers technically drink while on duty. She explained to the jury that sometimes it was easier to talk to sources or witnesses in somewhere like a pub, where they themselves felt comfortable. She left out the part that, on occasion, you would have a drink or two with your colleagues a little before you had theoretically finished for the day. It was a fairly common practice and, although Harry didn't really drink with the other officers, she had certainly seen him talk to people in the pub who could give him information.

Hunt listened to her and nodded slightly, apparently feeling as if his point had been made. Just for good measure, he added: 'Even if you were to meet with witnesses and the like in a pub, you wouldn't have to drink yourself, would you?'

'No,' Jessica had to admit.

Hunt was on a roll. 'Have you ever seen Mr Thomas act in a questionable way while on duty?'

It was the type of question that was difficult to answer. She had often seen Harry give his homeless contact money and food in return for information and what about the sealed brown envelope he had given to the same man whose tip had led directly to an arrest? Was that 'questionable behaviour'? Technically it could be seen as bribing a witness. She had seen him make vague statements in interviews, perhaps claiming to know more about a situation than he actually did. It was definitely a tad dishonest but was it 'questionable'?

'No,' she answered.

'Never?'

'No.'

Hunt's next question threw her. 'Have you ever acted in a questionable way yourself while on duty?'

She saw the steely twinkle in his eye as he asked, almost as if he had winked at her. He probably hadn't but there was an awful lot behind the question. She remembered Wayne Lapham and the interview room. The prosecutor leapt to his feet, objecting and pointing out Jessica herself wasn't on trial. The judge interjected but Hunt hadn't asked the question because he wanted an answer, he had asked it to wind her up.

He had switched from looking at the jury to looking at her, fixing her with a steady stare. If his previous question had rattled her, his next one was designed to push things even further. 'Have you ever been romantically involved with Mr Thomas?'

This time there was definitely half a smirk on his face as he eyed her. The jury wouldn't have been able to see it from the angle they were at. Another objection came but this time Hunt assured the judge it was a legitimate question to find out how closely the two knew each other. He pointed out that it could prejudice Jessica's answers if they had been romantically involved.

The judge ruled the question didn't have to be answered but Jessica looked at the jury and said 'no' in any case. She looked at the man on the end and the two women on the front row, the three people she wanted to convince, but knew her answer was irrelevant. Hunt hadn't asked it because he thought it was true, he had asked it to put the idea in their heads and make them doubt her. Jessica turned back to Hunt, who looked at the jury and then at her. 'No further questions.'

His smirk had gone but his eyes told the story. 'Take that.'

22

As she suspected, a catch-up drink with Harry never happened. The court broke for lunch shortly after her evidence and Harry had already left court by the time the prosecuting lawyer had finished speaking to her. Jessica thought there was every chance he simply didn't remember their conversation from Saturday. She hadn't smelled it on him but, given everything that had happened, maybe he had been lost to drink? He wouldn't be the first police officer to have succumbed to its lure.

Back at the station, everyone was already fully aware of how her appearance had gone. The desk sergeant's usual source, whoever it was, had apparently been spot-on about her showdown with Peter Hunt and everyone was well aware that, while she hadn't lost her temper and blown it, Hunt had got the better of her. Feeling in the mood to take her frustrations out on somebody, she tracked down Rowlands in the canteen. He was sitting at one of the tables chatting to the now not so new girl from uniform he reckoned he was taking out the previous week.

The girl laughed at whatever had been said to her as Jessica sat next to Rowlands opposite the female officer. She was young, blonde and good-looking, still clearly enjoying being a member of the police force. Jessica thought it wouldn't take long to disappear. Eighteen months maximum was generally what it took before fresh-faced optimism was replaced by cynicism and reality. Often it came as soon as you saw that the domestic violence victim you had spent time consoling had changed their minds about appearing in court and taken back their rat-faced boyfriend. Either that or some drunken scumbag who had called you every name under the sun had gone to magistrates' court and got off with a slap on the wrist. It wouldn't take long . . .

'You should watch this one,' Jessica told the girl, nodding towards Rowlands. 'I've heard that a lot of the girls he's ended up with complain of feeling a bit, erm, "itchy" down below not long afterwards.'

'Hey,' Rowlands said, putting down the fork he had been eating with.

The girl didn't seem too fussed. 'I've not had any of that.'

Jessica rolled her eyes and shook her head, nodding towards Rowlands again. 'Whatever. I need a few minutes with him.'

The female officer took the hint and stood up. 'See you later?' she asked him.

'Yeah, yeah,' he replied unconvincingly. 'I'll text you.' The girl scuttled off, beaming.

'Poor girl,' Jessica said to the constable now they were alone.

'What?' he responded with apparent indignation but a big grin nonetheless.

'Whenever you do muck *her* about, can you try not to muck her *career* about?'

'What makes you think . . . ?' Rowlands began to say but Jessica just looked at him, eyebrows raised. 'Yeah, all right,' he conceded. She went to speak but he carried on. 'I thought you were in court all day?'

'I've done that, now I'm back.'

'What do you want me for?'

'You remember your magician mate?'

'Yeah.'

'I figured that, as I'm off the clock anyway, it would be as good a time as any to go find out what the weirdo's got to add.'

'I'll have to check he's free.'

'How busy can he possibly be?'

It hadn't taken long for Rowlands to establish his pal wasn't over-encumbered with work and was happy to see them that afternoon. Jessica told Reynolds she was going to be out for the afternoon but didn't say where, making sure she reminded Rowlands to keep his mouth shut too. He insisted they go in his car, saying he didn't want to risk breaking down on the way if they went in hers.

'Haven't you got any original material?' Jessica asked.

'You're the gift that keeps on giving.'

'At least I don't drive some souped-up GTI twat-mobile.'

Rowlands's vehicle was exactly what she would have expected it to be: a smallish car that had been upgraded with any number of over-priced ridiculous parts.

'And you take the piss out of *my* exhaust?' Jessica said

as he started up the engine. His sounded as loud as hers, if not worse.

'Mine's deliberate.'

Rowlands's magician friend lived in a flat above a book-makers' shop in the Stockport area of the city. The neighbourhood was pretty grim but her partner didn't seem too bothered by leaving his car outside, which at least said one thing. They went around the back of the bookies' and the constable buzzed the intercom. The main door unlocked itself and Jessica followed Rowlands up the stairs to the inner door. As they reached the top and were let into the hallway, Jessica had to concede it didn't look like the typical type of accommodation you would expect to find over a shop. The first thing she saw was an enormous stuffed tiger's head hanging above the door facing them as they walked in.

'Oh yeah, he's into taxidermy too,' Rowlands said, as if that explained everything.

The man who greeted them was thin with shoulder-length long brown hair. He was dressed unassumingly in jeans and a T-shirt with some pattern she didn't recognise. Jessica did notice he was wearing a watch on each wrist as well as odd shoes. One was a bright white trainer, the sort you might go running in, the other blue and made of some kind of canvas material. He greeted Rowlands with a hug and an 'all right, Dave?' He also hugged Jessica. At first, she thought she would push him away but then just let him without reciprocating. She gave him a slight tap on the back as if to say 'all right, that's enough' but he was already in the process of letting go and hopped away, almost skipping through the door underneath the tiger's head. Rowlands was following him, so Jessica shrugged and did the same.

The room they had walked into was seemingly the living room. At first it didn't look as if there was anywhere to sit, just an assortment of throws and beanbags. The room was dark, with big thick curtains pulled at the back of the room and the only light coming from a selection of small electric lamps that looked like candles placed around the floor. There was a large elaborate chandelier on the ceiling but it was either turned off or didn't work.

The room was surrounded by tall heavy-looking book-shelves, most of which were packed with hardback books. On one of the shelves was something that looked decid-edly like a stuffed chicken. Jessica was going to ask if it *was* a chicken but figured she didn't particularly want to know the answer.

Most living rooms had some kind of central point – people pointed their furniture towards a television or something like a fireplace or fish tank. This room seemed to have nothing like that, not that there was any furniture anyway. There was certainly no TV and the only thing potentially central was a large round white shaggy rug. The colour stood out sharply against the rest of the dark shades in the room.

The whole flat smelled faintly of a substance Jessica would assume was incense but certainly had the air of something decidedly more illegal. She figured she would let it go . . . unless this guy really annoyed her.

The magician literally jumped onto one of the beanbags and sprawled himself out, bobbing up and down before arranging himself into a cross-legged sitting position. Rowlands seemingly thought nothing of this behaviour and sat on another beanbag the other side of the rug. With little other option, Jessica sat on a different beanbag. It reminded her of Caroline's flat at university when they first moved to Manchester with a distinct lack of furniture. There were beanbags then too.

Rowlands was smiling at her but Jessica didn't want to admit she felt a tad out of her depth, so asked the obvious: 'What's your name then?' She thought it was a simple enough question but the response made her less sure.

'My actual name is Francis but you can call me Hugo.' They had been there for less than two minutes but, not for the first time, Jessica figured she didn't want to know the answer. How could those two names be in the slightest bit connected? As if reading her mind, he added: 'Hugo's my stage name.'

'Are you on stage often?'

'Life's a stage, don't you think?'

She tried not raise her eyebrows but could see Rowlands smiling out of the corner of her eye. She ignored Hugo's response but shot the constable a look to let him know they would be having words later. 'Okay then, erm, Hugo, Detective Constable Rowlands says you may have some information that could help our investigation?'

She wanted to add: 'I personally doubt that very much, you mental case' but held her tongue. It was as if he hadn't heard her question anyway.

'Can I show you something first?'

'I'd rather you didn't.'

Rowlands took that moment to chip in. 'He's good, y'know.'

Jessica rolled her eyes. 'All right, whatever, go on.'

She was trying not to be sarcastic or obviously hostile but had felt her tone slip with that.

'Okay, hold this,' Hugo said, pulling an orange out from his pocket and tossing it towards her.

Jessica hadn't realised what was happening at first but caught the piece of fruit one-handed. If she hadn't, it would have smacked her square in the face. She shook her head but Hugo wasn't looking. He had leapt to his feet, motioning for Rowlands to do the same. Jessica stayed sitting on the beanbag, feeling more and more uncomfortable.

'Right,' Hugo said to his friend. 'How much money have you got on you?'

Rowlands fiddled through his pockets, pulling out his wallet. He opened one of the flaps and turned it upside down into his hands. A few coins fell out and he snatched a couple of notes out from the main part. He counted it all back into the correct place.

'Thirty pounds and eighty-two pence,' he said.

Hugo nodded along. 'Good, good. And you, Miss, er, Detective Daniel?'

Jessica didn't need to check. 'I've only got a tenner.' She didn't bother with change and only ever kept notes and cards in her purse.

Hugo kept nodding. 'Good, good.' He turned back to Rowlands. 'How much is that in total then, Dave?'

The magician's friend obviously didn't need much time to think. 'Forty eighty-two, I guess.'

'Hmm yeah, sounds about right,' Hugo said, plopping himself back onto his beanbag before instantly leaping to his feet again. 'Right, tea?' he asked, looking from Jessica to Rowlands and then back again.

'I'm fine,' Jessica replied, clearly confused.

'Me too,' confirmed the constable.

'I fancy some tea,' said Hugo, making his way back out of the living room before either of them could object.

Jessica was still holding the orange but, with the magician out of the room, looked to Dave. 'What are we doing?' she asked.

'I don't know yet.'

She nodded towards the shelf. 'Is that a real chicken?'

'Probably. I told you, he likes taxidermy.'

Jessica continued to shoot her colleague dirty looks while looking around the rest of the bizarre room. She thought there was something that looked like a stuffed rat or mouse on one of the other shelves.

A couple of minutes later, Hugo re-entered carrying a tray. On it was a small metal teapot with steam coming from its spout and three china teacups on individual saucers. Each was white with a flowery pattern. Jessica thought it was the kind of set you might expect somebody's grandmother to have. Hugo set the tray down in the middle of the white rug in between them. 'Right, tea,' he said.

Jessica started to remind him she didn't want any but figured it wouldn't do much good. 'Okay,' he added. 'I like mine with a hint of orange. Have you ever had it like that?' He was looking directly at Jessica.

'No.'

'Could you peel that for me?' He was indicating the orange still in her hand.

'Okay . . .'

Hugo threw her a handkerchief and Jessica started to peel the fruit, putting the pieces of skin into a nearby bin. As a kid she always tried to peel the skin off in one piece. Here she didn't care, tearing small strips off and tossing them away. When it was complete, she glanced back at the magician who stared at her. 'Can you squeeze a few drops into the pot?'

She was pretty much past caring what this obvious madman asked her to do. She got to her feet and went over to the tray. Hugo removed the teapot's lid and she gently squeezed the fruit, allowing a few drops to fall into the pot. As Jessica did that, she noticed something solid in the centre of the orange. She looked at the magician sitting on the floor in front of her who had an expectant grin on his face. Jessica pulled the segments apart and could now clearly see something that looked like a small poker chip. She pulled it out and set the orange down on the tray. The chip was round and black but on it was imprinted a pound sign, four digits and a decimal point.

'£40.82.'

She looked at Hugo, who was grinning smugly, and then at Rowlands, tossing him the piece of plastic. He caught it and looked at the number before exploding into laughter. 'That is fan-bloody-tastic,' he said.

Hugo didn't say anything but continued to smile. Jessica had to admit it was impressive. 'Pretty good. I've seen better,' she said.

Rowlands was still laughing. 'Love it, mate. Love it.'

Jessica let the mood settle. 'Okay, can we do what we came here for?'

Hugo had a knowing smile on his face but nodded at her. 'What would you like to know?'

Jessica didn't want to go into too much detail about the case, while Rowlands was still giggling to himself and rolling the chip around in his hand. 'What do you know about getting in and out of somewhere that is completely locked?' she asked.

Hugo nodded, taking her question in. He looked straight at her and she noticed that he was quite a good-looking guy despite his frame and weirdness. His face was nicely symmetrical and his smile was appealing and kindly. 'With any act of illusion, the obvious answer is almost certainly the correct one. Nobody can walk through walls or disappear from one spot and reappear in another. As an entertainer, my job is to make you think I can.'

'But how . . . ?' Jessica started.

'Think. When you're watching someone perform, it's not what you *do* see that matters, it's what you *don't* see. Is someone really flying just because you can't see the wires holding them?'

'But I know a man can't fly. I know somebody can't walk through walls.'

'We all know what a human being can and can't do.

215

The art of illusion is to make you question that. Look at me. What are the first things you noticed?'

Jessica rescanned him but knew what she was going to say. 'You're wearing two watches and odd shoes.'

'Exactly and while you're busy looking at my feet and wrists you're missing far more fundamental things.'

Jessica finally got it. 'So you're saying we're overlooking something straightforward?'

'I don't know; that's not for me to say but I do know that with anything that looks impossible, the obvious answer is almost certainly the correct one.'

23

Rowlands drove them both back to the station, still crowing about his friend's trick. He had kept the poker chip as a memento. Jessica thought about what Hugo had told her. The shoes and the watches were misdirection. She didn't know how he had done the trick but did feel as if she had learned something from him. In terms of progress, the meeting hadn't got her anywhere but she felt it could be useful in the future. For now, she just had to put his advice into practical terms. She still felt that the key to the case would be linking the victims. Wayne Lapham was a connection but there must be another. If she could find that link, she felt sure the rest of the pieces would click into place – including the mystery way the person had got into and out of the houses. It was that part she felt was the misdirection. While they were focusing on the method, they were not concentrating on whoever had murdered two people.

Hugo's words stuck in her mind as the week went on. The two people that had been given the task of linking the victims were reassigned as Jessica took on the job herself. She would take the files of Yvonne Christensen and Martin Prince home each evening, hoping something would occur to her which others had somehow missed. She went back over the notes of the interviews with the victims' family and friends and rechecked things such as bank and phone records. She even checked where the victims had gone to school to see if they unknowingly knew each other. It was dead end after dead end and she was becoming fully aware she was turning into a nightmare to live with.

Caroline's relationship with Randall had turned serious and they were sleeping over at either Randall's flat or theirs every night of the week now. Caroline asked her whether she minded but it was a bit late and Jessica wouldn't have objected even if she did; she was pleased her friend was happy. Caroline said that Randall's flat was a bit basic and theirs was much nicer. Jessica was allowing herself to be engulfed by the work. She would leave the flat early and either come home late, or return with the two files she knew off by heart. She had phoned Harry the evening after meeting Hugo but he had not answered. She also texted Garry Ashford that night.

'I owe you.'

In many ways, the week had gone well. Her court appearance was out of the way and the embarrassment over what had happened in the incident room the previous weekend was forgotten. Somehow, she was also off the hook over her relationship with the media. The irony was that she hadn't spoken to the papers when she was under suspicion but afterwards she actually *had* talked to Garry Ashford and was now not in trouble. It was odd how things worked out.

Of course there was one major problem: the investigation was still going precisely nowhere and even the press were bored now. Since visiting Sandra Prince after her release from hospital, Jessica had phoned the woman twice more. She wanted to let the victim's wife know she was trying her best. Each time they talked, Jessica could hear the devastation in the woman's voice. She said nice things and wished her well but Jessica felt guilty for her own lack of progress.

Caroline had noticed her friend's isolation and said she wanted to do something to cheer her up. Jessica had told her not to but eventually relented. Caroline had arranged a dinner party at their house, wanting to show Randall what a good cook she was. Not content with just cooking for two, she insisted Jessica be there too, while Randall had invited one of his friends along.

Jessica knew it was a sneaky way of getting her on a date of sorts but couldn't be bothered arguing. As promised, she had come home from the station 'on time'. She told Caroline that, if anything major was to occur, the plans would have to change but, much as she had willed it to, nothing had come up through the day. As she entered the flat, she smelled something inviting drifting from their kitchen. She yelled 'hi' and Caroline walked into the hallway, squealing: 'You're back.'

'I'm back.'

'Do you want to . . . get changed or anything?'

'Nope.'

Since going into plain clothes, Jessica had spent most evenings still wearing her work suits. It was a habit that went all the way back to school, where she would stay in her uniform from the moment she got dressed in the morning to the moment she got ready for bed in the evening. Her parents had tried to make her alter her ways but eventually realised they were fighting a losing battle. She wasn't bothered about making an impression on whoever Randall's friend happened to be. She thought she looked all right in any case. Her suit fitted her fairly well and she had washed her hair the night before. That, along with a little make-up, was about as prepared as she bothered to get when going out nowadays.

'Okay then. Can you watch the stove while I get changed?'

'What do I have to do?'

'Just make sure it doesn't boil over.'

Even with her limited culinary skills, Jessica felt she could manage that. As ever, she put her bag and shoes down inside the living room door on top of the two files she was carrying around more for comfort than anything practical. Caroline went off to her room as Jessica entered the kitchen.

Their kitchen wasn't massive but the end wall opposite the door had a cooker, which had eventually been brought in by their landlord after their complaints about the original one. It looked decent but Jessica had never bothered to learn how to use it. Her instruments of choice lay on the counter top next to it: a toaster and microwave. There were various cupboards lining the walls above the tops and down the left-hand side of the room. All of the doors matched the light yellow colour scheme of the room and Caroline did a great job of keeping everything spotless.

Jessica wasn't completely sure what was in the pan she was making sure didn't boil over by stirring it. Whatever it was, it looked potatoey and smelled good, as did whatever was in the oven itself.

Their flat had two bedrooms and a reasonable-sized living room but the kitchen had to double up as a dining room as necessary. Most of the time they ate from their laps in the living room but the option was there if they wanted to feel almost civilised.

There was a small table in the kitchen with a wobbly leg and Jessica sat fiddling with her phone, deliberately rocking the table and checking a few websites plus reading an email from her mum. Her parents had had the Internet installed a few years previously but it was only recently they were beginning to get to grips with its possibilities. With Jessica so busy and their phone calls becoming less frequent, her mum had taken to emailing. Her dad still wasn't too taken with technology, so her mother would write on behalf of them both. Each email was immaculately written. While language was evolving thanks to things such as shortened text-speak, Jessica's mother was certainly not one for abbreviations. Everything was spelled correctly with perfect grammar. Jessica always liked that when she read her mum's emails and it reminded her of being younger back at home.

The doorbell went and Jessica heard Caroline calling, 'Can you get it?'

As Jessica opened the door, Randall gave her a big grin, a hug and a 'hi'. He kissed her on the cheek as his friend followed him in. Jessica closed the door behind them and turned around, noticing the other guy for the first time. He was a little taller than her with short black hair and a nicely trimmed stubbly beard. He was wearing fashionable dark blue jeans and a nice loose-fitting linen shirt. It had an extra button undone at the top and his thick dark chest hair was clearly visible. He had a cheeky-looking grin already on his face as he eyed her nervously, keeping his hands in his pockets.

'How ya doin', Jess? This is Ryan,' said Randall.

'Hi.' The two of them shook hands.

'You're probably better waiting in the living room,' Jessica said. 'Caz is still getting changed and I'm on kitchen duty.'

Jessica returned to the kitchen but soon heard Caroline's bedroom door open and then the 'hellos' from the other room. Her friend then came back into the kitchen. She had clearly put a lot of effort into her appearance. She was wearing a short low-cut red cocktail dress with heels, even though they were inside, and had her hair tied up away from her face, which was impressively made-up. She looked adult and sophisticated, leaving Jessica feeling a bit silly in her work outfit. 'You look great,' Jessica said.

Caroline gave a half-curtsey. 'Thanks, do you reckon Randall will like it?'

'He'd be crazy not to.'

'Did you say hello to Ryan?'

'Yes.'

'What do ya reckon?'

'Of what?'

Caroline looked sideways at her friend. 'You know. What do you *reckon*?'

Jessica smiled. 'He's okay.'

'Do you know he's a vet?'

'So?'

'Y'know. Good with his hands, cares for animals, nice guy.'

Jessica ignored the insinuation. 'When's tea?'

'Soon. Go say hello to the boys.'

'Okay, fine. But let's open the wine first.'

Jessica went into the living room with her topped-up glass where Randall and Ryan were watching a show on television about American truckers. It wasn't the kind of programme she would usually have sat through. Randall was in the reclining seat, giving Jessica little option but to sit next to Ryan on the sofa. She would have to have words with Caroline when they were next alone. If she and Randall were going to try to fix her up with someone, they should at least try to be less obvious about it.

'All right?' she said as she slouched on to the sofa. 'Tea won't be long, apparently.'

'I'll go see how Caz is getting on,' Randall said, standing up and heading off to the kitchen.

'*Be more obvious about it . . .*' Jessica thought but said nothing. She suddenly found the television programme incredibly interesting but noticed Ryan looking at her and gave him a half-smile.

Ryan was smiling back at her. He really did have a boyish grin. 'So is it "Jess" or "Jessica"?'

'Either, I don't mind.'

'Okay then, "Jess", Randy says you work for the police?'

'Yeah . . . Er, "Randy"?'

'Ha. Yeah, Randy. It started off as a bit of a joke really but it kind of stuck.'

'How do you know him?'

'Just from out and about. Nowhere special.' There was an awkward pause. 'He's a nice guy. He likes your mate a lot.'

'He better.'

'I'm not sure he's really had a girlfriend before.'

'Really?'

'Well, I've never seen him go around with someone like he does Caroline.'

Another bout of quiet was broken only by the sound of the TV. 'So . . . police then?' Ryan tried again.

'Yes.'

'What is it you do?'

'I'm in CID.'

'Oh, are you . . . ? Oh yeah. You were in the papers, "The Houdini Hunter".'

Jessica sighed. 'That bloody headline . . . yeah, something like that.'

'That's pretty cool. You're famous.'

'Not really.'

Ryan's small talk was beginning to break through Jessica's apathy. It wasn't that she didn't think he was good-looking, she just wasn't interested in having a boyfriend or anything like that. She didn't like the fact Caroline and Randall had more or less forced her into the situation either. As for the actual talk, she didn't make a habit of chatting to anyone about her job but there was something about Ryan; he was persistent at least.

Jessica could barely believe she was saying the words. 'I hear you're a vet.'

She didn't even really like animals and had never been impressed by what people's jobs were. In the course of being a police officer, she had come across despicable people with terrific professions and lovely people who earned terrible money doing jobs most others wouldn't even think twice about taking. You learned to judge people on their actions, not their wealth, name or occupation.

'I work at a practice in the centre. I only passed out a few months ago and was lucky to get a job so quickly.'

'So you like animals then . . . ?'

'Yeah, it kinda comes with the job.' They both laughed but Jessica knew it was a stupid question. She would have been embarrassed if she had asked something so silly in an interview room. There she felt natural but trying to talk to someone normal felt alien.

'How long have you been with the police?' he asked.

'Seven or eight years. Two and a bit in uniform, two training as a detective, then three or so since then.'

'Do you enjoy it?'

'I don't know. Sometimes.' Jessica felt vulnerable admitting that. A chill went down her back. She did enjoy it, of course. She enjoyed the wins, the results, the convictions. She didn't enjoy the inertia and frustration, the acquittals and failures. She wasn't having fun at the moment.

She could feel Ryan looking at her, almost analysing her discomfort. It was broken by Caroline's voice from the kitchen. 'Tea's up.'

The dining table was fairly small for four of them but

the meal was fabulous. It certainly made a change from Jessica's usual diet of takeaways and microwaved food. The first course was some type of potato balls with a tomato sauce. The main course was a fish and rice dish, while dessert was a fully homemade cheesecake. It was a truly terrific effort. They all thanked Caroline for her work and Jessica volunteered to do the dishes. It wasn't something she would usually do but, seeing as her friend had put so much energy into the evening, whereas she had simply come home and been a bit grumpy, it was the least she could do.

Caroline and Randall went to relax in the living room. Jessica had now taken to calling her friend's boyfriend 'Randy' now she knew about the nickname. The poor guy seemed a little embarrassed but it was all in good humour.

Perhaps unsurprisingly, Ryan hung around in the kitchen to help out too. She found herself not minding. 'Your mate can't half cook,' Ryan said.

'Yup, she's always been a top chef.'

'Can you?'

'Cook? Yeah. Beans on toast or pot noodle and there's no one better.' She gave Ryan a grin. At some point during the evening another button on his shirt had come undone, possibly deliberately. Maybe it was the wine but Jessica seemed to think his chest hair had grown during the evening. His chin stubble certainly seemed to have done. His eyes were dark and friendly.

Jessica washed the dishes, while Ryan dried before they realised they hadn't thought it through, seeing as the guest didn't know where anything went. Given her lack of skill in the kitchen, Jessica was fully aware that she wasn't entirely sure where all the pots went either – but she at least had a better chance of getting it right than Ryan did.

They made more small talk and giggled to each other. Jessica finished another glass of wine and opened a further bottle from the selection they kept under the sink. 'Emergency alcohol' they called it. As they finished, Jessica took the bottle and went into the living room with Ryan. Randall was still sitting in the recliner, with Caroline cuddled across his lap, her short dress riding around her thighs. Jessica refilled her friend's glass and went to sit on the sofa next to Ryan. She wasn't complaining this time.

'You're getting on well, then?' Caroline suggested with a twinkle in her eye. Jessica and Ryan looked at each other and giggled but neither answered.

'We're going to go to bed,' Caroline said. 'Thanks for the company this evening.' She climbed off her boyfriend's lap and helped haul him to his feet. 'See you tomorrow, Jess. Have a *fun* night.' As she went to leave the room, she leant over and kissed her friend on the forehead, before departing hand in hand with Randall.

Jessica fumbled for the remote and turned the television on. Her late-night talk-show rerun was just beginning.

'Ha, you watch this too?' Ryan said.

'Not really.'

'Me neither.'

They both laughed and Jessica edged closer to their guest on the sofa. 'So do you reckon he's the father?' Ryan asked.

Jessica smiled. 'Course he is.'

They joked and enjoyed the show together but Jessica spent more and more time watching Ryan. He had a little crinkle around the corner of his eye when he smiled and he seemed to smile a lot.

The show reached its final advert break and Ryan turned to look at her. 'I'm going to have to go, the last bus goes soon. I could get a taxi I suppose . . .'

Jessica didn't let him finish the sentence. She leant forwards and kissed him. It was gentle at first but he kissed her back strongly and she let him. It felt good. Before she knew what she was doing, she had her hand inside his shirt on his chest. He tried to push her back onto the sofa but she stopped him, pulling away from the embrace. He looked a little confused for a moment but, as Jessica got to her feet, she made it clear why she was stopping. She held out her hand and led him to her bedroom.

Jessica slept well, thoughts of faltering investigations and dead ends as far from her mind as they had been in weeks. She woke in the early hours but it was nice to have someone next to her. She didn't make a habit of inviting strangers, or anyone for that matter, into her bed but she'd had a great evening. She closed her eyes and let herself drift back to sleep. It only seemed moments later but she awoke with a start. She opened her eyes as the light poured through the still too thin curtains.

She was alone on the bed.

'Ryan?'

She didn't say it very loudly but he clearly wasn't in the room. She opened her eyes fully and figured she would find out if he was still in the flat. She picked up a large jumper from the floor and put it on over the nightie she didn't remember putting on the previous night. It was a little chilly. She opened her bedroom door and walked out into the hallway before first checking the empty kitchen. She couldn't hear any voices but headed for the living room anyway.

As she opened the door she saw Ryan sitting on the sofa in his boxer shorts reading Yvonne Christensen's police file.

24

'What the fuck do you think you're doing?'

Ryan's head spun around and he dropped the file onto his lap, where the second file, Martin Prince's, lay. 'Jess. Sorry. I . . . they were on the table, I was curious.'

'What gives you the right? Do you get your kicks from this kind of stuff? From seeing dead bodies?'

'No, sorry, I just wondered what they were.'

Ryan stood and dropped the files onto the coffee table but Jessica's raised voice had obviously stirred Randall and Caroline. Caroline might normally have slept through the noise but Randall must have heard it. The two of them came into the living room, Caroline wearing an unfastened dressing gown which looked as if she had hastily grabbed it. Randall was just behind, clearly half-asleep and wearing just a pair of boxer shorts.

'What's happening?' Caroline started speaking but Jessica was still glaring at Ryan and cut her off.

'Get out now. You're lucky I don't arrest you.'

Jessica didn't know what she would have arrested him for but was annoyed at herself as much as anything. Taking the files out of the station could be a disciplinary matter, especially if you were as careless with them as she had been.

Ryan quickly moved past Jessica, Caroline and Randall. 'Sorry . . . I'll just get dressed.'

Jessica picked the files up from the table and started looking through them, making sure everything was still there. As well as the private information the police had on the victims and their families, there were photographs of the crime scenes and details of the interviews they had done. The link to Wayne Lapham was clear in both files. Most details were kept on the central computer system but, with the bigger cases, they still used hard copies.

'What did he do?' Caroline asked.

Jessica ignored the question, spitting a reply at her friend: 'And what did you think you were trying to pull last night? I told you I wasn't interested in meeting anyone.'

Caroline was clearly taken aback by the venom in Jessica's tone. 'Sorry, I just thought . . .'

'Well, don't.' Jessica stormed past the two of them, files in her hand, back into her room where Ryan was only half-dressed, still looking for his shirt.

'Get *out*.'

'Sorry, I'm going, I'm going.'

Ryan finally found his shirt and snatched it from the floor before leaving the room with a final 'sorry'. Jessica slammed the door behind him.

Her mood hadn't cooled by the end of the day. She had deliberately stayed at the station after hours and gone to the pub with a few of the other officers. She knew she wasn't great company and didn't even have the willpower to take the mickey out of Rowlands. The talk of the station that day was that the new girl had dumped him. That news had cheered her up a small amount but she was still in a bad mood.

She was annoyed at herself more than anything, aggravated she had let her guard down and not sent Ryan packing in his taxi last night; she didn't even know his last name. Jessica wondered if she had overreacted. At first, she thought it could be true he had just picked up the files out of curiosity but then she remembered she had left them underneath her bag on the floor, not on the coffee table. He had gone out of his way to look through them.

The only thing she did regret was the way she had spoken to her friend that morning; Caroline was only trying to cheer her up and hadn't done anything wrong aside from some clumsy matchmaking. Jessica was an adult and made her own decisions. She had certainly made the choice to let Ryan stay the night. It wasn't Caroline's fault but the worst thing was Jessica knew she was too stubborn to say sorry. As usual, she would wait for Caroline to apologise and then make a big deal over accepting it.

When she got home that evening, the flat was empty with a note on the coffee table that just said:

'Sorry. X'

Caroline was obviously staying at Randall's that night. In contrast to the day before, Jessica had a terrible night's sleep, waking up frequently before finally giving up in the early hours and going to watch the rolling news on television.

*

It was a Saturday the next day and, even though she could have had the day off, Jessica didn't want to be in the flat if Caroline returned, wanting to make her friend suffer a little longer. Jessica had already been up for hours and got dressed to go into the station. She was going to have to go in at some stage, having left her car there the previous day because she had been to the pub after work. She knew some officers would have driven home after a couple of pints, safe in the knowledge they were unlikely to be turned in by their colleagues. Everyone knew the ones who did and, while most didn't approve, they didn't want to be the one who said something. Breaking the law in such a blatant way was a line Jessica hadn't crossed and didn't want to.

The station was only a bus ride and five-minute walk away and she figured that she might as well put in a few hours if she was going anyway. When she arrived not long after nine in the morning, reception was busier than it usually was on a weekend. All the drunks and trouble-makers from the night before would be in the cells under the station and things were usually fairly steady by this time.

She asked one of the uniform officers what was going on. 'Nothing much,' came the reply. 'Probably a missing person. The call came in last night. We're off to support the tactical entry team.'

'Why?'

'I don't know. You now know all I do.'

Jessica checked the details with the desk sergeant, who seemed to be the bearer of all knowledge. 'That's pretty much it,' he said. 'A call came in from a woman last night who said she'd not seen or heard from her mother in a few days. She wasn't answering her front door and the daughter reckons she can hear her mum's mobile phone going off inside.'

'Why doesn't she let herself in?'

'I don't know. I suppose she doesn't have a key.'

'Why didn't you call me?'

'It's just a missing persons thing. They come in all the time.'

'Maybe. I'm going with them.'

'You're not in today, are you?'

Jessica didn't hear him and was already off to get the address from one of the men in uniform. Something seemed a bit too familiar. Missing persons reports *did* come in all the time but how many left their phones at home and locked the door before going missing? If you wanted to disappear, you just did it.

She got in her own car and headed towards the address. She knew roughly where it was but not exactly. It was generally in the same area as the first two victims but on a main road where you wouldn't want to be out after dark. The street was notorious for street prostitutes and kerb-crawlers and there had been a couple of vicious assaults in the past year or so. Jessica found the address fairly easily, mainly because there was a police van parked outside.

It was a ground-floor flat at the end of a row of dingy-looking shops. The main door was next to another on the side of the building which backed onto some sort of delivery yard for the shops. Beyond that was a patch of grass and some wasteland. Jessica went to talk to the two members of the tactical entry team, introducing herself and showing her identification. It wasn't usual policy but the tactical entry team said they were under instructions to wait for the uniformed officers to arrive. Jessica soon saw why; a girl who certainly looked as if she was still a teenager came storming up to her, pointing a finger. 'Are you in charge?'

'No.'

'Well, who is?' The girl looked back towards the tactical entry officer. 'Why can't you just hurry up and go through the bloody door? My mum could be hurt in there.'

Jessica quickly weighed the situation up. Tactical had arrived ready to go in but, given the daughter's hostility, had called in for uniform to escort them just in case. There was another woman standing on her own not far from the flat's front door smoking. She was quite a bit older, certainly in her fifties. Jessica first went to try the door handle but it was locked, so she walked across to the other woman.

'Hi,' she said.

The woman looked sideways at her without a smile, replying: 'All right?'

'What are you waiting for?' Jessica asked, trying not to sound too aggressive.

'I live upstairs,' the woman said, pointing towards a second door next to the first. 'Kim woke me up with all the shouting. She was round yesterday wanting to know if I'd seen her mum.'

'Have you?'

'Have I heck.' There was a clear hostility to the answer. 'You don't get on?'

'Would you get on with someone working as a whore in the flat underneath you? Door going at all hours of the night and all that *noise*? You lot don't do anything.'

Jessica hadn't introduced herself as a member of CID but the woman clearly knew. Jessica also had to admit the woman had a point. Kerb-crawling was illegal but prostitution in itself wasn't. Her 'lot' almost certainly hadn't done anything but there wasn't a whole lot they could do. The daughter who Jessica assumed was 'Kim' came pounding back across the yard towards the two of them. 'I bet you're loving this, aren't you?' she shouted at the woman.

'Leave me alone, Kim. I told you yesterday I haven't seen Claire.'

'Oh, piss off. You were always moaning, banging on the bloody ceiling. Calling the old bill.'

Jessica stepped in between the two of them, pointing towards a piece of grass between them and the tactical team. 'Okay, Kim, I think you should go over there,' she said. 'It won't be long.'

Kim glared at her. She was wearing jeans and a tight-fitting dark T-shirt. Her long blonde hair was tied into a loose ponytail. If it wasn't for the snarl on her face, she would have been pretty.

She turned from Jessica to the other woman, hissing a reply – 'You better not have anything to do with this' – before walking towards the spot Jessica had indicated.

'That's what I get all the time,' the woman said to Jessica. 'You'd think I was the one causing trouble.'

'How long have you lived here?'

'A year or so. I want to move out but am stuck on the housing association waiting list. Because I've got a place to live I'm not a priority.'

'Has the mother lived below you this whole time?'

'Claire? Yes – it's a convenient location for her, ain't it?'

There wasn't much else they could say to each other but moments later a marked police car pulled up next to Jessica's Punto behind the van. Two officers clambered out and crossed to the two tactical officers who were taking some heavy-looking equipment out of their van. The flat's door was double-glazed and very similar to the Christensens' and Princes'. From everything the locksmith had told her a couple of weeks ago, they weren't very easy to kick in.

As the other officers arrived, Kim again marched over to the tactical team before all four officers and the girl went towards the front door. Jessica joined them and everyone was asked to stand back while the team smashed their way through using a two-man battering ram.

The door took a fair amount of hammering before eventually succumbing to the brute force. Jessica wanted to be first through the door but Kim beat her to it, dashing inside and disappearing from view. Jessica started to lead the other officers in but, as she heard the ear-piercing scream, she knew exactly what they would find.

25

The woman might have been a prostitute and caused misery for her neighbours but she didn't deserve to die in the brutal way indicated by how she had been found. Jessica followed the screams into a room on her left as she saw Kim standing over a double bed, hysterical. Jessica's first thought was a selfish one; Kim had blood on her hands and had already contaminated the scene. The biggest uniformed officer physically picked up the shouting, kicking daughter and took her outside.

The woman sprawled across the bed was naked and face down. Aside from the unclothed limbs, there was a mass of bleached blonde hair spread out but discoloured in parts by the deep red blood. Jessica stopped any of the other officers from entering the room, waiting at its entrance. She told them to help calm down Kim, and ensure the woman who lived upstairs went nowhere either. Jessica took her phone out of her pocket and called the station to report what they had found and then called Cole. She would leave it to him to pass the news up the chain, while a Scene of Crime team would be requested.

Jessica took in the whole of the bedroom. The scene of this murder seemed much more vicious than the first two and Claire must have fought harder than the previous victims. The obvious first response was that whoever had killed her had been a client but Jessica knew full well that a locked door was no obstacle if the killer was the same as that of the first two victims.

With the rest of the flat empty, she took the chance to look around. The kitchen was a grubby room at the end of the hall. It had once been white but now had a distinctive yellowy-brown tinge. There was a round dining table in the centre of the room with four cheap-looking stools. Jessica could see a washing machine still full with a light flashing next to the dial at the top. It was bright white and looked new, standing out from everything else in the room. The floor itself was years old cheap linoleum that was peeling away from the surface. There was also an old-looking cooker, its top covered with hardened food stains.

Jessica scanned the scene and saw a handbag, mobile phone and some cash on the counter top. She didn't want to risk touching the paper notes in case the killer was a client and this was what he had paid. It seemed unlikely that their mystery man would have left such an obvious clue even if that was true but Jessica didn't want to risk it. She could see how much was there, a crumpled dirty ten-pound note and a much newer, crisper twenty. Thirty quid was the cost of someone's life nowadays, she thought, shaking her head.

Jessica saw a kitchen roll next to the sink and tore off a sheet, using it to cover her fingers while she looked through the woman's bag. She didn't have to look far and found exactly what she was searching for straight away – a set of keys in the main part.

Jessica moved into the hallway. She could still hear a

commotion outside as the officers presumably tried to calm Kim. She tried the door opposite the bedroom, still using a piece of kitchen roll to shield her fingers, entering a second room. There was another bed but this one was neatly made. The room had a lot of purple in it, both the duvet cover and carpet a matching colour. The walls were light and the room was full of clothes. Jessica didn't enter but scanned the scene from the doorway. She could see a wardrobe towards the back with the doors open. Even from this distance, Jessica saw it was packed with dresses, outfits and attire that would only be suitable for indoor use, or at best on the main road on the other side of the flat. The floor was scattered with more regular clothes, jeans and tops. Jessica's own room was messy but this was far beyond that.

She backed out and re-closed the door, then tried the other one leading from the hallway. It opened into a basic bathroom, containing a shower, toilet and sink. She could see a few soaps and shampoos but nothing out of the ordinary, so closed that door and made her way to the living room.

The main room of the house was cluttered but a lot cleaner than the kitchen and second bedroom. There was a large flatscreen TV pinned to the wall and a couple of large comfy-looking light pink sofas facing it. Jessica could see some assorted celebrity-type magazines on the floor but there were tidy racks full of DVDs and CDs. She scanned the titles, noticing names of films she had seen and liked. On top of the racks were some photographs. Jessica could see the smiling face of the woman most likely lying face-down in the other room. She saw a picture with a younger-looking Kim and another with a different young teenage girl. In the final photo, Kim looked around twelve and was with the girl from the other photograph and a boy. They were all young children, standing on a beach grinning at the camera. In none of the pictures was there a sign of a man or anyone who could be the children's father. Having seen the bedrooms and kitchen, this whole room was a contrast to the rest of the house.

Untainted.

It almost made sense to Jessica. When you gave up a massive part of your life in the way the victim apparently had, perhaps you needed something to separate yourself from it? Money was exchanged in the kitchen, while the first bedroom was where it was earned. Seeing as the lifestyle couldn't be kept away from the other bedroom, nor the bathroom, that left this one room as a haven of sorts.

She returned to the first bedroom to have a final scan before the Scene of Crime team arrived. The main light on the ceiling had been left on but a black lampshade ensured the room's dimness. The brightest thing was the victim's hair, despite the blood that had seeped into it. The bed had dark purple satin sheets but there were obvious blood-stains there too. Jessica couldn't see any cuts in the victim's neck as it was shielded by the woman's hair.

With little else she could do, Jessica left the flat. There was only one door in, while the only two windows were in the living room and the bedroom that didn't have a dead body in it. The curtains were pulled and Jessica hadn't bothered to see if they were locked but she knew they would be.

Misdirection.

Kim was allowing herself to be comforted by one of the officers as the neighbour spoke to one of the others. Jessica could hear sirens in the distance. She told one of the tactical officers that they needed to take both Kim and the neighbour to the station and that she would follow shortly.

'Don't arrest them or lock them up,' Jessica said. 'Holding room with an officer, not a cell.'

It was going to be another busy Saturday.

Back at the station, they first had to make sure Kim was eighteen or older. From her appearance, it was hard to tell. If she was younger, it would have been necessary to have someone there to act as her guardian. Although Kim had continued to veer from sheer aggression to outright grief, it had quickly been established there was another daughter who lived nearby. Once they had the full name and address, a police car was sent out to pick up her older sister: Emily Hogan. The other thing it hadn't taken long to find out was that there was definitely no father present.

'I don't have a dad,' was all Kim would say.

Jessica wanted to ask about the boy she had seen in the photos in the living room but figured that could come later. Kim clearly didn't like the police and hadn't been overly cooperative. She kept shouting: 'You lot never gave a stuff when she was alive,' and other similar phrases.

Jessica was torn between giving her space to grieve and actually needing to speak to her. The Scene of Crime team had taken over the flat and would be working on a time of death, as well as taking photographs and chronicling everything that could be relevant. Jessica hung around just long enough to see them gently turn over Claire's body and reveal the deep wounds in her neck, just like those of the other victims.

The neighbour had been spoken to first, with Kim given time to calm down in a holding room. The woman clearly didn't have an awful lot to add and had been released. She hadn't seen or heard anything out of the ordinary that week.

'The only thing different is that it has actually been quiet the past two nights', was perhaps the only useful piece of information she had. It gave Jessica a rough time of death until a more accurate one came in from forensics. Presumably that meant Claire Hogan had been killed at some point in the last forty-eight hours.

It hadn't taken long for Emily Hogan to arrive. She would have already been told about her mother's murder by a trained officer who collected her. Jessica met her in reception and took her through to see her sister. Emily and her sister looked a lot alike, although Emily was an inch or two taller. She didn't seem too upset but cradled her younger sister, who cried loudly.

Jessica gave them space until Emily turned to her. 'I presume you want to talk to us?'

Before Jessica could answer, Kim cut across them. 'Come on, Em, they were never bothered before. They were only interested in Mum when they wanted to bring her in.'

Emily had a softer tone than her sister. 'I know but that's gone now. We're not going to find out who did this on our own.'

Kim shrugged and sat down as Emily stayed on her feet. 'Do we do this here?'

'No,' Jessica said. 'The interview room's set up. You're not under arrest and can leave any time you want but sometimes it's better to get things on tape anyway. It's for your own protection.'

'Okay.'

Jessica took Emily to the interview room where she had sat across from Wayne Lapham just seven days ago. A uniformed officer was left with Kim, who hadn't run out at the mention of them being able to leave. Cole was already waiting for them and Jessica said there was a solicitor available if Emily wanted it.

'I've not got anything to hide,' Emily replied. Before Cole could start the tape, she added: 'Don't mind her. She's had it tough. She was always the closest to Mum too.'

Jessica nodded as Cole made the introductions. 'When did you last see your mother?' Jessica asked first.

Emily spoke clearly and eloquently. She was obviously intelligent and came across very well. 'Not for a while, we didn't really get on. Maybe a month ago?'

'Why didn't you get along?'

'I didn't approve of her . . . job.'

'I'm sorry to ask this but, for the record, can you say what she did?' Jessica knew the answer.

'She slept with men for money.'

Jessica didn't want to dwell the point. 'What was she like the last time you saw her?'

'The same as always. High.'

'She did drugs?' Jessica hadn't seen any obvious paraphernalia at the house but hadn't gone looking too closely.

'Where do you think all the money went?' Emily said as if it was obvious. 'She somehow scraped together enough to buy that dump a few years ago and the rest went up her arms.'

'How long ago did you move out?'

'I don't know. I didn't spend a lot of time at home anyway. Maybe five years ago? I'm twenty-three now so work it out. That place was never going to be big enough for us all.'

Emily went on to tell them that she lived with her boyfriend and year-old son in the north of the city. Somehow, despite everything, Emily had turned into a rounded adult. She and her partner had founded a promotions company and were apparently doing well for themselves.

'Tell me about your sister,' Jessica said.

'Kim? She's only eighteen, a kid. She just moved out a few months ago and got a job selling bags and stuff. I would have got her something better but she wanted to do it for herself. For a while I thought Claire was going to drag her down to her level.'

It was the first time she had directly referred to her mother. She hadn't called her 'Mum' or anything similar.

'Claire?' Jessica queried.

'If someone doesn't act like your mother, you can't really call them that, can you?'

Jessica nodded, trying not to give anything away through her expression. 'So your mother lived alone?'

'Yes.'

'No boyfriend?'

Emily laughed but not with any conviction. 'What do you think? A different boyfriend every night maybe, nothing more than that.'

'What about your father?'

'Who knows? He left a long time ago.'

'How long?'

'Eight or nine years back. Kim wouldn't have even been ten by then.'

'Do you know why he left?'

'No.'

'Wasn't it something you ever talked about?'

Emily shook her head. 'Claire did all of her talking through a bottle back then.'

'Have you seen your father since he left?'

'No.'

'Whose choice?'

'What choice? I wouldn't even know where to start looking. One day he was there, the next he wasn't. I was only fifteen or so. Claire spent the first two weeks telling us he was away on business.'

'How long has your mother been . . . working like this?'

'Not forever. We had a pretty decent childhood, believe it or not. Two-up, two-down, summers at the seaside and all that. Then Dad moved out and Claire eventually fell apart. A few years later we all ended up moving to that shithole. There was never much space for me, so I left straight away.'

Jessica took Emily's dad's name from her – they would check him out if possible. Some people dropped off the face of the earth when they walked out on their wife and kids. Others hooked up with different women and paid child maintenance but, given Emily said she hadn't seen her father in all that time, it seemed likely he would fall into the first category. Jessica doubted there was any Child Support Agency file on him and thought finding him would prove quite a task – and that was if he had even kept the same name.

She stopped to think what to say next. From what she had seen at the scene, the neck wounds and the way the flat was secured, her first thoughts were obviously that this murder was related to the other two. But while the first two had happened to people most of the public would consider 'normal', this was a bit different. That wasn't to devalue a life, just that a drug-addicted prostitute was always going to be likely to attract people who might see her as vulnerable and want to do her harm. Could Claire Hogan really be connected to Yvonne Christensen and Martin Prince in some way?

Cole had brought in the hard-copy files they had for the other victims, the ones Jessica had caught Ryan looking through. She took out a photo of Yvonne Christensen from before she had been murdered and handed it to Emily. 'Do you know who this is?'

Emily looked at the photo and narrowed her eyes. 'She sort of seems familiar.' Jessica felt her heart give a slight jump but her hopes were instantly let down again. 'She's been in the papers and on TV, hasn't she?'

'Yes.'

'She was killed too. This "Houdini" guy.'

Jessica still hated that nickname but it wasn't the time to argue about it. 'Yes.'

'Do you think whoever killed her killed Claire too?'

'I don't know.'

'I just thought . . . when the officer told me . . .' She tailed off, struggling to find the words. 'I suppose I've been expecting something like this for ages now. Given what she did for a living . . .'

Jessica let the thought evaporate and then handed her a picture of Martin Prince. Emily knew them both but only from the media coverage. 'Do you know of anyone who might want to harm your mother?'

'Her clients? I don't know. No one specifically. Kim is closer to her than I am. She visits her a couple of times a week.'

'Do you have a key for the flat, Emily?'

Emily laughed, again with nothing really behind it. 'I've never had one.'

'What about Kim?'

'I don't think so. You'll have to ask her. Claire never gave any of us keys – she didn't want anyone walking in on her. Kim used to come and stay at ours some nights when she couldn't get in. There was no room there anyway. When it was the three of them, Claire, Shaun and

Kim, Shaun used to sleep on the sofa with Mum and Kim sharing. It was ridiculous.'

'Is Shaun your brother?'

'Yes.'

'Where is he?'

'You should know.'

'What do you mean?'

'You lot banged him up two years ago.'

26

Shaun Hogan had been very easy to track down. He was currently three months away from potentially being paroled in HM Prison Leeds.

Jessica had first gone to talk to Kim and then returned to her desk to look up their brother. Kim hadn't been too keen to speak at first but they brought her sister in to sit next to her and the aggression level dropped. Much of what she said confirmed what they had already been told by Emily.

Kim lived in a flat half a mile or so away from her mother and had reluctantly admitted she'd had enough of living with her mum a few months previously. When she had lived at home, Kim wasn't allowed a key and there were certain hours of the day where she wasn't permitted to be inside, instead spending her time roaming the streets. Despite being only eighteen, she had done that for the best part of five years.

Kim obviously cared for her mother and had wanted to try to help but had reached the end of her young tether. As she cried and made her admissions, Jessica felt devastated for her. She was so young but her childhood had been ruined, having seen everything she must have done. Despite all of that, she refused to criticise her upbringing.

Given what connected the first two victims, there was

one question Jessica had been waiting to ask: 'Do you know if your mother was ever burgled?'

'What would you have cared?'

'We would always respond to something like that.'

'You didn't do much when those kids were harassing her.'

'I'm sorry about that.'

'You weren't too bothered when your lot were threatening to arrest her and scaring her off the street.'

Emily helped calm her sister and Jessica eventually got her answer. 'No.'

Jessica already knew Claire Hogan's flat wasn't one of the addresses Wayne Lapham had been caught in possession of stolen goods from but he was still their only link to the first two victims. 'Was' now seemed to be the appropriate word. If the prostitute's murder was linked to the other two, the one connection they thought they had – burglary – was no more.

Shaun Hogan was an interesting character though. He was now twenty-one and there were a few minor crimes on his record, things like shoplifting when he was in his teens. He had been jailed two years ago for a serious assault on a man outside a bar in Leeds city centre. Emily and Kim both seemed reluctant to talk about him but the older sister told them her brother left the area shortly after Claire moved into the flat.

For reasons that seemed obvious, given the lack of room, he had apparently not been too keen on living with his mother and younger sister. When Claire had moved out of whatever house she shared with her husband and moved into the flat, both of her eldest children had left home quickly, Emily at eighteen, Shaun at sixteen. Emily had somehow managed to turn her life around as Shaun had gone the other way, moving to another city and ending up in jail. Kim, meanwhile, had stayed at home for almost the entire time.

Jessica thought it was a very mixed-up family, while realising how lucky she had been to be brought up well. It put her silly argument with Caroline into perspective.

She called the prison, arranging to visit Shaun on the Monday. Someone would break the news about his mother to him in the meantime. After that, she spent the rest of the day in meetings with the DCI and Cole. At the moment, there was nothing concrete to link the latest killing with the previous two. The initial forensics results should at least confirm a similar murder weapon. Jessica felt sure everything was somehow connected and that the property had been locked almost to taunt them. Whoever the killer was could easily have got access to the flat given Claire's profession. Getting out might have been more difficult but whoever was responsible had set the scene up similar to the previous ones for a reason. If initial results confirmed a similar method of killing, the DCI said he would give another media briefing to ask for help.

A firm plan of action would be hard to come up with. Even if someone had seen a strange person entering Claire Hogan's flat it wouldn't have been anything out of the ordinary and the police weren't expecting too many of her clients to phone up either. It was going to be a hard thing to manage via the media. Getting members of the public to pay attention to a murder appeal for someone who seemed a bit like them, suburban and respectable, was easy. Getting people to care about the murder of a prostitute would be harder to pull off. It was the last thing they wanted to do but Cole suggested embracing the 'Houdini' name. Jessica hated the idea but had to admit it would keep the media on-side and give them their best opportunity of getting people to contact them.

As she emerged from the discussions to head home, she noticed there were three missed calls on her phone. She'd had it on silent all day, moving from interviews to meetings. The caller's identity was obvious, her only surprise being he hadn't called earlier. Jessica thumbed the redial button and the other person answered on the first ring.

'Mr Ashford,' she said. 'I've been expecting you.'

Garry Ashford still felt as if he was constantly riding his luck at work. The profile of DS Daniel had somehow managed to get him into everyone's good books. He even had a text message from her saying she owed him. He would have settled for any kind of communication that didn't involve copious but impressively creative swearing but that was even better.

He wasn't entirely sure how it was going to go down in the office but the editor had been upbeat about the piece. Garry had claimed it as an exclusive, even though much of it hadn't come from Jessica herself. That along with the background piece he had put together on Wayne Lapham had given him two more days of decent coverage.

The pay rise still hadn't materialised though.

Despite the text he received from DS Daniel, he didn't respond and hadn't contacted her since. Garry figured it was probably best to keep that goodwill stored up in case something else significant happened.

This particular Saturday he was hoping for a quieter day given what he had ended up being asked to do the past few weeks. When he saw his source's number ringing his phone, he groaned. He half-thought about ignoring it but then took the call. He listened to the details and wrote everything down, before hanging up and calling DS Daniel. There was no answer and he wondered if she was avoiding him. He phoned his editor and then set off to catch a bus out to the latest victim's address. His source said they didn't have a name but knew where the crime scene was. He tried DS Daniel one more time but there was still no answer.

'Another fine Saturday,' he moaned to no one in particular.

'Hi,' Garry said. 'I guess you know why I've been calling.'

'You're still going to have to tell me what you think you know.'

The journalist informed Jessica that he had visited the murder site and spoken to the upstairs neighbour. He knew Claire Hogan's name and that the woman who lived upstairs had been keen to talk about the dead female's chosen profession, as well as telling him how the police had smashed in the door that morning. He wanted Jessica to confirm this murder had been committed by the same person as the first two.

Jessica could answer that question honestly. 'I don't know that yet.'

'What do you think, though?'

'I think you're putting me in an awkward position. We don't have any results yet. I still shouldn't be talking to you.'

'I don't have to use your name.'

Jessica thought for a few moments. 'Who will you quote?'

'A senior source close to the investigation.'

'"Senior?"'

'Okay. A "source" close to the investigation.'

'"Close?"'

'Come on . . . You're taking the mick now.'

Jessica laughed. 'Yeah, I am. Okay, fine, I do think it's the same person but that is it. I owe you no more. We are even.'

'All right.'

'And no more phone calls. You've got to go through the press office like everyone else.'

'Really?'

'Yes! I know my sexy phone voice is a big turn-on for you but talking to the media can get me into trouble.'

Garry Ashford laughed awkwardly. 'Okay.'

*

When Jessica arrived home, Caroline was waiting for her in the living room, alone. Jessica had gone to leave her bag and shoes in the usual position, on the floor by the door, when her friend turned around to look at her. 'Hi,' Caroline said.

'Hi.'

'Long day?'

'Another body.'

Caroline raised her eyebrows in surprise. 'You're joking?'

'I wish.'

They looked at each other and there was a short pause that Caroline broke. 'Are we okay?'

'Yeah, of course we are.'

'I was only trying to help. I wanted to cheer you up.'

'I know.'

'What did he do?'

'It doesn't matter really.'

Jessica sat next to her friend on the sofa and hugged her. 'Where's Randy?'

They both giggled.

'I told *Randall* I wanted to spend the evening in with you.'

'That's nice. Is he still looking after you?'

'Yeah, he's a great guy. He was really upset the other morning. Neither of us knew what had happened with you and Ryan. You had both left. We were there staring at each other in confusion. He felt bad his mate had upset you.'

'It wasn't his fault.' Jessica moved slightly away from the embrace. 'Wine?'

They both laughed again. 'Of course.'

Jessica was feeling a lot better as she fetched a bottle from under the sink with some glasses. At some point, someone would call her with the results they were waiting on and they had Shaun Hogan to see on Monday. She was expecting a busy week and was pleased to have made up with her friend.

Back in the living room, she sat next to Caroline putting her feet up on the sofa and poured them each a glass of wine. 'So is it getting serious with you two, then?'

'Maybe,' Caroline said with a smile. 'He's been talking about getting a new job. He's had enough of working on the market now. He's better than that anyway.'

Jessica weighed up what to say next. She knew what she wanted to ask. 'Are you going to move in with him?'

It was something Jessica had been thinking about since she had first seen the two of them together, the way they looked at each other left the thought nestling in the back of her mind.

Caroline looked directly at her friend. 'It was always going to happen to one of us sometime.'

'I know. It's a shame. We've had a good run.'

Jessica could see a tear in her friend's eye but was determined not to cry herself after her recent sob fests. She put her arm around her friend. 'What type of job is he looking for?'

'I don't know really. He's only worked on that stall, fixing shoes and other bits and bobs. He's skilled though. Good with his hands.'

Jessica burst out laughing.

'Not like that,' Caroline clarified, giggling herself through a thin stream of tears. 'Dirty mind. He's only young, he'll find something.'

'So now you're admitting he's young?' Caroline smiled. 'Cradle-snatcher,' Jessica added with an even bigger grin.

'Jealous.'

'I'm pleased for you both.'

'We had talked about looking for a place when he gets himself fixed up with a better job. It was his decision. I said I could afford it at first but he reckoned he couldn't let me do that.'

'You're not going to move *away* away, are you?'

'Of course not. You're not going to get rid of me that easily.'

'Shame, I could get some good rent for that room.'

27

Jessica had never been a big fan of travelling by train. For one, she hated facing backwards while the train moved forwards; there was something inherently unnatural about it. She wasn't even too keen on the sideways-facing seats. Why was it so hard to have rows of seats that all faced the same way? They managed it on aeroplanes.

She was sitting next to Cole on their way to Leeds, facing backwards and feeling slightly sick. Travelling in a car across the Pennines was a nuisance at the best of times but during the morning rush hour on a Monday, traffic was at its peak. As much as she would never admit it to anyone, especially not Rowlands, Jessica rarely took her car on the motorway. She relied on it to get her a few miles to work and back and occasionally trusted it to complete a return journey to her parents' house, although only on the minor roads. She definitely didn't have faith for it to get her from one side of the country to the other. The force didn't like paying out expenses on car journeys either so a trip on the train it was.

The scenery thundered past as they made small talk. Neither of them seemed keen to speak about the case but Cole told Jessica about his Sunday out with his wife and kids. It felt like another world to her but made her think of poor Kim Hogan and how she hadn't had the opportunity of a proper upbringing.

Both she and Cole had seen the initial forensic test results. Claire's neck wounds were almost identical to those of Yvonne Christensen and Martin Prince, while the instrument was again some type of steel wire or rope. With that and the way the flat was locked, they were as sure as they could be that the murders had all been carried out by the same person. Forensics had once again failed to find any trace of the killer. There were no fingerprints, no DNA, no blood and nothing under Claire Hogan's nails. It also didn't look as if she'd had sex the night she died.

Either the murderer was very careful indeed, or he knew how to cover his tracks.

The cash that had been left on the side had at least six different sets of fingerprints between the two notes and traces of cocaine. The labs were working on isolating anything that could be useable but Jessica wasn't hopeful. Even if they did get something they could check, it would only rule people out unless they got a match on the National DNA Database.

At this point, Jessica would have been happy enough with someone to rule out.

She had seen Garry Ashford's name on the front page of the *Herald* again that morning. The other media outlets had the story too but Jessica doubted they had spoken to the woman who lived above the victim. In a good way for him, Garry was showing himself to be a bit of a pest. He was certainly persistent but she wondered who his source was. There were plenty of possibilities. Someone on the Scene of Crime team, maybe? They were the only people who had actually been to every scene that she knew of but then somebody had told him about her interview-room incident too.

The train steadily pulled into their destination but they remained sitting until the other commuters were off, a wall of suits, smart shoes and briefcases hurrying away almost as one. When it was clear, the two stood and made their way through the station, showing their tickets to the inspectors on the gate. They got a taxi but it was only a few miles to their destination.

HMP Leeds was a massive old Victorian building for B-class prisoners. The categorisation meant the authorities thought Shaun Hogan didn't need to be kept with the most violent offenders but he wasn't trusted enough to be in an open prison either. Jessica had read his file and knew the GBH he had been sent down for was something that happened all too frequently. It reminded her of Tom Carpenter but without the knife; two men fighting outside of a bar after drinking too much on a Saturday night. Shaun Hogan had ended up head-butting the victim, before kicking him in the head on the ground.

He was lucky he hadn't killed him.

Even with his guilty plea, he had been sentenced to five years in prison but he would be out in a few months because of time spent on remand and apparent good behaviour. He would have served just over half his sentence.

From the outside, the building looked like a castle with imposing cylindrical walls at the front. There was an enormous heavy set of wooden doors at the opening too, all of which added to the structure's intimidating appearance.

The taxi dropped them off outside and they walked into the reception area. It was a smallish office off to the right of the entrance. They showed their credentials and were searched. The fact they were police officers meant they were given a lot more leeway than most but everyone was patted down and had to go through the metal detectors – regardless of who they were.

The governor himself had come down to meet them both. He was a strict-looking man in his late forties with a short, tight haircut and fierce-looking eyes. He had a voice that, even with his Yorkshire accent, was a little too high-pitched and didn't quite fit. He introduced himself and shook both of their hands, saying he was taking them to the visitors' centre. He told them it wasn't visiting hours yet, so it would just be the two of them plus Shaun Hogan and the guards in the room.

He led them across the main yard, explaining that was where prisoners were first brought in and then took them through two sets of lockable doors before they emerged back outside into another yard. He told them about the facility itself and pointed them to the various wings as he did so, explaining where the old buildings ended and the new ones began. It obviously wasn't an inspection but the governor clearly wanted to impress them.

They crossed a second yard and went down a concrete walkway towards a separate building as the governor told them he had informed Shaun about his mother's death on Saturday.

'How did he take it?' Jessica asked as they walked side by side.

'He didn't even react. He nodded and asked if he could return to his cell.'

'Seriously?'

'He didn't seem upset at all.'

'How has he behaved since he's been with you?' Cole asked.

'Incredibly well. He's not been in trouble, he's done any jobs assigned to him and worked hard in class according to the tutors.'

'Is that normal?' Jessica asked.

'Sometimes you get the odd one but most people who want to cause trouble end up at Wakefield or one of the other Category A places.'

The governor led them into a building that was clearly newer than a lot of the prison, up a flight of stairs, before it opened into a large visiting area. The room was enormous, with vending machines lining the sides interspersed with posters that had words like 'Respect' and 'Think' written in large letters across them. The windows high on the walls were covered by metal bars and there were large banks of white strip lighting across the ceiling. Banks of grey and red plastic tables were bolted to the floor, with two chairs on each side. Everything looked very tidy and Jessica wondered if it had been cleaned for their benefit.

They were led to one of the tables near the front as the governor nodded to the two guards who were standing next to a separate door. One of them unclipped a radio from his belt and spoke into it as the governor said his goodbyes and left through the door they had entered through. Cole took out a notebook and pen and moments later they heard the door at the front being unlocked and a man was led in by two guards.

Prisons would often have their own interview rooms similar to a police station's but Shaun Hogan wasn't a suspect for any crime and they were talking to him to hopefully gain some background on his mother. Because of that, speaking to him in a more informal environment such as the visiting room, as opposed to an interview room, could perhaps get him to open up a little more.

The prisoner was wearing a grey sweatshirt and slightly darker tracksuit bottoms. He had short almost shaven dark hair but no other particularly distinguishing features. Jessica knew from experience you could look at some people and know they had spent time inside. They would have things like tattoos or scars and sometimes even the way they walked made them stand out from the rest of society. Jessica saw none of those giveaway signs in Shaun Hogan as he was ushered to sit in front of the two detectives, the four prison guards standing by the door again.

'Are you Shaun Hogan?' she asked.

'Yes.'

'My name is Detective Sergeant Daniel and this is Detective Inspector Cole.'

'Are you here about my mum?'

'Yes.'

'I'm not sorry she's gone . . .' The prisoner looked at Jessica, not in a threatening way but fixed enough to let her know he meant it.

'Why's that?'

'Do you know she never once came to visit me here?'

'Is that why you're not upset?'

Shaun ignored the question again, glancing away towards the bank of windows high up the walls. 'Have you spoken to Em?'

'Your sister? Yes we have.'

'She's been a few times. She even talked about helping me when I get out.'

'That's nice.'

'Yeah, it is. She's done well since she got away. I guess she told you all about Mum's *job*.'

'Yes.'

Jessica didn't know what she expected to get from the conversation with Shaun that she hadn't already heard from Emily and Kim, especially as he hadn't seen his mother for over two years, but she felt she had to keep prodding him. With a lack of other leads, he was at least someone who might have an insight.

'Why did you move out here?' she asked.

Shaun shook his head and then rubbed his forehead with his hand. 'I just wanted to get away. A few years ago Mum had moved out of our house 'cos she had no money and set up in that flat. She was always drinking and there was no room anyway. Em was a bit older and moved out straight away. There wasn't much there for me, so I went too. Some kid I knew from school that I still knocked about with reckoned there was some building work out here. It's not like I had anything better to do.'

'How old were you?'

'Sixteen. I ended up bunking in this disused pub for a

few months. We had a great time; the work was easy and we got paid cash. No one really said anything.'

'Was that the last time you saw your mother?'

'Nah, I went back a few times but she was still in that flat with Kim and she had moved on from the drink . . .'

Jessica let his answer hang for a moment. 'How did you end up in here?'

'It was my own fault. I'd been to visit Mum earlier in the day and we ended up arguing. I was doing okay then – earning a bit of money and I had my own place out here. It was nothing special but it was good enough for me. I'd said something about her having to sort herself out for Kim's sake. I know Emily had been saying it too.'

'What happened?'

'I don't know really. When I got back here, I'd gone out for a few drinks and things just . . . happened.'

'I mean what happened with the argument?'

Shaun looked at Jessica, then away from her again. 'She blamed me.'

'For what?'

'Everything.'

Jessica was clearly confused. She looked at Cole, who also seemed slightly bemused. It was the inspector who spoke next. 'Why did she blame you?'

Shaun closed his eyes and breathed out deeply. Jessica didn't know if he was going to say anything but then came a quiet: 'Because it's my fault.'

There were now tears in Shaun's eyes but Jessica felt there was something important still left to be said. 'Why is it your fault?'

Shaun spoke slowly and didn't look up from a spot on the table he seemed fixated on. 'When Dad left, we all held it together pretty well really. It was hard but Mum managed to keep us all in the house. Then . . . everything fell apart because of me.'

Jessica shifted onto the edge of her seat and leant in towards the table. 'What did you do?'

Shaun wiped his eyes with his sleeve and looked towards her. 'I can't tell you.'

'You can.'

'I can't. I'm about to get out. I want to sort things out with Em and have a normal life.'

'Shaun . . .' The prisoner looked up at Jessica, meeting her eyes. 'Someone killed your mother last week and whatever you have to say could be the key thing in finding out who that was.'

Shaun closed his eyes and breathed out deeply before opening them and staring at Jessica. His eyes narrowed slightly and he said two words softly but clearly. 'Nigel Collins.'

Shaun may have been one of the oldest but he struggled to keep up with the other three boys. They laughed and whooped as they raced across the patch of wasteland, cluttered with rocks, scrap metal and open patches of grass. Before he left, Shaun's dad had told him that this area used to be home to a few factories but they were now long gone. Scott led the way. He was the youngest but also the fastest, hurdling a displaced paving slab and willing the rest of them on.

Jon was next in line, the oldest of the four but also the quietest. He was the only one not cheering as they raced. He carefully watched his own footing, not wanting to fall and be laughed at by the others. Jamo followed, energetic and excited, aping Scott's calls and over-exaggerating the jumps. Shaun was at the back, out-of-breath but desperate not to show it. He copied the shouts too, not wanting to be left out.

He had struggled to make friends, especially after his dad left. The other kids took the mickey at school and, even though Scott did the same, he didn't mind Shaun hanging around with them. Shaun did his best to fit in, doing their dares and stealing chocolate bars from the local shop plus knocking on those old people's front doors before legging it. There was even a trick they pulled where Scott lay flat on top of some guy's porch and knocked on the door from above. The chap kept storming out the front but couldn't see anyone and was fuming. Shaun felt a little bad watching from the trees nearby but at least his friends weren't laughing at him.

The four of them were bonded not by age but by boredom. It didn't matter what year you were in at school when it came to booting a football around.

In every way imaginable, Scott should have been the kid who followed the others. Outwardly he was quieter, while he was certainly smaller. Most people who saw their group probably thought that but Jon, Jamo and Shaun knew different; Scott was the cool kid. He was the one with the sharp comebacks and the one who bunked off when it was sunny. He fought their battles for them as he was the one older kids thought they could pick on first but would end up paying a price for doing so. He was vicious and scary but reassuring at the same time, the type of kid you would rather be friends with than an enemy of.

The group tore across the concrete land, watching as the older kid they were chasing ran into an abandoned building which Shaun guessed was once part of the factory. Scott had stopped running and the other three had now caught him. The building was made of huge grey bricks, while a lot of the plaster that would have once covered it lay in dusty piles around the floor. Moss had begun to cover the lower part of it, the sun bouncing from the white concrete floor, making them squint as they stared ahead. The space the other kid had run through had no actual door, the rotting wooden frame having splintered at the top.

'We've got him now,' Scott said. 'The door at the back is blocked off.'

Shaun looked nervously at Jon next to him, neither of them wanting to say anything.

'Niiiiiiiiigelllllllll,' Jamo called loudly. Scott laughed as Shaun and Jon joined in half-heartedly.

Scott walked towards the entrance with the three of them behind him. Jamo was still calling Nigel's name loudly. Inside the building, the light levels dropped significantly and Shaun found himself blinking to readjust. Outside it was bright and sunny but the only light inside came through the partially destroyed roof. Patches of the floor were illuminated, piles of rubble flanking the walls. At first Shaun couldn't see anyone else in the room. He wondered if there was a second way out, or if they had somehow been mistaken when they thought they saw the older kid run into this building?

He hoped there was another exit but then saw a silhouette of a figure towards the back of the room crouching behind some of the rubble. He thought he heard a faint whimpering but no one else reacted. Jamo was still taunting. 'Niiiiiiiiigellllllllll.'

Shaun wondered if he was the only person who had seen the shadow at the end. He said nothing as the four of them scanned their surroundings. Scott's screwed-up face snarled as he looked from corner to corner, his features only half-visible because of the light from the doorway.

'Anyone see him?'

Shaun said nothing and Scott signalled for he and Jon to head towards the far end, the darker part where Shaun had seen the shape. 'You two look down there, me and Jamo will check around here and make sure he doesn't get back out the door,' Scott said.

The room was large but seemed so much smaller because of the rubble and wreckage. You could just about make out twisted pieces of metal and plastic that would have been tables at some point. Where there were holes in the roof, there were also patches of damp visible on the floor below. Shaun could hear the two boys behind them overturning pieces of junk and looking under things. He heard Scott cursing and making threats. Jamo was still calling but the word was getting longer and longer.

'Niiiiiiiiiiiiiiiiiiiiiiiiiiiiiiiiiiiiiiiiiigellllllllllllllllllllllllllllll.'

Shaun found it intimidating and it wasn't even his name being called. He felt his heart pounding and looked at the shape of Jon next to him. He couldn't make out his friend's features but could almost feel the fear there too.

'You go that way,' Shaun said, pointing towards the back left of the building. 'I'll go over there.'

He was sending Jon away from the silhouette towards the other corner. Shaun continued to walk towards where he had seen the shadow. He kicked a few random pieces of concrete to keep up the illusion he was looking and saw another small flash of movement. Nigel was less than ten feet from him. His eyes flicked towards the older boy and he could see the faint outline of a figure behind a mangled table. He thought he saw the person shiver but said nothing. They either hadn't seen or hadn't acknowledged him.

'See anything, Jon?' he called.

'No.'

Shaun could still hear the calls echoing around the room.

'Niiiiiiiiiiiiiiiiiiiiiiiiiiiiiiiiiiiiiiiiiiiiiigellllllllllllllllllllllllllll.'

He could definitely hear a slight sobbing coming from the person hiding by the table. Shaun realised he had been holding his breath and stopped to risk another look. This time the faint stream of light coming through the roof caught the two of them. Shaun looked at Nigel and the panic-stricken elder boy stared directly back.

Shaun tried to motion him to stay calm, to stay hidden where he was because he wasn't going to say anything but Nigel's eyes darted from side to side and he leapt up from his position. The thin boy's frame charged into Shaun, the pair of them stumbling backwards into a smashed-up cabinet. Shaun stayed still as Nigel clambered to his feet. The noise had alerted the others but, as Shaun peered across, he could see Jon rooted to the spot.

'Get him then,' Scott yelled from the other end but Jon didn't move and Shaun was on the floor. Nigel ran towards the door. Jamo had been taken by surprise and was still engulfed in darkness. Shaun could hear him struggling with something in the distance but couldn't see him. Scott was clambering over some old wreckage but Nigel was sprinting, head down in a straight line. Through the flashes of light that partially illuminated the room, Shaun saw Nigel's frame bolting. He was going to make it outside surely?

Suddenly Shaun heard the crunch, everyone must have done. Scott had cut across from his position and rugby-tackled Nigel to the ground feet from the door. The sickening sound of a bone snapping was instantly drowned out by Nigel's scream of pain. Shaun pulled himself to his feet and made his way towards the front of the building. He felt Jon close by as Jamo's laughing drowned out Nigel's agony.

Shaun felt sick. As he reached Nigel, he could see the older boy prone on the floor. His once-green T-shirt was covered in dust and ripped by the arm, his jeans bent out at an unnatural angle covering a leg which must surely have made the sickening crunching noise. The boy looked dazed and was crying. 'Please . . .'

Scott crouched down next to the boy and punched him hard across the face. 'Shut. Up,' he ordered. 'Stop crying.'

Nigel had his eyes shut, head to one side reeling from the blow. He was trying to catch his breath, trying to stop the tears. 'Do you know why we chased you, Nigel?'

The boy shook his head and whimpered. 'No.'

'You shouldn't have looked at my girlfriend like that, should you?'

Nigel was shaking his head, desperately holding back the tears. 'I . . . I . . . wasn't.'

Scott punched him in the face a second time, the sound echoing. Jamo gave a 'yeah'. Shaun continued staring at the angle of Nigel's leg.

'Don't lie to me, *freak*.'

Jon spoke. 'Scott . . .'

Scott turned around sharply, standing rigidly to his full height. He was shorter than Jon but stepped up to within an inch or two of him. 'What?'

The light from the doorway left them each half in

shadow, the only noise a faint whimper coming from Nigel. This was the moment for Shaun to say something too. If he and Jon stuck together, they could stop this now. He just had to open his mouth and say something . . .

28

Shaun Hogan was crying, not just small sobs but loud wails. The prison guards didn't seem to want anything to do with what was unfolding in front of them. They couldn't have heard anything specific given the distance from them to Shaun, Jessica and Cole but they had stopped talking among themselves and all four were watching the prisoner, presumably in case his sorrow became violent. His cries echoed around the empty visiting room. Jessica slid a packet of tissues from her bag across the table. 'Shaun . . . ?'

'I'm so sorry,' he said. 'I didn't say anything.'

The case of Nigel Collins had been massive news at the time and a total embarrassment for the force. A dog-walker had found a teenage boy's battered body on the site of an old factory. He was in a coma with one of his legs was broken. He had a fractured jaw and broken ribs. His face was so badly beaten that the walker wasn't even sure the victim was alive, let alone whether they were male or female.

Jessica had been in uniform at the time and most of the GMP's resources had been assigned to the case given its severity. The boy's face had been on the front of every national newspaper and at the top of every news bulletin. At first they had to find out who the victim was, which had taken a couple of days in itself.

Nigel Collins was an orphan who had lived in a children's home on the outskirts of the city since his parents had died in a car accident when he was eleven. They had left behind nothing but debts and Nigel. He had no relatives, no security and no future and was too old to realistically be adopted. Finding a foster family was always hard for a child on the cusp of being a teenager and the home had offered him somewhere to stay, even though he had never fitted in either there or at school.

After he had been identified as the victim, the police had followed all sorts of leads, from former school pupils to ex-housemates at the home. No one knew anything. Nigel was a quiet child and didn't talk much at the best of times. He lived in his own world with no friends and little contact with anyone other than the staff at the home. He had finished school at sixteen but was barely ready for the outside world. Staff had helped set him up with some-where to stay through a housing association but, given his personality, he hadn't achieved much else.

In the days after the media campaign, there had been plenty of reports of Nigel being harassed by other kids, younger and older. Some saw him on the streets and targeted the vulnerable, gawky loner. With his poor social skills, even adults would tell their children to avoid people like *him*. No one could give any specific details though and the police had to assume he had been attacked given the nature of the injuries and the place his body was found.

When Nigel regained consciousness, he either didn't want to or couldn't remember any details about how he had ended up there. He couldn't say whether he was attacked, let alone if he knew the people involved. A couple of the staff members from the home he had lived in as a child were brought in to speak to him but they couldn't get him to open up. As they pointed out, Nigel didn't talk an awful lot before the incident. Some officers believed he simply didn't want to say anything but no one could know for sure.

Five months after the attack he had been forgotten. He was released from hospital and, as he either couldn't or wouldn't cooperate with the police, any case against the people who had attacked him was dropped. It was another unsolved file in a large stack of them but with a victim who couldn't even point them in the right direction. The media had long since moved on to other stories too.

Jessica knew all of that off the top of her head. It had been ingrained into them as officers during the morning briefings before things had slowly been dropped. One by one they were moved onto other cases but those pictures of Nigel Collins' brutally beaten face were something that had stayed with her. He didn't even look human in the images, a mass of purple, black, blue and red all merging into one.

Jessica took a deep breath. 'Are you admitting to being part of a group who tortured Nigel Collins, Shaun?'

'Yes,' he sniffed.

Jessica didn't know how to phrase the next question so just asked it in the simplest way possible. 'Why have you told us all this now?'

'I don't know. I suppose I've been waiting to tell some-one for ages.'

'You do know everything you just told us could be used if the case is reopened?'

'It's fine. I deserve it,' he said quietly. 'But that's why it's my fault with my mum.'

'I'm sorry, Shaun, I still don't understand,' Jessica said.

Shaun was still sniffing but his sobs had died down. He spoke slowly and quietly. 'After it all happened, when Nigel had been found and was on the TV and everything, I couldn't keep it in. The four of us never really hung around together after that again but Scott told us all to keep our mouths shut. We were scared. *I* was scared but I told my mum . . .'

Things began to click into place for Jessica to explain the reason why Shaun believed the family falling apart was down to him. She didn't say anything and allowed Shaun to continue speaking. 'Mum didn't go to the police but it was never right. She never looked at me the same way; you could see it in her eyes. She had already started drinking after Dad left but everything was under control. After I told her though . . .'

Jessica let him tail off. He composed himself again and used another tissue to blow his nose. 'I'd just left school and was about to do my exams but I couldn't get the images out of my head. Scott made us all join in. That way, if any of us ever said anything, we would all be in it together. Jon – Jonny – he cried the whole time. Even Jamo didn't want to get involved when it got serious. As soon as my exams were done that's when Mum said we were moving. We all knew the flat she took us to was too small but I think it was just her way of saying she didn't want me there any longer.'

Jessica nodded. 'Is that what she said to you when you went to visit her on the day you ended up assaulting that man?'

'Pretty much. She had been drinking and was in the flat on her own. It was horrible. I had heard from Em that Mum had started *working* and I had shouted at her about it. I said it wasn't right what she was doing to Kim. She wasn't listening and just shouted back, "What about what you did?" It was the first time she'd ever said anything properly about it. She said it was my fault and that she couldn't even look at me because of what she saw every time she did.'

Jessica didn't know what to say. You heard all sorts of harrowing tales from people working for the police but this was right up there. No one came out well from this, Shaun or his mother. And what about the victims? Nigel Collins and poor Kim. Perhaps even Shaun himself and Claire were sufferers because of it all?

Shaun sniffed again. 'I felt so bad. It was the last time I ever saw her. I came back to Leeds that night and just drank. I didn't even know the guy I beat up. I've thought about it a lot since. I wondered if maybe I wanted to end up somewhere like here and punish myself? I don't know.'

There wasn't an awful lot they could say. They would pass on the confession to their superiors who might decide to reopen Nigel Collins' case. If that happened, someone else would come to visit Shaun to ask him to repeat everything he had just said. Even if he refused, Jessica's recollections and Cole's notes could probably be enough.

Jessica's mind was still working. 'Who were the other boys, Shaun?'

'I didn't really know everyone's name. It was all about nicknames and football usually, just having a laugh. It wasn't always just the four of us. Big groups of us would go off kicking a footy around. It was just that day it was the four of us bunking off. I'm still not really sure how it all happened. We were smoking around the back of this shop and Nigel walked past. We all knew his name and face just through him being around. Everyone took the mick and called him names and so on. He kind of half-knew us and our mums because we were all from the same area. He never seemed to forget anyone. Scott said he was the guy who had been looking at his girlfriend some other evening and we went with it. It was only a chase at first.'

'Do you remember Scott's last name?'

Shaun thought about it but shook his head. 'I'm not sure I ever knew it. It wasn't the kind of thing I would have asked. He was younger than me so we weren't even in the same class.'

'What about "Jamo"?'

'I don't know. That was what Scott called him.'

'Do you know if it was his first name, like "James"? Or last name like "Jameson"?'

'No, he was always just "Jamo". He was in Scott's year, which is how they knew each other.'

'What about Jon?'

'He's the only one I knew anything about. He was the

year above me in school and had already finished. He lived quite close by but was waiting to do his A-levels or something like that. I don't remember exactly. We didn't really talk again.'

'Do you know his full name?'

'Yeah I think . . .' Shaun looked up to the ceiling trying to remember. 'Price? Something like that.'

Jessica glanced at Cole and then spun around to look back at Shaun. 'Could it be "Prince"? Jonathan Prince?'

'Yeah, maybe. That sounds about right.'

29

It didn't take much working out for Jessica to figure out that 'Jamo' would be James Christensen, the son of Yvonne. That still left them Scott to discover but they knew three of the four gang members who had beaten Nigel Collins into a coma had now had a parent brutally murdered.

Jessica and Cole hurried out of the prison. One of the reception workers drove them back to the station and Jessica spent large parts of the car trip and train journey on her phone.

The first thing they had to do was find out who Scott was. What was his last name and where did he live? More importantly for now, where did his parents live? Someone had to find them to make sure they weren't the next victims. All they had to go on was that Scott was a few years younger than Jonathan Prince and Shaun Hogan and in the same school year as James Christensen. It should be easy enough to find out what school they went to, check the intake for that particular year and look for anyone called Scott. Unless he had changed his name in the meantime, it would give them maybe one person to look at if they were lucky but certainly no more than five or six if not. Complications could arise if people had moved but it still shouldn't take long. Jessica hoped the people at the station would have tracked down their man by the time the train pulled in. If any of that failed, they would bring in James Christensen to see if he could point them in the right direction to find Scott.

The next concern was to track down Nigel Collins. Surely he had to be their man? He was connected to all three murders and, depending on the way you viewed things, had the motive. She didn't know why he would target the parents instead of those who had hurt him though.

Aylesbury told Jessica over the phone he would be setting one team up to find Scott and another to find Nigel.

The train journey took the same time to arrive back in Manchester at lunchtime as it had to get to Leeds that morning but Jessica was on edge. Every stop at a platform had her seething, checking her watch and wondering what was taking so long. Again, Cole's coolness infuriated her. He didn't need to say anything, his posture said it all: Just wait, getting stressed can't help either of us. It was helping her, though. She watched people get on and off and had irrational thoughts about whether one of them was Scott or Nigel Collins.

Her phone rang as they pulled into the Oxford Road station. It was marginally closer to their Longsight base than the main Piccadilly station and Jessica thought they could get a taxi directly from there, saving them a few minutes. Cole shrugged and went with it as Jessica talked on her phone and bounded out of the station. The inspectors wanted to see her ticket but she wasn't in the mood to be stopped, pulling out her identification card instead and telling them in not too polite terms to move out of her way.

The phone call hadn't improved her mood. Far from finding 'Scott', it seemed as if the other officers had not got anywhere. Although he had returned to the area for a short while, James Christensen had gone back to Bournemouth University according to his father and no one seemed to be able to get in contact with him. They had his mobile number but he wasn't answering and a couple of local officers had been despatched to find him. Perhaps the only thing they had managed to do was confirm which secondary school James had attended. That information had come from his father who wasn't too keen to be giving out that kind of information according to the person Jessica spoke to. 'He kept asking if his son was under suspicion, then was banging on about his rights,' the officer told Jessica.

'What is it with people and their bloody rights?' Jessica said. 'Everyone thinks they're entitled to something.'

Officers had managed to go to the school and find an intake list from the year they needed, despite being told at first it was against the Data Protection Act. A call from the DCI had apparently straightened that out but the officers had been told the superintendent had also spoken to someone at the Local Education Authority before the papers had been handed over. The school had emailed a copy as well as handed over a photocopied version of the originals.

Even with that, the problem was that there were three people named 'Scott' in the same year as James Christensen. While Jessica had been on the train, the team had hit brick walls with all of their potential gang-leaders.

There was a Scott Hesketh, a Scott Harris and a Scott Barry. Those names were being cross-checked with birth certificates, the electoral roll and other easily accessible name archives. The school itself had a limited amount of information on past pupils. From what the officer told Jessica, it was basically just name, grades and home address. Given those addresses were six years old, that didn't give them much. Officers had been sent out to each of the three addresses to see if they could come up with something, while the other information they had was being run against their own police databases.

So far no links for any of the three had turned up and the situation with Nigel Collins was even worse. It was as if he had dropped off the face of the earth the day he walked out of hospital. They had checked the housing association records for the address he had been living at when he ended up in hospital but the association said he never returned. There were forty-seven Nigel Collinses living in the country and a team was currently working on bringing that number down based on age. It had already been established there were no Nigel Collinses fitting the age bracket living locally. That was the first thing they had checked.

'Great,' Jessica said, before telling the officer she was on her way back with Cole.

Jessica told their taxi driver they were both CID and that she was giving him her permission to do whatever it took to get them back to the police station as soon as possible. Cole simply raised an eyebrow as if to point out she couldn't authorise speeding in a private vehicle like that but she wasn't bothered. The driver was good and, after they arrived, she gave him a twenty-pound note without asking for a receipt or change and ran into reception.

There was no particular reason for the hurry – the team knew what they were doing and there wasn't an awful lot more she could add. Jessica wanted to feel part of things now they finally had a lead they had waited so long for and bounded past the front desk, past her office and onto the main floor where . . . everything seemed normal. Officers were on the phone and doing their jobs. She didn't know why she thought things would be different just because they were onto something.

Rowlands approached her. 'All right?'

'Yeah, what's going on?'

He told her that one of their three Scotts had been ruled out. Scott Barry had been found. He and his family had moved to a place in the Bristol area not long after he had finished school. He had become an auctioneer and one officer had struck lucky simply by searching for his name on the Internet. A quick phone call had established he was the person they were looking for and that his parents were alive and well living in Portugal.

That left Scott Hesketh and Scott Harris to track down. Apparently police officers had been to both addresses given on the school records. At the address they had for Scott Harris, there was no answer but the house was registered to a Paul and Mary Keegan according to the land deeds. At the other, whoever had answered said they had never heard of anybody with the last name 'Hesketh'. The occupants had only lived there a few months themselves.

'Has anyone been able to get hold of James Christensen?' Jessica asked.

'What do you think?'

Jessica went upstairs to tell Aylesbury what had happened that morning to find Cole already there. She had given him a reasonable outline over the phone but things still had to be done officially. As they were speaking, a call came through to say they had finally been able to get hold of Yvonne Christensen's son in Bournemouth. There was nothing sinister going on, he had been in lectures and had his phone off. His classmates would have had quite a spectacle as he was hauled out to be spoken to by police officers.

The call was patched through to the DCI's phone but he allowed Jessica to take the call. 'Is that James?' she asked.

'Yes, who's this? No one's told me anything here.'

'James, this is Detective Sergeant Jessica Daniel. I've been working on the case regarding your mother's murder.'

'Oh right,' the voice said sullenly, then quickly: 'No one's hurt my dad, have they?'

'No, your father's fine but I have to ask you about something that happened a few years ago.'

'Okay . . .'

'Does the name Nigel Collins mean anything to you?'

There was silence.

'James?'

'No,' he said.

'James, this is very serious. We can come back to Nigel another time but I need to ask about your friend Scott. What was his last name?'

The voice was quavering at the other end of the line. 'Scott? Oh God . . .'

Jessica spoke quickly, her heart racing. 'I'm sorry but you have to be calm, okay? Do you remember what Scott's last name was?'

'Oh God. Harris. It was Scott Harris. Am I . . . Am I in trouble?'

Jessica handed the phone over to the DCI, who would explain to James that nothing had been decided but he might want to get a lawyer. Jessica bounded down the stairs two at a time, charging through to the main floor where everyone was working.

'It's Harris,' she shouted. 'Forget Hesketh, find Harris.'

They knew the place he used to live was now owned by a family whose name was Keegan, so finding out where they worked was crucial too. The officer who had knocked on the door had been left outside the property in case anyone returned.

Jessica suddenly had a thought and went to stand behind Rowlands, who was nearby working on a computer. 'Did someone check the birth, death and marriage details for those names and addresses we had?' she asked.

'We got the birth certificates for all three of them.'

'What about the marriage records?'

'No, why?'

'Just check to see if there's any record of a Harris getting married in the past six or seven years.' Rowlands put the search into the computer and a list of a few hundred names came up. 'Now see if any of those Harrises married a Keegan.'

The constable tapped a few more buttons on the keyboard which left them just one name. He used the mouse to double click and bring up the full record but Jessica already knew which address it would throw up.

They'd had a police officer standing outside it for the past two hours.

30

Once they knew the Keegans were the family they were looking for, things moved quickly. Whether he was called Scott Harris or Scott Keegan, the son wasn't an instant priority. No decision had been made about reopening the Nigel Collins case but, given everything they knew, his parents could be in danger and getting them to safety was the first thing that had to be done. Jessica spoke to the officer at the scene to tell him to try the front door on the off-chance it was open and then to check around the back and look through the windows to see if anything was visible.

They discovered mobile phone numbers for both Mary Keegan – formerly Harris – and Paul Keegan. As she was being driven in a marked car to the house, Jessica tried both numbers. Mary's rang out with no answer but Paul Keegan answered to her silent relief.

It was now mid-afternoon and Mr Keegan told her he was at work in the council offices. Jessica didn't explain much but asked if he could return home to meet them. His instant question was: 'Is everyone all right?'

Jessica had no idea how to answer and didn't want to lie by giving a definitive 'yes', so simply said, 'We hope so.' It was a horrible way to reply and Jessica knew the poor guy would be frantic on his way home but there wasn't much else she could say. At best she would apologise in person if everyone was safe and well.

At worst . . .

The Keegans' house was once again in the same Gorton area as those of the first three victims. All four properties were within a mile's radius. The journey wasn't too far from the station but Jessica kept trying Mary Keegan's phone over and over. Every time it rang out. The car arrived and parked up on the road outside the Keegans' house behind the first police car. The officer who had been sent earlier was waiting for them.

'Any luck?' Jessica asked, wondering if he had been able to get in or at the very least see something.

'No. It's all locked up with the curtains pulled. I noticed a few neighbours taking an interest but nothing.' Jessica went to walk past him but his next throwaway line sent a chill down her spine. 'I've just been hearing a phone ring inside non-stop for the last ten minutes or so.'

'Shit.'

A third marked car pulled in behind them which would be bringing Cole and more uniformed officers. Jessica eyed the property. It was much the same as Yvonne Christensen's, a standard semi-detached house with strong imposing double-glazed doors and windows. The front garden was immaculate, surrounded by a small fountain and pond with lush trimmed grass. The Keegans were clearly very house-proud. Even the surrounding hedges were cut neatly, in stark contrast to some of the other properties on the street. Jessica walked down the path to the house and opened the letterbox. There were thick black bristles on the inside obstructing any view she might have. She used her fingers to try to push them aside but could see nothing. She next went to the bay window to the right of the front door and used her hands to shield her eyes from the glare to peer through. A thick net curtain meant she could see nothing of note.

Within a moment of calling Mary Keegan's phone again, Jessica could hear a muffled ringtone coming from the inside of the house. She leant with her forehead on the cool glass of the window and hung up.

She knew what they were going to find inside.

Jessica heard a vehicle screeching from somewhere nearby and moments later a large silver car pulled up in front of all three police cars. She saw a man quickly get out from the driver's side and run along the pathway towards her. 'Mr Keegan?' she said.

'Yes. What's wrong?'

Jessica ignored the immediate question. 'Do you have your house keys with you?'

The man was wearing black suit trousers and a white shirt with a blue criss-cross pattern. He was somewhere in his fifties and a few inches taller than Jessica, unshaven with carefully combed dark hair that was greying around his ears. He put his right hand in his trouser pocket and pulled out a key ring. 'Here. What's going on?'

'Do you mind if I borrow them for a moment?'

The man handed them to her and repeated, 'What's happening?'

Jessica said nothing but nodded to Cole and the waiting officers at the end of the path. Cole stood next to Mr

Keegan as Jessica pulled a pair of thin blue rubber gloves out of her pocket. She put the key in the front door's lock and turned it.

'Mrs Keegan?' she called as she entered with two uniformed officers following behind. There was no answer.

The door opened into what looked like a living room with a set of stairs immediately on her left. The room was spotlessly tidy with a neat pile of mail on top of a small table immediately on her right. At the other end of the room was a door that Jessica motioned the two officers towards as she went upstairs.

The stairs were made of wood, each one creaking noisily as she stepped on it. It was one flight to the top, which opened onto a hallway with three doors to choose from, two on her right and one straight ahead. She opened the door in front of her that led into a bathroom. As with the rest of the house, everything was immaculate, the white bath and shower cabinet gleaming as sunlight came through a small window. There was nothing else to see.

The next door opened into a bedroom. Posters of footballers and girls in bikinis were on the walls but the bunk beds directly across from the door were made in pristine fashion, the corners tucked and the blue duvets perfectly central. There were a few action figures on cabinets and dressers around the room but otherwise it was as tidy as the other rooms. Jessica wondered if this was Scott's room. Was this where he returned to after torturing Nigel Collins? She pulled the door shut, the bottom of the wood rubbing on the carpet as she heard one of the policemen's voices from downstairs. 'Clear here.'

One more door and she would be able to say the same. Jessica rested her hand on the final handle, held her breath and closed her eyes. She pulled it down and pushed the door open, forcing it against the bristle of the carpet. She breathed out and opened her eyes. 'No . . .'

On the bed was a woman's body face-down. Aside from the room's colours the scene was almost identical to what Jessica had witnessed at Claire Hogan's flat. Instead of a sprawl of bleach-blonde hair discoloured by dark blood spread across the bed sheets, Jessica could see long dark brown hair splayed out in a similar way. The yellow curtains were drawn and the room dim but Jessica could see the matching double-bed linen was stained by blood.

Jessica didn't need to see any more; four dead bodies were enough. She turned around and pulled the gloves off her hands, walking down the stairs back to the front door. The other two officers were standing in the living room, both looking at her.

'Don't go up,' she said, before adding, 'Someone call the Scene of Crime team.'

Jessica took it upon herself to tell Paul Keegan there was a dead body upstairs on their bed, likely his wife. She spoke slowly and gently but the man could only stare at her with his mouth open.

In any other circumstance his response 'Are you sure?' would have been ridiculous. In this one it was heart-breaking. Jessica could tell from the tone of his voice that he loved his wife enormously. Some people would have wanted to run past her into the house, race up the stairs and see for themselves. Paul Keegan didn't move from the spot on his front lawn. Jessica saw tears in his eyes and reached out to put an arm on his shoulder, before fully embracing him and letting the man cry on her shoulder.

After a few moments, he pulled away and tried to straighten his shirt. He wiped his eyes but the tears hadn't really stopped. 'Was it him?' he asked.

'Who?'

'Houdini.'

Back at the station things had been moving quickly. Jessica hadn't given Paul Keegan a yes or a no answer. Although it seemed likely, they weren't absolutely certain and they now knew Houdini was most likely Nigel Collins.

Paul Keegan hadn't wanted to go into the house but had agreed to an identification at the scene. It seemed harsh but for completeness' sake it was better being done there, rather than finding out a few hours later his wife was alive and well and some other dead body had been dumped in his house. He had clearly been upset at the brief look but had willingly come with them to the station for interview. Grief did odd things to people. Some reacted like Sandra Prince and were unable to communicate. For others, like Paul Keegan, it seemed to have the opposite effect, driving them to remember things they might not normally and to think with a level-headedness they might not usually have.

Jessica had a dilemma in whether to reveal his stepson Scott could in fact be indirectly responsible for what had happened. It didn't seem fair to add more grief quite so quickly. She had established that Scott was now at university in Liverpool, about to finish his first year studying forensic science.

'His mum was so proud of him for turning things around,' Paul Keegan said. 'He used to be a bit of a tearaway before we got together. I think he had issues with his dad.'

Jessica thought he didn't know the half of it, while the irony of Scott learning about how to deconstruct a body given what Shaun Hogan said he had done wasn't lost on her either. Another constable took notes as Paul Keegan spoke but Jessica said nothing about Scott. There was an older stepson too, Steven, who was just about to take his final accounting exam at Keele University. They were both due to return home in the next fortnight for the summer break.

Mary's husband spoke clearly and simply, explaining that his wife was a nurse and had been working late shifts that week, starting at ten at night and finishing at six in the morning. She would arrive home as he was waking up to get ready to go to his own job with the council for eight. They usually shared a cup of tea together, swapping notes on the previous twenty-four hours before he went off to work and she went to bed.

'I always hate it when she's on nights,' he said. 'It doesn't feel right sleeping alone.'

The present tense he spoke in was hard to hear. What he had told them explained why the body had been found upstairs rather than in the living room or anywhere else. It also indicated Nigel Collins must have been watching the house to have known the woman would be vulnerable during the day.

Thinking about it from the killer's point of view, Jessica could now see the pattern. Yvonne Christensen had been the easiest. She lived alone and slept at night like most people. If you could get into the house without alerting her, she would be fast asleep and provide no threat. Martin Prince was next in line because he was always on his own during the day but perhaps seen as more of a threat because he was a man? Claire Hogan would have been slightly harder to plan given that she lived on a main road and had a steady stream of visitors. And then there was Mary Keegan, who was the hardest. Had Nigel been watching and waiting long enough for her shift patterns to switch from earlies, to daytimes then back to nights again? If she was working similar hours to her husband, finding an opportunity to get either of them alone would have been a challenge. Nigel also didn't seem too bothered whether he was targeting the father or mother, seemingly going for whoever was easier. He certainly must have kept an eye on the comings and goings over the past few weeks or months.

Jessica hadn't done the checking herself but it had been established the doors and windows had been locked as with the previous three victims. The police officers had found Mary Keegan's keys with her bag in the kitchen but the reasons were less clear.

Alibis would be checked for Paul, Scott and Steven Keegan – the only others with direct access to the house. Paul had given them the details of Scott and Steven's real father too, Mary's former husband, but said he was now remarried and living in Scotland. Everything would be looked at but Jessica knew it would be a formality. The man they needed to find was Nigel Collins. Tying him to the four murders could prove more of a problem, given the lack of obvious evidence at the scenes but Jessica figured they would cross that bridge when they got to it.

After she had asked all of her questions and heard everything that was likely to be useful, Jessica added, 'Is there anything you would like to tell us?'

In interviews where the person had cooperated, it was always the last question you asked. In training, they had all been told a story of how a murder in the north east had been solved by a throwaway comment at the end of an interview. It was probably apocryphal, as so many of those training stories were, but the point had always resonated with Jessica.

Paul Keegan looked at her blankly and shook his head. 'How do you mean?'

'Sometimes when we interview victims and relatives, there are things they might remember that seem normal at the time but, in retrospect, could throw new light on something. People they've noticed and so on. Silent phone calls, things like that.'

'We've had a few problems with kids over the last few months on the estate, riding their bikes and being loud late at night and so on. You phone the police but nothing really gets done.'

It was a story Jessica heard all too regularly. On the one hand she knew how much of a blight it could be on people's lives but she was also aware the police couldn't be everywhere. With a lack of funding and targets that needed to be hit, things like this were often treated as a low priority. Again, there was no irony lost on Jessica, considering how Mr Keegan's stepson had seemingly behaved when he was younger.

'I can only apologise for that, Mr Keegan,' Jessica said. 'Is there anything else?'

'Not really, no.' Jessica thanked him for his time then broke the news that they would have to arrest and speak to Scott. She reassured him his stepson was not suspected of any direct involvement to his mother's death but couldn't add any more than that. They were arranging for Scott and Steven to come back to the area. Steven would be interviewed informally at a later date in regards to the killing of his mother although he wasn't a suspect. With the story breaking in the media tomorrow that their chief suspect was Nigel Collins, having Scott in custody would be a necessity. Even if the original assault case from almost six years ago wasn't reopened, they couldn't risk him running. He would obviously put two and two together but they would need to speak to him regardless – if only to formally rule him out of the inquiry into his mother's death.

Jessica had already arranged for Jonathan Prince and James Christensen to be cautioned in relation to the unsolved assault all those years ago too. Things really were getting complicated, with Nigel Collins being both a victim and suspect in two different crimes.

Back in the main part of the station, Jessica could see the search for Nigel Collins was moving, albeit slowly. The original list of forty-seven names had been brought down to just three who were the right age. Two lived in the London area, while one was in a small town not too far from Nottingham. An officer was going to visit the Nigel Collins who lived in the town but dealing with the Met Police in London was always trickier. Their structure was even more confusing than Greater Manchester's and there were always enough jobsworths to tell you that you were speaking to the wrong department. Anyone would think it was a different country they were trying to deal with. Eventually Aylesbury had become involved and two sets of two constables were now on their way to talk to the other two Nigel Collinses.

Jessica knew it was only a matter of time until they were ruled out. Whoever their killer was, it was someone who had been in the area very recently. Mary Keegan had been murdered that day but must have been watched for at least a few weeks previous. Their Nigel Collins wasn't someone who drove up from Nottingham or London, walked through a wall and then travelled home again.

Door-to-door inquiries were being made in the hope anyone on the street had seen someone acting suspiciously. An accurate e-fit could be their only hope. The police did have a photograph on file from the original case but it was only the one of the poor kid's battered face that had been on every news broadcast and in every newspaper at the time. It was no use for putting into a media campaign to find their prime suspect as you couldn't tell if the victim was male or female, let alone make out any features.

The children's home Nigel Collins had lived in didn't exist any longer, having been bulldozed a few years ago. Cole had already set some officers on the task of tracking down some of the staff who would have been there at the same time as Nigel. Even if they got hold of the right people, it seemed unlikely they would stumble across a picture from his childhood they could use. At best it would be six years old but Jessica doubted they would get anything anyway.

That left them with a name of someone who seemingly didn't exist, whose appearance they had no idea of and no idea how he got in and out of locked houses.

Nigel Collins really had set them quite a puzzle.

31

The next day was something Jessica had not been looking forward to. Every news bulletin on TV and radio had led off with the story that Nigel Collins was the 'Houdini Strangler'. The only photograph the police had to give out was that of Nigel's bruised face from almost six years previously, so it had been that staring out from the front of every newspaper, national and local, as well as the morning's broadcasts.

Jessica had been up at six in the morning to watch the coverage on a loop. She had found that watching things over and over could sometimes help clarify the facts in your mind. She first watched the BBC news, then changed channels and watched it on ITV, before returning to the BBC for the local take on it all. She also spent the whole time surfing news websites on her phone. In terms of information released, none of the stations had that much to go on. Aylesbury had hosted a press conference the night before. The first three murder victims' names had been previously released but Mary Keegan had been added to that list. The media were told Nigel Collins was the chief suspect but the link to the victims' children had not been revealed.

It would surely only be a matter of time before that got out and Jessica was only half-surprised she hadn't read the story on the *Herald*'s website that morning with Garry Ashford's byline. It was the type of story where he seemed to steal a march on everyone. Aylesbury had been keen to stress that the public were not at risk and the police didn't believe there was any need for further alarm. It was a fine line as they were pretty sure Nigel Collins had completed his killing spree but couldn't be sure. It seemed unlikely he would go back for the other parents but perhaps the people who actually tortured him could be targeted.

If it wasn't leaked, that information almost certainly would be revealed at some point in the next forty-eight hours. It seemed inconceivable the original case into the assault on Nigel Collins would not be reopened.

Randall had stayed over the night before and he and Caroline had got up an hour or so after Jessica and the three of them had watched the news together. 'Oh God, Jess. This is awful,' Caroline said as she cuddled into her boyfriend on the sofa.

Jessica had never really told her the full extent of the case and, though it had been in the media consistently through the past few weeks, this coverage seemed so much more real given the graphic detail everything was now being laid out in. 'It's okay,' Jessica said, giving her friend a half-smile.

'It's sick is what it is,' Randall said, gripping Caroline tighter and kissing the top of her head.

Jessica had to leave them to it. She had a feeling it was going to be a long day, something which was confirmed as she pulled her car onto the road the station was on. She could see a full media scrum outside the gates. She often took the turn into the station in third gear and one of the other officers once claimed he'd seen her car take it on two wheels. On this occasion, she had to stop and crawl through the mass of people. There were television cameras and flashes going off from photographers' cameras. She drove slowly, being careful not to hit anyone, and saw Garry Ashford off to one side as well. In the fleeting glimpse she got, he seemed slightly overwhelmed with the mass of people pushing and shoving.

Scott Keegan had been kept in the cells under the station overnight after returning from Liverpool late the previous evening. They could hold him for up to twenty-four hours without charge but the intention had only been to keep him in until the morning. By then the news about Nigel Collins would be widely known and they could speak to him.

Jessica parked and entered through the station's main entrance. In the reception area, there was a television high on the wall above a rank of chairs for people who had to wait there. A few years previously, someone had managed to steal an old TV from a similar spot, despite being in the reception of a police station. There had been much mickey-taking at the time. The replacement was usually turned off but had a rolling news channel switched on with the sound turned up as Jessica walked in. She glanced sideways at it and could see an outside shot of the door she had just walked in.

'They didn't get your good side, did they?' laughed the desk sergeant, who was pointing at the screen. Jessica ignored him, breezing towards the stairs to check in with

Aylesbury. Cole was also present, of course, and the morning update was as she would have expected. All three Nigel Collinses from the previous day had been ruled out, which left them with no one.

Initial forensic results were back, which meant someone would have been working late into the night. Mary Keegan had been strangled in the exact way as the previous victims but it was suspected, as with Yvonne Christensen, that she had been asleep. There was next to no evidence of a struggle. As Jessica had thought, all of the blood in the bedroom belonged to the victim, with nothing in the way of DNA from anyone other than the husband. In some ways that kind of evidence was irrelevant as they knew who they were after. But, if and when they found Nigel Collins, it would have been useful in tying him to the scenes for a trial.

The DCI did tell them that word had come down that the Nigel Collins assault case was going to be reopened. Given the way the two cases would be linked together, it was the only thing that could realistically happen. A separate set of officers would return to Leeds Prison to speak to Shaun Hogan again. When Jessica and Cole had spoken to him the previous day, he wasn't under caution as he wasn't considered a witness in the murder of Claire Hogan; he was behind bars after all. They had gone to talk to him to see if there was any background he could give them to help discover who killed his mother. The hope was that he would repeat what he had told them on tape and under caution. Having seen his demeanour the previous day, Jessica felt that he would.

After the meeting with her superiors, it was then the main team briefing. In itself, it threw up very little but there was at least a buzz considering everything that had happened in the past day. Rowlands had been sent back to visit Wayne Lapham. Although he wasn't a suspect, they still didn't know if he was linked to Nigel Collins. Given his record it could quite conceivably be true that he had happened to burgle from two of the four murder victims but how that could relate back to their prime suspect was just another mystery in a long list.

Following that, Jessica and Cole went to the interview room to talk to Scott Keegan. Jessica almost felt sorry for him when he was brought up. He was more or less as she would have pictured him given Shaun Hogan's story. He was short with sandy-coloured short hair but looked strong across his shoulders. That was undermined by his pale white skin and the bags under his eyes; he didn't seem as if he had slept much. He had been told in the cells he was entitled to legal advice. He hadn't wanted to speak to his father on the phone and, as he didn't have much money of his own, had opted for the duty solicitor. Jessica thought he already looked defeated as he was led in. There was no swagger and none of the cockiness someone like Wayne Lapham had.

Cole started the tape and went through the usual spiel but Jessica had conducted enough interviews to know the young man sitting in front of her was going to confess to everything. When he had finished speaking, it was Jessica's turn. 'Do you know why you're here, Scott?'

He didn't look up. 'Yes.'

'I want to ask you about Nigel Collins.'

No answer.

'Scott?'

He still didn't respond.

'Scott, you know that name, don't you?'

From nowhere, Scott exploded into tears. Jessica couldn't make out much in the way of words from him, only sobs. No one said anything, allowing his cries to echo. 'Are you okay, Scott?' Jessica asked.

It seemed as if the solicitor was about to step in but, as he reached forwards, Scott said: 'It's why she's dead, isn't it?' His words were still half-drowned by tears but could be clearly made out. Jessica saw no reason to hide the truth; he would know soon enough anyway.

'We think so, yes. We think Nigel Collins murdered your mother yesterday.'

The sobs got louder again but Scott was clearly trying to talk through them. 'It's all my fault. Oh God, it's all my fault. I'm so sorry.'

Jessica looked at Cole, who gave a slight nod and they waited for Scott to quieten down again. 'Are you okay, Scott?' Jessica asked when he had.

'Yes.'

'Okay. I need you to tell me what happened with you and Nigel.'

Scott spilled everything, confirming pretty much everything Shaun Hogan had told them the previous day. He even took responsibility, saying he made up a story about seeing Nigel look at his girlfriend and admitting he had carried out most of the attack, pressuring his friends to join in. He spoke with very little interruption for over twenty minutes, Jessica just asking him to clarify a few points.

Maybe it wasn't crucial to either of the investigations but at the end she felt she had to ask the question, if only for her own benefit. 'Why did you do it, Scott?'

The fact he didn't even need to think about it was chilling in itself, though the way he said it did at least sound remorseful. 'It was something to do. Everyone knew he was just that weird guy who hung around and I thought it would be a laugh.'

All of *this* because some kid wanted something to do, thought Jessica.

'Why him?' she asked.

'I don't know. He was just there. Everyone knew he was a bit weird. There wasn't a reason.'

'Is there anything else?'

'No . . . just . . . I don't know why it happened. I was different then, angrier. Dad had left and . . . I just don't know. I'm so sorry.' He swallowed another sob before continuing. 'I've thought about it every night since but, at the time, I couldn't stop myself. I was hoping everything was over, going to uni and all . . .'

Jessica almost hated herself for the twinge of sorrow she felt for him. He had done something horrendous and unforgivable years previously and made it worse by coercing his friends into it too and covering everything up. But she could tell from the way he spoke that he genuinely had agonised over it in the years since. Scott would only have been thirteen at the time and now, years on, all these lives had been ripped apart.

Cole stepped in and formally charged Scott Keegan with attempted murder. The feeling was the charges would be revised down to grievous bodily harm before it got to court as there was no Nigel Collins to give evidence. They still had all the medical details on file from years before, plus the confession. It would be up to the CPS to decide. There would be a media release later to explain the link and Scott would be up in front of magistrates in the morning. Jonathan Prince and James Christensen had been arrested within the hour and would most likely join him whether they confessed or not; the evidence they had from Scott would be enough to charge them. Shaun Hogan might or might not appear via video link, Jessica didn't know. Given the fact they would all be feeling responsible for the murder of one of their parents, Jessica fully expected Jonathan and James to confess too.

What a mess.

Cole had gone to pass on the news to Aylesbury that they had a confession, while Jessica headed off to the main floor to see if any progress had been made on finding Nigel Collins. She couldn't help but feel they had traded in not knowing who the killer was to simply having no idea where to find him. There had been no luck with tracking down extra photos. Two members of staff from the children's home had been found but they had no mementoes and no idea who else would have anything. His previous schools had been visited and, though year photos he should have been in had been discovered, he wasn't in any of them. Jessica didn't think it was a surprise given the way he had been ostracised.

She did laugh when someone told her one of the officers had been in contact with the *Herald* to check their archives relating to the car crash that killed Nigel's parents, just in case there was a photo of him as an eleven-year-old. There wasn't of course but it was worth a try. She thought going to the paper would have simply given Garry Ashford another tip to follow up. From the *Herald*'s website that morning, she could see he had done well. Not only was there all the standard information everyone else had been given but he had somehow managed to get himself a chat with Kim Hogan. Jessica wondered how Garry had talked the girl around. It certainly seemed as if he'd had more success talking to her than she had.

Rowlands was bringing Wayne Lapham back to the station for a follow-up interview. They weren't expecting to get anything in relation to knowing Nigel Collins but it had to be done. For obvious reasons, Jessica wouldn't be taking part in that interview. She didn't know if Peter Hunt would be present. The jury had gone out in Harry's case the day before, so it seemed unlikely as he would still be at Crown Court waiting for a verdict. Besides, Wayne Lapham wasn't likely to be getting all the media coverage, considering the press had Nigel Collins and his four torturers to focus on now.

Jessica started to make her way back to her own office but a constable stopped her before she could reach the door. 'The DCI wants to see you,' he said.

Jessica went up the stairs, knocking and entering her

boss's office. Cole was still there. Usually his face was hard to read as he gave so little away but, as she looked at him sitting in the chair across the desk from Aylesbury, she thought he looked angry. There were visible worry lines across his forehead and he was shaking his head. She had never seen him like that before.

'Sir?' she said, looking at the chief inspector.

Aylesbury told her to sit down too, his own look stern. Her boss took no time in cutting straight to the point as his first three words made her heart sink and instantly explained Cole's expression. 'Serious Crime Division.'

32

It had been something that had been in the back of Jessica's mind pretty much since they first started working on the case. The Serious Crime Division always had it in their remit to step in and take on crimes of this magnitude, especially if solving it wasn't proving too easy, but their timing was something that was hard to take. She and her team had already done the hard work – they had found the connection between the victims and knew almost certainly who the killer was. They had even solved a case from six years ago, albeit accidentally – but that wasn't the point.

'Why are they talking about this now?' Jessica kept repeating.

Aylesbury let her vent all those feelings with very little response, nodding to show he was taking everything on board. Cole didn't add anything but even he seemed sympathetic. Aylesbury did explain the decision was going to be taken by people higher up the chain of command than him and assured her he had done his best through his dealings with DSI Davies to put her very views across. She doubted they were *exactly* her views, given the amount of off-the-cuff swearing she had just pulled out.

As it stood, nothing had been decided for certain but he told her things would be sorted out within the next twenty-four hours and they would most likely have a decision by the morning. Jessica would have put a lot of money on knowing precisely what the outcome would be. Given it had already been a long day and everyone was left in something of a limbo, the DCI told them both they may as well go home. He was going to be in talks for the rest of the evening, while there was still a press release he wanted to draft along with the office. The only thing Jessica had to console herself with was that, if she stuck her foot down on the drive out of the station, she might strike lucky and get a cameraman or two under the wheels.

Back at her empty flat, Jessica stomped around, slammed a few doors and generally took her aggression out on as many inanimate objects as were to hand. Or foot. At first, she'd had vague visions of somehow stumbling across Nigel Collins on the street outside her door.

It was ridiculous, of course, she didn't even know what he looked like. But perhaps he had some sort of scar or something? Maybe he wore a big sign around his neck with his name on, or a large top hat with neon flashing lights and a giant arrow? She knew it wasn't going to happen but thought how good it would be to find him that night before the SCD could take the case away. Then she could march in tomorrow morning, past the reporters, photographers and TV cameras and plonk Nigel Collins down in reception and give a big, collective middle finger to anyone who had doubted her. Of course, given she was the person who doubted herself the most, that middle finger would be as much for her as anyone else.

As her irrational fantasies got more and more out of hand while Jessica sat on the sofa stewing, she heard the front door go. 'Hi?'

'Oh hi,' Caroline's voice called out. 'You're home.'

Randall was with her too but Jessica didn't mind. For once she actually felt like some company. After saying their hellos and some brief small talk, Caroline said she would cook for them all. Jessica hadn't eaten all day and wasn't particularly hungry but her friend said she didn't mind if there were leftovers. Jessica shifted over to the recliner and they all ate off their laps, watching some soap opera on television that none of them apparently followed. Jessica would have had anything on TV that wasn't the news. The food was good, some sort of rice dish, and they laughed together at a preposterous story twist involving a long lost uncle, while she tried to forget about events at work. It must have been clear she wasn't in the mood to talk about it as neither Caroline nor Randall asked her how the day had gone.

After they had eaten, the two women did the dishes while Randall joked he was exempt from kitchen duties. 'A woman's place . . .' was all he said with a grin. Caroline bashed him around the head with her hand and told him that, in that case, he should be out skinning a bear or something similar to provide for them.

They shared a bottle of wine as they lounged in the living room when everything had been tidied away.

'Jess, can we talk for a minute?' Caroline said softly.

Jessica knew from the tone it would be something serious but she wasn't ready to listen to things straight away. 'You're not pregnant, are you?'

Jessica and Randall laughed but Caroline peered down and started stroking her belly. 'No, why, have I put on weight?'

'Well, I didn't want to say anything . . .' Jessica said.

'Oi! Cheeky.'

They all laughed but, when the mood had settled, Caroline tried again. 'Seriously, can we talk for a minute?' The two girls looked at each other and Jessica knew what was coming. 'Randall quit his job today. He's been offered an apprenticeship with a design company in the city.'

'That's great, congratulations,' Jessica said, looking across to the man on their sofa. He had a small grin on his face.

'That's not all though. We had been talking about it but, when he got the news, he went out and put a deposit down on a flat we're going to rent while we look to buy somewhere. We want to know we can live together before we make too big a splash.'

Jessica had known it was coming but still felt something in her stomach. It was an odd feeling. She was delighted for her friend but there was a part of her that selfishly wanted them to stay living together until Jessica herself had found someone.

'I'm so pleased for you both,' Jessica said, getting up from her seat to hug the pair of them. 'You make a great couple.'

'Is it really okay?' Caroline asked.

'Of course.' As she finished hugging Randall, Jessica also gave him a playful smack on the head. 'But none of this "Get in the kitchen" malarkey, yeah?'

They all laughed again but Jessica had to force it as she sat back down.

'We're not going straight away,' Caroline said. 'We've got a month so we are going to move things in bit by bit.'

'So I've got to put up with your dodgy cooking for another four weeks?'

'I'm afraid so, yes.'

'So it's all marriage, kids, the works then?'

'Get out of it. Not yet.'

Caroline and Randall snuggled closer on the sofa and Jessica strongly suspected the 'not yet' part was critical. Looking at them, she didn't think it would take long. 'The big question is what does his mum make of you?' Jessica said. 'There's got to be a bit of competition there now for his attention. You're going to be the tart who stole her precious little boy away.'

'Mum and Dad live abroad,' Randall said. 'I reckon they'd be big fans though.'

The wine bottle was empty so Caroline sent her boyfriend off to the kitchen to get another. 'And get used to waiting on me hand and foot,' she called after him. They heard the toilet door go while they were waiting.

'Are you sure you're going to be okay?' Caroline asked.

'Of course. I'm a big girl and all that.'

'Are you going to stay here?'

'I don't know. Probably. I can afford the rent on my own. It's close to work, which helps.'

'Maybe you can get some fish for company?' Caroline had a mischievous look on her face.

'Yeah, right. I don't think I'd trust myself to look after some other living creature.' She remembered the stuffed chicken from Hugo's house, thinking that was just about her limit.

'Is everything okay with . . . the case?'

Jessica didn't want to get into things, so just nodded. 'Yeah, it's fine.'

Jessica felt like a condemned woman on the drive to work the next morning. Rain was lashing down which at least meant the full press pack wouldn't be outside the station's gates in such force. 'Journalists,' she said to no one in particular while driving, 'a group of people on a never-ending quest for the truth . . . unless it's pissing down and then the truth can go bugger itself.'

There were a few people outside the gates but nothing like the day before. She weaved in between a couple of television cameras and made sure that the car shielded her from any unwanted long camera shots when she parked up. Even though she felt sure the case was going to be taken from her, she had still spent the morning watching the news. The tragic story of Nigel Collins was everywhere, while the link had obviously been made to the three young men who were going to be in court that morning and the one who was already in jail. Jessica realised that was probably why the throngs outside the gate had thinned so much – everyone was at the magistrates' court instead.

She first went upstairs but Aylesbury saw her through his office window and waved her away. He was on the phone and most likely deciding her future. She returned to reception and spent a few moments watching the rolling news on the mounted television. There were some outside shots of the courts but nothing much was happening. There was still some presenter talking frantically as the drizzle poured in shot behind him. 'Just go indoors,' she said quietly.

Jessica grabbed a copy of the *Herald* from the reception desk and disappeared off to her office. Reynolds wasn't around, so she took off her shoes and leant back into her chair to read it. The front page was a given so she flicked straight past that but inside Garry Ashford had another background piece, this time with Paul Keegan.

It was labelled as an exclusive and Jessica couldn't help but be impressed that the journalist had managed to get both Kim Hogan and Paul Keegan to speak to him in successive days. He hadn't phoned her since she'd told him not to and, in some ways, she felt a bit sorry about that. As annoying as he was, his phone call after each find had almost been the proverbial kick she needed to get things moving properly. It also allowed her to blow off some steam with some choice words too, of course.

The article itself was mainly a tribute to Paul Keegan's wife. It skirted around the details of Scott's involvement, which had been written about elsewhere, but included things about charity work she had done and how many years she had given to the nursing profession. It was nicely written and Jessica couldn't help but feel her emotions stirring, thinking what a waste of life it was.

She flicked through the pages and thought how odd it was that one news story could be about something so dark, yet overleaf was a light-hearted article about some world record cross-stitching attempt; it was bizarre.

There was a knock at the door. 'Yep. Come in.'

Aylesbury entered and Jessica quickly wheeled around in an attempt to not look quite so casual. She put the newspaper down over her keyboard. 'Sir.'

Her superior sat in Reynolds' seat across the desk from her. He looked around the room, clearly taking in Jessica's messy half, but said nothing.

'I've just been to see Detective Inspector Cole,' he began. Jessica knew where the rest of the conversation would go. She stared at a spot on her desk, refusing to meet his eye. 'After speaking to Superintendent Davies this morning following various discussions last night, it has been decided that the Serious Crime Division will be taking over responsibility for finding Nigel Collins.'

Jessica said nothing, continuing to focus on her desk. 'I'm sorry. Everyone appreciates the work you and the team have put into this investigation.' He paused as if to give her an opening to reply. She didn't trust what she might blurt out, though. 'Jessica?'

He had never once called her by her first name, always 'Detective' or 'DS Daniel'. She looked at him and, perhaps for the first time, saw him as a man, rather than a policeman who was her superior. He was staring at her with his head slightly tilted to one side. 'I'm proud of you. I don't think anyone could have expected more.'

Jessica felt a lump in her throat. She wanted to speak, if

only to tell him to leave so he wouldn't see her burst into tears but no words would come out. Surely, she couldn't cry again? Not in front of her boss. She blinked hard and fought not to lose it. 'Thank you, Sir,' she managed to croak out.

He must have seen how close to tears she was but didn't react. She knew it was highly unprofessional. 'There will be other cases. You have proven to everyone you can handle serious matters.'

Jessica nodded but still couldn't speak.

'Okay. I've got to go and speak to a few more people and then arrange for exactly how things are going to work. Feel free to finish up any paperwork you have outstanding and liaise with Detective Inspector Cole.'

He swiftly stood up and turned around, exiting the room and closing the door behind him. Jessica didn't move but could hear the hum of people working outside. She blew her nose and then closed her eyes and breathed in deeply. She didn't know if she was angry or upset. Another knock came on the door shortly after and, thinking it was Aylesbury back for some reason, she again composed herself. 'Come in.'

The door opened and it was Rowlands.

'All right?' she said.

'Yes, come on. The verdict's due.'

He dashed back out of the room, presumably expecting Jessica to follow. She was confused at first, thinking Scott Keegan and co had only just appeared for their first appearance that morning, then she clocked it was Harry's case at the Crown Court. The jury had been out for two days and must have returned.

She quickly put her shoes back on and followed after Rowlands into the reception area. It seemed ridiculous that members of a modern police force were waiting in their own entrance foyer watching a small portable TV screen high on a wall. There were other televisions around the station but none specifically hooked up. There were various health and safety guidelines about setting up electrical items and, even if there weren't, Jessica suspected a lot of the crew wouldn't have been able to figure out where all the leads went anyway. Rather than mess around everyone had dashed to the nearest working screen.

She could see a presenter standing outside a different court to the one from that morning. He was being shielded by an umbrella as the wind blew his hair around. Across the bottom of the screen scrolled the words: 'Tom Carpenter verdict due'. The sound was up but Jessica couldn't hear what was being said over the expectant chatter. A library photo of Peter Hunt appeared on the screen to enormous boos and various insults that rhymed with 'Hunt' around the room.

Jessica knew that if the jury believed Tom Carpenter had been attacked first or thought he might be, they could decide he was allowed to use 'reasonable force' to defend himself. In most cases a knife would not be reasonable but, given the way Harry had been portrayed as out of control, they might just be swayed.

There was no doubt Carpenter had stabbed Harry but, according to the desk sergeant, Carpenter had claimed on oath that Harry had come at him with a glass. The knife was in his pocket and he had acted instinctively. Jessica knew that didn't sound like Harry to her but, with all the witnesses conveniently being in the toilets at the time and no one to say any differently, it was Harry's word against Carpenter's. That meant it would come down to the jury but Harry certainly hadn't helped himself. If they believed the force Carpenter had used was reasonable, they would find him not guilty.

Jessica thought of the two female jurors on the front row and the man she thought would be the foreman. She wondered if any of them had been swayed by her. Had the man on the end been pushing for a guilty verdict or did he believe Harry had been a threat?

Suddenly the scrolling text at the bottom stopped and it was as if everyone held their breath collectively. The room was silent as the presenter frantically looked behind him. The breaking news ribbon began to move along the bottom of the screen again, the words scrolling in slow motion.

'Tom Carpenter found not guilty.'

As soon as the words had been revealed, the room erupted with shouts of derision and cries of unfairness. Jessica thought she swore a lot but some of the language shocked even her and that was nothing compared to the outrage as Peter Hunt emerged from court side by side with Tom Carpenter.

Jessica tried to shush everyone as the camera dashed towards the two people in the court's entrance. Microphones appeared in front of them from all directions and finally everyone in the station quietened down.

Hunt was beaming even wider than his client. He had

clearly made a special effort with his appearance that morning just in case this moment came. He looked more polished than ever and had some unnamed aide holding an umbrella over him. Jessica thought she wanted to listen to it but as soon as Hunt's first words came, 'This is justification . . .', she drifted away from the pack back towards her office.

Poor Harry.

33

For the rest of the week, the papers and news bulletins had been full of both Tom Carpenter's acquittal and the force's failure to find Nigel Collins. Peter Hunt had a field day, appearing on a breakfast news programme, both of the major twenty-four-hour news channels and at least two national newspapers. He had been the main guest for a radio phone-in where the question was: 'Are Britain's police incompetent?' As she listened to the broadcast on her drive to work, Jessica wondered what kind of lonely lunatic rang these types of show, spouting ill-informed mindless nonsense. She reckoned they would be on the phone pretty sharpish if they needed the police's assistance. The presenter's smug annoying tone, 'So are Britain's police a total bag of useless shits,' he might as well have been saying, drove her crazy. She made a mental note that if she ever came across an emergency call from someone called 'Sue from Bromsgrove' she would quite happily ignore it.

'We'll see who's incompetent then, you old hag,' Jessica told the radio.

If that wasn't bad enough, Tom Carpenter had sold his story to a red-top tabloid. 'CRAZED COP GLASS TERROR' put across his version of events in all its made-up glory. Harry had been painted as an out-of-control drink-fuelled corrupt officer. She had tried calling Harry half-a-dozen times since the verdict but his phone wasn't on.

It summed up Jessica's week. Even though the SCD had taken their case, her department was still getting hammered on two fronts. She had been forced to brief one of the SCD officers the day after handing the files over, talking them through her notes and letting them know where everything was on the computer system. The smug git spent the entire two hours with a 'We're cleaning up your mess' look on his face that Jessica had felt desperate to wipe off.

She had been put on the case of a man who robbed an off-licence with a weapon. The shop's owner had been smashed in the face with a claw hammer and had his week's takings ransacked from the safe. Jessica had spoken to the distraught victim who kept repeating he was pleased his wife hadn't been present as she often worked that shift. Jessica did her best to work as she usually would, gathering the CCTV footage and so on, but could feel her heart wasn't in it. Every time she was driving, whenever she went to bed at night or had a quiet moment, her thoughts drifted back to Nigel Collins. She felt bad for not focusing fully on her job but had invested so much energy in the 'Houdini' case, it was hard to forget.

By the Friday night, she was sick of the week as a whole and pledged to curl up at home with her old friend: the local supermarket's own-brand cheap rosé wine. Caroline and Randall had gone off to set a few things up in their new flat, ready to start moving, and she had the place to herself. She was halfway through watching a repeat of some talent show she had no interest in when a thought dropped into her head. She had gone through two-thirds of the bottle by herself, which she was pretty sure was influencing her decision-making. She picked her phone up from the coffee table, scrolled through her list of contacts, and pressed the 'call' button when it reached Garry Ashford's name.

It rang twice before being picked up. 'Hello?'

'Garry, it's Jess Daniel.'

'DS Daniel?'

'Yeah, call me Jess.'

'Okay . . . Are you all right?'

'Wanna come keep me company?'

'Sorry?'

'One-time only offer.'

'Er, yeah, I guess . . .'

The poor guy sounded scared stiff. Jessica gave him her address. 'Oh and Garry,' she added. '*Don't* wear the tweed. *Do* bring your notes about Houdini and *do* bring wine.'

She hung up.

Garry Ashford arrived forty-five minutes later with a carrier bag full of notebooks and two bottles of wine; one red, one white. 'I didn't know which you preferred, so bought one of each,' he said.

'Actually I usually go for rosé,' Jessica replied with a wink, taking the bottles from him.

In the time before him arriving, she had phoned up the takeaway a few streets over to order some curries. The first bottle of wine had begun to kick in and she really fancied something hot to go with it but they hadn't arrived.

As Garry walked in, Jessica thought he was actually dressed like a functioning member of the human race that evening. He was wearing a pair of regular blue jeans with a red T-shirt. She let him into the flat and led him into the living room, before leaving one of the bottles of wine off in the kitchen and opening the other. She took an extra glass into the living room and handed it to her guest, before filling both his and her own.

He was sitting on the sofa and had started taking his notebooks out from the carrier bag. Jessica sat next to him. 'Christ, Garry, did you make all this effort for me? Your hair looks as if you've only been dragged through a hedge once tonight instead of the usual three or four times.'

Garry smiled. 'I feel privileged now I've finally achieved the Holy Trinity of insults.'

'Huh?'

'You've now taken the piss out of my name, dress sense and looks.'

Jessica did actually feel a bit bad, realising not everyone would get her sense of humour. 'Sorry, I was only joking.'

Garry looked at her. 'It's all right. At least I don't look as bad as that photo we used of you on the front page. I mean what kind of crazed woman grins underneath a headline about a murder?'

Jessica playfully punched him in the shoulder. 'Oi.'

They both laughed and then Garry asked the obvious question: 'Why am I here?'

Jessica downed the rest of her glass in one and looked

at him. 'To be honest, I'm not sure. You know they've taken the case away, don't you?'

'Yes.'

'I've looked over my notes and the files and it's been in the back of my mind the whole time that I've missed something obvious. I guess I just thought . . . I guess it's because you're not police. Before I'm ready to let it go completely I suppose I wondered if you might have picked up something I missed.'

'I doubt it. I've only been following where you lot have been, talking to the same people and so on.'

'Maybe . . .'

Garry took out his first notebook but as he did the doorbell went.

'Curry,' Jessica said.

'Oh, right.'

'Don't worry, I got you something mild and wimpy. I thought it seemed your style.'

Garry shook his head slightly but then answered. 'Yeah, you're probably right.'

After Jessica returned with a grease-soaked paper bag and some forks from the kitchen, Garry opened his first notebook. Jessica had a peek at the contents just in case she could make out a name that could be his source.

The journalist clocked her doing so. 'Their name isn't written here, y'know.'

'Whose?' Jessica replied with a half-smile.

Garry nodded and started to talk her through some of the people he had spoken to and what they had said. Jessica knew she probably shouldn't but, given she was now off the case, she filled in some of the blanks for him. He asked if he could make new notes on what she had told him.

'Okay, fine,' she replied. 'But only because you brought wine.'

They ate as they worked. Jessica had gone for the hottest chicken dish on the menu but Garry struggled with his mild lamb meal. Jessica laughed at him while he told her she stank. It seemed like a childish insult but was probably true.

The journalist spoke about Stephanie and Ray Wilson and how Stephanie hadn't had too much to say but had genuinely seemed disturbed by the loss of her friend. He said the husband had phoned the paper every day for the week afterwards to remind them he and his wife were available for photographs if the paper needed them.

As he got to his notes about the meeting with Jessica herself, he veered off to tell her about the pressures he was under and how his career hadn't turned out the way he had hoped. He talked about his editor and how sales were affecting all of the staff. Until the last few weeks, he had been thinking of quitting and would have done already if it wasn't for the money.

'What else would you do?' Jessica asked.

'I don't know really. Write? I have no idea. It's not easy to just drop everything. You don't want to end up going back to your parents to admit you've made a right mess, do you?'

Jessica couldn't disagree with that.

Garry told her about his meeting with Marie Hall and

the way he had been bullied into buying a host of drinks to get any details about Wayne Lapham. Jessica admitted she hadn't known who the woman was before but laughed at Garry's pub story. Then they both dissolved into giggles when he spoke about the dressing gown the woman had been wearing.

'Was it peach?' Jessica asked.

'Eew, yes. She hadn't fastened it completely either.'

'Oh God, you couldn't see . . .' Garry didn't answer but the look on his face made Jessica explode with laughter. She went to put the empty food cartons in the kitchen and get the other bottle of wine Garry had brought. By now she was feeling decidedly tipsy but refilled both of their glasses and let the journalist continue.

'Then I finally ended up speaking to you,' he said, flicking through pages and pages of notes. 'You were very, erm . . . revealing.'

Jessica felt a bit embarrassed remembering her phone confessions to him. 'You took advantage of a distressed young woman, Garry. You should feel ashamed of yourself.'

'Young?'

'Oi, you cheeky . . .' For the second time that evening Jessica playfully punched her guest in the shoulder. 'How did you end up talking to Kim Hogan?' she asked as Garry opened another notebook.

'It was an accident. I was at the house talking to the neighbour who was spilling everything. The other girl stormed up and started swearing at the both of us.' Jessica thought that sounded familiar. 'Anyway, I said that she could put her own version across if she wanted. She asked if there was money involved . . .'

'Really?' Jessica interrupted.

'Yeah. Sometimes people are like that, no matter what the circumstances.'

'Did you pay her?'

'I gave her twenty quid. It was all I had on me. I ended up walking back to the office because I didn't have anything left for the bus.'

'Doesn't the paper pay for things like that?'

'You must be joking. You're lucky if they pay for notebooks and pens.'

'What was she like?'

'I've had worse interviews but not many. She was okay really but it was hard for her. There was just lots of swearing. She hates your lot and kept going on about kids bugging her mum and how you never did anything.'

'What about Paul Keegan?'

Garry let out a massive sigh. 'It was horrible. I didn't want to knock on his door but the editor basically told me to do it. I thought the guy would tell me to get lost but instead he invited me in and went to put the kettle on. It was surreal.'

Jessica had thought that the whole time she had spoken to Paul Keegan. She could see that inside his heart was broken but outside he was almost normal. Some people in the force would see that type of behaviour as how guilty people acted. She just thought everyone was different but did wonder how he was really coping behind closed doors, especially with what had happened regarding his stepson.

'He talked and talked,' Garry added. 'He said they had only been married a few years ago. He showed me all the photos and told me everything that ended up in the article. He was a really nice guy and told me to call back if I wanted to check anything, He phoned on the day of the article to say "thanks". He said he was going to keep the paper and reckoned it was a perfect tribute to her.'

'Poor guy.'

'I know. I felt so sorry for him. You don't know what to say, do you? He said they'd had problems with kids in the area but he thought your lot had done your best. Bit of a difference to Kim and Marie.'

Garry gave a small laugh but Jessica didn't. 'Hmmm,' she said.

'You all right?'

'Yeah, just too much of this,' she said holding up an empty glass. 'Shall we call it a night? I'll even pay for your taxi.'

'It's okay. I reckon I'll get another story out of the bits you've told me. "Senior source", yeah?'

'Source.'

'Whatever.'

Garry packed his things back into his bag and gave a little wobble as he stood up. Jessica could feel the alcohol inside her too. She walked him to the door and found herself giving him a little hug as they said goodbye. She thought his cheeks had reddened slightly afterwards but it could have been the booze for him too.

'Thanks for your help tonight, Garry.'

'No worries, Det . . . Jess.'

'Good night.' Jessica closed the door but instantly took her phone out and typed a reminder into the calendar for the next morning. It was probably nothing and possibly just the wine doing her thinking but she'd had an idea and didn't want to forget it when she woke up.

34

Jessica had never had big hangovers in her life. There was always the odd morning after when Caroline had been at university and the two of them had gone out but nothing crazy and she had never lost days or anything silly like some of the stories people could tell.

She woke up on the Saturday morning with an aching neck, a world-class headache and the distinct taste of last night's curry in her mouth. The room was ridiculously bright and she again cursed herself for not contacting the landlord. She fumbled her way out of the cocoon she had made of her duvet and realised she was still wearing the clothes she'd had on the whole of the previous day and evening. Craving water, she staggered out of her bedroom and made her way groggily towards the kitchen.

'Caroline?'

She hadn't heard her friend and Randall come in the previous night but, considering how much she had drunk, that was no particular surprise. There wasn't any answer anyway, so presumably the two of them had stopped the night at the new flat.

Jessica turned on the sink's tap and almost hypnotically watched the water gush out and hold her attention. Vague memories of her chat with Garry the previous evening came flooding back. Had she hugged him? She saw the three empty bottles of wine next to the bin.

She shook her head and snapped her gaze away from the water, snatching a glass from the draining board and filling it up. She downed the whole glass in one and filled it back up again. After that, she hunted around in the drawer under the sink for some aspirin and took three along with another full glass of water. She was pretty sure the recommended dose was two tablets but that was surely for a standard headache?

Regardless, she fumbled her way back to bed and lay down. The ceiling was still spinning but not too badly and she could hear a buzzing noise from somewhere. She looked from one side of the bed to the other, confused by the sound, before realising it was coming from her phone, which was face down on the nightstand. Her head had started to clear slightly but she still struggled to pick her phone up, unable to figure out what the specific tone was. It was definitely a different noise to her alarm and text message sounds. Her fingers didn't seem to want to do what her brain was willing them to but she eventually managed to unlock the screen and saw there was a calendar alert and a separate text message.

She read the text first: it was from Caroline.

'Been called into work CU later. X'

Jessica then pressed the button to read the note she had left herself the previous evening.

It may have been the ramblings of a drunk woman but she had nothing better to do – as soon as she'd had a shower, Jessica resolved to follow the note up, even if she did end up looking stupid.

'Sorry, who are you?'

Jessica was listening to an irate voice from the other end of her phone.

'Kim, it's Detective Sergeant Daniel. We spoke at the station. Do you remember?'

'What do *you* want?' Kim Hogan's tone didn't indicate she was overly receptive to being called by a member of the police.

'I just wanted to clarify a point or two with you if that's all right?'

'I read yesterday your lot had been booted off the case or something like that. Some super cop people brought in to clean up your mess and find that Collins psycho.'

'That's not really true, Kim.' Jessica realised that in essence it actually was correct but she still wanted the girl to answer one question.

'What do you want? I told you everything last time.'

'I want to check one thing with you.'

'Fine. Just get on with it.'

'You know when you told me we hadn't done much about kids harassing your mum, what did you mean?'

'Well, you didn't, did you? Your lot wouldn't even come out.'

'To what, though, Kim?'

'It doesn't matter now, does it?'

Jessica was already feeling exasperated and glad she

hadn't gone to see the girl in person, as had been her original plan. She'd had to phone the station and ask for a favour on the quiet to get someone to pass Kim's contact details on to her. There were a few people she trusted to keep something like that under the radar.

'I'm not trying to trip you up, Kim. I just want to make sure we've checked all angles.'

'Fine. Look, it went on for a while. There was always kids knocking on the door and running and all that and harassing her on the street. But then one of them put glue in the front-door lock one night. We had to climb out the window. Your lot hadn't done anything before and were always hassling Mum on the street so she couldn't be bothered. She just got . . . someone she knew to fix things.'

Jessica's heart was racing, all signs of a hangover long gone. 'Who?'

'I dunno. I wasn't even in. Just someone she knew.'

Jessica didn't want to ask the obvious but couldn't see a way around it. 'One of her clients?'

'Piss off. Don't talk about her like that.'

'Please, Kim. I . . . Look, it could be really helpful.'

'Whatever. I don't know. It was just someone she knew.'

Jessica apologised for the call, ignored the sweary response and hung up. She was in her living room, sitting on the sofa in a still-empty flat. She took a deep breath, her heart still charging. She would have to make at least two more phone calls with the first to Garry Ashford to get Paul Keegan's phone number. She didn't want to risk another call to the station to get information that technically she wasn't entitled to any longer. It most likely wouldn't have got her in trouble but she didn't want to alert anyone to the fact she was still doing background work on the case.

She kept the call to Garry short and didn't give him any reason why she needed the number. He sounded more hungover than she did but text-messaged her the number. Straight away Jessica phoned Paul Keegan. The poor guy sounded shattered on the other end and she just couldn't bring herself to ask him anything over the phone. She asked if he could spare an hour or so and they arranged to meet in a cafe local to him. He sounded grateful to be getting out of the house. Jessica thought about driving but didn't want to risk still being over the limit from the night before. The place they were meeting was only a bus ride away and she figured it would give her time to consider how best to approach things.

Paul Keegan was already waiting for her when Jessica arrived. The place they had arranged to meet was his choice, a greasy-spoon establishment just off a main road not too far from his house. Jessica could smell the fat as she walked through the door, instantly reminding her of childhood. She and her parents used to spend two weeks every summer in Blackpool. At the time, the sea front was lined with places like this, dirt-cheap cafes competing to sell the cheapest cup of tea and fighting to get as many people in as possible to play bingo. This was the sort of place that had once been the lifeblood of a city like Manchester but had largely died out in the last few years, replaced by posher, more expensive chain restaurants. There were still a few remaining, mainly on the outskirts where defiant locals would still go for a fry-up and a brew a couple of times a week.

There was a low chatter as Jessica spotted Paul Keegan off to her right, not far from the counter. He had a mug of tea on the table in front of him. She said hello and asked if he wanted anything to eat or a refill but he shook his head to both. Jessica ordered and paid for a cup of tea, although she wasn't entirely sure it would be of a much better standard than the ones from the machines in the station and then took it back to sit opposite Mr Keegan. 'Thanks for coming,' she said.

'No worries, it's fine. It's nice to get away from the house to be honest. We weren't allowed back for a couple of days and now it doesn't feel right.'

Jessica didn't know how to begin to respond to that. It was a horrendous thought to have to return to live in a house where your wife was murdered. He was clearly trying to sound positive but it was obvious he was struggling to cope. She didn't think going straight in to ask the one question she wanted to would be that tactful.

'How are you doing?' she asked.

She knew the answer wouldn't be terrific but she didn't want to ask directly about his stepson. Magistrates had refused Scott initial bail, fearing he and the other two who admitted to assaulting Nigel Collins could run. They had all confessed to the crime and it was just a matter of time until it came to court.

'I don't really know,' he said. 'It's Steven I feel sorry for the most. He's had to go back to do his final exams with all this hanging over him. With all the funeral arrangements and everything I've not really stopped for the past few days. I even went to see Scott yesterday . . .'

Jessica must have looked surprised because he felt the need to justify what he had said. 'He's not a bad kid. He had a bad time when his dad and Mary split up. Don't get me wrong, I know and he knows that what he did was wrong but . . .'

He didn't finish the sentence but Jessica knew what he was alluding to. Most people did something stupid when they were younger. That wasn't to excuse what Scott had done in any way but one stupid immature decision when he was barely a teenager had now cost him any semblance of an adult life. She couldn't help but be impressed by his stepfather. Paul Keegan had every right to hate a son that wasn't his own flesh and blood but had indirectly caused the death of his wife. Yet he didn't; it seemed he had already forgiven him. Jessica was stunned by the man's compassion.

'Do you want another?' she asked, nodding towards his now-empty cup on the table.

'Yeah, okay.'

'Anything to eat?'

Paul Keegan shook his head.

Jessica thought he looked as if he could do with a meal but knew she couldn't force him. She went to the counter and ordered a new mug of tea before returning to the table. When Jessica sat down, he asked her why her team had been removed from the case. She gave the best answer she could, trying to sound professional and remarking that the Serious Crime Division had more training in this type of area now it had essentially become a search for one man. She thought it sounded good, even if she didn't believe it herself.

'I just wanted to check one thing with you, if that's okay?' Jessica said.

'No worries.'

'Do you remember when you told me you'd had a few problems with kids recently, what kind of problems did you mean?'

'Oh, the usual. Kids out and about at night, just noise and that. Someone ended up putting Super Glue in our locks. We had to climb out the window, plus get someone to change them and get a bunch of new keys cut.'

Jessica struggled to respond. How had she not asked this question before? She went to speak but stumbled over her words. It almost seemed as if time had slowed down before she finally managed to reply. 'How long ago?'

The penny had clearly dropped for Paul Keegan too. 'Why, do you think . . . ? Umm, a few months, five or six.'

'Do you know who fixed the locks?'

'No, I was at work while Mary was off but um . . .' He stopped speaking and was clearly mulling something over. 'Yeah, yeah, I remember. Here's the thing; we got this flyer through the door literally the day before it happened. It was some kind of special offer thing. Mary always kept the mail and everything so neatly on the table next to the door. It seemed like a piece of good fortune at the time.'

Jessica's mind was racing and she prayed the answer to her next question would be positive. 'Did you keep the flyer?'

'Oh . . . I don't know. Mary usually kept things like that just in case. I don't know if it was one of those things you had to hand in.'

'Can we have a look?'

'Of course.'

Paul Keegan quickly stood up, clearly understanding what could be happening. He marched towards the door, Jessica just behind. His house was only a few minutes' walk away and Jessica followed him along a cut-through towards the estate. Neither of them said a word. Jessica could feel the nerves in her stomach. Suddenly things seemed to be making sense, at least for the final two victims. Nigel Collins had tracked down Claire Hogan and perhaps befriended her as a client. Then he had sabotaged the lock on her front door by squirting glue into it and just happened to be there to fix it for her. It would have been so easy to keep a copy of the key for himself. He could have either let himself in, murdered her, then left, locking up on the way out, or he could have gone to her as a client, killed her and locked the door behind him.

Even the 'why' seemed clear. It was as Hugo had told her – misdirection. While the police were busy trying to find out how the crimes had taken place, they weren't focusing on what linked the bodies. He had even used the trouble with local kids as another way of directing attention away from himself but this time for the victims. The victims had blamed local children for the trouble, not bothering to trust the police to do anything.

Something similar would have happened with Mary Keegan, except Collins had been even cleverer, all but ensuring the Keegans would come to him to get their door fixed. He cunningly posted a flyer through their door offering a cheap deal and then damaged their locks not long after. It wasn't entirely foolproof but everyone liked a good bargain.

It would be a pretty good bet the Christensens and Princes had to have had their locks changed after being robbed too. Most people obviously wanted it doing for their own piece of mind but it was usually an insurance requirement after a burglary anyway. How Collins had managed to make sure he had a key for those properties wasn't exactly clear and there were still gaps, such as how he knew where everyone lived – but she knew she had figured out a large part of everything.

Now she just had to figure out the final but largest part of the puzzle – where was Nigel Collins?

Paul Keegan unlocked the same front door Jessica herself had done not that long ago when she had discovered Mary's body and they both went in. She remembered the tidy stack of post on the table next to the front door and it looked as if it had been added to. She was led into the kitchen and Paul opened a drawer to the left of the sink. 'We keep things like menus and vouchers and so on in here. If it's not here, it won't be anywhere.'

He pulled out a big pile of glossy pieces of paper and put them on the kitchen table. Jessica was on one side as he sat opposite her. They each started looking through a very large heap. Jessica worked quickly. She could see from some of the vouchers that the expiry date was years old. The whole house was spotless but this seemed to be something of a forbidden drawer, where all sorts of miscellaneous junk was thrown just in case. Her dad kept a similar hoard at home.

She didn't want to seem disrespectful and copied Paul by putting the pamphlets that weren't useful in a separate pile. Her stack was twice the size of Mary's husband's, who was taking time to read each piece of paper, while she was far more ruthless. There were lots of menus, plus vouchers for money off fried chicken and pizza, various flyers for local supermarkets or the off-licence on the main road. Between them the initial selection was down to around a quarter of its original size.

Jessica started to put one more sheet on her discard pile and then she saw it. She had been so close to tossing it away but stopped in mid-action and brought the flyer back towards her so she could read it. She scanned the words, her eyes flicking from side to side and reading the contents twice over.

She knew where to find Nigel Collins.

35

Paul Keegan watched her take the flyer. He had stopped sorting himself and glanced up. 'Have you found it?'

'Yes.'

'Can I see it?'

'I'm not sure that's a good idea.' Jessica didn't think he was the type to go storming off looking for revenge but she didn't want to risk giving it back to him just in case. It looked as if he understood anyway.

He nodded gently and simply made one request. 'Just make sure you get him,' he said sadly.

Jessica followed the details on the flyer to the address it had given. Things almost made sense, though there were still gaps. The location listed would have almost certainly been the place closest to all four homes if they wanted to get keys cut. As well as being the nearest place, there was a good chance it would be the cheapest too. All of the victims were local and would have been well aware of those facts.

It was quite possible the person that ran the place would have had the skills to replace a lock for Claire Hogan too but, even if he didn't himself, there was still a very reasonable connection. Jessica didn't know if she would ever truly know the whole story – unless Nigel Collins was willing to talk after he had been caught. There was perhaps still some coincidence but maybe she just didn't know the whole story yet.

The biggest problem Jessica had was that she couldn't find the place listed. She knew she was roughly in the right area but found herself walking in circles. She had made at least two laps of the site, weaving in and out of the people and checking each possible location individually. She didn't understand how she could be missing it.

Eventually she decided she just didn't have enough knowledge of that precise area and that she should ask someone who did. She walked up to the closest person, took out the flyer and held it up to the man in front of her.

'Hi. I was wondering if you knew where this place is?'

The man squinted to look at the paper in her hand. 'Hang on a minute, love. I'll need my glasses.' The man fiddled with a pocket on the inside of his jacket and took out a case, before removing a pair of bifocals. He put them on and reached out for the flyer. Jessica was reluctant to let it go, given it could be used as evidence at some point, but released her grip nonetheless. The man took it and scanned through the words. 'Sorry love, I'm only here on Saturdays. Not a clue.'

He gave it back but Jessica was silently fuming. 'Why didn't you just bloody say that in the first place,' she thought to herself.

She decided to ask a woman close by, walking over and holding the flyer out once again. 'Hi. I was just wondering if you know where this place is?'

The woman took the paper from her and gave it a read.

'Do you know the offer's out of date?' Jessica felt like shaking the woman. 'Of course I bloody know,' she thought. 'I do know how to read. Just answer the question.'

Instead, she actually said: 'It's okay. I was looking to find the place rather than use the offer.'

The woman shrugged at her, pointing the way Jessica had come from. 'It should be on the end just over there.'

Jessica took the flyer back, put it in her bag, said 'thank you' and turned around. She was puzzled as she knew she had checked each place behind her. She figured the woman knew better than her, so walked back the way she had come and paid even more attention to her surroundings.

She reached the place on the end, where the woman told her she should be looking and got as close as she could without drawing too much attention. The woman must surely be wrong – this place didn't deal with locks . . .

And then Jessica saw it.

It did deal with locks. It also engraved signs and trophies, plus sold batteries and various leather goods but that wasn't the main function of the Gorton Market stall.

Now she could see why she had missed it. Each time she had walked past before she had simply seen the sign for shoe repairs.

And then she knew exactly who Nigel Collins was.

There had been no better feeling than ditching the name Nigel Collins. It was something that reminded him of being weak and pathetic, of seeing those fists pounding down upon him until he woke up in hospital. People had thought he was stupid and weird but there was nothing wrong with being quiet. His parents had died for crying out loud and he had been left in a children's home he despised. What did people want him to say and do? He had only been a child and all the other kids picked on him.

That was a few years ago now and he was finally getting things together. The main thing was getting rid of that name, which had taken a while. He never would have felt able to get on with his life the way things had been after he had left hospital. Luckily, he had made friends living on the street. It was funny that people who were overlooked could be so resourceful. Some of them were lost to drugs but that had never appealed to him. One of the people he had met had told him he could get him a new ID and national insurance number. You never knew whether to believe what you heard on the streets but his friend had come through with a brown envelope containing the few basic documents he would need.

He wouldn't be able to drive without risking being discovered, or leave the country, but that could change with time. When it came to other homeless people you rarely got anything for nothing but Nigel had found that passing on money from begging and the odd bout of slippery fingers got him what he wanted. You learned all sorts of new tricks when you needed to.

With a new identity, things had started to come good. He got himself a flat. It was horrible but a roof was always better than no roof then he got a job. It was nothing special, just fixing shoes, engraving and cutting keys on the market but the stall's owner had been great with him, looking to pass on his skills so he could semi-retire but still take the income. He had found out lots about himself; how practical and creative he could be. With a new name, somewhere to live and a job, he had found his confidence growing at last. He started making friends and creating a new life.

Talking to girls.

And then, within days of each other, two people walked into his life as if to taunt him, a reminder of a past he had forgotten. He recognised the faces as parents of the people who had destroyed his life. Names weren't a strong point but he never forgot a face. These were features he knew but they had looked through him, not knowing or caring what their children had done.

First a man, mumbling something about having been burgled and needing new keys, pretending he didn't know who he was talking to. You didn't usually need to take name and address details but people rarely questioned you when asked. Every now and then he had got a few girls' names and numbers in a similar way. When the man returned, he got his keys – without knowing about the extra one that had been cut.

At the time, the man formerly known as Nigel Collins didn't know how it could come in handy in the future but then there was a second gift.

Two days later a mother of one of his other tormentors also pretended she didn't know who he was and came to him with the same story. She said she had been burgled but wanted to chat, without even acknowledging who he was. She had been only too happy to give over her address details and another key had been pocketed.

He wondered if the other two would walk into his life, two more gifts, but they hadn't so far. Maybe fate or God was telling him he had to find the other two himself? Perhaps it was time to be Nigel Collins for one final short period of his life and then he could get back on with things, find a career and a girlfriend and settle down.

FIVE MONTHS AGO

One of the hardest parts of leaving one identity behind was choosing yourself a new name. It had to be something you felt comfortable answering to but also something you actually liked. After the tedium of 'Nigel', he wanted to be more memorable; not weird but something not exactly regulation either. Although he had decided on his new moniker a few years ago, he had really begun to feel it sticking recently. He felt his senses moving quicker when people spoke his name. The acknowledgment they meant him was becoming instant and natural. He liked it.

The plan that started forming seven months ago was beginning to work too. The other two he wanted to target had not come directly to him, so he had to make sure they did. The first was easy, the woman even lived in the same house as years ago, although he didn't recognise the man with her. He resolved then it would have to be the woman he took; the man could be completely blameless but not her. He had begun to watch the location and realised it would be difficult to get the right pattern of when she was alone. The first two would be easy but this would be a lot harder. He felt sure the right opportunity would come if he waited long enough.

He had thought of a way to try to make sure she came to him in the first instance, giving him complete access to her. Everyone loved to save a bit of money and a good offer. In his head it would be successful and if fate kept favouring him, it would work.

The other woman had been harder to find. Like someone who was homeless, whores could almost live in plain sight with many people driving and walking past but pretending not to see what was in front of them.

He had used the Internet to check the final name on his list and saw the tormenter was in prison, where he belonged. But that shouldn't let him off the hook. Finding anyone close to him had proven hard though. He didn't even know if they lived in the same area now. He had been waiting for fate to guide him with little luck. He did not want to continue with a plan that only contained three of the four people he wanted.

And then he saw what he had been wanting to see for all these months – and she had been right in front of him the whole time. He had walked past her row of shops on many occasions as he went home. He usually kept his head down. He had even heard her voice, 'Do you fancy . . .' as he hurried past. Then one night he glanced up and saw what he had been looking for the entire time. A familiar face from years before, a face he remembered walking young Shaun to school. Befriending her was easy; money tended to do that. Afterwards she wanted to be friends, offering him cigarettes and complaining about the local kids.

Then everything just appeared to him, a way to get access to both his final places. The owner of his stall had taught him some very useful skills in the past eighteen months, wanting someone to run the business for him but still keep the profits for himself. He had learned those skills willingly and now he had used them. He repaired the lock he had damaged the night before and pocketed a third key, and then the final woman came to him on the stall and the fourth and final key had been created.

Now he just had to wait and watch. He didn't even know if he were capable of doing what he planned. He would have to be focused and think of what had been done to him in the past. He would have to build up his strength first, develop his body and keep a close eye on the comings and goings of his targets. When the time came he would have to be careful not to leave a trace but he could plan and wait for the perfect time when there would be little chance of him being discovered.

And then, when all four were gone and he could live with himself again, he could finally say goodbye to Nigel Collins and start his life over. It would be his tormenters who had to live with the wreckage they had caused, not him.

36

Jessica didn't recognise the old man standing on the stall but then she instantly knew why not. The person who had worked there had got himself a new job. Emotions flooded through her and she kept repeating to herself over and over that she must be wrong. She had to be sure and approached the stall. She had been staring at it trying to take everything in and the holder must have been anxious as she reached the point where she was directly in front of him.

'Are you all right, darling?' he asked in a local accent.

Jessica couldn't think straight. 'Yes, sorry. I was just wondering about a man who worked here . . .'

The man half-smiled at her. 'Heh, you're not the first. I think a few of the girls around here have had their eye on m'boy over the past couple of years.'

'*Your* boy?'

'Oh not my son or anything but, yeah, he's a good lad. He has a new job, so I'm sorry he won't be around any longer.' Jessica didn't know what to say but the man clearly misunderstood the look on her face. 'Oh don't worry, it's a good job. I'm pleased he's sorted himself out. It just means I've had to come out of retirement until I can find someone else to take over.'

Jessica hadn't been listening but said thanks anyway.

Her mind was racing and she felt as if she were in a trance. It couldn't be . . .

She felt she had to hear someone else say it before it would be true. She had taken a few steps away from the stall but turned around again and walked back towards the man. 'Could you tell me what his name was?'

'You didn't even know? I didn't think he was that shy. It was Randall. Randall Anderson. Maybe you'll get lucky and come across him one day? I think he's got a girlfriend so you might have to wait in line.'

The man laughed but Jessica didn't. She moved quickly away from the stall, fumbling with her bag to pull her phone out. Once again, just as she needed to move quickly, her fingers betrayed her. She finally pulled it out of her bag but it caught on one of the handles and she dropped it.

Her heart froze as she saw it fall almost in slow motion. There was a small crash as it hit the ground. She bent down and snatched it up but the screen had a slight crack across it, although it seemed slightly responsive. Jessica pressed the button for her contacts list. The phone was being slow and the scroll was only half-working but she managed to get up a list of recent contacts then pressed the 'call' button next to Caroline's name.

'Answer, answer, answer,' Jessica said quietly but out loud while the phone rang. She heard a click and for a moment thought her friend was about to speak. Instead, it was her voicemail message. While she listened to her friend's voice, Jessica remembered that morning's text saying her friend had been called into work. As the other end of the line beeped, Jessica spoke frantically.

'Caz, it's Jess. Look, wherever you are, go somewhere safe or somewhere public. If Randall is with you, make some excuse to get away and call me back? It's urgent.'

She hung up and swore, much to the annoyance of a woman walking nearby with a young child. What did she do now? The obvious answer was to do what she always told everyone else to do – phone the police – but Jessica was thinking of her friend. What if there had been a mistake? She would be risking throwing away their friendship and perhaps her own career.

Ultimately, she wasn't worried about treading on toes considering the case had been taken from her. It was better to be wrong and get a telling off than be right and do nothing. But if she ended up making allegations that turned out to be untrue, especially if it looked as if it were designed to coincide with Caroline moving out, their friendship would surely be irreparable. More practically too, if the police were looking for the killer and he got wind of it, he could go to ground and disappear. He had done it before and Jessica couldn't risk that happening.

Jessica decided she should head back to the flat to see if Caroline had returned from work. If not she would at least be able to pick up her car and drive to her friend's office and then the two of them could go to the police station while people senior to her decided what to do. From the market, the journey would only take ten minutes to get home and that might even give her a chance to see where she had gone wrong. There was a taxi rank next to the market and Jessica jogged towards it, before opening the door on the first one.

She gave the driver her address and then attempted using her half-working phone again. She called Caroline over and over with no luck but there wasn't much point in leaving further messages.

As the taxi drove, she tried to think of things that might not fit but instead could only come up with things that justified her fears even more. Caroline had never met Randall's parents. He said they lived abroad but it was an easy thing to say to get out of having your girlfriend meet them. And what about Ryan? He claimed he had found her files on the coffee table after she had left them under her bag but maybe he did find them where he said because Randall had already gone through them first? It was a horrible thought. It could have been her carrying those files around that led to Claire Hogan and Mary Keegan being killed quicker before the police could find the connection.

The taxi driver was good and Jessica gave him a ten-pound note before dashing out of the car towards her flat. She put the key in her front door, thinking about how a key had been turned by Nigel Collins or Randall Anderson to let himself into the victims' homes.

She pushed the door open and went inside. 'Caroline?'

There was no answer. Jessica put her bag on the floor next to the front door and took her phone out, putting it in her pocket and then went to pick up the car keys from her room. As she moved, she thought she could hear some sort of rustling sound coming from Caroline's room. At first her heart leapt, with her instant thought being her friend was at home but then something far more sinister occurred to her.

Jessica crept along the carpeted hallway. She knew where the squeaky floorboards were and moved to avoid them. She passed her own bedroom door and carefully approached Caroline's. It was mostly shut but there was a crack and she could definitely hear something moving inside. Jessica held her breath and tried to peer through the gap where the hinges met the wall but could see nothing. She looked through the already open part but could only see one side of Caroline's bed. She slowly pushed the door open to reveal more of the bed through the widening crack, squeezing silently through the gap and looking behind the door.

Randall was standing there, his hands reaching into the built-in wardrobe but his face turned to look at her with a puzzled look on his face. 'Jess? Sorry I didn't hear you come in. Caroline was called into work but left me her key so I could start moving things for her. Didn't she text you?'

Jessica felt frozen to the spot. What did she do? Randall was bigger and stronger than her. It wasn't as if she could just go straight in and accuse him of being Nigel Collins and call the police. She already knew what he was capable of doing, having seen all four bodies. Not only that but, if he did kill her here, the police would just assume that Collins had come to deal with the officer assigned to his case. Even if Randall's DNA was found at the scene, that would be expected as he was Caroline's boyfriend.

She would have to be careful but couldn't risk leaving the flat or letting him leave and losing him for good.

Jessica tried to keep her voice calm. 'Hi. She sent me a message this morning. I've just been out and about.' She thought her voice had faltered slightly but, if it did, Randall said nothing.

'Do you want to help me?' he asked. 'I don't really know what I'm doing with all these clothes and things. I've got these boxes but I have no idea how it should be sorted or anything.' He indicated some cardboard boxes on the floor by his feet and was smiling.

Jessica tried to return the smile but it was excruciating. If she could just get away from him for a few minutes, she could call the station and get help.

'No worries. I just want to get a drink. Do you want anything?'

'Yeah, just some water would be fine.'

Jessica walked backwards out the room, her heart racing. She turned around and went into the kitchen, putting two glasses on the draining board letting the tap run as she took her phone out from her pocket. Even if he were nearby, perhaps he would hear the water and not her?

Her cracked phone screen was still not properly working. She pressed the screen to view her contacts but it wouldn't load. She used one hand to fill both glasses, using the other to jab at the front of her phone ever harder. Eventually she had both glasses filled but left the water running anyway. Finally the phone started to respond. She needed to use both thumbs but got the list of names scrolling down. She could see her hand shaking and felt sick but kept telling herself to focus. She got to the entry 'Station' and pressed call. She put the phone to her ear and turned around to face the door.

Randall was standing there looking directly at her with a pair of scissors in his hand.

37

'Are you all right?' Randall said. 'You've been a while.'

Jessica heard the call connect and the desk sergeant's voice say 'hello'. In that fraction of a second she weighed up blurting out as much as she could, saying, 'It's Jessica Daniel, I've got Nigel Collins in my flat, send help.' Could she hold Randall off for long enough until help arrived? Would the sergeant understand everything in time? Was it worth the risk?

She hung up and put the phone in her pocket. 'Yeah, I was just trying Caroline to see if she knew when she was going to be finished. There was no answer though.' Randall looked as if he was weighing her up. Jessica thought she might have been imagining it. Could he know? She hadn't said anything that could give her away.

He motioned the scissors in his hand. They had long blades and were sharp on the end. 'Do you have any tape? One of the boxes just broke.'

'Yeah, hang on. Here's your water.' Jessica offered him one of the glasses and turned the tap off. She focused hard on not letting her hand shake as she gave it to him, not showing she was nervous. He took it from her without saying anything and drank. She took a few sips from her glass then tipped the rest away. She felt sick.

Randall emptied the glass and offered it back to her. 'Thanks.'

'No worries. The tape is in that drawer behind you.'

Jessica pointed to a cabinet next to the door. Randall turned around and opened it, reaching in and rummaging. There was a knife rack above the drawer he was looking in. If he had figured things out, she knew she was in big trouble.

She watched him but he didn't make any sudden movements and quickly pulled a roll of tape out of the drawer. 'Got it,' he said. 'Are you coming?'

'Yeah.' She wanted him to turn around and walk out of the door first; that way she could at the very least pocket one of the knives.

He didn't move and stood holding the door open for her. 'After you.'

She moved slowly, looking at the knives out of the corner of her eye. She didn't necessarily want to stab him but she wanted something that would give her an advantage if need be. She thought about the distances. There was no way she could pick something up without him noticing but could she grab a weapon and back him into a corner? Even if she did, what then?

Jessica walked past the knives, in front of Randall and through the open door towards Caroline's bedroom. She could feel him moving behind her but kept her cool and went back into Caroline's room, waiting by the side of the bed for him to go past her towards the wardrobes. He did what she expected and pulled one of the boxes onto the bed before taping it underneath where it had broken.

Jessica watched him carefully. He had put the scissors on the bed but then picked them up to cut the tape and pocketed them.

'Right, where do we begin?' he asked as he turned back around to the wardrobe.

Jessica couldn't believe she was going to have to make small talk. This was a man who had killed four people. 'I reckon put all the trousers and skirts and stuff in one box, then the tops and dresses separate.'

'Heh, I was going to group everything by colour. Good job you're here.' Randall laughed and Jessica tried to join in but there was no substance to it. 'Can you fold?' he asked.

'Okay,' Jessica said. 'If you take them out, I'll fold and you can pack.'

The situation was almost laughable. Jessica was looking for a way out. Could she somehow lock him in this room then make a call? Once again, she had been stupid. She should have phoned the police in the first place.

They started working in tandem but to Jessica it was like an out-of-body experience, a bit like being back in the interview room with Peter Hunt and Wayne Lapham. Her body was folding the clothes but her mind was somewhere else, desperately trying to think of how to handle things.

'How's the job going?' Randall said out of the blue. Jessica stopped halfway through folding a pair of jeans and looked up at the man in front of her. He had just put another pile of clothes on the bed and his hands were free. 'I know you were taken off that Houdini case, it was all over the news but I just wondered how things were now.'

Jessica said nothing but folded quickly and put the trousers down on the bed. 'It's okay,' she said. 'I've been working on other things.'

'Not one of those TV cops who keeps working a case then?'

She thought she detected something in his voice and tried to laugh but her voice cracked. 'Nah, not me.'

'What's the flyer about in your bag then?'

She glanced up quickly and saw it in his face. He knew.

Instinctively, Jessica raced towards the door but Randall was faster. He pinned her against the wall, his forearm across her chest, shouting in her face: 'Why couldn't you leave it be?'

She could smell his breath and aftershave.

Jessica didn't have time to think but acted instinctively. She couldn't raise her arms properly but had enough leverage to smash the side of her hand hard into his windpipe. He instantly reeled back with a vicious cough and released her. She wriggled down away from his arms and escaped out of the bedroom, dashing for the front door, having no idea what to do next. He was quickly on her, bringing her down with something like a rugby tackle in their hallway. She tried to turn over but felt his fist punch her hard across the face as she did so. She saw stars, blinking to try to clear her head while hearing him continue to gasp for breath. She thought she could feel a trickle of what was almost certainly blood on her top lip.

Randall was now sitting astride her, his knees digging into her elbows so she could barely move. Her legs were relatively free but she knew she wasn't strong enough to flip him over.

His breathing was tight but his blue eyes were staring right at her. 'It was over!' he shouted. His tone was lighter and he didn't scream as he had done in the bedroom. 'It was over. I just wanted to get on with things, settle down with Caroline.'

Jessica could feel the pain in her head from the blow but could just about focus. 'Why did you do it, Randall?'

There were tears in his eyes but he still had a fierce look on his face. 'It was Nigel. I had become Randall and was getting on with things but then two of them came to me on the stall. It was like a sign. A way to finally say goodbye to Nigel and get on with my life.'

Jessica realised he must mean the two burglary victims. They had gone to the closest place to them to get new keys cut after Wayne Lapham had broken into their homes but their appearance must have reminded Randall of a part of him he had buried. The part that still remembered being Nigel and feeling helpless.

'How did you recognise them?'

'I don't forget faces.'

'Really?'

'I guess that's part of being "weird".'

'Why didn't you kill the boys who hurt you?'

Jessica felt the body astride her tense up. 'What?' It was almost as if he hadn't heard her correctly. He used one of his hands to rub first one ear, then the other, the grip with his knees returning to what it was.

'Why didn't you go after the ones who had hurt you instead of their parents?'

'They didn't kill me, did they? They made me live like this.'

Jessica couldn't move her body enough to nod but in some ways understood what he meant. If he killed their parents, the ones who had hurt him would at least have to endure the emotional pain.

'How did you change your name so easily?' she asked.

His volume went up again. 'It wasn't easy. It wasn't just a name, it was everything associated with it: being pathetic and weak.'

'But how did you manage to become somebody else?'

'I lived on the streets for a while. Someone helped me, they reckoned they could get new identities sorted.'

Jessica had a chilling thought of Harry handing over a brown envelope to a homeless man on the street. She remembered Peter Hunt's wording in court. 'Have you ever seen Mr Thomas act in a questionable way while on duty?' She had said 'no' but was suddenly confused. Had that act indirectly led to all of this?

Her expression must have changed. 'What?' Randall said.

'What are you going to do now?' Jessica asked, hoping he didn't force her to answer.

She felt his grip lighten ever so slightly. He blinked away more tears. 'I don't know.'

'You don't want to kill anyone else?'

'I love her . . .' Jessica knew he was talking about Caroline. He leant back slightly and she felt even more pressure release on her elbows. She could feel pins and needles but could probably free her arms if she needed to.

'It's why I wanted to get it all finished,' he continued. 'She came along and I wanted to leave Nigel behind. Once the four of them were finished with, we could have a life together. It was all over with.'

Jessica was playing for time. If she could get him to relax further, when the feeling came back into her arms, with her legs already free, she could surprise him and possibly get away. 'Why did you lock all the houses after you left?'

Randall rubbed his ears again. 'I didn't want to get caught. I thought if your lot were busy looking at family members and trying to figure out how it all happened, you would forget to look for things like Nigel Collins. It worked, didn't it?'

Jessica would have admitted that it had but didn't want to let him focus on anything positive. 'Can I ask you something?' The directness clearly shocked him as he would have felt in control of the situation being on top. She didn't give him time to answer. 'Do you remember when the three of us were watching the news together that morning? You said the coverage was "sick" . . .'

'I was talking about them using that old photo. With my face . . .' Jessica knew he meant the one of him as a teenager with his features bruised and swollen. At the time she thought he had been talking about the murders themselves.

Her bluntness had worked and his tears stopped as he relaxed even further. The feeling had returned to both of her arms and the blurriness had cleared from her head. She thought about her options. Talking to him about letting her go or anything to do with the future would most likely anger him. He must know deep down his chances were hopeless. The only thing he could really do was either kill her and run for it or kill her and hope the investigators blamed it on Nigel Collins, not knowing he and Randall were one and the same.

Either way, her chances didn't look good. She had to keep him off-balance. 'How did you meet Ryan?'

It was a question completely out of the blue, something he wouldn't have expected. He rubbed his ears again. 'Ryan?'

'Yeah, he was a nice guy.'

Randall shook his head slightly and stroked his neck with one of his hands. 'Oh yeah, just around. We started playing pool together and . . .'

Jessica didn't let him finish. She lunged forwards, using the spring of her free legs to propel him away from her. He yelled as he crashed backwards but as Jessica turned to run the few feet left to the front door, he flicked out with his foot and tripped her. She stumbled into the door, fumbling for the handle to open it. She had to take a step back to open it inwards but he slammed into her, crushing her between his weight and the door. Her arms were free and this time she reeled back and punched him as hard as she could in the windpipe. He stumbled fully back, obviously dazed.

Jessica let go of the door handle with her other hand and hammered the base of her palm upwards as hard as she could into the base of his nose. It was just as Harry had taught her and the same thing she had threatened to do to Wayne Lapham. Blood exploded over her arm and Randall's face. She saw his eyes blink and close and quickly turned back to pull the door open, thinking she was free until she felt a hand grabbing her hair. Jessica's face was slammed hard into the frame once, then twice as she felt consciousness slipping. She tried hard to focus, feeling her head yanked backwards.

She couldn't open her eyes because of the pain but could hear Randall's furious voice shouting behind her. Jessica couldn't make out anything he was saying, his nose was most likely broken and his throat would certainly hurt from her two blows. She could hear him wheezing but couldn't stop herself being dragged away from the door into her own bedroom and onto the bed. She was aware of what was going on but helpless to do anything about it, her head dazed and her limbs unresponsive. Jessica opened her eyes and could see him on top of her, tears running down his heavily bloodied face.

She thought she heard him say 'I'm sorry' and then felt his hands on her throat, squeezing. She could feel the pressure and was struggling for breath, not even able to kick her legs any longer.

And then she heard the front door open.

38

Jessica felt as if she was dreaming, her head hazy, like waking from a vivid dream and not being sure which reality is the correct one.

'Rands? Jess?'

It was Caroline's voice. Jessica was groggy but the pressure was instantly released from her throat. She could see a fuzzy grey colour but felt the weight lifted from her and get up from the bed. She tried to sit up but everything was in slow motion. There were voices from the hallway. She could hear shouting and thought she heard Caroline say something like, 'What's going on?'

Jessica managed to sit up and eventually stand. There were still voices coming from the hallway. She stumbled towards the door and into the hall, her vision still grey but she heard Caroline scream clearly. 'Jess!'

As she looked across from her bedroom door towards the living room, Jessica's vision began to clear, although her throat was on fire and breathing painful. Randall was standing behind Caroline with his front to her back but his left arm across her, hugging her into him. His face was a mashed-up mess. The red of the blood smeared across his features seeped into the grey that was affecting her vision and helped clear it. Jessica could feel blood on her face too. She must also look a mess.

Caroline had a terrified expression on her face. Her eyes were wide, her bag dropped by her feet and the contents spilled across the floor.

'What's going on?' Jessica clearly heard Caroline say this time. Her voice was faltering and then Jess saw why.

Randall didn't just have his left arm around his girlfriend, he had the scissors in his right hand placed next to her neck.

'Stay calm,' Jessica said. She couldn't speak clearly and her thoughts were scrambled. She was speaking to Randall as much as Caroline. 'Just stay calm.'

Randall had more tears running down his face, blending in with the blood and causing vertical streaks to form down his skin. 'Why couldn't you just leave it?' he said.

Caroline clearly didn't have a clue what was going on. She kept staring across the hallway at her friend. 'Jess?'

'It's him,' Jess said softly. 'He's Houdini. He's Nigel Collins. He killed those four people.' Jessica saw Caroline's body slump.

'What . . . ?'

Jessica didn't know what else to add. Caroline was wearing a grey work suit and Randall's blood had begun to run onto her shoulder. She was shaking her head despite still being gripped by her boyfriend and having the scissors held to her neck.

Randall coughed loudly, spluttering more blood. He moved his body around so his back was to their front door. 'You're going to let me go,' he said but his words weren't coming easily. He coughed loudly again and Jessica saw his head twitch once, twice. Caroline had clearly felt his grip slacken as she must have moved before being snatched back hard into her boyfriend's body.

'Where are you going to go, Randall?' Jessica said. Her own throat still felt sore but her vision had more or less cleared. She knew she was pushing her luck.

Randall shook his head and blinked rapidly. 'I . . . it doesn't matter. I'll start again.'

Caroline was whimpering, clearly not able to process everything that was happening.

'Let her go,' Jessica said, taking a step forwards. Her eyes were on the scissors in Randall's hand. She saw his fingers tense on the grip but not move any closer to her friend's neck.

'Stop there,' Randall said.

'Just let her go. You told me you loved her, remember?'

Randall peered up and coughed again, before another furious blinking fit. Jessica took a few more small steps towards them as he struggled. She was around eight feet away from them.

The man's grip on the scissors was still tight but, if anything, his grip on Caroline had slackened. 'No closer,' Randall said but his eyes were not backing up his words.

'What's wrong, Randall?' Jessica said. She could see the confusion on Caroline's face and shuffled a little closer as Randall tried to control his blinking. He snatched his left hand away from Caroline but moved the one with the scissors in so they were touching the front of her neck. Using his left hand, he first rubbed his eyes, then hit his own left ear a couple of times before putting his hand back across Caroline and holding her close to him while again moving the scissors a little further away from her.

Jessica simply watched, before taking another small step forwards.

Six feet now.

'You need to let her go,' Jessica said, carefully watching Randall, trying to catch his eye. He looked at her, still blinking.

'What have you done?' he asked.

'There was an aspirin in your water,' Jessica said, edging forwards. 'The pain you thought was from me hitting you in the throat is actually your windpipe swelling. You need to let her go then let me call you an ambulance.'

Randall stuttered something but Jessica could see his eyes had widened. He dropped the scissors but put his right hand tighter around Caroline's throat, using his left to fumble with the front door handle.

'Randall . . .' Jessica said. He launched into a coughing fit and Jessica flung herself at him, carefully targeting the left side of his body with Caroline held to his right. She caught him with her shoulder and his head cannoned back into the door. Caroline fell to the floor but was free, while Jessica used her feet to kick the scissors away. Randall was on his knees, spluttering and struggling to breathe.

39

The funeral had been far more emotional than Jessica had expected. She sat next to Caroline, with her arm around her for large parts of the ceremony. So many more people had turned out than Jessica would have expected. The marks around Jessica's throat had already begun to fade and the cuts on her face would heal in time. The mental scars her friend must be feeling would be something that took a lot longer to fix.

Jessica had never discovered if it was in fact Harry who had provided the method for Nigel Collins to change his identity; she didn't want to know. If it were true, part of her personality as a detective, the parts she had learned from Harry, would be destroyed. She had not phoned him, nor visited, and never would.

Gradually the police had filled in the gaps between Nigel Collins leaving hospital nearly six years ago and the first body turning up. He had tried to reinvent himself but, with his memory for faces, had recognised the parents of his tormentors. At first it had been something of a co-incidence that two of Wayne Lapham's victims had gone to him but he had seen it as a sign and followed things through to a conclusion.

'Thank you for coming.'

Jessica was standing with Caroline in the church's hall

after the body had been put to rest. Paul Keegan was in front of them, offering his hand for them to shake.

'Mary would have liked it, I think,' he added.

'It was lovely,' Jessica said. 'Are you going to be okay?'

'I think so. Thank you, you know . . . for catching him.'

Randall Anderson, or Nigel Collins as he had previously been called, was currently in isolation and on suicide watch while on remand at Manchester Prison, formerly known as Strangeways. As he had crouched struggling for breath on the floor in their flat, Jessica called 999 and an ambulance as well as what seemed like most of the Greater Manchester Police force had been sent to her flat. The paramedics had arrived in time to save him but he was in no state to fight or escape.

Since then, he hadn't said a word to anyone. Jessica had been offered leave, given her injuries and the severity of the case. She wouldn't have wanted any part of his police interview anyway, even if it had been offered to her. Not that he had spoken about anything. He hadn't confessed and offered no details of how things had been conceived. Some of the plan would never be known.

The police had raided both his old flat and his new one. It had been awkward because he didn't seem to own much and what little he had was in boxes at the new place, while the old one had been cleaned out. They had found a small coil of thick metal wire in the wheelie bin at the back of the block where he lived. Tests had shown it was very similar to the implement used to kill the four people, with the assumption he had cut pieces off to use for each victim. The owner of the stall where he worked said it was the exact kind of wire they would use to help bind together shoes they were fixing. Two days later and the bins would have been emptied and the evidence lost. On first thought it seemed careless to ditch something like that in a bin so close to his flat but from Randall's point of view, it must have seemed as if he was in the clear. Not only that but he was moving anyway.

Building a case would be hard given the lack of DNA but the trail from the locks to his stall, plus the wire and her evidence – and his refusal to speak – should be enough in court.

In terms of Jessica herself, everyone had been so concerned about her that no one had brought up anything about her following up a case that wasn't hers. She didn't know if there would be some sort of disciplinary action down the line but didn't care either.

Caroline hadn't coped well. Jessica didn't really know how to deal with things but eventually her friend had gone to stay with Jessica's parents for a couple of weeks. They said they saw her as a daughter anyway.

And now, a few weeks later, the two of them were at the wake following Mary Keegan's funeral, along with many members of the investigating force. Cole had left not long after the ceremony had finished but Aylesbury had now come over to speak to the dead woman's husband. Jessica guided Caroline away towards some plastic seats to leave the two of them to it. Jessica felt guilty for her early attitude to her boss. She could now see what an asset he was. He had been terrific looking after her following the arrest. The first instinct would have been to interview her and find out everything she knew but he had shielded her.

Garry Ashford meanwhile had written a string of stories about her bravery. She didn't know where the details had come from and felt largely embarrassed about it. He had been at the funeral too, a few rows across from Jessica. She had seen his solemn face during the readings, thinking he was someone else she had misjudged.

Caroline sat down and Jessica went to take the seat next to her. Her friend waved her away. 'It's okay. You go mix. I could do with a few minutes on my own.'

The woman gave a thin smile and Jessica kissed her forehead. She turned around and walked over to Garry Ashford, who was standing on his own drinking from a plastic cup near the door. 'Hey.'

'Hey.'

'You can take the piss out of my looks now if you want,' Jessica said, pointing at one of the cuts on her face. 'It looks like I've gone a few rounds with a heavyweight boxer, doesn't it?'

Garry smiled. 'Maybe a middleweight. Your nose is only horrifically deformed off to one side, not fully smashed up.'

Jessica grinned, fuller than she had done in weeks. 'Oi.'

Rowlands came over to join them. 'Garry, this is Detective Constable Rowlands. Detective Constable, this is Garry Ashford,' Jessica said. The two shook hands.

'How are you doing?' Rowlands asked her.

'Not too bad. Why? Are you concerned about me?' she asked sarcastically. 'That's lovely . . .'

'If you're not back fit and healthy soon, I'm going to have to find someone else to take the piss out of.'

Jessica laughed. 'Cheers. You're all heart. I'm surprised you're not over there trying to cop off with one of the nieces or something.' She pointed towards the buffet table where two pretty twenty-something girls were chatting to each other.

'I'm not that low,' Rowlands said, glancing towards them. 'Still, they are next to the food and I'm feeling a bit peckish.' He rubbed his belly and grinned, before giving her a wink.

'See ya, Dave,' Garry said.

Jessica shook her head, smiling. 'One day he'll get his comeuppance,' she said.

Garry shrugged. 'So are you okay then?'

'Yeah. It'll all be fine.'

Garry took a deep breath. 'How about a drink one night then?'

Jessica looked back at him. 'Are you using a wake as an opportunity to ask me on a date?'

'Maybe.'

Jessica looked away and gave a very audible 'Umm' intended for his benefit. 'If I say "yes", are you going to explain to me how you know Detective Constable Rowlands's first name?'

Afterword

The final version of what you have just read has perhaps as much of a tale behind it as the story itself.

In 2010, I had the incredible misfortune of turning thirty. Wrinkles appeared overnight, all-new silvery strands of hair providing a taunting reminder that my youth was all but gone. Joints that once allowed me to run around being terrible at football now ached, still allowing me to be equally terrible at football. All of a sudden, teenagers started listening to music I'd never heard of and I had an overwhelming urge to talk about how things were better 'in my day'.

Anyway, despite thirty 'being just a number', inside I had a sense that I hadn't really done much with my life – not unless you count being pretty good on the PlayStation and carefully cultivating a palate for ice cream, which most people wouldn't. I figured I could either meander through the rest of my life and wonder what I might have managed to do had I bothered, or I could actually try to do something.

So I made a list of everything I reckoned I was half-decent at, thinking that if I failed at the first then I'd move onto the next until I found something that made me happy.

It seems a bit crazy now but I never got beyond the first thing on that list – writing a book. I always thought I could, not because of the saying that 'everyone has a book in them' – which I don't believe is true – but simply because I had a lot of ideas.

Over the next few months, each time I heard, saw or thought of something I found vaguely interesting, I wrote it down. Sometimes it was something as small as a name I liked, other times a news story, or perhaps a small flash of an incident. After a while, I had many Post-it notes littering my side of the bed and my car.

Back at school, my most impressive works of fiction had been the excuses I had for not doing my homework, why I was late, why I had missed a lesson, or why I was generally being disruptive. I hadn't written anything even approaching a story since then but soon thought I had enough to start stringing something together.

I'll leave out all the boring sitting-around-on-the-sofa-while-typing bits – because they basically involve me being boring and sitting on a sofa. It may well be what you're doing now. It's pretty boring, isn't it? But it was a good feeling when I finished something so completely different to anything I had done before.

If I had written it a year earlier, there is every chance the document would still be sitting on my laptop now, gathering digital dust. As it was, I was messing around on Amazon.co.uk one day when I saw a 'self-publish with us' link at the bottom. I had a quick read and figured I may as well give it a go.

There are a lot of books on Amazon, over a million in fact, but with mine something strange began to happen: people bought it. I'm still not entirely sure what started things rolling but I began receiving emails from strangers within weeks, saying they had read it and wanting to know if there was another one coming.

My Giant Pad of Ideas, which by this time was actually a

pad, had plenty left on it and was continually being added to. I have written more or less every day since – sometimes for half an hour, one time for eighteen – but I always have something on the go.

The most astonishing thing is that people have bought, and continue to buy, the Jessica Daniel stories. Within three months, I had the number one fiction book – not just ebook – on the whole of Amazon UK. The sequel to *Locked In*, *Vigilante*, was second only to its predecessor in the crime chart. Somehow I was in Amazon's top ten list of British authors worldwide for 2011, despite not having a book out in the first seven months of the year.

Everything happened incredibly quickly, culminating in Pan Macmillan buying the rights to the Jessica Daniel series in early 2012.

If you like what you have just read, books two, three and four should all be out with more to come.

Essentially, almost everything that has happened to me over the course of the past year and a bit is down to readers such as yourself. Saying a simple 'thank you' doesn't seem quite enough. You might say that to the person who held the door open for you this morning, or whoever made you a brew – even if they did put too much milk in it. The words themselves become a cliché, so you'll have to take my word for it that I really do appreciate everyone who has bought the books and liked them enough to tell someone, buy the sequels, leave a review, or write me an email, tweet or Facebook message.

I've had emails from teenagers and parents alike; people who have heard about Jessica from their nieces, nephews, cousins, uncles, aunties, grandparents, parents and children; someone whose cab driver told them about my books, someone who read one while recovering from a serious illness, someone else whose midwife talked about the books . . . and so on. Lots of very normal people reading and passing the message on.

Essentially, the last few months have shown me how fundamentally great the majority of people are.

So these few rambling paragraphs are to offer my appreciation to all of you readers who have been so involved in making Jessica's stories as popular as they have become.

Thanks to you all.

Kerry Wilkinson

VIGILANTE

Jessica Daniel Book 2

A killer behind bars is still killing . . .

Dead bodies are piling up for Detective Sergeant Jessica Daniel.

Usually when a serial killer is on the loose, the pressure would be building to find the perpetrator but the victims are all hardened criminals themselves.

The national media can't believe their luck with an apparent vigilante on the streets, while Jessica's new boss seems grateful someone else is doing their job for them.

But things aren't so straightforward when forensics matches blood from the apparent killer to a man already behind bars.

An extract follows here . . .

ISBN 978-1-4472-2566-9

1

The sun was just beginning to rise as Detective Sergeant Jessica Daniel walked from her parked-up red K-reg Fiat Punto towards the thin white tent which had been put up around the crime scene. She had been told on the phone it was a dead body so had a reasonable idea what to expect. Given the particular area of Levenshulme in Manchester it had been found in, it wasn't necessarily a surprise either. The youths who lived here seemed to spend large parts of their free time finding new and ingenious ways to hurt either themselves or someone else who happened to look a little different to them.

They rarely went as far as killing each other though.

It had still been dark when Jessica had taken the call to come to see this particular body. Being a DS meant she was only phoned if something serious had happened. Her sleeping patterns hadn't been so great over the past year or so anyway but it seemed pretty typical that some poor guy had got himself stabbed on one of the few mornings she had been fast asleep.

Jessica reached the front of the tent and saw one of the Scene of Crime officers walking out wearing a white paper suit. They had obviously been quick off the mark that morning even though their department was notoriously under-staffed and relied on volunteers to stay on top of Greater Manchester's policing needs.

Noticing a familiar face towards the back of the tent, Jessica walked around to join Detective Inspector Jack Cole. 'Bit early for all this, innit?' she said. Cole shrugged. 'Have you seen inside?' Jessica asked, nodding towards the tent.

'Yes, I got here about two minutes before the SOCO boys.'

DI Cole was Jessica's immediate superior. They had been promoted at the same time eighteen months ago. He had gone from DS to DI, with her bumped up from Detective Constable to her current DS position. DI Cole was well known in the station for not wanting to get his hands dirty and preferring to work from his desk. Some people saw that as a negative and, although Jessica had at first, it did enable her to get more involved in things. Despite that, he was loyal and one of the people she trusted the most at the station, even though she didn't really know much about him.

Jessica was in her early thirties but the fifteen or so years between her and Cole couldn't have been wider. She was still living in a flat with next to no savings and taking things as they came. He was settled with two kids and a wife he clearly adored but kept that side of his life completely separate from his professional career. She had never met his partner or children and, as far as she knew, neither had anyone else in the station. He was a normal, unassuming guy who you wouldn't look at twice if you didn't know he was a detective.

Jessica acknowledged Cole's reply with a nod and moved around to the front of the tent. The white material was encircled by the standard police tape on a pavement, with marked police cars parked nearby shielding their position from easy view. A couple of uniformed officers milled around near to the vehicles. As the morning began to get lighter people had started to come out of their houses and flats to gawp at the police scene. Jessica noticed a couple of young teenagers in school uniform on the opposite side of the street. The schools had only gone back after the summer holidays a few days previously and, while it was still early in the morning, it wasn't necessarily a surprise to see kids out at this time, certainly not in this area. The bigger shock was the school uniform as the estate the body had been found on was one of the roughest in the neighbourhood and just getting the youths to school was an achievement, let alone in uniform.

Jessica ignored them and walked around the tape to the tent's entrance.

The Scene of Crime team's job was to make sure any suspicious incidents were catalogued. Bodies would be cautiously removed from a murder site, photographs taken and everything measured and carefully chronicled. Things like fingerprints would be checked for, as well as blood or hairs that might belong to the perpetrator. It was very specialist work and the team didn't like having their scenes trampled upon.

There were two people working around the site and Jessica recognised both of them. She didn't know their names but people got used to seeing each other due to the nature of their overlapping jobs. Some people got closer than others but the ins and outs of dead bodies had never appealed to Jessica. Although she felt the crime scenes sometimes helped clarify her thoughts, she was more than happy to read a report rather than see the gory parts for herself.

Despite this, seeing as she was there anyway, she asked to have a look.

The person in the white suit standing by the tent's opening was a woman a few years older than Jessica. 'I'd rather you didn't.'

'I won't touch anything. If the light's okay, I won't even go past the entrance.'

The relationship between the teams was awkward. Technically Jessica could walk in if she wanted but, if she contaminated a scene, it would be a very serious matter. That meant that CID and other officers, no matter how senior, often deferred to the wishes of the Scene of Crime team.

The woman eyed her up and then turned around, ducking slightly and looking back into the tent. Jessica often found that you were more likely to get what you wanted if you asked nicely in situations like this.

The person in the white suit stood back up and peered at Jessica. 'All right, fine. But stay around here, okay?' She indicated the tent's entrance and Jessica nodded, stepping forwards as the flap was held up for her.

Inside a separate lamp had been set up to illuminate the body but the gentle sunlight was now coming through the thin sides of the tent in any case. Jessica could see all she needed to pretty easily. A young man's body was slumped face-up on the pavement. His legs were straight out below him but one of his arms was bent towards his neck, the other limp by his side. He was wearing jeans and some sort of black sweatshirt. Even though the top was dark, Jessica could see an even murkier stain on the man's chest, matching a circle of deep red spread out on the ground. There was an obvious gash in the middle of his neck where he had likely been stabbed and another hole was just about visible in his chest. In total there were two, possibly three, knife wounds and a very dead victim.

Jessica stepped backwards and thanked the woman for holding the flap up for her. 'Have you found anything yet?' she asked.

The woman shrugged and gave a small smile. 'Bit hopeful, aren't you?'

'You never know.'

'There was something under a couple of his fingernails on the arm you see raised; he might have grabbed his attacker. There were a couple of other odds and ends but it will take a few days. It should be easy to identify him though. His face is fairly clear and it's not rained or anything to mess up the scene. We found this in his pocket too.' She used a rubber-gloved hand to delve into a plastic container on the floor, pulling out two sealed plastic pockets. One had a small bag containing what looked like cannabis, the other had a canvas money-holder in it.

'There's ID in the wallet,' the woman added. 'Do you want the name?'

'I know who it is.' Jessica said. The woman clearly looked a bit confused, so Jessica continued. 'I reckon ninety-five per cent of the Greater Manchester Police force would recognise that angelic face.'

It was fair to say Craig Millar was well known to the local police. Even though Jessica hadn't had the pleasure of arresting him herself, he had a face most of the local officers would know straight away. Jessica didn't know his exact age but was confident he was in his early twenties. Off the top of her head, she reckoned he had a criminal record for drugs possession, actual bodily harm, common assault and a drunk and disorderly or two. If she checked his full file, she would be fairly certain of finding more on there and probably a few police cautions or on-the-spot fines thrown in for good measure too.

And that was just what he had been caught doing.

His friends would no doubt have similar records and owe hundreds of pounds in unpaid fines to the courts. Once young people like Craig Millar got caught in the cycle of criminality, it seemed to continue until they ended up permanently in prison or, if they really annoyed the wrong people, dead on a pavement somewhere. She wondered who he could have upset. Maybe he was dealing drugs in an area he shouldn't? Or back-chatting out of turn to someone a bit higher up the criminal scale than he was? Or perhaps it was a stupid drunken argument with a friend who wouldn't remember much about it the next day?

Jessica found herself shaking her head as she walked back towards Cole. He clearly saw it in her face. 'Recognise him then?' he asked. His head was at a slightly sideways angle and she found his face difficult to read.

'That Millar kid. You noticed him too then?'

'I couldn't remember his name but the face was familiar.'

'What do you reckon? Whoever it was didn't bother taking his wallet so it wasn't just a mugging.'

'Drugs? Fighting? Who knows? If you're sure of the name we should probably get the address and find out if he lives with anyone before word gets around here anyway.' Cole indicated behind him and Jessica could see faces at windows of the block of flats that backed onto the road, with other people passing by on the other side of the road trying to get a glimpse.

Jessica said she had confirmed the victim's name with the officer who had the wallet. 'Who called it in anyway?' she added.

'If you had twenty quid on you, who would you put it on?'

'What makes you think I don't have twenty quid on me?'

Cole smiled. 'Reynolds reckons you still owe him a tenner and never bring money to work just so you don't have to pay him back.'

DS Jason Reynolds was an officer Jessica shared an office with. She grinned back at the inspector and gave a small laugh. 'It's got to be a dog-walker who called us.'

'Bingo.'

'I reckon we need a new way of investigating things like this. In future, let's just assume the bloke out walking his dog did it and work backwards from there; it's the perfect alibi.'

Cole's smile widened. 'I'll call in for the victim's address. It will almost certainly be around here anyway.'

*

Cole got Craig Millar's last-known address by phoning their Longsight base. It was a flat somewhere nearby but neither of them knew exactly where the place was and, from the records, they weren't completely sure if the victim lived alone. According to their own files, there were other Millars associated with the address but unsurprisingly no one was on the electoral roll. Jessica knew that anything seeming slightly authoritative would be roundly shunned in this area and doubted there were too many accurate records of who lived with whom.

Jessica crossed the road and asked the two teenagers in school uniform for directions to the victim's address. She didn't give the exact flat number but asked where the block was. The pair pointed her in what she assumed was the right direction without much of a protest and she and Cole set off to find out who actually lived at Craig Millar's address.

They crossed back over the road and cut through an alleyway that separated one set of flats from another. Jessica thought the whole area seemed fairly depressing, even with the sun now up and shining. The estate was a mix of red-brick two-storey blocks of flats and small houses. Most of the area was administered by a housing association, with signs all around bearing the organisation's logo and strict instructions that 'Ball games are not permitted'. Jessica knew full well from various newspaper reports and word-of-mouth around the station that, even if the association got tough on ball games, they weren't so bothered about low-level drug dealing and other misdemeanours as long as rent was paid on time.

Everything looked the same and the small scraps of

land that hadn't been built on had patchy, muddied grass, graffiti littering many fences and walls. They continued walking and Jessica noticed a run-down children's play park on the opposite side of the road from them. She could see a pair of swings had been wrapped around the top of the frame they hung from and guessed that much of the rest of the equipment was unusable or vandalised.

It was easy for the police to blame the people who lived here for making a mess of their own estate but Jessica knew well enough a cycle of poverty was hard to escape from. Kids would struggle to get jobs, so sat around bored and hung about in gangs. Then when they were mature enough to have children of their own, which wasn't that old for some of them, the cycle would start over. Even if you wanted to get out, you would be up against it. A place like this would have a reputation, so it was easy to get left behind when it came to funding for things like education or anything else that might aid social mobility.

It didn't help either if you had to live close to criminal scumbags who cared about no one but themselves.

Jessica and Cole followed the teenagers' instructions and soon came across the row of flats they were looking for. He pointed out that the ground-floor apartments all seemed to have even numbers, so they took the nearby stairs up to the first floor. The concrete entrance to the stairwell stank and Jessica avoided looking towards the back of the area where the bins were overflowing. The stairs opened out onto a full row of odd-numbered properties on their left and a wooden rail running the full length of the building on their right plus a hard stone floor underneath them. The first thing

Jessica noticed was a bank of satellite dishes overhanging the rail. It seemed as if every property had wires running from their front door across the ceiling covering the walkway and back down to their own dish.

They made their way halfway along the row until they reached the door they were looking for. Jessica knocked and waited but it didn't feel very sturdy. Most modern properties had double-glazed entrances and windows but the whole rank of flats had old-fashioned wooden doors.

Jessica had grown to like working with DI Cole, although his coolness did sometimes unnerve her. When they ended up working together, he was the calm thoughtful one while she went in running her mouth off. She had spent the past year trying to calm those instant reactions but it was a work-in-progress. In most situations, there was a tacit agreement between the two of them that Jessica would take the lead when it came to talking to witnesses or suspects. It wasn't a tactic they had ever spoken about, more something that had happened.

There was no immediate answer so Jessica knocked again, louder the second time. This time, she heard a voice from inside but couldn't make out what was being said. It didn't sound too friendly. The door was wrenched open and a woman stood there in a light pink dressing gown. She had greying brown hair and was scowling before Jessica had even bothered to get her identification out.

The flat's occupant rolled her eyes. 'What's he bloody done this time?'